A Kiss Is Still A Kiss
and other stories

BARRY CALLAGHAN

McArthur & Company
Toronto

This edition published in 2002 by
McArthur & Company
322 King Street West, Suite 402
Toronto, Ontario M5V 1J2

First paperback edition published by Little, Brown and Company
(Canada) Limited 1996

National Library of Canada Cataloguing in Publication Data

Callaghan, Barry, 1937-
    A kiss is still a kiss / Barry Callaghan.

    Short stories.
    ISBN 1-55278-027-9

    I. Title.

    PS8555.A49K58 2002   C813'.54   C2002-906055-9
    PR9199.3.C266K57 2002

Cover by Tania Craan
Composition and Design by Michael P. Callaghan
Printed in Canada by Transcontinental Printing Inc.

The publisher would like to acknowledge the financial support of the
Government of Canada through the Book Publishing Industry
Development Program (BPIDP) and the Canada Council for our
publishing activities. The publisher further wishes to acknowledge
the financial support of the Ontario Arts Council for our publishing
program.

10 9 8 7 6 5 4 3 2 1

Everybody wants to laugh,
Nobody wants to cry,
Everybody wants to hear the truth,
But still they want to lie.
Everybody wants to know the reason
Without even asking why.
Everybody wants to go to heaven,
But nobody wants to die.

— Albert King

Or some other trouble
Comes in the ashes
Like in that old light
The face in the ashes
That old starlight
On the earth again.

— Samuel Beckett

CONTENTS

I

I

. . . A Motiveless Malignancy.

— John Milton, *Paradise Lost*

Because Y Is A Crooked Letter

There's a Hole in the Bottom of the Sea

*I*t began over a year ago. I was going to drive to the foothill town of Saratoga to stay for two weeks in a rambling, spacious house and try to have lunch every day at a table under the tent at the old gabled racetrack. I had renegotiated the mortgage on the house and bought a new pair of tinted prescription sunglasses so that I could read the racing form in the glaring sun. Marina had packed several oblong dark bars of wax and her slender steel tools. She is a sculptor. I am a poet. We went out the back door of our house, through the vine-covered and enclosed cobblestone courtyard, and decided to move the car forward in the garage, toward the lane. I turned the key and the Audi lurched backward, breaking down the stuccoed wall, dumping concrete blocks and cement into the garden. I looked back through the rear-view mirror into an emptiness, wondering where everything had gone, and I heard the whisper of malevolence and affliction on the air. I did not heed it.

The car was fixed. Mechanics said that wires had crossed in the circuitry. We drove to Saratoga where every morning in the lush garden behind the house I wrote while sitting in the shade of a monkey puzzle tree:

> *pain and pleasure are two bells,*
> *if one sounds the other knells.*

The house was a brisk walk from the racetrack where shortly after noon grooms started saddling the horses under tall spreading plane trees, and then they led the horses into the walking ring and people pushed against the white rail fence around the ring, the air heavy with humidity. Some horses, dripping wet, looked washed out, with no alertness in the eyes. It is a sign, but it is hard to know if a horse is sweating because of taut nerves or heat, so I looked for the blind man.

I stood against the rail along the shoot from the walking ring, at a crossing where the horses clopped over hard clay. The blind man came every season on the arm of a moon-faced friend, and they always held to the rail as the horses crossed, the blind man listening to the sound the hooves made. "Three," he said at last, "the three horse." The horse was dripping wet from the belly but I went to the window and bet on the blind man. The horse got caught in the gate, reared and ran dead last. A warning, I thought, but before the next race the blind man said sternly to his friend, "I can't close my eyes to what I see." I moved closer to him. The other horses he heard during the day ran well. He called four winners and I strolled home to the big house and Marina and I drank a bottle of Chateau Margeaux, 1983, a very good year. A few more winners and I might be able to pay for our trip.

That night I dreamed of butterflies swirling out of the sky and clouding the track. "It's all our lost souls," Marina said. The days passed. I worked on poems in the morning and forgot the blind man and the butterflies. I wrote about my dead mother, who would sit in candlelight, her sleeves stained by wax, and play the shadows of her hands like charred wings on the wall.

The sun shone but did not glare. I did well at the track and bought a Panama hat.

One morning, the phone rang and it was Marina. She had driven through town along the elm-shaded side streets. There had been an accident. When I got to the intersection I found our Audi had been T-boned by an elderly man from California who was driving a Budget rental car. "I was listening to Benny Goodman on the radio," the man said, "*Sing, Sing, Sing*. It still sounds great." He had gone through a red light, slamming the Audi up over a sidewalk and on to a lawn, smashing it into a steel fence. Marina had stepped from the car unscathed but stricken. The car's frame was bent and twisted and it was towed to a scrapyard where it was canni-balized and then reduced to a cube of crushed steel. There was a whisper of malevolence and affliction on the air but I did not heed it and we went back to our home in Toronto where I was cheerfully sardonic about the hole in our garden wall. "There's a hole in the bottom of the sea, too," I said, and laughed and then began to sing, *There's a hole, there's a hole in the bottom of the sea . . .*

LIKE MY BACK GOT NO BONE

Our house was in Chinatown, a red brick row house built about 1880 for Irish immigrants. It had always been open to writers who dropped in on us of a morning for coffee, and a little cognac in their coffee; sometimes I made pasta or a tourtière for two or three editors; and since Marina was a splendid cook, we had small suppers for poets from abroad and often we held house parties, inviting forty or fifty people. It was a friendly house, the walls hung with paintings, drawings, tapestries — all our travels and some turbulence nicely framed, but one September afternoon the front door opened and a young man with bleached hair spritzed like blond barbed wire walked boldly in, his eyes bleary, and one shirtsleeve torn. He stared sullenly at the walls, spun around and walked out without a word. Marina was upset. She began to shake and I felt a twinge, a warning, but I was too absorbed in getting ready to give readings in Rome, Zagreb and Beograd, and then I was to go on to Moscow and St Petersburg before coming home in late November for an exhibition of Marina's sculpture. We decided to relax before I went away by celebrating Thanksgiving at the family farm near a town called Conn.

We loaded food hampers on to the back seat of our new Audi parked in the lane (Marina's car was in the garage). I looked back through the broken wall, through the jagged hole. There had been no time to cement the blocks back into place. I felt a vulnerability, as if in the midst of my well-being, I'd forgotten to protect myself. Before she died, my mother had warned me, "People who buy on time, die on time, and time's too short." I checked the dead-bolts and locks on the house doors. An old, fat Chinese woman waddled along the lane watching me with a stolid impassivity that made me resentful. She was my neighbor but I knew she didn't care what happened to me. As she passed, I felt a sudden dread, a certainty that she belonged there in the lane, between the houses, and I didn't. I remembered that my father, whenever he felt cornered like I suddenly felt cornered in my own mind, used to sing:

> *rock me baby,*
> *rock me baby like my back*
> *ain't got no bone*

> *roll me baby,*
> *roll me baby like you roll*
> *your wagon wheel home*

THE QUEEN FALLS OFF HER MOOSE

Our farmhouse was on a high hill surrounded by birch and poplar and black walnut woods. The back windows of the house looked over a wetland, a long slate-colored pond full of stumps and fallen trunks lying between gravelly mounds. The trees on the hills were red and ochre. There were geese on the pond. At dusk, we ate supper in the dining room that had old church stained-glass windows set into two of the walls, sitting under a candelabra that burned sixteen candles. "I think there's a song about sixteen candles," Marina said. "Or no, maybe it's sixteen tons, about dying miners, or coal, or something like that." For some reason, we talked about violence, whether it was gratuitous, or in the genes, or acquired, and whether there actually was something called malevolence, evil. I read something I'd written that morning to Marina: *I love darkness that doesn't disappear as I wake again but leaps a distance, unseen and then as the sun sets, draws near. I see someone approaching: emerging from the dark, merging into the dark again.* I smoked a pipe and we listened to Messian, *Trois Petites Liturgies de la Presence Divine,* and then we went to bed. I lay awake for a long while hearing the night wind in the eaves and a small animal that seemed to be running up and down the east slope of the roof.

In the very early morning, the phone rang. It was a neighbor from the city, a painter who had made a name for himself by painting portraits of the portly Queen wearing epaulets and seated side-saddle on a moose. He was a shrewd, measured, ironic man, but he sounded incoherent, as if he were weeping. "Come home," he said. "Come home, something terrible, the house, it's been broken, come home." I phoned our home. A policeman answered. "Yes," he said, "you should come home, and be prepared. There has been a fire. This is bad." For some reason, as we drove through Conn, I started hearing in my mind's ear Lee Wiley singing over and over: *I got it bad and that ain't good, I got it bad . . .*

A DREAMBOOK FOR OUR TIME

We pulled into the lane behind our house (after two tight-lipped hours on the road). I felt a terrible swelling ache in my throat: there, alone and in pairs and slumped in sadness were many of our friends. What were our friends doing there? They came closer and then shied away, as animals shy from the dead. The police were surprised. They were expecting Marina's red car (it was gone from the garage), and at first they didn't know who I was, but then a detective took me aside. "You should get ready before you go in . . . I don't know if your wife should go in, it's the worst we've ever seen." I looked through the gaping hole in the garage wall. "She's not my wife," I said. "We've lived together for twenty years."

"Do you have any enemies?"

"I don't know."

"It looks like it."

"Why?"

"Because it looks like somebody's tried to hurt you."

"Really."

"We'll have to go around to the front of the house to get in, they never did break the dead-bolt on the back door."

"I've got a key," I said.

"Oh right, sure," the detective said and another cop tried to lead Marina away, but she broke free. "No one's keeping me out of my own home." In the kitchen, a long black-handled carving knife had been stuck into the wall over the telephone; two fires had been set, one on the floor, the other on the gas stove, and the house had the sour reek of smoke; papers and broken glass and crockery covered the floor tiles; the television set was gone. In the dining room, the armoire doors hung open, armloads of old family crystal and china had been swept out on to the floor . . . but I saw that a portrait of me, a painting by Kurelek, had not been touched and I said warmly, "They're not after me, otherwise they would have slashed that."

"Don't be so sure," a cop said smugly. "It doesn't look like you."

"The red car's been stolen," another cop said. "It's just been reported in a hit-and-run accident."

We went into the living room with its twelve-foot high ceilings: the black sofa was hacked to pieces; an engraving by my old Paris friend, Bill Hayter, had been hammered off the wall and lay in a scorched heap; a tapestry I'd brought from Cairo, carrying it through the Black September war in 1970 when I was a war correspondent, was slashed open down the center; the floor was littered with boxes, broken crockery, papers, broken frames, torn cloth, broken records and cassettes, a Chinese vase and ripped books; the lace curtains in the bay window (*Lace curtain Irish*, Marina had liked to call us, since she was Lithuanian) had been set afire, charred; and in the vestibule, a turquoise funerary piece that had once been in a pharaoh's tomb, the pharaoh from the time of Moses, lay broken and beside it a Phoenician bronze bull that had been crushed under a heel, or at least there were well-worn black shoes left beside the bull, and I realized my leather cowboy boots were gone.

"The son-of-a-bitch," I said, laughing grimly, "he's not only cut and slashed his way through my house but he's gone off in my goddamn boots and left me his lousy Goodwill shoes."

"This is terrible," Marina said. We shied away from the grand piano. A fire had been set under it. I could see the blackened veneer, the warped lid.

"It's worse upstairs," a cop said.

"Well, lead on Macduff," I said. The cop looked at me quizzically.

The second floor *was* worse; they had torched a vase of antique silk flowers and a Kashmir carpet on the landing; the word processor was stolen (a literary prize I'd never learned to use, didn't want to use, and was secretly glad to see gone); my books were spilled on the floor, yanked out of their shelves (they'd tried to set a fire in the study by using two books: *Child of the Holocaust* by Marina's cousin, Jack Kuper, and *A Dreambook for our Time* by the Warsaw novelist, Tadeusz Konwicki); in the bedroom, they'd thrown a pioneer child's pine chair through one of Marina's large brush drawings of tangled lovers; Chinese porcelain figurines that my dead maiden aunts had brought from Shanghai in the late 1920's were smashed; and they had ransacked the bureau drawers for jewellery . . . all the silver and gold . . . rings, charms, bracelets . . . all were gone . . . all our bindings of love . . .

The third floor studio walls were soot blackened: dozens of Marina's frames and drawings smashed; an enormous black and brown oil painting by one of her former lovers, *Homage to John Kennedy on his Death* — slashed; the sofa bed springs had been pulled apart with a claw-hammer, the sofa pillows burned; plaster casts hacked open or broken; and the floor was slick with a sludge of burned, scorched, and then doused papers . . . they'd started a fire in an old Quebec armoire . . . acting like a fire box, it had funnelled flame to the ceiling and had burned through the roof of the house, the heat blowing out the windows . . . and all my papers, so assiduously kept over the years; letters, manuscripts, transcripts . . . twenty-five years of intimacies, words chosen with care, exactitude . . . a wet grimy ash.

"We had the water on her three minutes after the alarm," the fire chief said. He was pleased, full of self-approval. "Thank you," I said. He had a grey bristle moustache. Marina asked me if I thought he trimmed it in the morning with little silver scissors. "When we got here the whole house was full of black smoke . . . luckily the front door was open, luckily a woman across the road saw the smoke coming through the roof . . . "

"Who would want to hurt you?" the detective, a Sergeant Hamel, asked again.

"I don't know. All I know is the Dom Perignon is gone." Marina went downstairs from the studio and then came back. There were tears in her eyes. She does not cry easily. "It's the piano," she said. The piano had been given to her by her laconic father before he died of throat cancer, a cancer he'd contracted during the War when he'd enlisted as a boy, too young, having lied about his age, and he'd been gassed and buried alive for several hours in a rat-infested trench. A rat had gnawed on his left little finger. He'd told her two things: "Always listen to music no matter what, and never tell anyone you're Jewish." He'd given her the piano, a 1912 Mason & Risch, a mahogany grand with a beautiful fiddleback grain and carved legs.

The fire under the piano had burned down into the hardwood floor and then up an antique silk shawl draped from the lid. When the lid was lifted, the piano was a burned-out, warped, gutted box.

"It's gone forever," she said.

"No it's not," I said.

A standing whalebone shaman, a drummer figure who had the four eyes of the mystic, done by Ashevak, the finest of the Inuit carvers until he died of tuberculosis, was still on the piano but the drum was broken, the beater scorched black.

"Don't you feel violated?" a newswoman friend, who'd come in from the lane, asked. "Don't you feel raped?"

"No," I said.

"You don't?"

"No, and you're a woman, you should know better. This is a house. No one's entered my body, no one has penetrated me. This isn't rape . . ."

"Yes, but . . ." she took off her glasses and then put them back on. She was offended, as if I had been difficult when all she had intended was sympathy. But I *was* being difficult, because I believe, especially in times when there are charred shadows on the walls, that exactness is one of the few ways I can make a stand in the ditch against sentimentality, self-pity, falseness.

"But the rage," she said. "Someone attacked your place in a state of rage."

"It looks that way."

"How do you account for such rage?"

"I don't know."

"Any ideas?"

"Motiveless malignancy," I said. A cop, who I noticed had cut his neck while shaving, took me by the arm, smiling a tight little angry smile. "We've got one of them," he said.

"You have!"

The cops, while driving down a lane behind the El Mocambo tavern, had seen a shabbily dressed man sitting huddled in a doorway, and he was clutching two bottles of Dom Perignon. "We knew right away that something was sure wrong," a cop said. They had handcuffed him. Strung out on crack, he'd said that he would show them the house he had broken into that morning, and now he was in the backseat of the cruiser in the lane.

"I don't know whether I want to see him," I said.

"Oh, you can't see him."

"Why not?"

"I don't want an assault-and-battery charge on my hands too."

But I did not want to beat anyone. I felt only the torpor that comes with keeping an incredulous calm in the face of brutality. Rage, imprecations, threats were beside the point. I had seen in my life what skilled and sanctioned soldiers or thugs could do to

22

a house in Belfast or on the West Bank or in Beirut. I felt curiously thankful that so much in our house had survived. But I knew some people, and particularly some cops, had their own expectations: I quickly learned that I was a suspect . . . because I was too detached, too self-contained. "He's got to be in on it," a cop, who smelled strongly of Old Spice after-shave cologne, told Sergeant Hamel, who said that he had tried to explain: "No, no. He's a writer. That's what writers do. They stand back and look at things."

WHAT OLD PROFESSORS KNOW

*T*he suspect was named Lugosi ("It looks like he's a cousin of Bela Lugosi," another detective insisted), a young man "of no fixed address." Lugosi had fought in the cruiser, kicking out the rear window, punching, biting and spitting. He had fought at the station. He had seemed driven by rage. The officers had had to go to Mount Sinai hospital for hepatitis shots.

Sergeant Hamel, ingratiating yet reflective — a cop who did not look at you with that wry solicitousness so close to a sneer that is the mark of the cop who knows we all have a criminal secret — opened the trunk of his cruiser. "They set seven fires," he said. "Firebugs. The worst we've seen." He reached into a bag and took out several small bronzes . . . funeral ornaments for a mummy's breast from a pharaoh's tomb, a Phoenician clown's head . . . and then an alabaster fertility monkey from a scent dish

. . . all things that I had bought years ago in a desert town outside Cairo from an old disgruntled professor of archaeology who had stolen them from his museum.

"These yours?"

"Yes."

"It's terrible, things like this being broken."

"Yes. Lasting this long, suddenly smashed."

"I want you to think about your enemies."

"I'm not sure I have any."

"You've written a lot, some people are pretty crazy."

"I'll think about it."

I did not think about it.

"We've got to go where there's water," I told Marina, and we went and in the morning we woke up in the Hotel Admiral on the waterfront, and as we sat up, with the dawn flaring red across the water, we were suddenly flooded by light. "I had an old philosophy professor," I said, "and he always talked with his eyes closed, but when he forgot where he was going he'd open his eyes and say, `Well, we'll lick the lips and start afresh.'"

We went back to look at the house. Standing alone in the sooty squalor of the rooms, I knew we had lost things that connected us to the past, but they would be nothing compared to the loss of the future. I wanted to sit at the piano as I had on other dark and sombre days and play in a minor key. I wanted to shuffle on the black notes, singing, *Rock me momma in your big brass bed, rock me momma like my back got no bone* . . . but it was charred, and then the expert piano restorer, a man named Rob Lowrey, came into the house, shook hands, and then shook his head as he lifted the lid. "Burned to a crisp. It'll cost more to fix it than it's worth, it'll cost $30,000 if we can do anything, and we can't." He hung his head. "The insurance will never pay for it."

"I don't care," I said, "we'll work out something." Lowrey's men carried the piano out of the house. "If we come back," Lowrey said, "it'll be in a year, and if we come back at all, it'll be a miracle."

"You bring the loaves," I said, "and we'll bring the fishes."

EURYDICE DESCENDING

We lived in the hotel for over two months. It was small and elegant, charmingly run by young women, and one wall of our room was glass facing over the water, facing Ward's Island and Hanlan's Point. Every day we came back to the room after sifting through rubble and refuse in the house, and we sat and stared as the sun leaked out of the autumn sky, and then we dressed for supper . . . it was a determined elegance of spirit, a determined refusal to yield to the lethargy of dismay, regret, self-pity, or blame (all the questions asked by the police or insurance adjusters — even the simple question, Why? — contained a hint of blame, of accusation . . . and it was even suggested by a friend that we had asked for it: our house had been too open . . . and another friend wondered whether we wouldn't at last learn that such expansiveness, such openness in a home, was a vanity, and vanity was always punished), but we did not blame ourselves. We ate well at a table beside the wide harborfront window and watched the island airport lights flicker on the dark water. There was a pianist who played out in the lobby, out of our sight, and it was like listening to the ghost of our piano playing, our piano being rebuilt, and ironically, we knew that before our house could be rebuilt, it had to become the ghost of itself: walls washed down, the quarry-tile floors stripped, the broadloom ripped out, the hardwood floors sanded . . . as if a deep stain had to be eradicated, as if a cleansing had to be done (and all the while, we went through the dreary listing of each broken or missing thing . . . each thing the ghost of a moment from the past — like counting razor cuts on the skin that were so fine they could hardly be seen though the wounds were deep to the bone). Papers had been hosed down by the firemen and letters turned to sodden ash in my hands; rolled drawings were scorched funnels that fell apart . . . leaving only a drawn fingertip, a lip . . . all stacked in a hundred boxes piled in the basement . . . two lives, boxed and stacked, and then, a few days later, the police told us that they had arrested a second man named Costa. In a determined gesture toward normalcy, we bought a new television set and put it in the kitchen, a dead grey eye but a promise of sound . . .

On a crisp December morning we woke and ate breakfast and watched the long, lean harbor police boat leave on patrol. The harbor was icing over but there were still geese on open patches of the gunmetal grey water. We drove to the house and discovered that the back door was open, the television set was gone, some jewellery trinkets and a fox fur jacket were gone. We had been robbed again (when a house has been hit, a cop on the phone said, the word goes out on the street: thieves know television sets will be replaced, and an empty house is a sitting duck). So we were being watched. We were a word on the street, a whisper of affliction on the air.

A detective came by to dust for fingerprints. He was wearing a narrow-brimmed hat, a brown suit with narrow lapels. He was lean and close-mouthed, gruff and meticulous. "Yes ma'am," he said. "No." Dust and fingerprints. For a moment, Marina said she thought she was losing her mind, except she couldn't stop laughing quietly, and she mumbled to me, "Go ask Jack Webb if he thinks we'll ever catch these guys."

"No," the detective said. "Not likely. You got the first guys but not these guys."

I could see that this affliction was going to go on for a long time. I could hear the blind man talking to the butterflies. Disconsolate, I went back to the hotel, and then down to the shore, to the breakwater in front of the hotel and I sat watching single-engine planes drop out of the watery gray sky to the island airport. I'd finished a new poem, my dead mother following a dogwood trail:

> *until she reached brushes and eelgrass,*
> *a cover of slate grey water.*
> *She undressed and slid*
> *down a stone shelf*
> *into the shallows,*
> *dragging shore-slime and fronds,*
> *and splashed cold water over her belly and breasts,*

staring at the sky
moth-eaten by light, pale stars.
She eased into the slough.
It had the feel of ointment
as she scissored down
to the braided roots on the bottom,
eyes closed, ears singing,
her drowning voice filling her lungs, swelling,
until the sound became a searing light
behind her eyes
that drove her crashing
into the air,
gulping down the dark
as she crawled ashore.

GUMBY GOES TO HEAVEN

We knew that this tawdry, soft mockery of our life was going to go on for at least a year: certainly, we would outlast it if only because we could still laugh, that raw laughter down the snout, the *Haw* of laughter at laughter itself — but I was now full of a dark rankling alertness to all kinds of signs and signals of affliction: for instance, one day at Dundas and University streets, I saw through the car window a tall memorial monument to the dead airmen of the War. I was suddenly enraged. I heard myself hissing the name of the very rich man who had paid for the monument. *Hal Jackman* . . . a local man known for his wealth, his collection of antique lead soldiers, and his sterling political connections, a man who had used his connections to erect a monument to his moneyed influence, and his trite taste. Children had nick-named it *Gumby Goes to Heaven*, after the cartoon character, Gumby, who had been steamrollered flat by life. In every aesthetic sense, since it was so safe, so conventional, so banal, the monument was a sculptural affront to all the men who'd fallen out of the sky on fire, the lost souls it presumed to celebrate. I could rebuild our house, and someday — if Rob Lowrey could work his miracle — I would play the blues on the piano, but I was going to have to confront that selfserving monument for as long as I lived in the city. It was a permanent offence, a tin-soldiering view of life and death.

Luck Bird in a Monkey Puzzle Tree

*B*efore Christmas, on a cold, clear day, we drove to the old city hall (a dank labyrinth of pea-green and pallid yellow courtrooms) for the preliminary hearing. We had not thought much about the two men who were doing dead time in the city jail (my own contact on the street, a musician — a black horn player I'd known for years — told me that six men had been in the house, that six men had been in Marina's stolen car). We wondered about their faces and pondered the old question: was this a hired hit? And if so, who hated me so much? And if money for the moon plant and crack were the motive for the break-in, was the raging assault on the house a malignancy without malice?

We sat in an overheated room with the fire chief, several detectives and officers, a woman who said she was Lugosi's girlfriend, a Vietnamese bricklayer who had come face-to-face with Costa as he hauled suitcases full of our things out the front door, hauled them out to be fenced and melted down by some scumbag uptown swine who fed off junkie break-and-enter kids . . . melting down our bindings of love . . . and the woman who had seen the smoke and turned in the alarm, a stout woman who was the desk clerk at the Waverly Hotel on Spadina Avenue where Lugosi had rented a room, another woman with confetti in her hair who sat beating a tin cup . . .

As we went up the wide marble stairs to wait outside Courtroom H, a courtroom next to the marriage bureau, I was told several things by several people: that when looking for Costa, two officers had cornered a man in a cappuccino bar on College Street and the man had flattened them both, driving one cop into the street through a plate-glass window . . . the detectives confessed that they felt very sheepish about this; also, Lugosi had checked into the Waverly Hotel before breaking into the house and he had checked in under my name; the house had been cased by a man, a light-skinned black man, named Bo . . . and Bo — who was known to the cops — had probably been in the house at least once before it was hit; Bo apparently had his own business cards — "Surveyor and Estimator" — and would work for any "interests" who would hire him; Lugosi had come back into the hotel after leaving the house in the morning, waving a blowtorch, threatening to set fire to the hotel "just like he had torched a house on Sullivan Street;" several men were waiting in a blue car at the hotel and got into Marina's car without

Lugosi and drove off; Costa had made several trips to the fence who operated out of a Dunk-A-Donut shop on Spadina Avenue during the night using Marina's car; Lugosi's old girlfriend, saying he had done her grievous harm, not only wanted to testify to that harm but also said she could explain why he had savaged our house: it was all, she said, because of an incident in August when I was seen taking the ferry to the park on the island in the city harbor, and Lugosi, who worked with a punk rock band, had spoken to me and I had snubbed him: "He said he would get you for that." The only problem was, I hadn't been on the ferry to the island for four years and in August I had been writing poetry and handicapping under a monkey puzzle tree in Saratoga.

As the afternoon passed, as we waited to be called into the courtroom to at last look into the faces of the two men, to say to them and to the court what we had been through, what we had lost inside ourselves, what music and private liturgies had been stilled, we listened dryly to the sullying confidences of the street while very young couples — most of them black and surprisingly alone, without friends or family — strutted by, beaming, untarnished and newly wed. The woman with the confetti in her hair beat on her tin cup. Then, after all the witnesses had been heard in the closed courtroom and the afternoon had waned, we sat alone on the bench, uncalled, in silence: the doors opened and Sergeant Hamel, looking pleased, explained that everything had worked out to his satisfaction. "The two of you are unnecessary. It's being sent to trial." Lugosi was led to the elevator; slender, head bowed, penitential;

31

Costa, less shrewd, smirked with bravado and stared brazenly at Marina. The elevator doors closed, and so, with nothing left to do in the shadow light of the old city hall corridors, we went Christmas shopping.

"This is all lunatic," I said to Marina. "Everybody's doing what they're doing without ever asking why."

"Because Y is a crooked letter," she said.

On Christmas Eve, after we were told that the sanded hardwood floors in the house had been stained, we stood at midnight in the vestibule, pleased with the wet, dark sheen. "It'll go beautifully with the piano," Marina said.

On Christmas Day, though there was no furniture in the house, we moved out of the hotel, leaving the waterfront behind. Two old Chinese women stood in the lane watching us unload books and papers and clothes. The women said nothing. One was wearing a T-shirt under her open jacket. There was lettering on the shirt:

IN FREEDOM
LUCK
BIRD

I realized that in our four years of living in Chinatown not one Chinese neighbor had ever spoken to me, not even the people who ran the corner Mom and Pop store, who sold me cream and detergent and paper towels. We had handed dimes and quarters back and forth, but I didn't even know if they could speak English. I was angry at Lugosi and Costa but loathed the political culture that encouraged people like the two old women to close in on themselves in a language from another country. Getting to know such neighbors would be like climbing a monkey puzzle tree.

LIMBO LIKE ME

*S*eparate trials took place in February. The Crown Attorney, a pert young woman, was eager: she had a solid case; break and enter, theft and arson, fingerprints and a witness. She thought she could get a substantial sentence. A plea bargain was struck: Lugosi would not contest his guilt if I would agree to five years. "Yes," I said, "I suppose five years will do." (But what, I wondered to Marina, did five years mean?—What did this curious attachment of penitential time to a crime mean? . . . Not the inflicting of corporal pain, but the religious notion of "serving time" in a monkish cell; and I recalled the idiotic notions of my childhood catechism and the confessional — two years off in the purgatorial fires for . . . five years off in purgatory for . . . we were pale souls smiling wanly, innocent but sullied by an eyeless firebug desert god who was always itching for a final conflagration.)

We sat in an almost empty courtroom. Two men I'd seen around the Waverly Hotel sat beside me, and a lone woman, and a detective. Lugosi sat in a box, head down. I looked at Lugosi for a while and felt little or nothing: no witnesses were called before Judge David Humphrey. Police photographs of the house were entered as evidence of wilful havoc and the seven fires. At the court's request, I had written a note about what it was like being a victim. It was for the judge to read. Time, I told the judge, was our punishment, too. Guilty of nothing, we were being punished. Time was the real bond between criminals and victims: "Having survived three months' dislocation we realize how disruptive the devastation has been . . . the endless sorting through drawings, papers — charred, destroyed, these are the tissues of our life, our spirit. We have been robbed of time, it is a robbery that goes on and on . . . Creative time, insights — those fleeting moments of inspiration — they are gone forever . . . The dispiriting loss of time — and we cannot help each other — for Marina, as an artist, has suffered exactly the same loss as I have. We are doing time, and we get no time off for good behavior. The terrible irony is that these two men may well do less time than we will. For us, the loss of time spirals . . . each week implies a month of lost writing, sculpting . . . every two months a half-year, a half-year two years, a year will become five. Together, we may do more dead time than they will. There is the real crime committed against us . . . " The judge expressed his stern dismay; Marina said nothing; Lugosi said nothing. He was sentenced to five years.

A few weeks later, Costa was tried. His defense was hapless: he said that all the damage had been done by Lugosi after he'd left the house for the last time at nine o'clock in the morning. The fire alarm had been turned in at 9:03. That meant Lugosi had savaged the house and set seven fires on three floors in under three minutes. The judge shook his head, embarrassed by the ineptness of the argument. Costa was a young immigrant, a crack addict, a child of the moon plant, his life ruined, on his way to the brutality of prison. I wanted to say something but had nothing to say. The judge told Costa that he was sentenced to two years in a dark clock, the penitentiary.

BETWEEN THE STRUCK KEY AND THE STRING

"A t last," Marina said, "I feel safe." She stopped looking for addicts in the windows at night where she'd see only her own reflection. We took no pleasure in the sentencing. It had to be: the arson demanded it; the police — for their own morale — needed it; as victims we were witnesses to it; but we took no pleasure. Vengeance, like jealousy, is a second-rate emotion, which is why I told the Crown Attorney that I had always found the old Jewish tribal stories of blood-letting and sacrifice — "an eye for an eye, tooth for a tooth" — so twisted. "Esther was a murderous lunatic," I said. "Esther who?" the Crown Attorney asked. I was no pacifist, but vengeance gave me no pleasure, no satisfaction. We felt only a hollow in the house, and the need to fill it with laughter, meditation and music. But every morning, all day, there was only repairing, hammering.

Drilling.

Waiting for workmen to show up.

Waiting. Life as repair.

Realizing the repairmen were padding their bills.

"What d'you care, Mac, it's all covered in the insurance." Expediency. Grease for the wheels.

Nothing done on time, time meaning nothing, till in the summer we went to Rob Lowrey's to see the piano: it had become, in our imaginations, more than scorched fiddleback veneer and charred legs; after opening the lid on its inner parts, so scarred and warped and twisted by fire and supposedly beyond repair — it had become the embodiment of our own renewal. Mahogany could be turned and trimmed, as we had turned ourselves out for dinner every night at the waterfront hotel, but only we knew the ashes, the soot we could still feel on the covers of books, taste on our breaths. So the piano had to be cleansed and brought back to life. The stillness that lies between the struck key and the string, the stillness that contains the note, had to sound.

Rob Lowrey, who had said in dismay that restoration would require a redeeming miracle, greeted us with a subdued eagerness, a caution that comes from dealing with damage. But he had a solid, rounded playfulness as he moved quickly and soundlessly into the aroma of varnish and glue in his workroom, standing in his white apron, obviously relishing his young workers' bashful way of laying their hands on wood. There were men at several pianos, each striking a note, listening, head half-cocked, then malleting a tuning peg into a pin plank, threading thin wire through the peg . . . slowly tightening, tuning the treble and then the heavier bass strings . . . twenty-four tons of tension in those strings, all our anxiety struggling toward the inner harmony that is always the mystery of the piano, the piano in tune with itself.

I stood staring into the hollow guts of our piano as if I were looking back through a jagged hole into the months that had passed, the veneer peeled down to the glue-stained frame and new wood held by vices, the bridges and ribs, the pin planks all laid out . . . and Lowrey, smiling said, "September. We've had to send the legs to Cleveland. No one here can carve those old legs . . . "

"September?"

"Don't worry," he said. "It'll play like a charm."

"I'll have a party, then, open up the house."

"Why not?"

We felt safe: the lane and the garden were flood-lit at night, the garage door could be opened only from inside, the garage wall was rebuilt, all the glass doors had jamb-bars, the rooms had all been wired to an alarm system of motion detectors, and we were four: we had got a young, powerful golden retriever, and called him No Name Jive, and we'd got a regal Irish setter, C-Jam Blues. They slept with us and whimpered if they weren't petted but snarled at any sound outside the door and chewed our shoes as we retrieved our losses.

We had been fortunate to have a good man — fair and accomplished — as our insurance adjuster: a man with close-cropped hair and alert eyes, John Morris. His efficient cheerfulness puzzled us: more than for a priest, it seemed to me, disasters came like tumbleweed across Morris' desk . . . an endless array of mishaps and malevolence that he had to adjust. Perhaps, I said to Marina, that is what a priest really is or should be: an adjuster. In his middle years, he had heard every slick story and dealt with every scam, yet, for all his rigor, he had been fair and sympathetic, and the insurance company had accepted all his recommendations. We would never recover all our losses, but the company was going to honor their obligations without argument.

To Erewhon and Back

*B*ut as we prepared to drive south again to Saratoga, to renew the ritual of daiquiris in the garden and the saddling of the horses in the walking ring, and the blind man, our insurance company, Trafalgar, announced it would not renew their coverage, shedding us, leaving us completely vulnerable. So be it, I thought. Our agent tried to make arrangements with other companies. To her astonishment, to our rage and sudden fear, no one would insure us. Not Trafalgar, not Wellington, not Guardian, not Laurentian, not any company approached. At the same time, the mortgage company wrote asking for confirmation of fire insurance, a condition of the mortgage. Without insurance the mortgage would be called. Never mind the blind man. We would be broken by debt, driven out of the house. "Because," I was told, "you're a controversial writer, even I remember what you said about the settlements on the West Bank, the bigots in Belfast." This was worse than any street thuggery. Even our insurance adjuster, unbelieving, tried to get us insurance with his contacts: the answer was No. There was nothing to be done. Though I had paid house insurance into the industry for twenty-five years, as soon as I was hit — as soon as what I was insured against happened — those companies all closed down on me. Insurance men weren't low-life junkies, strung out and hooked on crack; no, I raged at Marina, they were the blue suits, the actuaries money-crunching the odds on death, shrewd men who were kissing cousins to the California auto insurer for Budget Rent-a-Car — who still, a year after the Audi had been compacted to the sound of *Sing Sing Sing*, owed us $1,200, and still they refused to pay, stalling and stalling until time, the statute of limitations, the clock would run out. These men were bigger sharks than any dipso break-and-enter kid: these were men who had earned their pin-stripes, men who intended to leave us twisting in the wind, defenceless. I knew where I was. I was in the land of Erewhon, Samuel Butler's Erewhon (Nowhere misspelled backwards), where "ill-luck of any kind, or even ill-treatment at the hands of others, is considered an offence against society, inasmuch as it makes people uncomfortable to hear of it. Loss of fortune, therefore . . . is punished hardly less severely than physical delinquency." We had committed an offense by becoming victims. The insurers were going to punish us in ways harsher than any druggies had ever dreamed of . . . the motives behind their institutional malignancy were clear. "The insurance companies are protecting themselves," a broker with pale, almost colorless eyes, said with disarming openness. "If you weren't who you are, there'd be no problem."

"If I wasn't who I am," I said to Marina as we drove past the monument to all the dead airmen, "I'd blow the bastards up."

Then our adjuster found us a sensible, elderly, experienced woman in the insurance business — who reminded me of the way good bank managers used to be: she did not have an MBA from a business college and she was unafraid of her own judgment — and the problem was solved.

"What's required is a blind eye," she said.

"Of course I understand . . . I'm a nobody," I said, and we both laughed.

She wrote on the form: "No known notoriety." I let out a raw laugh, a loud *Haw*, down the snout.

"How come you don't think like these other gonzos around here?" I asked.

"Actually," she said, "I was not born around here. I was born outside Munich, on the edge of Dachau, but that's another story." The woman winked. "They make very good porcelain in Dachau, you know."

The house was insured by Chubb.

BEYOND FIELDS OF ASPHODEL

On a September Saturday afternoon, two men levered the legless and lidless body of our piano on to a sling and lowered it out of a truck on to a trolley and rolled the trolley into the house. They malleted the pins that hold the legs and set the piano in the bay window, all the light catching the grain, so that Rob Lowrey could tune the strings, and then in the early evening, Doug Richardson, a friend for more than thirty years, came in. I had known him back in the days when I'd hung out with a woman

called Crow Jane in a black dance hall close to
Augusta Avenue, the Porter's Hall, run by a gap-
toothed man called Kennie Holdup, and Doug had
played his horn there, and now he played flute, too,
and he had a pianist with him, Connie Maynard.
"You get to christen the keys," I said as Connie sat
down and worked through several chord progres-
sions, and then stood up, beaming: "Very nice.
Beautiful sound. Quiet touch."

"Quiet, I like quiet," Doug, who had an impish
wit, said. "I hate noise, noisy cars most of all.
Expensive cars are noisy. Who'd want a Ferrari? How
could you ever hold up a bank in a Ferrari?"

The house was beginning to fill with friends carrying flowers and wine, crowding into conversation
in all the rooms, friends who were writers and news-
hounds and gamblers, editors and the two carpenters
who had meticulously trimmed the house, professors
and maitre d's and film producers, and after Marina
said, "This'll be strange, being hosts at our own resur-
rection," I drifted happily from room to room pouring
wine, all the slashes on the walls healed, while hearing — I was sure — each note unlocked from the stillness between struck key and string. I introduced
Sergeant Hamel to the crowd. He bowed in a courtly
way from the waist. Doug, mischievous as ever,
stopped honking on his sax and spread-eagled himself beside the door. "All niggers up against the wall,"
he cried. Everyone laughed and the laughter was an
acknowledgment that there is a little larceny in all of
us, and in the cops, too. I had given Sergeant Hamel
my new book of poems and he said he wanted to hear
something said aloud because he didn't know how to

read poetry. "It's not like reading a report," he said. With Doug and Connie on the piano backing me up, I chanted in the voice of Sesephus the Crack King, a whacked-out hustler:

> *Get down, get down,*
> *you got to get down*
> *on your hands and knees*
> *and keep your ear close to the ground.*
> *There are druggies*
> *who honey-dip around parking lots*
> *playing the clown*
> *instead of the clarinet, looking for*
> *peddlers of high renown*
> *as in H,*
> *or dealers doing sap of the moon plant,*
> *crack and smack. I used to dial a vial*
> *myself,*
> *a little digital digitalis,*
> *the speed I dropped*
> *absorbing the absence*
> *in the air*
> *with a light so rare*
> *it baked the shadow of despair*
> *on a wall that wasn't there.*
> *God almighty, it was a time*
> *in fields of asphodel . . .*

In the early morning hours, after our friends had sung a last song around the piano and had gone home and Marina had gone to bed and the dogs were asleep, I stood on the upstairs back porch staring down into the darkness of the lane, the dark split by a shaft of light from the new high-beam lamp on the garage. The two thieves had come up on to the porch out of that darkness to break and enter into our lives, but as I stood there staring at the light I remembered my childhood and how at night when the light from a kitchen door fell across an alleyway, I'd crouch on one side of it — as if I were a mysterious traveller — and then I'd leap through the light and go on my way unseen, unscathed. The year had been like that light; we had leapt through it and with our secret selves intact we were now travelling on.

II

What he has now to say is a long

wonder the world can bear & be.

Once in a sycamore I was glad

all at the top, and I sang.

Hard on the land wears the strong sea

and empty grows every bed.

— John Berryman, *The Dream Songs*

OUR THIRTEENTH SUMMER

*T*his is a story that comes out of my childhood when I saw what I saw and said what was done and did what I was told.

I was a child during the war and we lived on the upper floor of a duplex in what was then called a railroad apartment, which was a living room at the front end and a sunroom at the back end and a long hall with rooms running off the hall in between. The apartment below was the same. "The same," my father said, "but not exactly the same." A chemist and his family lived there. He was an expert in explosives, working with the war department. He was not old but his hair was white. He told my mother that he was working on "a bomb so big that when it hit, when it blew, the war would end up on Mars."

He was called George Reed. He was a chain smoker and his teeth were yellow and irregular. He had a portwine stain on the back of his left hand. He often kept his left hand in his suitcoat pocket. He didn't talk much. He seemed to be shy and reticent but I always felt that he disapproved of me, disapproved of all of us, but he didn't want to be forced to say so, and so he hid how he felt behind his shyness. Sometimes his left hand fluttered in his pocket, and sometimes he couldn't stop it fluttering, not once it got going. "It's like he's got a trapped bird in there," my mother said. As for his wife, I heard my mother tell my father once that "she looks like someone who's been swept over by sadness and has gone strange."

She was from Vienna. That's what she had told my mother and father. I didn't know where Vienna was. "That's where it all began," my father told me, "Hitler's town, except she's Jewish." She was short and had thick black hair. When she talked she got excited. She leaned down and breathed into my face, she peered into my eyes, like she was looking for something that was way beyond me, beyond my mother and father, like she didn't know what she was looking for and yet she was sure it was out there, whatever it was, long gone and lost. And one day, she breathed in my face and said, "I'm not Jewish," and her son Bobbie told me the same thing. "My father's English and nobody's Jewish." Bobbie and I played together on the front lawn. He had his father's wine stain on his neck, just below his left ear. We played war games with soldiers and tin tanks in the rockery. There were no flowers in the rockery, only mud and stones because the landlord refused to spend money on flowers. He said money was too scarce because of the war. But Bobbie and I didn't want any flowers. We wanted the mud and the stones. We could spend a whole afternoon shifting our soldiers from ledge to ledge, country to country. We took turns being the enemy. Whenever he had to be the Germans, even though they always lost, he always said, "Don't tell my mother, don't let my grandfather hear us."

Every day at ten-thirty in the morning and at four in the afternoon his grandfather came out of their sun-room which was below my bedroom. Bobbie said he slept there and studied his books there with the shades down and then he would come out and take one of his walks, shuffling in his slippers from our house to the end of the street and back. He never spoke to Bobbie. He never spoke to me. He was dressed all in black, in a black suit. He had a long pale face and a long blade nose. He sometimes wore a black broad-brimmed hat and sometimes a shiny black skull cap, and he had long curls of hair that hung down beside his ears. He didn't wear shoes, he wore his black leather slippers.

"If he isn't Jewish, I don't know who is," my mother said.

"We're not Jewish," Bobbie told me.

"Sure you are, you gotta be," I said.

He punched me as hard as he could in the chest. When I got my breath, when I wiped away the tears that had come to my eyes from the punch, I told Bobbie to put up his dukes. My father had taught me how to box. He had bought me boxing gloves, and kneeling down in front of me, he had sparred with me, teaching me how to jab and hook, and how to block punches and take a punch. He'd hit me really hard two or three times. "That's so he'll understand that getting hit never hurts as much as he thinks it's going to hurt," he told my mother. "Once you know that then you won't worry about getting hurt and you can learn how to hit and hit real good."

Bobbie put up his fists. I flicked a left jab in his face. He didn't know what I was doing. He didn't look scared. He looked bewildered, helpless as he tried to duck his head. I hit him with a left hook. His nose began to bleed. He tasted his blood, he looked astonished, and then when he saw blood all over his shirt, he was terrified. "My mother will kill me." He began to bawl, but he was afraid to run into the house. His mother came running out. Her black hair was loose and long and flying all about her head. She screamed and pulled Bobbie behind her, to protect him, but I didn't want to hit him again. I felt sorry. I wished he hadn't hit me and I hadn't hit him.

"Why?" she screamed.

"Because he said I was Jewish," Bobbie said.

"Because he's Jewish . . . He's not Jewish," and she swung and hit me in the head, knocking me down. She hauled Bobbie into the house. I looked up from where I was, lying flat on my back, and the old grandfather, who was wearing his skull cap, was standing by their open front window, staring at me, twisting one of his long curls in his fingers.

Later, when I told my father what had happened he said to my mother, "I know they're terrified, I know they're from Vienna, but that's not the point," and he went downstairs and stood very close to Mr. Reed and said through his teeth, "If either one of you ever hits my boy again, I don't care how big your bomb is, I'll knock your block off."

•

*T*here was a Jewish family up the street, just north of us. Mrs. Asch was plump, almost fat. She wasn't too fat because she didn't waddle, but she had a huge bosom and she would hold my head to her chest. Mr. Asch worked with furriers. He was, my father said, "A cutter." It sounded dangerous, like he should be on *Inner Sanctum Mystery* radio. But he didn't look dangerous. He was small, had pasty-colored skin, a round closely-cropped head, and always wore his skull cap, even under his hat. He came home every evening at six-thirty, sat down looking sullen, ate cold chicken that was shiny and pimpled in its boiled white skin, and drank Coca-Cola. We never drank Coca-Cola in our house. "Rotgut," my mother called it, so I drank Hires Root Beer, telling my friend, my pal, Nathan Asch, that it was a kind of real beer. He didn't believe me but sometimes we put aspirins in it to give it a boost and he drank it with me and usually he said, "This is living," and we got a headache that we called a hangover.

Nathan, who was plump like his mother, had one leg shorter than the other. He wore an ox-blood boot with a double-thick sole and heel. He couldn't run very fast and he could hardly skate at all, and so, because I wanted to be a baseball pitcher, he was my catcher. His sister, who was a lot older and very pretty and worked in a fur salon modelling coats, had bought him a big round catcher's glove. It was the best glove anybody on the street had and Nathan knew it and he was proud to be a catcher and I was proud that he was my catcher because he was good at blocking any curve balls I threw into the dirt.

On the weekends when Bobbie Reed's mother
and grandfather walked up the street together to the
grocery store on Dupont Road, they would pass the
Asch house and most of the time in the summer the
Asches would be sitting out on the front porch listening to Mel Allen broadcast the Yankee games on
WBEN Buffalo, or Ruth the daughter would have her
portable record player set up by the porch stairs,
playing Frankie Lane singing:

> *My heart goes where the wild goose goes,*
> *wild goose, mother goose,*
> *which is best,*
> *a wandering fool or a heart at rest . . .*

and the old man dressed in black would sometimes
get a hitch in his step and hesitate and glance up the
walk to the porch. He always wore some kind of
white tasselled cloth under his suitcoat that looked
like a piece of torn sail. If Mr. Asch was sitting on
the porch, he'd glower at the old man and if Mrs.
Reed looked at him, then Nathan's father would get
up, still small no matter how tall he tried to stand,
and he'd push his chin out and down and spit. This
seemed awful to me, particularly because Mr. Asch
was no good at spitting and whatever he hocked out
of his mouth it always went splat and sat there on
his own porch stairs. I didn't understand why he
was so angry and why he was spitting at a woman
and I didn't understand spitting on your own stairs.
I didn't understand any of this at all. The second
time it happened, I asked Nathan and he said, "It's
because Bobbie and the whole bunch of them tell

everybody they're not Jewish. My father hates them for that."

"I never heard the old man say he wasn't Jewish," I said.

"He don't say nothing," and Nathan shouted, "You don't say nothing," hoping the old man would hear him. "You might as well be from Mars."

I watched Mrs. Reed thrust out her chin and quicken her stride as the old man unbuttoned and then buttoned his suitcoat, shuffling away from us, and he looked bonier and sharper in the shoulder blades than I'd thought he was, but then, I'd always thought of him as slumped through the shoulders and he wasn't slumped. His shoulders were very straight, though he did push his feet along the sidewalk like he was tired when he walked.

"Just look at him like he's not there," my mother said. "That's best."

"But he is there," I said.

"So you say," she said and laughed.

About two months after Nathan shouted at the old man it was time for Nathan's birthday. August was always a big month for the kids on the street. August was the last month of the summer holidays and Nathan's birthday was at the beginning of the month and Bobbie's birthday was at the end and all of us were always invited to wear paper hats and blow whistles and bob for apples and eat cake and play hide-and-seek down the alleys between the houses after dark, before we went to bed. I didn't like my birthday because it was in February and it was too cold to play outside. But this year, Nathan's party was different. It was smaller. There were kids there that I didn't know and the kids I knew and expected to see weren't there. Nathan told me that this wasn't going to be his real birthday party, his real birthday party was going to be his *bar mitzvah* because he was turning thirteen and he was going to be a man. After we ate the cake and his mother's cookies, when I said goodbye to him at the door and he thanked me for my gift, a Yankee baseball cap my father had brought from New York, he said, "I can't see you so much anymore."

"What?"

"My father says I can't see you so much, not now that I'm a man."

"Why?"

" 'Cause you're a *goi*."

"What's that?"

"One of the *goyim*, you eat unclean food so you got unclean hearts."

When I came home early, surprising my mother, she was standing alone out on the sidewalk under a street lamp that had just come on. I was crying quietly, not quite sure why because I had done nothing wrong, or maybe it was because Mrs. Asch was never going to hold my head against her big bosom again. The Reed front windows were open and there was loud music coming from the windows as I told my mother what had happened with Nathan and she folded me into her arms and said, "There, there, there's nothing you can do with some people." She sounded very sad but I could tell she was also very angry. As we walked up to our door into the duplex I could hear the music and see the Reeds spinning and twirling, Mrs. Reed with her head thrown back, laughing, and I asked my mother, "What's that they're doing?"

"Waltzing," she said. "That's the way they dance in Vienna, they waltz."

"Like that?"

"It can be very beautiful," she said.

•

*A*t the end of August, Bobbie turned thirteen, too. I was playing more and more by myself. Once or twice I lay on my bedroom floor with my ear to the floor to see if I could hear Bobbie in the old man's bedroom below me but I never did hear him. Sometimes I heard the old man complaining and singing a kind of moan and once, as he was going out walking, he paused beside the rockery and looked down at me as I lined up two Lancasters at the bottom of the stones. I looked up and he looked down. "Bombers," I said, and another time I had my baseball and my glove beside me and I asked, "Hey, you wanta play catch?" He looked startled and then he laughed. Not a loud laugh, but quiet, like a chuckle. "You speak English?" I asked. He took two steps away and then stopped, turned around, and said in a voice that seemed to be as much heavy breathing as it was a voice, "Of course," and then he kept on walking without looking back.

I asked Bobbie if he was going to have a *bar mitzvah*, too. He sneered at me and said, "Of course not. What d'you think I am?" Then I realized that every night, just before supper, Bobbie and his father were putting on boxing gloves in their living room and

Mr. Reed, who probably didn't know anything about boxing, was trying to teach Bobbie how to box. One late afternoon as I stood out on the lawn watching their heads and shoulders duck and weave, I realized that the old man was standing near me and he was watching, too.

"Hi," I said.

He just looked at me, a strange look, like for a minute he thought I was someone else that he was surprised to see, but he didn't say anything. He sighed and went into their house.

Two days before his birthday, Bobby's mother stopped my mother. Usually they said something nice to each other without meaning it, but this time Bobbie's mother didn't bother. She said, "From now on, nobody calls Bobbie Bobbie anymore. His name is Robin. A man's name. Robin Reed." Bobbie looked kind of mopey, so I said, "Well Robin, I don't hardly see you anymore, not even on the weekend."

"I go with my father on Saturdays now."

"Where?"

"To his lab. He takes me to his lab."

"What for?"

"To teach me chemistry, to teach me what he does."

"Terrific," I said. "He makes bombs."

"He doesn't let me make bombs," he said. "Not yet."

On the afternoon of his birthday, I was all alone. My father was away again and my mother was out shopping. Mr. Reed came home early, his head down, his left hand in his suitcoat pocket, fluttering.

I thought he was home to get ready for the party, but not long after, Robin came out on to the front lawn wearing boxing gloves and carrying another pair for me. I thought it was really strange, the gloves were the exact same color as the wine stain on his neck. He said his father had told him that he had to box me before there could be any party. "He says I'm turning thirteen, you know."

For the first time in my life I just suddenly felt all tired, like my whole body was tired. And sad. I was laughing while the two of us stood there with great big gloves hanging off the ends of our arms, but I felt so sad I was almost sick, and though I could tell right away, as soon as Robin put up his gloves, that he was still the same old Bobby, that he didn't know how to box at all, I only remembered the last time I'd hit him, the blood, and how sorry I felt, and I was half leaning toward him while I was thinking about that and he swung a wild looping left that caught me behind the ear and knocked me down. I wasn't hurt, and he didn't know that I knew he couldn't hurt me no matter how hard he hit me because my father had taught me how to take a really hard punch and not to be afraid. So I got up and pawed the air around Robin, trying not to let him hit me, not really punching him because I felt too tired even if I had wanted to punch him, and then he cuffed me a couple of times, but he didn't know how to punch off the weight of his back leg, so I staggered a little and I saw that Mr. Reed was standing in their front window, his hands flat on the glass, a great big glad smile on his face, but the old grandfather had come out on to the cement stoop beside the rockery. He had on his broad-brimmed black hat and he stood with his arms folded across his chest, the torn sail hanging out from under his arms. He was silent and intent. I let Robin take a bang at my body. I was glad my father wasn't home. He'd have been ashamed and angry and I would have had to fight, had to really beat up Robin or Bobbie or whoever he was. Instead, I wanted to cry. Not because I was hurt. I just wanted it all to be over so that I could cry and so I sat down on the lawn and stayed there because no one I loved could see me, no one I loved was there to make me do anything I didn't want to do, and at last, Robin, totally astonished, turned and ran into the house, ran into his father's arms.

I got up and went down the lawn to the sidewalk and sat on the curb and slowly undid the laces to the boxing gloves with my teeth and pulled the gloves off. I wasn't really sniffling. The Reeds were crazy if they thought I was going to get up and go to Robin's birthday party, but I didn't know why they were actually crazy. Then I heard shuffling leather slippers behind me. I thought he'd gone into the house, too, to be with them, but he was standing close behind me, and when I turned and looked up I was almost angry at him but he was smiling, looking down from under the wide brim of his hat and shaking his head with a kind of bent sorrowful smile.

"It's not so easy to hurt you," he said.

"Nope," I said.

"You would make a good Jew," he said.

"How would you know," I said, real sharp, "you're not Jewish."

"No, that's right," he said, smiling a little more, and then he leaned down and whispered, "I'm the man from Mars."

Up Up And Away
With Elmer Sadine

1

*E*lmer Sadine was sent to Saigon and assigned to a squadron of Phantom F-4s, but he did not see battle action. He saw sullen men under propeller fans in bars, sitting on the edge of their chairs waiting for the end of the war, for their flight home, men who sweated too much as they talked about morphine sul-phate. Elmer hitched a ride on a helicopter recon flight and as the gunship followed a mustard-colored river, he fired off an M-79 launcher and watched a rocket grenade explode in a clump of trees. A lance-corporal laughed. "Now," he said, "when it's all fucking over they're sending us the sharpshooters." Elmer was offended. "Up your ass," he said. The lance-corporal punched him in the face and stuck his .45 in Elmer's mouth. "Suck this," he said.

Elmer met a nurse, a woman older than he was. He met her outside a whorehouse. She asked him how he'd got his swollen eye, and if he wanted her to look after it. The whorehouse was surrounded by old vines and flowering trees. He didn't know the name of the flowers, but he said they looked like orchids. "Damned beautiful." The nurse said they weren't orchids, the trees were common as weeds in Saigon, but the real little flowers were in the whorehouse. She told him she had worked for two years with medivacs near Da Nang but now she was living in the whorehouse and looking after the young girls, testing them for infection. "It's my penance. Our guys carry more shit in their veins than the world can handle," she said. None of the girls was older than thirteen. She tested Elmer and then made love to him. She liked to undress him in her room and she was meticulous about his body. After they made love she fondled and washed him tenderly, which aroused him again, but she always smiled at his arousal and turned away. "Too much of a good thing and you go blind," she said.

One day when he came by the whorehouse she swallowed a green capsule and told him he could watch as a child prostitute made love to her. The child smelled of Tiger Rose Pomade. Then she sent the girl away and undressed him, made love to him, and washed him. He forced her back on to the bed, bruising her wrists. "You're raping me, you know," she said. Then she laughed, and sang snatches of songs and then she cried a little. She wouldn't kiss him.

"You're wired," he said. "Fucking wired."

"Never mind that, never mind the girl. It was just something to do," she said, "something before the weeping and gnashing of teeth."

"The gnashing of teeth?"

"Yes."

"What if someone's lost his teeth?" he said, trying to make her laugh.

"Teeth will be provided," she said.

He went back to his room and got drunk and wrote her a note, saying he couldn't see her anymore. "I don't believe in much and you don't believe in anything," he told her. He blamed her for their breakup but he did not send the note. He burned it. For some reason he kept the ashes in an envelope. He put them with his military papers and went for a walk in the night, close to a rancid, stagnant lagoon where there were thousands of squatters' shanties. He was carrying a .45 under his raincoat. He fired a single blind shot into the dark toward the shanties. He didn't know if he'd killed anyone or not. Two days later the whole shanty-town went up in flames. A cooking stove had exploded. Then most of his squadron shipped home. The nurse went with them. He stayed on and took a room for a week in the whorehouse. He slept with the children, grew a moustache, and then left. He plucked a flower from the tree and pressed it between his papers.

2

When he came home from Saigon, his father, a successful stockbroker, said, "I know you. You don't want a job, you want a position. You should go into local politics." His mother thought that was a wonderful idea. "I'd love to see your picture in the paper," she said. "Yes, and you could present yourself as something of a war hero," his father said.

"A hero?" Elmer asked.

"Sure, nobody knows who our heroes are now, a picture in the paper, a sign of the times," his father said and laughed.

"You're laughing at me."

"No, no, I'm laughing at the times."

"Your father loves you," his mother said.

"You're my only son, I've left everything to you," his father said. "What else can I do?"

"Nothing," Elmer said.

He knew his father was not mocking him, that his father loved him. But he also felt his contempt, perhaps because his father had a quiet sneering contempt for everything. He was glad he did not feel close to him. It was safer to talk to his mother about his father because she was always cheerful, even about her own disappointments, and whenever he'd had an angry word with his father she would bake a big cake, chocolate or maple walnut, and then he and his father would sit at the dining room table in silence and eat cake while she sat in the kitchen and sang quietly:

> She wheeled her wheelbarrow
> Through streets broad and narrow
> Crying cockles and mussels
> Alive alive-oh . . .

Every October, his parents took a short holiday; they drove into the Caledon hills to see the changing leaves on the trees. He drove a Buick, they wouldn't have any other car, and they stayed in regular motels as long as the motels had swimming pools. They never went swimming. "But sitting by a pool drinking your morning coffee kinda makes it feel like California, or the movies," he said. Since Elmer had just come home from Saigon, they asked if he wouldn't like to come along. "No," he said. "I seen jungles full of trees." They said, "We thought you might like to visit with us," and set out and as they drove along highway 401, they were killed, crushed when a transport trailer truck broke an axle and overturned on to their car. The truck, carrying tons of watermelons, burst into flames, the diesel lines rupturing at the fuel tanks under the trailer. In the intense heat, hundreds of exploding watermelons blew open the trailer doors.

They were crushed and burned, *scorched*, the police said. Their bodies were put in bags and then in closed caskets. "Gave up trying to get watermelon seeds outta their bodies," the mortician said. "I understand," Elmer said. "I guess you would," the mortician said, "you being in that war like you said." As Elmer stood at attention in his airman's dress blues, he looked down into the twin graves, and what he suddenly remembered was a black soldier in Saigon, a grunt who had bobbed his head drunkenly, saying, "Life's like a black woman's left tit, it ain't right, and it ain't fair." As Elmer left the graveyard, the minister asked, "Well, Mr. Sadine, what'll you do now?"

"Politics," he said.

"Really?"

"Sure."

"Well, that's some job."

"I don't want a job, I want a position."

He shaved off his moustache and settled into the house. It was a big house with many small rooms.

He did not like to go into bed. He left a light on in their room all night, and usually kept their door closed. Sometimes, stretched out on a sofa in the upstairs study, drinking several glasses of whiskey to ease himself to sleep, he stared at the bedroom door. Then one night, for no reason, he opened it and went in and looked under their bed. There was a bugle, his father's. He'd never heard his father play the bugle. He left it there and entered politics.

3

*H*is election slogan was: UP UP AND AWAY WITH ELMER SADINE. He stumped the narrow row houses of Ward 9, the downtown ward. He talked about family values in public life. He wore his flier's wings on his lapel. He made speeches at several Legion Halls but he did not find it easy to be with other airmen, other fighter pilots who had fought in other wars. His eyelid fluttered when they talked about air strikes and carpet bombing. He shuffled his big feet. When he was asked one night why he had wanted to fight for another country in another country's war he said that he had nothing to say about war because war was like a black seed that they all carried in their bones, everybody, Americans or Canucks, and whenever he said this he broke into a cold sweat. He could not blame the sweat on fatigue or dreams of a free fall through the air in flames. Whenever he had to talk about war he felt dead on his feet at the podium.

The campaign lasted six weeks. The voting results in the ward were close. After a recount he was elected as alderman by 9 votes. He'd run in Ward 9 because his only opposition was a florist with a lisp, and also because he had been born on the 9th day of the 9th month. He appeared at a breakfast prayer meeting one week after the election and said that he hoped to serve the city for nine years. He said that while standing under a cold shower that morning, he had brooded on the number 9, looking for a meaning, and he had seen that no matter how you looked at 9 in all its multiples, it always added up to 9 (9 x 8 was 72, which was 7 + 2, a 9; and 6 x 9 was 54, 5 + 4, a 9; and 9 x 9 was 81, 8 + 1, a 9). No other number, he said smiling happily, was so self-contained. "I can assure you, I'm my own man," he said.

The next morning, his photograph appeared in the newspaper: OLD NUMBER NINE TAKES HIS SEAT. He was startled to see such a big picture of himself in the paper and, though he knew his mother would have been pleased, he was slightly offended. He did not think he looked old. He studied his face in the mirror. He was a young man. He had his father's nose and his father's eyes. He looked hard and long into the mirror. He heard the grandfather clock in the hall chime. He'd been looking into his own eyes for nearly half-an-hour. "Son-of-a-bitch," he said. He laughed loudly at that and then he remembered that his mother had always said, "The loud laugh bespeaks the vacant mind."

He started wearing flight glasses, not just on the street and to nursing homes and old folks' homes, but to council meetings. He wondered what people thought. "I like them," his secretary said. "They

give you a certain *je ne sais quoi*, a certain elan. They
go with your wings." He thanked her. He decided
to look up those words to see what they meant. He
asked her to write them down. That's what he told
his secretary to do when anyone asked him a question, "Write that down." He soon had a large filing
box full of questions. He'd say, "Oh yes, I remember
you, the question you asked." He did not pretend to
have answers. He gradually became known as a
tight-lipped spokesman for reduced taxes. "There's
no such thing as loose change," he said. "There's
loose morals but no loose change." During Lent, a
reporter from *Your Catholic Neighbor*, writing about
morals in civic life, asked him what he believed in.
"The number 9," he said. The reporter did not
laugh. "Don't worry, I won't quote you," the reporter
said.

4

*T*hree years later, the Mayor, Mort McLeod, who
had been elected to bring casino gambling to
the city, suddenly died of heart failure in The Dutch
Sisters, a cheap lakeshore motel. It was whispered in
the Council cloakroom that he'd been found in bed
with a high school baton twirler. Sadine had only
contempt for cloakroom gossip. *Shitheads*, he said to
himself. Then he told several newspapermen that he
was his own man, a *hands-on man*, "And I trust what
I can touch, what I can see. I trust these here sandstone walls, that battleship linoleum." During the
conversation with the newsmen, he said to a startled
fellow alderman, "That's a fine door, a fine glass

door you've got there, and the mayor was a fine mayor."

The requiem mass for the mayor was said in the cathedral. The De La Salle high school drum and bugle corps blew their silver bugles at the elevation of the host. Sadine wished that he'd had bugles blown over his mother and father's graves. Taps. We're all fallen warriors, he thought as he stood at the cathedral's center door beside the Monsignor. He said to the Monsignor in a loud, clear voice, "Good work is public work. And the public work is our private work. And our work was the Mayor's." The Monsignor looked doubtful but smiled and said, "I'm sure you must be right." Sadine, as he shook hands with the parishioners, felt a sudden bond with the Monsignor. Though he wasn't Catholic, he thought he might start coming to church. His eyelid began to flutter wildly, so he put on his flight glasses. The Monsignor turned to him and made the sign of the cross, saying, "May the Holy Mary, Mother of God, and all Her angels and saints, bless you." Sadine went home feeling pleased, so pleased that he was afraid that something was going to go wrong.

5

*A*s the sitting alderman from the central ward he was asked to take over the Mayor's chair until an election could be called. "I'm just sitting in," he said expansively to a news photographer, "sitting in for the next eight months or so." He agreed to meet with a rakish old Chinese real estate broker at Bistro 990 on Bay Street. The broker said, while winking and spooning ice cream into the bruised mouth of a delicate-boned young man, "A fool and his money are soon parted. I should like to play the fool in your life." The broker offered him a trip to Hong Kong if he would help to ease the stringent garbage collection regulations in Chinatown. Sadine said, "I've already been to the Far East, thanks." He declined cash, but a week later, he accepted shares in an established chain of funeral homes that asked for his help in re-zoning several new parking lots. "You name me a better bet than death," the broker had said. Sadine, now that he had such a secure income, decided to invest the money he'd inherited from his father in the first Sadine's Dry Cleaning Store. The store's motto was: *Let the Mayor take you to the cleaners*. His aides said the motto was a political mistake because he wasn't really the mayor, but he said, "You don't understand how popular a dumb joke can be."

As acting Mayor he refused to support the extension of an elevated cantilevered concrete skyway along the east-end lakeshore. Trying to make a joke, he said the skyway would desecrate the memory of the dead Mayor by casting a shadow over The Dutch Sisters motel. Then he stood up in Chambers, stroked his chin, and said: TAXES, TAXES, TAXES and sat down. Later, at a large fundraiser in Little Italy, Igidio Ciparone, a construction executive said, "How do we get this guy's nose into joint?" Ciparone's wife, a woman who had plump, swollen arms, said sourly, "Look at your shoes, Sadine. Only a low-flying bore like you would wear shoes with such thick heavy soles." He shuffled his big feet and looked down at his shoes, wondering why anyone would be interested in the weight of his footwear, and he said, "Sensible people wear good solid shoes." He went home. "A lot she knows," he said. He went out to the garage where there were rows of shelves on the walls, the shelves lined with model airplanes. He'd started building the planes shortly after becoming an alderman. Sometimes he stood in the unlit garage and stroked the taut paper bodies of the planes, chanting in a whisper: up up and away with Elmer Sadine! Sometimes, while waiting for the glued struts to dry, he wondered why he'd never played with model planes as a boy. He wondered why his fondest childhood memory was sitting beside his mother, holding her hand, watching squirrels run across the garage roof and up into the branches of the big sugar maple. "Tree rats," she'd said. "Just common rats who look loveable because they have bushy tails and run around in the air." He felt a cold chill. He missed his mother. He went back up to his study and sat down and doodled several 9's on a piece of notepaper. After half an hour, he said, "When all's said and done, there's nowhere to go but up."

6

*H*e ran for Mayor because it was expected of him. But he'd lost interest, going from meeting to meeting feeling lethargic, bored, and angry at his own lethargy. It was how he'd felt in Saigon on the night when he'd gone out to the shanties beside the lagoon and fired a blind shot into the night. His mind wandered on the hustings. In the middle of a speech to the Knights of Columbus, he suddenly started talking angrily to his nurse in Saigon. "Teeth will be provided," he declared. There was loud questioning. "You mean clackers?" someone yelled. Everyone laughed. He didn't care. He was deeply upset because he couldn't remember the nurse's face. He could smell the flowers around the whorehouse. He remembered the smell of the child-whore's hair, Tiger Rose Pomade, and her fingers. He remembered the final two days in Saigon, lying in bed with three little girls as they stroked him and kissed him and giggled. And he could remember the Mayor's face, though they'd never had a conversation alone. But he couldn't remember the nurse's face. He was sure he could remember his mother's face. Or perhaps, he thought suddenly in a panic, he was confused. Maybe he could remember the nurse but not his mother.

He went home and had several glasses of whiskey. An empty whiskey glass fell out of his hand and he heard his mother say, "Oh dear! You're drunk." He heard his father laughing in the bedroom. "Son-of-a-bitch, I'd kill you if I knew where you were," he said. He went and got the bugle from under the bed and blew a loud *BRAAAK*. The next day, as soon as the polls closed, he conceded defeat. When asked by a reporter how he felt, he said, staring straight into the TV camera, "I have no shame at how I did." He was astonished when the reporter turned to the camera and said, "Well, there you have it. At last a politician who admits he has no shame."

7

*T*hough he was still a young man, Sadine quit politics. He wept when the Organization of Funeral Home Directors, at a lunch, told him that they would make sure a small, little-used park close by his house would be named Sadine Park. He felt so good he stood up and cried, "Up, up and away with Elmer Sadine!" Everyone laughed. He went to the bank. He was told by the manager that he was in a very good position financially. He opened another Sadine's Dry Cleaning Store, beside the funeral parlor. He did not change the store's motto: *Let The Mayor Take You To The Cleaners*. He thought that it was still a very good joke.

When he wasn't at his stores, he stayed at home and worked in his study at a long pine table with an exacto knife and boxes of balsa strips and tubes of glue. Then he went out to the garage. The garage was empty because he didn't drive a car. There were more than fifty model planes on the shelves. Every Saturday, he went to Sadine Park on the edge of a ravine. He flew his planes in the park.

One morning a tall, lanky man came into the park through the gate and pointed at Sadine with his walking stick. Sadine was standing by a cluster of honeysuckle bushes with several model planes at his feet. He stepped back into the bushes but the man came directly to him and reached over the bushes and grasped him by the hand. "The name's Mellens, Martin Mellens. I wanted to meet you. I wanted to know what kind of a neighbor of mine sleeps with a light on in his house all night." He said he lived in a coach house down near the old iron footbridge that crossed over the ravine.

He was older than Sadine. He had long spindly legs, a tanned skin that was tight on his skull, and cropped hair. Sadine stared at Mellens. He didn't like his house being watched. "I was sure," he said dryly, "that I was out of the public eye." Mellens laughed, took his hand again, and said, "My young Mr. Mayor, I'm not the public, I'm your neighbor." He strode back to the gate, calling out, "And if I can't be your neighbor, I'll be your friend." Sadine, seeing the older man's spindly long legs and boyish bounce, thought, "The man walks like a water spider who's run out of water."

Sadine asked the postman about Mellens. The postman said he was Russian, a widower whose young wife had died after giving birth to a son, and the baby had died, too. But when he asked a neighbor across the road, the neighbor said, "No, he is not Russian, he's Latvian, and not only is there no baby, but the wife, a young woman, she ran off with an evangelist who goes in for holy roller services, preaching out of his motor-home church." The neighbor laughed. "She swapped Mellens for a Winnebago," and he slapped his thigh at his own joke.

8

On the next Saturday, Mellens knelt by the planes at Sadine's feet. He helped inject fuel into the tiny stainless steel motors. He grinned. As the humid afternoon passed, he mopped his brow with a big white handkerchief and told Sadine that he had made his money in the nursery business, not shrubs and flowers, but a pesticide he had developed that was not toxic but killed grubs. "I don't mind telling you, I've got a streak in me that's a touch flamboyant. See this, my walking stick? That's a grub," he said, putting the ivory handle of his stick into Sadine's hand. The handle had been carved into the shape of a maggot. "Mellens is the name, grubs are the game." He laughed. Then, late in the afternoon, he suffered short uncontrollable fits of shaking that started in his hands. His whole body shook. He grinned and said, "Pay no attention. It goes away." Sadine was glad to hear that. Without thinking, he began to sing:

> *She wheeled her wheelbarrow*
> *Through streets broad and narrow*
> *Crying cockles and mussels*
> *Alive alive-oh . . .*

"Sometimes," Mellens said, "there's a pain that comes with the shaking. It's almost as if it were right in the center of my bones. Unbearable. Nothing works on it. Aspirin. Cocaine. Nothing."

Sadine stroked his chin. At last he said, "You should try morphine sulphate. Get your hands on that. I've seen how it works in Saigon. I was in Saigon."

Mellens began to stop shaking. He leaned on his stick.

"You were?"

"Sure."

"Must've been quite terrible."

"Nearly got killed. Charlie punched me in the face, stuck his pistol right down my throat."

"Jesus."

"Nearly shit myself."

"I'll bet."

"Nearly fucking shit myself."

"I'm sure."

"Long way to go to shit yourself."

"They say travel broadens the mind."

"Right. Well it concentrated mine. I was tonguing the hole in the barrel."

"Jesus," Mellens said, looking at Sadine with what Sadine thought was a wry smile. Sadine suddenly feared that Mellens knew he was lying, about Charlie, about ever coming close to getting killed, and Sadine, astonished at himself, wondered why he had twisted the truth of the story.

"The travelling I like to do now," Mellens said, "is the cruise ships. You ever been on a cruise ship?" He fitted a fuel injection needle into a motor. Sadine said, no, he had not. Mellens told Sadine that he had met a young woman on a cruise to Curacao. "Changed my whole life," he said. After a night of shipboard dancing, she'd come to his cabin. She'd started to sing as she undressed, and he'd begun to shake. "It was like having a high fever. She held me all night, asking me no questions." She had towelled the sweat from his body until dawn. Drained and calm, he'd fallen into a deep sleep. He'd slept through the whole day and into the next night, and then they'd gone dancing again. They'd made love. She'd come home with him, home to his house, and they'd got married. "But now I'm not with her. I

don't sweat, I don't dance, I just shake." He laughed
as one of Sadine's model planes, a Spitfire, circled
over their heads. It flew in low. The motor's ratch-
eting noise forced Sadine to yell. "You're a lonely
man," he cried.

"I suppose I am," Mellens said, smiling.

"I suppose you are," Sadine said.

"It's kind of like tonguing that hole you were
talking about," Mellens said.

9

Sadine sat at night by his bedroom window staring into his own reflection in the dark glass. He
distrusted Mellens, a man so free with his feelings, so
openly full of himself in the generosity of his friend-
liness. "Alive alive-oh," his mother had sung.
"Crying cockles and mussels . . . " Sadine poured
himself a glass of whiskey. He felt the soundless
weight of emptiness in the house. He'd never felt
this emptiness before. He thought of his mother. He
had come home once late at night and found her
wearing a black bonnet with jet sequins, peering
through the bay window curtains, whispering,
"Albert, Albert, fly away home, your house is on fire,
your son has no shoes." He'd laughed. He'd always
had shoes. His mother had been drunk. She'd
looked up at him and said, "Don't you know how to
pray, son? So you can put on the shoes of the fisher-
man." It was dark. He saw himself in the glass. He
wasn't wearing his shoes. He was in his bare feet.
Everything was still. He blamed Mellens for this
sudden sense of silence in his house. He walked into

his parents' bedroom and looked around. There were no more bugles under the bed. Nothing else had been touched. His mother had always been cheerful, wary and cheerful, sometimes almost feverish in her cheerfulness. He realized he'd never gone to see the Monsignor, never gone back to the church to mass. *TAPS.* He decided that a lone bugle blown in the night might be the most beautiful sound in the world.

He went back into his bedroom, rummaged in a drawer and found his military papers and lifted out the pressed flower, dry pink petals with streaks of mauve. He held it to his nose. There was no smell. He began to cry, remembering Mellens' laughter in the park, the sweet mournful look in his eyes as he'd talked about his wife, Lucinda, talked about how beautiful she was. "She came out of nowhere to me," he'd said. Then Sadine laughed as he lay down on his bed, seeing the spindly-legged Mellens coming out of nowhere through the park gate, wagging his walking stick at him in the air. "I wanted to know why my neighbor sleeps with a light on in his house all night." Sadine got up, went into the bedroom, and turned off the light. "Fuck you," he said.

10

*A*s Sadine walked into the park, Mellens was standing by the honeysuckle bushes, singing happily, quietly to himself:

> *There's a husky dusky maiden in the Arctic*
> *And she waits for me, but it is not in vain,*

For someday I'll put my mucklucks on and ask her
If she'll wed me when the ice worms nest again.

"What kind of song is that?"

"That! That's you. You're from here, this country, that's your heritage," Mellens said and immediately put his head down and went to work on the
motors. Sadine stood back. The sun was shining
brightly, so he put on his dark flight glasses.
"Heritage my ass." He'd been watching old war
movies on television the night before. He was tired,
and he was irritated because a very old couple had
begun coming to the park, sitting on a bench close to
a clump of lilac trees. They sat watching Sadine
every Saturday, pointing at the planes, laughing.
Mellens completed the fuel injection. Sadine sent the
radio-controlled planes up into the air. The planes,
swooping and dipping, rose and circled the rim of
tall spruce trees around the park till he checked his
stop-watch for fuel time and drew two of the planes
down to a safe landing. The old couple under the
lilac trees applauded, but they snickered cruelly
when the last plane ran out of gas and plummeted to
the grass, crushing its nose cone and a wing. He
couldn't stand the way the old couple giggled.
Mellens, wagging his cane, said, "Don't let those
crazy old coots get to you." Sadine nodded. "Okay,"
he said as Mellens picked up the fuselage and then
carried the broken pieces of the plane back to
Sadine's garage.

11

*I*n the garage, with rows of model planes parked behind him on plain pine shelves, Mellens stood staring up into the stillness of wings suspended from the ceiling by black linen threads. "You know what this is like? It's like staring up into Alaska," he said.

"I've never been to Alaska," Sadine said.

"You should go."

"I don't want to go."

"I went for a cruise once to Alaska," Mellens said. "All sorts of people sitting there in chairs beside windows that were sealed up so you could see the big high slopes full of trees but you couldn't smell the air, sitting there sealed in amber, so I sat down to say 'Hello' to some of these kindly folks in their golf shirts and pretty soon the man beside me, he said, 'Well, there are a lot of them trees out there,' and he rubs his hands together and says, 'Do you think that those trees is natural or man-made?' and I said, 'I don't know, they must be natural,' so he says, 'Now that's what I was saying to Edna, they gotta be natural, because if they was man-made they could never of got 'em that close together.'"

Sadine laughed. He felt a pang of envy, wondering why he'd never had such easy conversations with strangers, or if he had, why he couldn't remember them. His memory never seemed to give him what he wanted. He could hardly remember anything his mother or father or the nurse had talked about, and when he visited the managers of his dry cleaning stores he had little or nothing to say. Only the week before, a prominent funeral director at a curling tournament supper for funeral home handlers and embalmers had patted him affectionately on the shoulder. "Our man's a born listener. It's a gift," he said. "Now if only my wife had the gift."

"I wish I could remember a joke," he said to Mellens.

"You do?"

"Yeah," he said as he laid a line of clear glue along a balsa wing-strut and secured a joint, searching his mind for a joke. "I remember at this curling tournament they asked me what I thought about curling and I said it looked to me like a bunch of caretakers on ice. They thought that was pretty funny." Mellens howled with laughter. Sadine was taken aback. "You want to talk about ice," Mellens said, "the miles and miles of ice up there in the glacier bays, sometimes when the air is squeezed out of the ice the ice absorbs all the light into pockets of turquoise, it all looks like the broken fingers of the earth, that's where only the ice worms live, it's a big brutal serenity out there . . . "

There was a drop of glue on Sadine's forefinger. "That's funny," he said, as the glue began to harden.

"What?"

"I just remembered something else."

"What?"

"Something I did. Like what you're saying."

"What'd I say?"

"Where you were, a big, brutal serenity, except this was out on the prairies." He peeled the glue from his fingertip. "Empty space, that's what it was, or whatever that great big thing was, it didn't care a hoot about me, that's what I remember, an emptiness so tight in my chest I was almost afraid to breathe." He paused, and then winced, as if he'd got a sudden pain in his side. "I hate my father," he blurted out. "I hate the prairies and I hate my father." He moaned, staring up into the dark well of the garage, into the wing spans. Mellens said nothing. Sadine took a deep breath, shrugged, and said, "He was a kind of caretaker and he sure had an attitude."

He did not go on to tell Mellens how afraid he had been of that prairie emptiness, how he had walked up and down the streets of the town, afraid, filled with panic. He'd hired a hooker at the hotel and taken her to his room and there, she'd led him into the bathroom so that she could wash him. "A girl's got to keep clean," she'd said, and the fondling with warm water and soap had aroused him. The girl had held him in the palm of her hand. "You can play with that," he'd said. "Sure," she'd said, "and I can whistle a happy tune on it, too."

Mellens, lifting one of the fragile planes from a shelf, turned it over in his hands, a Stuka dive-bomber. Sadine remembered how grimly he had made love to the hooker, till he had rolled over exhausted and heard her say as he fell asleep, "My God, ain't you something."

He had wakened in the prairie hotel feeling so refreshed that he didn't care when he found that the girl had taken fifty dollars from his wallet. "She was damn good for me." After that, every Friday night, he had booked a room and a hooker at the King Edward Hotel, and he always had a dozen chrysan-themums delivered to the room. He liked the lush

expansiveness of flowers. Sometimes he tore a handful of petals from the flowers and spread them on a
pillow and then went into the bathroom.
"Cleanliness is next to godliness," he said, laughing
as he stood by the sink, wearing his flight glasses,
waiting to be washed. "Up up and away," he said,
aroused.

Mellens held the frail body of the Stuka against
the garage light, running a finger along the wing-
tips. "I'm glad you've come back," Mellens said.

"What?"

"Wherever you went in your head."

"I was thinking."

"I am sure you were."

"I was."

"Thinking of what?"

"Soap," Sadine smiled.

"You were thinking of soap?"

"I was," Sadine said.

"Soap."

"Yep."

"I was in the war, too," Mellens said. "You
know that?"

"I didn't know," Sadine said.

"Not your war. The World War."

"You're kidding. That makes you old enough to
be my father."

"Not quite."

"Where're you from?"

"Riga."

"Where's that?"

"Latvia. And I ended up in a concentration
camp. Hard labor. I was sorry for myself, I was

sorry for the Jews. There was no point feeling sorry for the pansies. Everybody hated the pansies. The gypsies hated them. The Jews hated them. What was hardest was to live with how filthy everyone was. Shit. Lice. You don't know how lousy life is till you know that you've learned to actually sleep with your own lice. To lie in shit and sleep with your lice. Nobody dreamed about whipped cream and eclairs in there, we dreamed about soap. And one day, a particular guard said to me, 'My garden is dying. You fix my garden and I will get you a box of soap, a big box.' So I fixed his garden and I got this box of a dozen bars of soap and I kept one bar for myself and gave the box to the Jews in my barracks and at the bottom of the box, after they took out all the bars, there's this particular card saying JEWISH SOAP. They had a ceremony, they buried the soap and said prayers over the dead, and that was that."

"That's all?"

"Yes," Mellens said.

"So you became a gardener."

"Me and the worms, we made a life."

"Here?"

"In my mind, in worm country. Wherever the ice worms are, up in Alaska. Anywhere. That's where I am. Ice makes you wonder, you wonder about wormholes," he said, holding a slender Phantom F-4 up to the light. "The physicists, they say the universe is a great big transparent sac like a skin and there we are in this sac except there are wormholes out there, holes that go right through the world's skin out into other worlds." He circled Sadine, saying, "We could get out of this life alive, we could almost get out of this world alive if we could find the wormholes."   Sadine heard a sharp, brittle crumpling sound and Mellens, with a sheepish smile, held up the Phantom F-4, the belly spars collapsed in his big fist. "Damnation," he said, "now that's dumb." He handed the broken plane to Sadine, who yelled, "You broke it!"

"So, it can be fixed," Mellens said, shrugging.

"It's broke," Sadine said, surprised that he was so angry.

"If it's broke, fix it."

"Fix it. The man says fix it, he's got no shame," Sadine cried. "You've got no shame."

"Shame," he said.   "You want to talk about shame?"

"No. There's nothing to talk about," Sadine said.

"Why not?"

"Because I've got nothing to be ashamed of."

"Then shut up," Mellens said. "It's a paper plane, for Christ's sake. There are bigger things," and as he turned to leave the garage he began to sing:

> *She'll be waiting for me there*
> *With the hambone of a bear*
> *And she'll beat me*
> *'Til the ice worms nest again.*

12

A week later, Sadine had to go downtown. He needed to get new leather soles put on his shoes. He took a taxi rather than walk past Mellens' house. In the shop, a man at the counter said he wanted to get a pair of riding boots repaired. He was wearing a red hunter's jacket, a hard, black riding cap, and he was carrying a bugle. Sadine spoke to him and the man explained that he was the bugler at the racetrack, that he took the bus out to the track every noonhour, going in full dress because it meant curious people always talked to him. He liked to talk to strangers. "Never had a lonely bus ride yet," he said.

"How hard is it to learn to play the bugle?"

"Learning to blow is one thing, learning to play the bugle is another."

"My father left me his bugle, he left it under his bed."

"No kidding," the bugler said. "The only time I put my bugle under there, it was a woman I loved so much I never wanted to get out of her bed."

"You're kidding."

"Look, learning to play your father's bugle, that's nothing."

"It's the bed that's a problem," the shoemaker said.

At home, Elmer put the bugle to his lips. He had the peculiar feeling that he was kissing his father for the first time. He blew into the bugle, making a loud braying flatulent sound. "Fat fucking chance I can play this thing," he said and laughed. He went downstairs and out to the garage and began to rebuild the Phantom F-4, paring the balsa strips with his exacto knife. When he was done, he set the plane on a table. He stared at it a long time and was surprised that he felt no satisfaction. He felt grim. He felt he was being watched, *a light in the window*, he caught a glimpse of his mother's face in the overhead well of wings. "What are you doing there?" he screamed. He brought both fists down on the plane and crushed it and shook his head because he felt a sudden tiredness, a lethargy so deep in his bones that he wanted to lie on the floor and cry. He wondered if he had actually killed anyone on that night when he'd fired into the shanties by the lagoon.

On Saturday, he went to the park with only one plane. He flew an F-86 in low circles over the trees. The old couple, seeing how grim and tight-lipped he looked, left him alone. Mellens did not appear. The air was humid. The plane had no lift. It crashed. Sadine walked home carrying the broken wings, disheartened, his eyelid fluttering. "Some goddamn pilot," he said. He was astonished that a stupid argument with Mellens had left him so troubled. He poured himself a drink and opened his mail and was startled by a big white pamphlet that had 999 embossed in bold black on the cover. He remembered telling the reporter that all he believed in was the number 9. Then he realized he was holding the pamphlet upside down, that it was an evangelical tract promising the imminent end of the world under the sign of 666 — *the numbers of the apocalypse*. "Three 6's are 18," he thought, "and 9 and 9 are 18, so maybe it'll all even out."

He opened another Sadine Dry Cleaning Store and then went to the bank with a large unexpected dividend cheque that had come in from the funeral homes. "Boy, the dead are really dying," he said. He was so pleased he booked a room in the King Edward Hotel in the middle of the week. The girl turned out to be very young, probably too young, which was dangerous, but Sadine felt incredible arousal as she crouched on her hands and knees and he mounted her from behind. Then, almost immediately, he became preoccupied with the taut smoothness of her skin and his own flabby paunch, and though he thought, *I'm still young*, he heard himself wheezing for air. He wondered if he was bored. He wondered what had been in the green capsule that the nurse had swallowed in Saigon. He decided he would ask for two girls on Friday so that he could watch them. "It was just something to do," he heard the nurse say. With a loud laugh, he gave the girl a hard slap on the buttocks, and then another slap. The girl leapt up. "None of that fucking shit," she yelled. "None of that fucking shit, man. Nobody hits me," and she gathered her clothes, dressing so quickly that Sadine, still on his knees with his eyes closed, didn't realize she was dressed until she was at the door. "No, wait," he cried.

"Wait for what?" she said, her hand on the door knob, "This bitch is on wheels, man."

"I wasn't trying to hurt you."

"Who the fuck cares."

"I do."

"Don't give me that shit, man. You gonna beat on me, you think I was born yesterday, man."

"No, I was," he said.

"Very funny."

"No, it's not," he said. "It's not funny at all. I wish it was funny. I wish I could tell you a joke."

"This is a joke, this whole fucking night's a joke."

"No it's not," he said.

"So what d'you want?"

"I usually get washed."

"Washed?"

"Yes. With soap."

"You want me to wash you?"

"If you want."

"No, no, no, no man. It's what you want, not what I want. It's what you pay for."

"I don't care anymore. I'd just like you to stay, that's all."

"So what're you gonna do if I stay?"

"Nothing. Talk. You can talk to me."

"I don't talk. I fuck."

"Try talking."

"What's to tell. It's all shit. I don't shovel shit for dead men."

"Nobody said I was dead."

"I didn't mean you were dead, man. It's just a way of saying. Don't take it personal."

She came to the side of the bed. She looked at him very shrewdly, smiled, and stepped out of her high heels. "I ain't telling you nothing, man. I bet you could do me dirt. I ain't telling you nothing about me."

"So don't."

"Nothing."

"Whatever you want," he said.

She took off her dress and lay down beside him. "I can tell you about tricks, all the lunatics I meet," she said.

"Whatever," he said.

"Like you," she said.

"What?"

"You're a lunatic."

"Is that true?"

"That's a maybe."

13

When Mellens came through the gate, Sadine was embarrassed because he knew he was smiling warmly, but he didn't mind being embarrassed. Mellens, striding across the grass, began to talk at the top of his voice, wagging his grub-handled cane, saying, "What a trip, what a trip, people of our kind, Sadine, our kind, successful, big rolls of fat under their arms and under their chins. They play bingo! They play bingo. Can you believe it? All afternoon in that cruise ship, not caring about the sea, and when the bingo caller called out, 'Under the I, two little ducks — 22,' they all cried, *Quack, quack.*" He hooted with laughter. Sadine quickly sent a Hurricane fighter plane roaring straight up into the air, driven by a booster motor.

"'Under the O — twin 5's, the number 55, and so big,' and what did these fine people of ours call out? — *Dolly Parton!*"

He told Sadine stories about his trip until the sun sank behind the trees. All the planes landed safely. As they walked home along the heavily treed streets, past limestone rockeries, they were subdued and reflective, but inside the garage, as Sadine shelved the planes, regretting that there was no repair work to be done so that they could stay there, Mellens said, "You know the strangest thing I saw? You should've seen this ship's casino, it was sitting there totally empty except for this nice looking old man at the end of the craps table, and when he threw the dice, the croupier, he calls, '*Hard Eight*, your point is 9.' The old man had his cane hooked to the edge of the table and it's a white cane. He was blind, he's a blind man shooting craps all alone, and suddenly, when the old blind man says, 'Double my bets,' the croupier took his money from the rack and counted it out very careful and I felt right there, felt what I'd never understood before, the complete wonder of human trust, the trust in life as it is. Life as it is is better than no life at all. A blind shot in the dark. That's how we learned to sleep in shit with our own lice. I could see it in the cane hanging on the lip of the table as though it was hanging on the edge of the world, a crazy blind man, beautiful, in a world he'd never seen."

"A blind man shooting craps!"

"Yeah, and a winner."

"He made his point?"

"Yeah, and later, I thought about you."

"You did?"

"Your planes. Once we left Acapulco, I was standing on deck late at night somewhere outside Panama City and all these planes are coming in, lights blinking, and I thought of you, that light you keep on all night in your house."

"Not anymore," Sadine said, as he stepped out of the garage into the pale shadows of dusk. Mellens followed, his cane clacking on the interlocking brick driveway.

"It's strange," Sadine said.

"What?"

"How one thing leads to another." He walked down the driveway, suddenly wanting to tell Mellens

that he was seriously thinking of really learning how
to play his father's bugle. Instead he said, "One night
I was in Calgary for some alderman's convention or
other, staying out by the airport. You could see all
the landing lights from the window, and I hired a
hooker . . . "

"You went with a hooker?" Mellens said, grinning,
so that Sadine could see the line of his dentures.

"A girl who wore silver stockings and she had
braided hair with little beads in it, and a sequined
purse. Funny how I remember that."

"What was her name?"

"I don't know. I never asked her, she was from
Detroit, I know that. She was a black girl from
Detroit and I suddenly told her I wanted to watch
the planes come in, I wanted to stand out in a field in
the dark somewhere while she was doing me and
watch the planes come in. So she drove me to this
side road and she said, 'There's no planes at one in
the morning,' but I said, 'There are always planes,'
and I stood there staring at nothing in the sky happening while she knelt down to do me and the next
minute there were these great goddamn rabbits
going by in the night, a herd of rabbits."

"Don't be crazy."

"Big like this," and Sadine opened his arms.

"They must've been hares."

"Who cares, they were the ghosts of something
going by."

"You're seeing things."

"Sure I was seeing things," Sadine said. "I'm
hauling my pants up around my throat and I'm seeing things and they've got big red eyes."

"Maybe they were ghosts getting out of town."

"They were going straight downtown. They were screaming. You know that? Rabbits scream, and all of a sudden, standing there holding my pants so I wouldn't fall down, I yelled, 'Sweet Jesus, get me out of here!'"

Mellens laughed and put his arm around Sadine's shoulder. "I'd never have guessed that you've got this low-life taste for hookers." Sadine stiffened, offended. He would never be able to make Mellens understand that his use of hookers was essentially a practical matter, that he'd always left the hotel rooms feeling braced and buoyant. Cleansed. It was nothing personal. He'd learned in politics that people who took things personally ended up wounded, enraged, and belittled, but he wanted to protect himself so he tried to sound lighthearted. "I give her the number 9," he sang, "drive it home, drive it home." They stood side-by-side on the sidewalk, smiling like secure old friends. He wished, as he stepped out of Mellens' embrace, that he'd never told him about the rabbits, their screaming and their red eyes.

14

Mellens telephoned later in the week. He said he was sick, a congestion in his chest. As Sadine hung up, he realized that they had never talked to each other on the phone before, and though they were neighbors who'd met for weeks in the park, they had never been in each other's house. "And probably a good thing, too," Elmer said. He took Mellens' phone call as a sign, a warning. Late one night, after several glasses of whiskey, he thought he heard Mellens' step on the stair, and then he was certain he heard Mellens talking to his father in the bedroom. He thought they were arguing and he put down his whiskey and got up and stood in the hall to listen. He heard nothing. They had stopped. Perhaps they knew he was there. "They're fucking hiding," he said. In two weeks, in early October, he talked to Mellens again. Mellens phoned and asked, "You still there?"

"Where else would I be?"

"In the grave."

"Don't be ridiculous."

"That's what's left," Mellens said.

"What?"

"Being ridiculous."

On Saturday, Sadine was shocked by Mellens as he came through the gate, wizened and yellow under the eyes. "Sick, sick as a dog," he said, pulling the shawl collar of a woollen sweater-coat close to his throat.

"With what?"

"With life, with nothing."

"Nonsense."

"I'm dying," Mellens said, jabbing his cane at Sadine and then saying, "Get going, let's get this act of ours up in the air."

Sadine had to wait as the elderly couple strolled across his take-off path. He was shaking, his eyelid out of control. He suddenly wished that Mellens had met his mother, had met her before she had put on her black bonnet with the jet sequins. "My mother was a lonely woman," he said. "Today, she would probably have baked us a cake. She had this peculiar faith in cake."

"You don't say."

"Yes. The more I think about it, she was very lonely. She used to sing *Alive, alive-oh* . . . " He sent a Mirage bumping across the grass and up into the sun. "So you're feeling really sick," he said to Mellens.

"The ghosts got me, I guess."

"Ghosts?"

"Those rabbits of yours. My wife, she came home and got me, too."

"You saw her?"

The Mirage swooped low over clumps of dogwood bushes. "Sure, it was just like she'd come back down a wormhole and stood there at the foot of my bed."

"She's come back to haunt you?"

"That's exactly what I said the first time I ever saw her. *Here is a haunting beauty.*"

"I don't believe in ghosts."

"If you've got no ghosts, you've got no life," Mellens said grimly.

"I still don't believe."

"Sure you do."

"Nope."

They heard a smack. Under the lilac trees, the old woman had slapped the old man, knocking him down, and now the man was up and shambling from the park, weeping. "Ah, young love," Mellens said. His laughter made him look so gaunt that Sadine was ashamed that he'd ever been angry at him. "Wait'll you see this," he said. "I've been working on it for weeks." He drew a cloth back from a sleek black swept-wing plane. "Stealth," he said.

"What?"

"It's a Stealth bomber, the great night fighter. No radar can track it."

"Really."

There were twin motors in the belly of the bomber. It rose slowly, in a long graceful low flying arc. "You know what I've been thinking about while I've been sick," Mellens said, shielding his eyes from the sun and following the flight-line of the plane. "That trip to the glacier bays, those glaciers growing like they do at two or three hundred feet a year, their damned relentless lifeless growth . . . it's exactly what God's mind must be like, a great big white silence, those huge tongues of ice with their roots in the sky."

"Mellens, for Christ's sake!"

"What?"

"We're flying planes. We're trying to have some fun flying planes."

"You fly and I watch."

"Right."

"Because you got your wings," Mellens said, chuckling. "But I've got your number. Yessir, Mr. Mayor. You ever seen my number? I never showed you my number."

"What number?"

The Stealth bomber pulled straight up over the trees, their leaves all changed in color, pulling into the sky and disappearing for a moment in a sun flash. "You want to see something, look at that," Sadine cried. "Look at that," and the black plane reappeared out of the sun, diving at high speed.

"Camp numbers," Mellens said.

"Oh."

"4-6-2-3-5-3," he said, showing Sadine his bare arm.

"You got no 9's," Sadine said.

"Who needs 9's?"

"I like 9's."

"I'm talking concentration camps."

"I'm not."

"Why?"

"Because I don't want to."

"You're scared."

"No I'm not."

Mellens suddenly cried, "There it goes! Heading straight for the wormholes!"

"Cut it out, you and your goddamn wormholes," Sadine yelled, looping the plane back over their heads.

Mellens drove his cane into the soft earth. It stuck and quivered. "Yeah, well you know what? I don't think any Viet Cong stuck a pistol in your mouth, and you know what, maybe I've never been on a cruise ship. What d'you think about that?"

"Nothing."

"What d'you mean, 'Nothing?'"

"Be careful," Sadine said.

"I'm too old to be careful."

"Then be nice."

"Nice. What's nice? What a dreadful word, nice."

"Get a life," Sadine suddenly screamed. "For Christ's sake. Get a life."

Mellens hurried across the lawn. "I told you I'm dying." He left his walking stick in the earth. He turned at the gate. "You remember, Sadine, there's a great big white silence out there," he cried. He went through the gate and Sadine sent the Stealth bomber, its twin motors shearing the stillness in the park, straight up in the air again. But then it went into a series of tight turns which he had not sent by signal, so he levered a new flight pattern into the control panel but the bomber widened its circles and picked up speed until it levelled off. It crossed overhead and disappeared between the tops of the yellow and ochre and red trees, heading downtown. Sadine took off his flight glasses. He stood rooted to the ground for a long time, staring off between the trees, waiting for the plane to come back. "Something about those leaves," he heard his father say, "they're so beautiful they make you wish life wasn't the way it is." He picked up the Mirage and the control panel and he drew Mellens' walking stick out of the ground. The ivory grub handle was warm in his hands. He felt so heavy-footed he used the cane for support on the walk home.

15

*A*ll week, he worried about what to say to Mellens and what to do about the plane. He scanned the newspapers to see if there might be a story about a model Stealth bomber that had showed up out of nowhere in a child's backyard, but there was no word, and he had no idea where to look for the plane. A week passed and he decided that he had to see how Mellens was feeling.

When he telephoned, a woman answered. She said that she was his wife. "Are you a friend?" she asked.

"Yes," he said, almost defiantly.

"Well, in that case, the burial is tomorrow morning. You'd best come."

16

*S*adine drank six glasses of whiskey but did not fall asleep. He dreamed that his mother was hiding a cowering Mellens under her pleated white skirt, and then he saw Mellens as a scrawny long-legged boy in a concentration camp, a boy baring his arm, the blue numbers that were all 6's, grinning as if he'd known that they would meet, saying, "Sadine, Sadine, teeth will be provided." Sadine was sopping wet, shivering. "For Christ's sake," he said. He heard his mother singing, his mother who had bathed and washed him as a child. He thought of the women who had washed him and then taken him in their mouths, swallowing his semen. His seed. He had no children. No one to wash. He'd never wanted a child. He and Mellens had no children. They shared that. And the black seed they carried in their bones, he could feel the seed inside his body, like soot along the bones. "But at least I'm still alive," he said. He got up, his hands shaking as if he'd been accused of something shameful. He went into his parents' bedroom and lay down again and went to sleep.

17

When he awoke, he began to shiver, dreaming — though he knew that he was awake — that he was lost alone on the runway of a wilderness airport in a snowstorm and there were red warning lights all around him, but then he realized that the warning lights were eyes, the red eyes of the dead, the dead who were so white he could not see them. He could see the whiteness of everything, including the dead, and yet he could not see anyone. He was certain that Mellens was standing in front of him but he couldn't see him. The clarity of seeing nothing stayed with him as he showered and then put on his dress blue uniform, folded away for years so that it still smelled slightly of cleaning fluid. He was a little flabby and the belt was tight but he hadn't put on too much weight. He drank a cup of black coffee and called a taxi. He sat in the backseat of the taxi with Mellens' cane across his knees. He was in a cold sweat again, trembling. He had pricked his thumb, drawing a drop of blood as he had fastened his wings to his lapel. He'd sucked his thumb to stop the bleeding. He was still sucking his thumb as he got out of the back seat of the taxi.

18

He crossed the grass to the graveside, his shoulders back, his head held high. There was a minister at the grave, whose red-white-and-blue Winnebago was parked under a weeping willow, and there were six professional pallbearers. He noted that they were not from his funeral home. A young woman who had long auburn hair was wearing a veil so that Sadine could not see her eyes. There was a white orchid on the lapel of her black suit. He was wearing his flight glasses.

"You must have been a very good friend," she said, noticing the cane that he carried under his arm. "If he gave you his walking stick you were a very good friend."

The minister ended a brief prayer, asking flights of angels to carry Mellens home. He blessed the coffin as it was lowered into the earth.

Sadine went to salute but stopped. He didn't know what to say. He wanted to do something. He was furious with himself for not having learned to play the bugle. "I would have played *Taps* . . . " he said. The veiled woman looked startled. "Pardon?" she said. Then he tore the wings from his lapel, ripping the cloth, and he dropped the wings down into the hole. The metal clunked against the coffin. His feet sank into the soft, loose earth. His eyelid fluttered. "From time to time," he said, "we flew together."

A Kiss Is Still A Kiss

*A*n old blind man shuffled his feet under a chokecherry tree, trying to get out of the shade of the tree, tapping his white cane as he hunted for the sun, for a warm bench in the park where other men lay sprawled asleep on the grass, their hats in the crook of their arms and empty beer cans between their legs. A seagull stood close to the sleeping men. Another perched on one leg on the stone sill of a large display window across the road from the park. The window was on the ground floor of the Household Trust tower. It was noon and a woman sat at a carillon inside the window, and because there were speakers in the high branches of the trees in the park, the old man could hear her playing. He sang the words as he tapped his cane:

> *You must remember this,*
> *A kiss is still a kiss . . .*

He kept tapping until he began to feel strong heat on the back of his neck, sunlight by a bench at the foot of a two-storey wall that had been painted, ochre fields and green foothills, clouds and white birds, and leaping out of the painted sky was a rainbow that fell to root behind a bench where a young woman sat alone, her face tilted to the sun, alone until a young man sat down beside her. He was in his late twenties. He wore a black felt hat and had gathered his long black hair into a tooled silver clasp at the back of his neck.

"You're looking good," he said to the girl. She was wearing high-top black policeman's boots and a mottled battle-fatigue jacket that bore a hand-stitched patch over her heart: *May The Baby Jesus Open Your Mind And Shut Your Mouth.* Her head was shaved clean except for a hedge of yellow hair and she had braces on her teeth. "You some kind of Indian?" he said.

"No way," she said. "No Indian looks like this."

"Maybe not."

"You a doper?" she asked.

"Nope," he said.

"Only a doper would figure me for a Indian. I don't look nothing like those guys lying on the lawn."

"Right."

"Fucking right," she said and tilted her face to the sun again.

"This park gives good place, eh?"

"Whatever you say, man," she said.

"You a punker?"

"Get real," she said, eyes closed.

"Would if I could," he said.

"There's punks, and punkers," she said.

Hunched forward with his elbows on his knees, he said, "You mind what I wanta ask you?"

"Talk be cheap, man."

"How come you got those tinker-toy tracks on your teeth?"

"You mean my braces?"

"Yeah."

"My old boyfriend, he figured they were prime, man, so fucking prime he got himself some braces too. He don't need no braces. He don't need nothing. He got himself beautiful teeth. He don't care about nothing. He's just doing what he does."

"What's he do?"

"He don't really do nothing."

"Me too," he said. "I don't do nothing. Not if I can help it."

"Perfect," she said. "Fucking absolutely perfect."

"What's your name?"

"I don't deal names, man. Not with no strangers."

"What kinda paranoid is that?"

"The right kind, man. The right fucking kind because I got the fucking facts."

"So tell me your name, for a fact."

"What for?"

"For nothing. I can't talk to nobody that's got no name."

"I ain't nobody."

"Right."

"Cindy," she said. "Cindy Witchita."

"That ain't no name, that's a town."

"I can't help that, man. How can I help that?"

"That's a town in the movies."

"I ain't no fucking movie, man. No way. No fucking stupid movie is happening inside my head. So, if you're so smart, what's yours?"

"Abner," he said. "Abner Deerchild."

"Fucking unreal," she said. "Absolutely fucking unreal."

"What?"

"You're a fucking Indian name."

"Right."

"You panhandling or you on the pogey?"

"I just kinda steal, you know, like I steal what I can."

"Like you're a real thief?"

"Naw, I just look out for myself."

"Like we all do, man. Keep your fucking eyes open."

"Right. Quick fix."

"So don't fuck my head, man," she said.

"Why would I do that?"

"I don't know, like, suddenly we're talking to each other, so just don't do it."

"Okay."

"So what's with you? How come you sit down beside me, like outa the blue?"

"Nothing. Nothing I'd want to say right out."

"Why not?"

"Not right out."

"Why not?"

"You might get mad."

"Big deal."

"I better not."

"Why not?"

"I'd like to fuck you."

"Very funny."

"I'm not trying to be funny."

"Yeah, so why not?"

"Because I'm not."

"So why you want to fuck me?"

"You got great hair."

She laughed. "There's some dudes," she said, "some underdogging dudes who lose their lunch looking at my hair. Lose their fucking lunch. Freak out, they fucking freak out. That's what everybody is, scared shitless of their own shadow and they figure right off the bat that I'm their shadow." She opened a canvas sack beside her on the bench and pulled out a floppy leather-bound book. She put it on her knee. "Check it out. This here, that's my grandmother's Bible."

"Bibles weird me out," he said.

"Bibles are the word."

"They still weird me out, right out of my skull."

"This here's the light," she said, tapping the book cover with her finger. "When you got the light, when you got the blessed fucking light beaming on you, you don't get so shit scared of your shadow, you don't get so scared in the dark."

"The dark don't scare me." He smoothed the nap of the crown of his hat with the flat of his hand, straightened the orange feather in the black suede band, and settled the hat on his lap.

"I don't scare," he said again, leaning back and stretching his long legs and crossing his leather cowboy boots.

"Everybody's scared," she said.

"Not this dude."

"Sure you ain't a dope head?"

"Naw. No way. I got my shit in gear."

"You carrying some shit?"

"Naw."

"Know where I can snag some?"

"I told you, I don't do dope."

"You ain't never done no dope?"

"I done dope, every dickhead's done dope, but I don't do no dope now."

"Too bad, man. Like, I could die for some shit right now."

"If I die I'm gonna die like I wanna die," he said.

"Don't matter which way you wanna die, man, when you die, you're dead."

"Nope," he said.

"What's this nope?"

"Not my grandfather. He's not dead."

"Who's your grandfather?"

"He got himself hung," he said. "Hung for murder, out by Bowmanville, and the judge, he promised he'd let us lay his body out in the old way, up in the air in a tree. But the judge lied. He fucking lied. A priest buried him."

"Don't shit me, man. Nobody sticks dead bodies up in trees around here."

"Look," he said, nodding toward the men curled asleep on the grass, their faces swollen, "we're drinking ourselves fucking dead as doornails so that when we die you can bury us in the ground." He laughed and then spat. "That's what you lardasses want, you wanna trap our spirits forever."

"Like fuck," she said.

He leaned closer to her. "But the dead don't stay dead. My grandfather's not dead. There's been graves opened." He was very close to her, whispering. He saw the old blind man sitting in the sun under the rainbow. The old man smiled. "Even in the old cemetery right here downtown," he said, "there's people who've dug open the graves so the spirits are free."

She bent over and rubbed the dust off her boots.

They heard the carillon, a new song, and the old man sitting on the bench tapped his cane between his feet and sang:

> *Sometimes I'm happy,*
> *Sometimes I'm blue,*
> *My disposition*
> *Depends on you . . .*

She suddenly gave him a pecking kiss on the cheek. "I don't kiss so good with my braces on," she said. Her hand was on the Bible. He covered her hand with his.

"I haven't been kissed like that since my little kid kissed me."

"You got a kid?"

"I been a daddy since I was sixteen. I ain't seen my kid for two years, but I ain't seen my own daddy since I was six."

"I wish I had a kid," she said. "I tried once to get a kid but I got trouble in my tubes, you know, so I pray and I pray a lot."

"I don't pray your kinda prayers," he said. "They pray," and he pointed at the men asleep on the grass. "They all got rosaries."

"I ain't no Catholic," she said.

"Neither are they."

"This here's my grandmother's Bible, I'm her kinda Christian."

"No shit."

"I wouldn't shit you about Jesus."

"What kinda Christian?"

"Not one of them weird Pentecostals, man, they's always looking for blue smoke on the floor," she said. "That's what my father is, and my mother, though she just goes along for the ride, like she's scared, too, collecting prayer cloths, always on the road pretending she's Rose of Sharon looking for the next miracle."

"They got some kinda road map for miracles?"

"They got an old bunged-up trailer, that's what they got, and they're always looking for some shit-for-brains preacher who just got the gift of tongues."

"I got the gift of tongue."

"I'm talking miracles, man."

"Me too."

"Don't make no mistake, man. Don't play me for dumb. You remember Dumbo. He was a baby elephant. He had big ears. I don't got big ears. I hardly know you."

"You're looking for miracles."

"I believe I'm a miracle, like, we're all miracles."

"No shit."

"All of us being here is a miracle, man, and some of us are even washed in the Blood of the Lamb, except most people are fucking well scared shitless of being alive." She opened the Bible. "See," she said. "Second Timothy, one:seven, *'For God hath not given us the spirit of fear; but of power, and of love . . .'* I'm not scared of no love." She put the Bible back in the canvas sack.

"Let's split," he said.

"Where you wanna go?"

"Around."

They walked past the painted foothills, past the old blind man, out on to a boutique mall where office clerks on their lunch hour from Household Trust were browsing among polyester Blue Jay bird hats, plaster lawn pigs the color of candy floss, satin embroidered GENERATION X cushions, and desktop models of the Skydome designed to hold elastic bands or safety clips. At the end of the mall a balding man wearing wide red suspenders over his yellow shirt, beckoned to them. There was a sign over his head: *Put Your Polaroid Face On A Genuine Porcelain Plate*. "Come on," Abner said, "it's only a couple of bucks, it'll be like getting married."

They sat on a red plush velvet sofa. "Everybody comfy?" the balding man asked. He took their photograph. Then they picked a purple and gold-rimmed plate from a display rack. Their polaroid print was trimmed and pasted over the white moon in the center of the purple plate.

"That's sweet," she said. "Real sweet."

"You bet your sweet ass."

"My ass ain't so sweet," she said coyly. "I got a big butt."

"I like your ass."

"I like my hair, and I like your cowboy boots," she said.

"You two should be honeymooners," the balding man said, handing them the plate.

They put the plate in her canvas sack beside the Bible and they walked down the mall past Taco Time and Chubby Chicken and two sapling lindens, the trunks wrapped in protective plastic webbing.

"You wanna go up to the glass house?"

"No prob," she said.

They crossed the mall to the brass doors of the Household Trust tower. He sang along as they heard the woman in the window play:

> *Somewhere over the rainbow,*
> *Way up high . . .*

They rode a chrome escalator to the second floor, a glass-enclosed garden of shrubs and dwarf trees and shallow pools, ferns, pink hydrangeas, laminated benches, and serpentine walks made of interlocking ochre bricks. They sat down on a bench in the wind-less and humid air. Nothing moved, no leaf, no fern, no breathing sound in the dense ground cover. All they could hear was the rush of motor-driven water in a pond.

"I think I love it here," she said.

"I could see you'd like the outdoors thing," he said, and he stretched his legs and then smoothed his black jeans along the inside of his thighs. "I mean it's peaceful, like it's almost really real, you know."

"The trees are maybe real," she said.

"Yeah, but really real still ain't like this."

There were little bronze deer standing in a pond close to a tiny red bridge.

"Can I ask you something? I mean, seeing as how you asked me about my braces."

"Okay."

"I was looking at the guys lying on the lawn, you know."

"Yeah."

"And one of them woke up and was looking at me."

"Right."

"He was looking at me like I was weird."

"Right."

"You know a lot of white men?"

"Some."

"What d'you call white men?"

"What d'you mean?"

"How do you call them? White people?"

"Lardass."

"No, like in your own language. You got a fucking language?"

"It don't come out in my language like *white people*."

"What's it come out like?"

"It's a long story."

"How long's long?"

"Pretty long."

"So, I got all fucking day."

"What my grandfather told me, is white people got no color, so the word we use is *K'ohali*, like it means a certain part of animal fat, right, like the white part of the fat, the color of fat people, lard."

"I ain't fat."

"All white people are fat, like, you know, you live off the fucking fat of the land."

"Ain't no fat land around here, man."

"Shit, all you white people got life ass-backwards."

"You're telling me I'm ass-backwards and you're, like, sitting here like a regular goddamn fucking warrior clomping around in cowboy boots?"

"That's got nothing to do with nothing."

"My boots are better anyway."

"You probably like this glass shit-box better than the woods, all the trees you never seen."

"I seen trees."

"What d'you mean trees?"

"Trees."

"This goddamn city's got no trees, it's more like what we call a wilderness. I got to watch out for animals going by, that fucking car, because maybe it'll swallow me up or run over me and kill me. Somebody's got to haul ass here." He put his arm around her, cradling her. "Salvation for the nation, that's what I say, the United Iroquois Hour . . . "

"You Iroquois?"

"Ojibwa. Way north, Lake Superior."

"You miss the water."

"Life goes by calmer when you're close to water."

"We got fucking water all around us."

"These goddamn piddly pools ain't water."

"I don't mean here. I mean in all the windows."

"What the hell you talking about?"

"There's waterbed stores all around here."

"So?"

"Half the city's out there sleeping on their own fucking little lakes." It was very humid in the enclosed garden. She laughed as she undid the buttons to her fatigue jacket. He saw that she had a small tattoo, a cross, between her breasts. "I meet this guy a week ago," she said, "and he tells me he's got five waterbeds. Couldn't stand them, except his wife and kids love 'em and every night he says he's dreaming he is drowning because he's never learned how to swim and when he told his wife that they had to get rid of their waterbed because he couldn't sleep, she told him he had to learn how to swim."

He laughed loudly. A young clerk with a pencil moustache, who had bleached his close-cropped hair, snorted with irritation, closed his cardboard carton of french fries, and moved down the path to a Chinese waterfall wheel.

"Can you swim?" He still had his arm around her and he could smell talcum powder on her shaved head.

"No. And I don't need no lesson," she said fiercely. "I already been saved."

"I was just talking talk." He hugged her again.

"Absolutely no one talks to you fucking Indians except us punkers, so be nice. Like, don't pretend, man. Like, we're all part of the same thing, man, the fucking grateful dead, man."

"No shit."

"No shit. You guys are like ghosts, you listening up, man, all the dead fucking Indians who are still alive, you're ghosts. You figure that out, man, you're so fucking brain dead."

"Who's brain dead?"

"You are, otherwise you wouldn't ask me smart-ass questions like you ask me."

"What questions?"

"I'm not scared of you or anyone, except Jesus. I'm scared of Jesus, so I don't try to pretend nothing."

"Who's pretending?"

"You better not be."

"I'm not."

"Okay," she said, mollified. "That's cool."

"We're cool?"

"Yeah."

"You're not mad at whatever you were mad at?"

"No."

"Can I ask you a question?"

"You wanta know how I shave my head?" She opened her canvas sack. "I got a straight razor."

"Naw, a real question."

"There ain't no real questions, man."

"Sure there are."

"So ask me one, like a real one."

"You're saved, right? Born again."

"Right."

"How did you know you were saved?"

"What do you care?"

"I want to know."

"See my boots." She stretched her legs. "That's my old boyfriend, he taught me how to varnish my boots. He was in the army."

"Okay, I love your boots. I love your hair and I love your boots."

She crossed her legs. There was a long slit in her denim skirt. He could see the white of her thighs. She rested the canvas sack on her knees. "I got this big window in my bedroom, see, facing east, man, and there were these cross-bars in the window and the sun used to come through the window in the morning." She laid her hand on the sack, on the Bible in it. "And one morning standing in the sun I could feel the fucking heat, man, and the shadow of the cross from the cross-bar in the window on me, on my boobs, and like, I felt full of joy. I knew right then that I was saved, that I had the mark of the cross on me, and I bear witness, man, I bear witness to the joy in the Lord wherever I go."

He pursed his lips like he was thinking hard and cracked his knuckles.

"You think that's joy, eh!"

"That's what I felt that day," she said.

"Life's one day at a time, right, that's what you say."

"Right."

"One day."

"Absolutely fucking right," she said. "Fucking dead on, man."

"I got myself a joystick," he said, and he spread his big hand over hers.

"You looking to fuck me?" she said.

"I don't wanta just fuck you."

"What you wanta do?"

"I wanta give you that baby."

"What baby?"

"The baby you said you was wanting so hard to have."

"You watch out. Don't go fucking overboarding on me. Nobody just fucking-well has babies."

"Sure you do. That's what real fucking's for."

"The days are coming, man, the final days, so don't you go bottom feeding on me, man."

"My grandfather, he told me that all the time."

"What?"

"The world's gonna end."

"Yeah, so how?"

"He told me when I was a kid, he told me to take this here little pail outside and bring some sand in to him and when I did he poured the sand into piles and said these are the cities and there'll be bigger cities in the future and then there's gonna be a punishment, but the only thing we don't know is when we're gonna get punished but it's gonna happen."

"Fucking real, a grandfather like that."

"They hung him."

"That's what you get for going around killing people."

"He didn't go around."

"He went somewhere."

"The priest said he went to Hell."

"You know what I can't figure about you?"

"What?"

"Why a guy with a moccasin mind would wear such pretty cowboy boots, and you think my hair and braces are weird." She laughed, gathered her canvas sack, and got up.

"I stole them off a white drunk," he said.

"You're fucking kidding."

"Naw. He was lying drunk in a crapper in a bar so I took his boots off and left him my running shoes."

They went down the escalator, came out on to the mall, and saw the lady sitting at the carillon in the Household Trust tower window. She was smoking, and then she stubbed her cigarette in an ashtray and started to play:

I ain't got nobody and nobody I know's got me . . .

They walked through the park. A shadow from the tower had fallen across the painted ochre fields and the white clouds and the rainbow. The blind old man was slumped on a bench, sound asleep in the sun, snoring. Others were still huddled on the grass under the shade trees. It was two o'clock. The lady at the carillon shut down the loudspeaker system. It made a pop, like a pistol shot heard from a long way off.

"So where's home?" he asked.

"The Wilton Hotel."

"You kidding me?" he said.

"Cindy Witchita never kids."

"I copped a bed there a couple of months ago," he said. "Or maybe it was last year." They walked arm-in-arm along the sidewalk toward the old hotel, passing pawnshop windows cluttered with fishing gear, clocks, chairs hung from the ceiling, wedding rings, birth stones.

"What room you in?" he asked.

"319, man."

"Really?"

"End of the hall."

"We were neighbors when I was there, so how come you never visited me?"

"Because I didn't live there then, man. Anyway, I don't butt in. I mind my business."

"Me neither," he said. "Too many people always butt in."

"But like, when I wake up at fucking two in the morning it's what I wanta do."

"But somebody might be sleeping."

"Right, so either I chase dust bunnies across the floor or I make me a coffee instead."

"Then you really don't get no sleep."

"It's not the coffee that keeps me awake," she said, moving closer to him.

"It ain't booze either."

"If you got nothing to do and go to sleep too early, man, you wake up too early, so what're you going to do?"

He laughed and squeezed her hand. "You ain't scared of me, eh?"

"I never been scared of no love," she said.

"You still look like all the goddamn Mohawks I ever seen in the movies," he said.

"Yeah, but they weren't real Indians like you are, man." She skipped up the stairs of the hotel, surprisingly light on her feet in her shiny policeman's boots.

Once they were in room 319, he set his broad-brimmed black hat on the bottom of a straightback chair, the only chair in the room. She draped her battle-fatigue jacket over the end of the bed and took the purple china plate with their photograph from her canvas sack.

"Where'll I put our picture?"

"Top of the TV."

"Nice," she said. "We look real nice, man. Happy," and she took her grandmother's Bible out of the sack and put it under her pillow and began to undress.

"How old are you?"

"Nineteen," she said.

"Spring chicken."

"Don't call me no fucking chicken, man. I hate chickens. I ain't nobody's fucking chicken. Only pimps got chickens."

"Sorry," he said, drawing off his tight black jeans. Naked, he stepped back into his cowboy boots.

"I gotta tell you this," she said. "My real name's Alice." She sat on the edge of the bed, pulling off her boots. "Cindy's a name I stole from a movie star."

"Yeah, well, my real name's Falling Moon Feather. Goddamn priests at the mission school named me Abner."

"They hurt you? Those fucking priests." She lay down on the narrow bed, tucking the other grey pillow under her hips.

"Naw, this guy Father Marshal, he used to give me whisker rubs and kiss me a lot but he never hurt me."

"I had an uncle named Abner."

"Was he cool?"

"He married a moron, man, like she was a big woman, you know, but she had a fucking midget mind. He always called me his little Cindy and touched my tits, always telling me how unhappy he was, and how fucking unhappy God was. And he's busy touchin' my tits."

Falling Moon Feather knelt on the bed beside her. "All that stuff about my grandfather, that's bullshit," he said.

"He didn't get hung?"

"Naw. They don't hang nobody nomore. They ain't hung nobody around here forever."

"So why you tell me all that?"

"It's good Indian shit, it goes over good."

"Take your boots off, man," she said, laughing. "You gotta take your boots off."

"They're not my boots," he said, and kicked them off toward the window where a seagull was standing on the window sill. Falling Moon Feather was sorry that there was no music in the trees. He began to hum *You must remember this, a kiss is still a kiss* as he brushed his lips against her breasts and throat, his long black hair falling over her face. He kissed the cross tattooed between her breasts.

"That's nice," she said.

"That's what the priests taught me," he said, "to kiss the cross."

"I knew there was something totally right between us," she said. "I knew right away when I was sitting there with my eyes closed."

"Me too."

"You didn't have your eyes closed."

"No, but I knew. I was watching a blind old man sit in the sun and when I sat down beside you, even though he couldn't see us, man, he smiled at me. Like it was a good sign."

"I can't stand bad signs."

"Bad vibes, man."

"How come you ditched your wife?"

"Bad. She turfed me."

"How come?"

"She's a good woman but a good woman can go bad. Her heart can go bad on her."

"That's what I say. It's what's in your fucking heart that counts."

The seagull rose from the sill and flew off into the red sky reflected in the glass wall of the Household Trust tower.

"Except now she says I should go home to her because she hears I'm happy."

"No shit?"

"No."

"She's unhappy . . . "

"She's unhappy because I'm happy."

"That's the way it goes, man. Most people aren't happy unless we're unhappy."

"I tell you, Alice," he said, as he kissed her and entered her and she accepted the weight of his body in her arms.

"What?"

"Unhappiness is fucking overrated."

INTRUSIONS

1

Dusk, and once again Mildred Downs, dressed in a black blouse and a long black skirt, sat in a rocking chair on the front veranda of her stone house. She clutched a blanket around her shoulders and settled her Siamese cat in her lap. The dark green blinds in the windows of the big house were drawn. When she wanted to close herself off completely from the street, she unrolled a canvas awning down to the old wisteria that grew along the veranda railing, clusters of pale mauve flowers hanging from the vines.

Her husband had drowned in the spring in Lake Scugog, and since then she had taken to sipping sherry in the afternoon and straight gin at night. Sometimes on hot nights she put a cube of ice in the gin. She slept fitfully at night, afraid that if she fell soundly asleep she might forget to wake up. She believed that several light sleeps during the day were good for her. She liked to sit as still as she could in the rocking chair, holding the cat in her lap. "I can keep my body so breathless," she whispered to the cat, "that I don't even hear the beating of my own heart." When she slept she moaned and rocked in the chair.

As soon as she fell asleep, the cat leapt to the floor, went down the flagstone stairs and crossed the lawn and climbed into the tall sugar maple tree. Her son, Henry, was standing in the shadow of the awning. He was lean and angular and in his early thirties and he had his mother's pale, almost color-less blue eyes. He didn't like the cat. "Let it fend for itself," he told her when she woke up and wondered where the cat was. "It kills birds." As he said this, she touched the hollow of her cheek and sighed. "There are hard truths," she said. "Hard truths you've never had to deal with, thank your lucky stars." He stepped back into the shadow of the low-ered awning, tying the cord into little loops. He offered to make tea. "No," she said, "I'll have a glass of gin. There's a time for everything."

"So there is, mother. So there is. Go back to sleep."

When she woke, the sun had gone down. Though it was a moonless night, the sky was blue. She heard the shrill cries of children chasing each other in the dark at the back of the house. "They sound like seagulls," she said. She was angry. She had heard seagulls crying when they'd brought her husband's body ashore, broken by rocks in the cold lake. Bloated lamprey eels were fastened to his legs and stomach. "This is unfair, this is unfair," she had cried over and over, beating her fists on the sand. "Goddamn unfair." She had boarded up the win-dows of their summer cottage and nailed the doors shut, and then suddenly, with an air of vengeful disdain, she had sold it at a loss. "Let some other fool get the blood sucked out of him."

The screeching children were at the side of the house, hooting and crying. Mildred picked up a small mallet. There was an oak end-table by the veranda railing and on the table, a brass bell from the bridge of a small yacht. Henry had bought the bell years ago in a pawnshop and had given it to his father as a birthday present. His father, who had been a ham radio operator and had built small-scale model schooners as a hobby, had laughed and said, "Whenever there's trouble, bang the bell. Lord knows, no one will come, but bang the bell anyway."

Mildred banged the bell. She listened to the echo clang down the lane. Then there was silence. Her heart was pounding. "You stupid children," she called out, "get away from here. You're a menace. I won't have it." She held her breath, listening. When she was certain the children had crept back through the trees, she went into the house and called upstairs to Henry, opened the liquor cabinet that was inlaid with copper and tortoiseshell, and poured two glasses of sherry. She always had Hunter's sherry before supper.

Henry stood in the center of the living room, facing the drawn blinds in the bay windows. He had long arms and large hands and a loping stride that made him seem boyish. Mildred adjusted the hour hand in the brass *boulle* clock on the marble mantelpiece and then lit a match. "It's bad luck," he said, "to chase young children away. They'll come back to haunt you." She lit the six candles of a candelabra that was standing on a side table. Like his mother, he had high cheekbones and hollows in his cheeks and something mournful in the way he stood with his head cocked to one side. "I've come home for good," he said. "I'm home to stay for good."

"Have another sherry," she said. "And whose good do you have in mind?"

"I need a whiskey," he told her. "I need something strong."

"Well, water it down," she said. "Your face flushes all red when you drink whiskey. Your father couldn't drink either, he was always flush-faced."

Since her husband's death, she had held off loneliness and the panic of loneliness with a stern composure, a composure that gave her a severe but attractive dignity. Some mornings when she woke and lay in bed with her eyes closed, she was sensually aware of her own stillness, her repose, and in repose, she thought, she could actually feel the comforting weight of silence, a weight like the spent body of her husband after he'd made love to her. That was when she had felt closest to him, when he'd lain exhausted and thankful on her body. She regretted that she had not learned this composure earlier, because her husband, Tom, so bluff and good-natured and full of yearning and rash bursts of generosity, had always embarrassed her, suddenly giving her gifts and wanting to know her thoughts. "If I talk to the whole world on my radio at night, why can't I talk to you?" he'd said, sitting beside her on the bed. "So tell me what you're thinking." This had left her feeling sheepish and guilty. Twisting the silk straps to her nightdress, she hadn't known what to say, what he wanted to hear. "I love you," she'd said at last, but he'd said, "No, no, not that. What are you really thinking?" She had hugged the pillow and said, "Nothing," and he had yelled, "Don't lie to me. Not in our own bed." Now, she wished that instead of telling him the truth and weeping, she had been able to confront him with the stern composure she'd shown on the day that they had buried him. Even the winds had been still on that day on the high cemetery hill, so that the sun had felt closer and stronger and, shielding her eyes with her hand through the prayers, she had felt suddenly in touch with her own strength. The young eager priest had said, trying to console her, "Well, he's in the embrace of God." She had startled him, saying, "He wanted to know me and I don't think he ever did, because he didn't know he knew all there was to know, and that's a fact."

"A fact?" he said.

"That's right. And facts hurt."

She turned away from Henry and put her glass of sherry on the side table and laid her hand on a small hunched dark bronze figure standing to the side of the candelabra. "Your father was a generous man," she said. "I remember when we were in Paris and we went into a gallery somewhere around rue du Bac and I had always loved Rodin, and there it was, this very maquette of the big Balzac statue that's up by La Coupole, and so he bought it for me. Oh, that was years ago when no one wanted Rodin and you could get him for a song. He was a very kind and generous man."

"La Coupole?"

"Really, Henry. You shouldn't be coming home, you should be going away, out into the world, out of yourself."

"My father didn't know any more about La Coupole than I do."

"That's no tone to take toward your father."

"He didn't give a damn about Paris. He wanted to go to Vladivostok."

"Where?"

"Vladivostok. With Nikolai."

"Oh, that dreary little man. He had one of those dreadful flat faces. Thank God he disappeared. I still wish I could find out what he stole."

"He didn't steal anything. He just took off. And that's what Dad wanted to do, too, though I guess he did it the only way he knew how."

"Oh," she said and clapped a hand over her eyes. He let her stand there like that, her long bony fingers covering her eyes, and then he said softly, "You're peeking, that's no fair," and he laughed, saying, "I miss old Nikolai." He had been the gardener around the house and summer cottage, a hunched old handyman who'd been in the Czar's navy as a boy in Vladivostok, and then he had worked for years in mining camps inside the Arctic Circle. At the cottage he'd crouched on his haunches at the end of the dock and told Henry about men who'd got lost in the long Arctic nights of deep snows and then when they were found in the spring they were only skeletons hanging by their snowshoes, the shoe-webbing tangled in the top branches of the trees after the snows had melted. He'd seen a government handbill that had said: COME TO SASKATCHEWAN and because he didn't know where Saskatchewan was, he'd gone, working on a feed-and-fertilizer tanker out of the Black Sea, but he'd never gotten to the prairies and the town of Moose Jaw, and he'd said, "Even men who have two good legs dream they are cripples," and he'd laughed and tousled Henry's hair and Henry's father had said, "What a terrible hard life you've had, Nikolai."

"Hard, okay," Nikolai said. "But no terrible."

"No?"

"No. You'll see in one hundred years it could be very beautiful, this life."

Then, Nikolai was gone. There was no word, no note, only a pair of canvas work gloves tacked to the garden shed door. For weeks Henry's father was strangely unsettled. "I think somehow he was my legs," he told Henry. He talked for hours in the night to towns all over the world on his ham radio, suddenly angry and berating people he didn't know, people he had never talked to before. Then he wandered into the spare room that his wife had covered from floor to ceiling and wall-to-wall with mirrors, a black steel ballet bar bolted to the walls — and when he'd walked into the room and found her limbering up wearing black leotards, seeing that her image disappeared down reflected tunnels of cold light, he'd said, "Jesus, it's like being swallowed up inside a Fun House."

"This is my room," she'd said. "I expect to be left alone." He had gone out on to the veranda and given the bell one good clang and had never spoken of Nikolai again.

"He had a flat face," Henry's mother said. "You cannot trust people with flat faces. Your father had a good nose, what they called a blade nose, and a good firm jaw."

"And he had a good life," Henry said softly.

"Yes," she said, ignoring the wryness in his tone, "but you're too morbid about him. It's morbid the way you ring that bell in the morning and sit scrunched up in his chair in his study with the door closed, suffocating with those model boats. I never understood the hours he gave to those boats."

"He sailed the seas in the palm of his hand, Mother."

"It was the oddest thing," she said. "I saw him staring so hard one day at a boat in his hand and he suddenly crushed it, and then smiled at me as if he'd made a mistake, some kind of big mistake that had nothing to do with the boat, like when we were children and did something wrong and we wanted it to be right, but you knew it never could be right."

"He had his own reasons. I never understood why he was so generous."

"It seemed perfectly straightforward to me," she said.

"Maybe it was a kind of despair," he said. "Maybe he gave things away so he could be sure that there was at least a little generosity somewhere in the world. That's when I felt close to him."

"It's not how I knew him."

"No?"

"He was never desperate with me."

The cat leapt into her lap. "It's strange, Henry, that you should feel so close to him and not to me because I was the one who always made sure you were sent away to the best boarding schools. Let me tell you, your father's generosity was just his way of hiding away from all of us. He hid who he was, and he turned whatever he gave us into a kind of blackmail. We were always in his debt. Sometimes, when I couldn't stand it anymore, I mean his silence, and I was just about to scream at him, he'd suddenly give me something so beautiful I wouldn't know what to say. So I wouldn't say anything, and he'd get really mad at me. And sour and sullen. All those gifts of his became like little deaths, hoarded little deaths. And, certainly something died in me when he died but now I don't owe him anything. And," she said, reaching out to Henry, "you come home from one of the finest teaching positions in the country, with no woman and no ambition. It's preposterous. Your father became a rich man by making men believe they owed him something, and now you come home as if you owe no one anything, not even an explanation. It's unfair."

"Of course it's unfair," he said.

"What do you mean, of course? You had everything, everything I could give, and now that you're home you insist on sleeping in the attic room, as if somehow you're in the wrong house, trying to hurt me."

"Why would I want to hurt you, Mother?"

"I just feel it," she said with a little coquettish whine. She lifted the cat out of her lap and pulled a quilted comforter around her legs. A window was open and there was the tang of early snow in the air. "I don't know," she said. "I honestly don't know why you'd want to hurt your mother."

"Well, if you don't know," he said, touching her shoulder and then her cheek, "who does?"

He poured himself another whiskey.

"You know what Nikolai used to tell me," he said. "It was some kind of old proverb . . . *If you meet a Bulgarian, beat him. He will know the reason why.*" He laughed so hard he got a stitch in his side and had to hold his breath until he could straighten up, and he stood in front of her stirring the ice cubes in his glass with his finger.

"What a terrible habit, Henry," she said with a little curl of disdain in her lip. "Where in the world did you pick that up?"

"Out in the wide, wide world," he said. "At school. You pick up all kinds of bad habits from children. They attach themselves to you, they cling to you." He tugged the cord to one of the green blinds in the front bay window and it clattered up into a tight roll, but there was no sudden burst of light. It was the dead of night outside. "Don't you think," he said, "that this is all a little too deliberate, I mean keeping the blinds down all the time."

"This is the room where I sat after he died."

"In the living room," he said, and laughed quietly.

"I swear I don't know what's going on in your mind," she said. "I don't know why you say the things you do or what you think about anything."

"I may not know either," he said.

"Well, it's not necessary to mock me," she said, brushing a wisp of hair away from her face. "It's not necessary to come home and mock whatever contentment and control I've been able to find."

"Are you content, Mother?"

"At least I know how to show some composure," she said. "Now take your finger out of your drink."

"You love to talk to me like I'm a child," he said, watching the cat lick its forepaws.

"Well," she said, "you are my child."

"I am indeed," he said.

"Well, don't forget it," she said.

"I won't," he said. "I can't."

She sipped her glass of sherry and settled into a heavy wingback chair, her eyes closed. With her head to the side, she was soon asleep. He began to hum, a dirgeing sound, and then to sing quietly, staring down at his mother:

> *My eyes are dim,*
> *I cannot see,*
> *I have not brought my specs*
> *With me,*
> *But there are rats, rats,*
> *Big as alley cats,*
> *At the door, at the door . . .*

2

*H*e stood in front of the large bathroom mirror, drawing silver-handled brushes that his father had given him through his hair, and then he buffed his nails and went downstairs to the dining room where his mother, with a silk shawl around her shoulders, sat at the long oak table. He was late, having changed his shirt and trousers after playing games with children in among the trees behind the house. She was reading a slender book and seemed in a state of such repose that he hesitated on the last stair, unsure if he should enter the room and disturb her silence. She looked surprisingly frail and shrunken and dry, as if she had never been young, and as he rubbed his big hands together he found it hard to believe that he'd ever come out of her womb, come out from between those thin thighs, but then she stirred and snapped her book shut, and he strode to the table, saying with loud heartiness, "And what are you reading tonight, Mother?"

She closed her eyes, straightening her shoulders, and then she smiled warmly, looking up as if she were pleasantly startled and had just seen him for the first time in a long while. "Saint Theresa," she said.

"I didn't know you went in for the lives of saints."

"I don't," she said, lifting the lid of the silver soup tureen, preparing to serve him. "I found it among your father's books."

"Really," he said. "I didn't know he went in for saints either."

"He certainly did," and she smiled coyly.

"I don't know, I get my saints confused, but wasn't Theresa the little girl who slept with her mouth open until one day a bee flew into her mouth? It buzzed around but it didn't sting her?"

"I really wouldn't know."

"And Christ is the bee with His blessed little stinger."

"He is?"

"Sure, but He's come and gone. The rest of us got stung."

She handed him his bowl of soup, a steaming fish soup, and for a moment he lost his breath because he thought he saw an eye floating in the broth, but it was only a bubble that suddenly broke, and with relief he said, "Well, what does little Miss Theresa have to say?"

"It's quite wonderful," she said, ladling soup into her own bowl. "She says that if God hadn't created heaven for Himself, He would have created it for her."

"There's a ripe little bitch."

"Oh, I don't know."

"You think that's wonderful?"

"I find it amusing."

"Sounds like she's having a wet dream," he said, and spread his napkin over his knees.

"Really. You can be so crude," she said, and scowled.

"All right, a dry dream," he said.

They ate in silence, their knives and forks clicking on the bone china, the cat scratching and mewing by the back screen door. He wondered if the cat had brought a dead bird to the door mat again. As his mother cut her meat into tiny pieces, he suddenly felt queasy and had the uneasy sense that he was on the verge of swirling into deep sleep, slipping down into an inner twirling cocoon, the walls of this cocoon just beyond his touch, and because he was afraid that he was going to pass out, he almost reached out to hold on to his mother, but then the spell passed and she crossed her knife and fork on her plate and said, as if there'd been no length of silence between them, "I think we should take coffee in the other room." There was a slice of veal on his plate, untouched, but he got up and followed her.

They sat in maroon leather easy chairs in the living room, with a silver coffee pot and a silver plate of little cupcakes on the pedestal table between them. "You still haven't told me," she said, "why you've come home, why you've quit teaching."

"Home is where the heart is."

"Don't be facetious."

"You want me to tell you the truth, now that we're done with supper?" he asked. She dabbed the corner of her mouth with the napkin.

"I'm not sure," she said.

"Let's just say that when you love children too much you make childish mistakes."

"Do you?"

"Yes, you do," he said. "That's what love is, a mistake. All the best things we do are mistakes."

"I did my best with you," she said.

"That was probably a mistake, so who could blame you?"

"I honestly don't know what you're talking about, except I know your father would not agree with you," she said.

"Oh yes he would," he said, getting up and coming around behind her chair so that he could lean over her, into the lamplight. "Yes he would. He did all the right things all his life and he knew every one of them was completely wrong. He should have been a man of the sea, a real captain, instead of frittering his life away with all those hours of dreaming, making his model boats, his little toys," and he whispered in her ear, "that's where his heart was, with his toys."

"Oh," she said. "Your father was not a childish man. And he loathed people who made mistakes." She straightened her collar. "Imagine, thinking you could know what was in your father's heart better than I could, the woman who listened to his heart in his bed. I can still sometimes hear the pounding of Tom's heart."

"Ah, yes, the bed," he said. "It all begins in the bed."

"What does that mean?"

"Nothing," he said, and he took a cigarette from a black lacquered box. He lit it from the candle on the mantelpiece, blowing a smoke ring. He watched it dissipate. Then he blew another ring.

"You can't say something like that and then just say, 'Nothing,' " she said.

"What's there to say," he said. "That I used to lie there on my bed when I was a boy, pretending to be asleep, watching you watch me."

"What do you mean, watch you?"

"Just that. You stared and stared, with some stern little hairball of a thought inside your skull. How could I know?"

"I loved you very much," she said.

"Of course you did. You were my mother," he said. "It's just that I hadn't seen that look of yours for a long time."

"What look? When?"

"When the headmaster at the school agreed I should quit teaching boys, he stared at me a long time and all I kept thinking was, where have I seen that look before?"

"What look?"

"Your look," he said. "Distaste."

She sat with her eyes closed. He stood blowing smoke rings in the silence, and then, after a long time she said softly, "Put on some music, Henry. A little

Schubert, perhaps. Schubert is so simple, so intimate, so much the way the heart is." She set her cup and saucer aside. "We'll have to get to know each other again, Henry. Do you still have trouble sleeping? I used to listen to you when you came back as a boy from boarding school. It was frightening, listening to a grown young man cry out in his sleep."

"Sure it's frightening," he said. "Sometimes I used to walk through the student dormitory at the school," and he drew away from her, a pained look in his eyes, "early in the morning, before dawn, listening to the smaller boys cry in the night, but it wasn't so much crying. More like a whimper. It's terrible to think that a child, free in his dreams, ends up whimpering."

"And what do you think's wrong with them?" she asked.

"They know they have two legs," he said, "but they think they're crippled."

They sat listening to Schubert for nearly an hour.

"I think," he said at last, "I'll take a bath."

In a little while, she snuffed the candles and went upstairs, pausing at the top of the stairs. She heard a voice and slowly went down to the end of the hall and stood by the bathroom door, listening to a low intoning that soothed and enticed her, so that without thinking and full of curiosity, she quietly opened the door to the large tiled room, the window filled with hanging potted plants, and saw Henry in the big old claw-foot tub, reading aloud:

> *Hear the tolling*
> *of the bells, iron bells!*
> *What a world of solemn thought*

their monody compels.
In the silence of the night,
how we shiver with afright . . .
at the bells bells bells . . .

"How beautiful," she said, "how very beautiful."
Then, she saw that Henry was surrounded by his
father's model boats, all of them afloat. He rose out
of the water, glaring, astonished, and the book
slipped from his hands and sank and water streamed
from his naked body, swamping the boats, and she
was astonished at how much black hair there was all
over his body, wondering as she backed out if he
could really be her child with all that hair, murmur-
ing, "His boats, his silly little boats." Henry
screamed, "How dare you, how dare you," as she
backed down the hall to her bedroom.

3

*T*hrough the following week, she slept late in the
morning and began to take a sip of sherry
before coming downstairs. She wore the same black
blouse for three days. He wasn't sure if she was
washing in the morning. Then she appeared for
lunch wearing a black lace mantilla around her head.
She ate very little, only green salads and bowls of
steamed rice with honey, and she insisted on carrying the cat in her arms from room to room, though
the cat mewed and sometimes struggled to get away.
Henry watched her, head cocked to the side, with an
almost languid aloof sadness, as if he were bored,
and he played with a little silver pocket knife while

he sat silently across from her in the late afternoon on the veranda. There was menace in the way he toyed with the tiny knife. It looked like he was trying to frighten her, but he was only keeping his nails clean, the cuticles cut back. He didn't want to frighten her at all. He only wanted to watch her, in silence. He wanted her to feel his presence. The weight of it. The bulk of it. "I am a bit of a bastard," he said to her quietly one day, but she said nothing. The cat started to spit. She let the cat go.

Then, one afternoon she kicked her comforter away from around her legs and suddenly pulled the cords to all the blinds in the living room, flooding the room with light. "You're just like your father," she said. "You think I owe you an apology. You want me to feel as if I'm in your debt, but I'm not in your debt. I am your mother."

"Whatever you say," he said and opened the door to the veranda. The clusters of wisteria were still in bloom but fading. He sat outside, and she came out, too. They sat side-by-side for a while, bundled against the chill of the autumn wind, saying nothing, and then, at dusk, because it was so cold, they went in and she poured a glass of gin and a glass of whiskey. "Cheers," she said. In the bleak light from the bay windows, he saw that a large painting on the east wall was hanging crooked and when he straightened it there was a clean slash of white left on the wall. "We can't have that," he said. "It looks like a scar." He moved the frame so that it was crooked again and the scar was hidden. The painting was of barley fields and a setting sun that was bathing a white stone cottage in a sepia light.

"That's my painting. I love it," she said with sudden eagerness.

"It was hanging crooked," he said, tapping the ornate frame with his forefinger. "It's only the same old stone cottage it's always been."

"Only a stone cottage to you," she said.

"That old butcher general, Kitchener, he used to say the heart of the empire was the stone cottage."

"The empire my foot. What the devil do we know about empires?"

"We know," he said, "that they fall down," and suddenly he sang out:

> *London Bridge*
> *Is falling down,*
> *Falling down,*
> *My fair lady-o.*

"There are times," she said, "when you sound like a lunatic."

"It's my childhood," he said. "A childhood song. Anyway, that's what's lovely about anyone's childhood, it was always a little on the lunatic side."

"You think so?" she said coldly.

"Sure. As soon as you grow up everything turns into a lie, a good sensible lie, so everybody can get along. There are even crippled men who will tell you they've got two good legs," and he laughed.

"You are a lunatic," she said.

"Too long in the noonday sun," he said.

"There was one summer month," she said, "before I got married, that I rented a stone cottage. Alone. I was very happy there alone. That's the truth and it's still true even if you think everything's a lie," and she closed her eyes, saying, "You are much crueller than your father."

The cat was curled in her lap, staring at Henry, purring. "Tomorrow's my birthday," he said, but she did not answer and he realized that with her empty glass in her hand, she was sound asleep. He took the glass out of her hand. "You should pay more attention, Mother," he said sourly. "You never paid attention." The cat leaped away as he stood up. He wanted to hurt the cat, beat it with a stick, break its back. He didn't know why he hated the cat, because he didn't really care about the birds that it killed. He cared about the mess of bone and feathers on the mat. He felt so enraged that he suddenly wanted to cry, to beat his fists on the table, overwhelmed by sorrow, by a terrible sense of being cheated. "I don't care, I don't care, I don't care." He felt ice cold. He saw himself hanging by snowshoes tangled in tree branches, upside down, gleaming in the spring sun, a skeleton. He began to sing:

> *There are rats, rats,*
> *Big as alley cats,*
> *At the door, at the door . . .*

Early the next evening, with his loping boyish stride, he hurried up the front walk carrying a cardboard box. His face was ruddy from the wind. He'd been away all afternoon. "Hello, mother," he called, but as he got to the top step, she said, "Hush, hush, only badly-bred children yell like that." He gave her a dry laugh and went into the house. She could hear the faint crying out of children in the trees back behind the house. She suddenly wanted to cut down all the trees, so the children would have to go away forever. They would have no place to hide. No place to seek.

In about half an hour, Henry came out on to the verandah. Her head had fallen forward and she was dozing with a smile on her face. He banged the ship's bell, two good clangs that resounded down the lane, and she bolted up, dazed, crying, "Tom, Tom." She sounded so vulnerable, so afraid, that he suddenly felt reluctant and full of remorse though he'd done nothing to her, nothing except wake her up, but then she wheeled on him with disdain. "You're not Tom. You're not my Tom." He said, "No, no," and laughed and took her arm. "I'm glad you stopped wearing that damned mantilla," he said, and led her into the house and down the dark hall, past the cabinet of rare porcelain that Tom had bought for her.

"Henry, I think your life has been too easy," she said, "so easy that you've turned into someone quite hard." They went into the dining room. She had regained her composure as she sat down at the head of the table, facing the french doors to the garden. "No, not hard, Mother," he said. "Hard's the wrong word. I've just learned to love kids the way my father loved his toys." The chandelier lights were on and the sideboard candles were lit and the long table, covered with a lace cloth, was set with silver and Crown Royal china. She was too startled by the light and the table to say anything. She sat with her mouth open, gaping at an enormous birthday cake.

"Close your mouth, Mother," he said. "Or you'll get stung." On top of the cake, she saw a ship made of marzipan, surrounded by little candles. "I knew you wouldn't want to forget, Mother," he cried. "You wouldn't forget my birthday," and then she heard shuffling and muffled giggling outside, and someone clanged the bell out on the porch as the french doors were thrown open and a huddle of small boys, all wearing colored paper hats and blowing plastic police whistles, broke into the room, crying, "Happy birthday, Henry, happy birthday . . . "

They sped around the table, squealing and banging into one another, terrifying the cat, picking up forks and plates and waving them in the air. They also had wooden whistles with rolls of paper attached to the ends, and when they blew, the paper unfurled into long colored stingers and they spun around her, bees stinging one another with glee. *Buzz . . . Buzz . . .* Henry, beaming at his mother, drove the silver cake knife into the heart of the icing, crying, "How do you like my little darlings, Mother?" She clasped her hands to her throat, unmoving, stricken by a pain, a closure on her lungs that she had not known since childbirth, a pain that burned through the arteries in her neck so that she felt her collarbone was cracking, and she tried to choke the pain off with her hands as the boys piled cake on their plates and let forkfuls of icing slide on to the carpet, hooting and hurdling over one another, clutching at her legs, fat little boys fastening on to her ankles until she closed her eyes and cried, "It's unfair, it's unfair."

Seeing her stricken, he pried her hands from her throat. Two of the boys let go of her legs and backed away. She began to pound the table, pounding with her eyes closed, her face ashen, whispering, "It's unfair, it's unfair." All the boys were backing away, not just from her but as if they were suddenly uncertain of Henry, even afraid of him. He was enraged by the wariness in their eyes and yelled at them, telling them to go away. As they trailed out of the room, he pulled his chair in front of hers and sat down. Their knees touched. He looked at her thin legs, shaken by how thin she actually was, and how big he was. "How in the world did I get born?" he asked, and reached to the cake and flicked a fingerful of icing into his mouth and said, "Look, Mother . . . "

She stared at him, her mouth open, her pale eyes unblinking, and he put a finger full of icing in her mouth.

"Look," he said, as she licked his finger, "in a hundred years life could be very beautiful."

BUDDIES IN BAD TIMES

*A*rthur Aneale stood over the body of his dead friend, Trent. He was astonished. Trent had been sick for two years, he had looked sallow and hollow-eyed and frail, and yet lying dead in the casket he seemed only to be sleeping soundly, in the flush of health. Aneale wanted to talk about Trent, he wanted to talk about how alive he looked, but as he drifted through the men in the room, most of them dour and uneasy, and some looking sick themselves, he felt like a stranger, sullen and alone. He sat down by the door and stared at his feet. Whenever he was by himself and feeling lonely he stared at his feet because his feet seemed too big, as if they weren't his, too big and cold. It was cold by the door. He could feel the cold in his toes. "You'll catch your death sitting by the door," a man wearing a black leather Harley Davidson jacket said as he came in out of the wintry night.

Aneale saw a tall young man shuffling back and forth beside the open casket. He had a handsome pale face and he smiled as he looked around the room, the eager smile of a stranger, as if he were hoping someone would talk to him, and so Aneale got up and walked back to the casket. "Are you a relative?" he whispered.

"No, I'm sorry."

"Don't be sorry. Not on a night like this. It's too cold, colder than a witch's tit," he said. "Let's get a drink," and he took the young man's arm and led him by the elbow to a sitting room in the funeral home where there were tall stainless steel coffee urns standing on an oak sideboard. "I've got a real drink here," Aneale said, grinning amiably and slipping a silver flask from his suitcoat pocket. He got two cups from a water tray beside the urns and poured whiskey into the cups and they sat down on a small sofa.

"My name's Arthur Aneale."

"And mine's Jeff Trainer."

"I just could not stand it in there any longer, all mope and pick-pick and no flounce, I mean, what's beyond belief is how he's lying there looking so absolutely puckish, toujours the little prince in his casket, when the real dead, let me tell you, are the angry little sluts skulking around the room."

"I'm glad you look at it like that," Trainer said, his eyes shining. "It's exactly how I feel. But it's not for me to say." He leaned toward Aneale and Aneale, loosening his tie, grinned and tapped Trainer on the wrist. "I don't know why we let ourselves die and get laid out like drab and dowdy are the only dress of the dead, just so a bunch of bitches can gawk at us."

"I guess it's the custom," Trainer said, smiling.

"It's not my little frisson, just in case you happen to be on the avenue when I die. It's shut the coffin door on me," he said. "Here's to Trent, one of the dear departed, he was a peach."

"Here's to him," and Trainer raised his cup.

"He certainly would like this, the two of us sitting here so absolutely très vite, drinking to his health even if he did just die."

"That's how I feel," Trainer said. "I didn't know him so close like you did, but he certainly came across to me, strong. Earth. I just felt the earth in him."

"He certainly loved his gardening," Aneale said.

"Really?"

"The last time I saw him he was out there in his tank top in that garden, clomping around in his Greb boots, deadheading."

"Dead who?"

"Cutting dead heads off the flowers, he always said they'd bloom better that way, come the spring."

"Really?" And Trainer, settling into the sofa, crossed his slender long legs.

"Such is life, he used to say," Aneale said. "Cock of the walk one week, dead head the next. He said that every time we took a trip." He told Trainer about a summer holiday that he and Trent had taken on the Gaspé. "I remember a boy, just a kid, not exactly a chicken, we picked him up outside a ruined old church and this little sweetheart of a kid cottoned on to Trent and the next thing we knew we couldn't get rid of him for the life of us and so we had to take him along." Trainer was listening with his head tilted to the side, as if he were comparing Aneale's memories with his own impressions of Trent. "I mean, the crazy thing was, we couldn't even talk to the boy, he only spoke French."

"I could have spoken French," Trainer said, holding out a hand for no reason, but just holding it out, as if he were always ready to be helpful. Aneale saw that he had soft, very white, puffy hands. He was wearing a severe black suit and a silver silk tie and white french cuffs, but a red Mickey Mouse wristwatch. Aneale found the little watch endearing. Trainer saw him staring at Mickey Mouse and said, "It's nine-fifteen in Disneyland. Mickey's going out to meet Pluto." He giggled and then, as if he didn't want any break in their conversation, he asked Aneale if he ever watched the afternoon soap operas. "I'd like to think we liked the same things," he said, touching Aneale's knee, and he seemed so considerate, so unassuming and available, that Aneale said, "I'll certainly be around town for a couple of weeks more. I mean, why don't we see each other? You, me, and Pluto?"

"I'd love to."

"My name's Arthur, I'm going to call you Jeff."

"I certainly wish you would."

"Let's have dinner, Jeff. At the Byzantium."

"I thought you'd never ask, Arthur."

"So let's just get secretarial for a minute and let's have your phone number," and while he was writing down the number in his *Gauguin In Ferarra* notebook, Aneale said, "Remember now, we've got ourselves a date," and then he asked, "By the way, where are you from?"

"Where was I born?"

"Right."

"A little two-bit town deep in the Ottawa Valley."

"Well, no wonder I couldn't place your accent."

"My mother was part French."

"What do you do for a living? I mean, it's so absolutely boring to ask, but how did you run into Trent?"

"Me?"

"Right."

"I'm the undertaker's assistant."

"The undertaker?"

"Yes," he said with a soft, wry smile, waiting, as if he expected Aneale to be so uncomfortable that he might get up from the sofa, breaking their sudden intimacy. "You surprised?" he asked, touching Aneale's wrist again.

"No, I mean, well yes I am, a little bit, but after all, I mean toujours le monde so why can't you be an undertaker if you want to be?

"I know the look, I've seen it before," Trainer said, and he stared at his shoes and then shrugged as if he were full of resignation and regret, though he had done nothing.

"I was wondering," Aneale said, wanting nothing to impinge on their amiable warmth, "how'd you get the job?"

"I got it when I was fifteen."

"You mean you've been handling stiffs since you were a kid?"

"I sort of grew up with them," he said, smiling and moving close to Aneale again, telling him that there had been only one undertaker in his town when he was a boy, and often the undertaker had been so busy that he'd needed help. "At first my father used to help him." His father had had a small convenience store so that there were times when he was too busy to go with the undertaker. "When I was fourteen, my father sent me over one day when he couldn't go himself," he said. "After that, it worked out simple enough. When the undertaker in his busy periods couldn't get my father he took me." While the other boys in town who had to work after school were delivering groceries or papers, he was busy embalming. "The whole thing really got going good when the undertaker needed a permanent assistant," he said. "I was awful unhappy for a week. I was sure my father would get it. I'll never forget the day the undertaker came over to the store. As soon as I saw him I knew he'd chosen my father. My father was sitting on a big packing box of Kellogg's Rice Crispies and then the undertaker asked my father if he could drive a car, and because my father knew what that meant, he shook his head like he was real sad, and he was sad, because the store hardly paid its way, see, and he wanted that job, but I got it," he chuckled, "because I could drive a car." His eyes were bright with the memory of that afternoon.

"You wanted to dress up stiffs for the rest of your life?"

"It's real interesting," he said simply.

"But why? I mean, don't you get tired of, like, touching the dead?"

"Listen," he said, eager to explain himself. "People don't get what's got to be solved each time I go to work. It's serious, I can't let my work repeat itself. If I do, then it's just a job. And I don't want to do just a job. So, there's people who end up in here in pretty bad shape, right. I mean it's terrible these days. I can't tell you how bad some of the men look. So, suppose I let them go out in their caskets looking awful? What'll their people who love them feel?" Aneale stared at him in wonder. "I've got to try and get a clear picture in my mind of what people expect to see," Trainer said. "I've got to try and find out what I can about the person I'm fixing, and I'd never want to boast, but you might be awfully surprised by some of the results I've got while knowing almost nothing at all." He had his hand on Aneale's knee. Aneale was appalled by his candor, and fascinated by the respect Trainer had for his work.

"You're absolutely out of this world," Aneale said.

"I'm glad you think so," he said, delighted. "Take your friend, Trent, he was quite sick, I mean, he'd been sick. Big-boned, but when I saw him dead, what I saw, well it was skin and bone country, he weighed only about a hundred and twenty pounds. So supposing I hadn't got a sense of him, hadn't got him right, how would you have felt? We'd never have talked." Getting up, he said quietly, in a calm measured intimate tone, "Come on back to the casket, I'll show you up close what I mean. Tricks of the trade."

Aneale put his flask in his suitcoat pocket and followed Trainer to the crowded front room. Several men were weeping. From others, a muffled laughter. Aneale and Trainer stood beside the mahogany casket, bent over the body in contemplation of the dead man's face.

"I'll bet he looks almost like you knew him," Trainer said.

"He took my breath away when I first saw him," Aneale admitted, confused because he was sure that two angry looking men dressed in black suits and black shirts were pointing at him and whispering.

"It's not bad for the little I had to go on. Just a couple of snapshots. But if I had got close to him like you . . . "

"Me?" Aneale asked as Trainer put his soft puffy forefinger under Trent's chin and pushed the flesh up. "See," he said, looking into Aneale's eyes, his smile boyish, "there's a trick . . . "

Aneale tried to smile but he felt a sudden chill and buttoned his suitcoat. His feet were cold. He was suddenly sure that Trainer, ingratiating and polite, had only been looking at him so intimately because he wanted to get a feel for his face. *Jesus Christ, he can't help it, he's been looking at me the whole time like I'm dead, already in the box.*

"Let's blow this pop stand," Aneale said desperately, easing away from Trainer. "I think I'd better go."

"Okay," Trainer said, checking his Mickey Mouse watch. "But it's only ten after ten."

Aneale turned away to talk to one of Trent's old lovers, a humorless, unshaven and paunchy man that he didn't like, a man who went in for chrome studs and leather hats, but he stood close to him and after a few minutes, as they left the funeral home, they went out the door together. At the sidewalk, a man called from a car parked by the curb, "Mr. Aneale, Mr. Aneale."

Trainer was leaning out of the open window of the car, the blinking neon funeral home sign lighting his face. "Can I give you a lift, Arthur?" he called. "Go your way?"

Aneale was shocked, even a little frightened, to see him sitting there, waiting, so available, holding out his puffy white hand. "No thanks," Aneale said curtly.

"He a friend of yours?" Trent's old lover asked.

"No, we were just killing time back in there," Aneale said.

"Well, we're all buddies, buddies in bad times. Talk helps."

"Trash talk, that's all," Aneale said, "that's all it was." He watched the car pull away. Trainer had looked very hurt, and puzzled. Aneale promised himself that he would speak to Trainer at the funeral.

In the morning, as the burial chapel bell tolled eleven, Aneale stood at the grave in the wet snow watching Trainer attach a small wreath of lilies to the gray steel box that encased Trent's casket. Aneale hunched his shoulders against the wind and stared down at his feet, tight-lipped and stern, feeling very lonely. Trainer, cradling the small crucifix that he had removed from the lid of the casket in his open, pudgy palm — so that he could give it to the grieving family — looked trim and elegant in his mourning clothes, his tailcoat and striped trousers. He had to step close to Aneale as he moved around the steel box and as he did so he looked intently at Aneale, hesitating, so that they stood almost toe to toe, but Aneale refused to look up. Aneale stamped his feet in the snow. He was cold. His toes were cold. He stamped his feet again. He didn't want Trainer standing so close, only a step away.

MELLOW YELLOW

The McBrides lived in a comfortable house in a row of red brick houses on the south side of Amelia Street. There were tall sheltering elms and a stone wall on the north side of the street, a wall that enclosed the old cemetery, and beyond the cemetery was a railroad track, a single line that was used only early in the morning when Marie-Claire would waken to a low train whistle and get up and draw back her bedroom curtains and look out over the stones, many of the thin slabs tilted and broken. She'd played in the cemetery as a child. She had never been afraid of the graves, not since she'd stretched out on her stomach and called down into the earth and listened, and called again, and listened. No one had answered. She'd decided that no one was there, that she was safe inside the walls, so the first time she'd let a boy touch her naked body had been in the long tufted grass, lying between the stones, but he'd been so frightened of the dead and her white body in the failing light of dusk that he'd suddenly stood up and run away to the doorway in the wall.

At nineteen, her full breasts trembled when she walked quickly. She had long legs and auburn hair down to her shoulders. Boys whistled at her when she walked down the street. She didn't mind. Sometimes she put two fingers to her mouth, as her father had taught her, and whistled back. She didn't like young men her own age. She liked men who were old enough to be serious, but that didn't mean she liked old men. Older men weren't serious, she said, they were worried about dying. She never thought about death, even when she went for a walk in the graveyard. She felt wonderfully alone and at ease with herself among the stones, alive and eager to see the world. That's why she thought the morning train whistle was like a call and on some mornings as the train rumbled slowly past the yard, she leaned against her window pane and let out a low muffled wail, calling to the train, giddy with expectation as she went down to breakfast where her mother said to her, "Whatever in the world are you going to do with your life?" and she said, "I don't know, but I'm going to live it."

She brought Conrad Zingg to the house to have supper with her mother and father. She had been seeing him for several months and her mother had said that she wanted to meet him. "This is Conrad," she said, and her mother smiled because he was tall and slender with a lot of black hair, a firm mouth, and steady dark eyes. "Call me Connie," he said, taking her father's hand but smiling at her mother. He seemed very sure of himself, very amiable and yet aloof. "Yes, all my friends call me Connie," he

said and stepped back, shoving his hands into his
suitcoat pockets. Her father stepped back, too, disconcerted. "Connie, eh," he said. "Connie what?"

"Connie Zingg."

"Zingg, what kind of name is Zingg?"

"Viennese. My parents came from Vienna when
I was a child."

"So you grew up here, then?"

"This is my town," he said.

"And here you are," Mrs. McBride said, "at
home in our house for supper," and then she said to
her husband, "And doesn't Marie-Claire look
happy." Conrad said, "Zingg went the strings of her
heart." Mrs. McBride laughed and took him by the
arm and led him into the small dining room. Marie-
Claire was startled. She felt a tinge of betrayal. She
didn't think they should be talking about her heart,
taking for granted how she felt, even though she had
wakened that morning wondering as she listened to
the train, if she didn't love him.

She tried to think of how she would tell him after
supper that he shouldn't joke about her feelings, but
then as they stood by the table her thoughts drifted
back to the afternoon they had spent together on the
bay. They had laughed and laughed, riding the
ferry, not getting off, but pretending that they were
docking at all the great cities, and as she had stared
at the sunlight on the choppy waves, she'd felt that
she was wonderfully safe beside him, safe in the
shelter of his self-possession, safe to dream that she
could be anywhere she wanted to be in the world.
"Well, sit down," her father said. "Marie-Claire, she

says you work at being a traffic consultant. What's that?"

"I design the traffic downtown."

"You dress it up?" her mother said.

"No, no," he said affably. "Computers, I work out the timing, the red and green lights, trying to get the flow."

"Stop and go," her father said.

"Right."

"You're in charge of the stop and go?"

"Right."

They ate their supper. It was a good supper of pot roast and potatoes. Marie-Claire was pleased because her mother was happy. She knew her mother was lonely for company. She also knew that her father was morosely uncomfortable, eating with a stranger in the house. He didn't like having strangers in his home. He thought a home was a safe place for friends where he didn't have to explain himself. He did not have many friends. But Conrad had been very attentive to her father's silences. He had not talked too much or been overbearing. At the end of the evening, after saying goodnight to her parents, he kissed her lightly at the front door and said, "Salt of the earth, your people, salt of the earth."

Her father was still at the table as she passed to go upstairs, content that she'd shown her parents that a successful young man could be attracted to her and could want to court her, but her father called out, "It doesn't work."

"What?" she asked, startled.

"The stop and go. Any damn fool can see that."

"Nonsense," she said angrily.

"He may have designed it, but it doesn't work."

She got into bed feeling wounded, as if her father had passed judgment not only on Conrad but on her, and for a moment she wanted to rush downstairs and say as cruelly as she could, "What do you know, what have you ever designed?" but she was naked in her bed and too tired to get dressed again. "Tomorrow is another day," she said and went to sleep.

She admired Conrad's confidence, and how sure he said he was that he had a future. Her mother and father had always talked about the future as a day to be afraid of, a day when everything would go wrong. As she listened to Conrad talk she tried to keep a grave expression on her face. She wanted him to take her seriously. He talked about traffic, and how his control of where and when people went was crucial to the control of chaos. "Red and green, in themselves they don't mean anything," he said. "It's like right and wrong. We agree to agree about what's right, and what's wrong. Red and green. Life's that simple, and that hard."

"I like yellow," she said, though she'd never thought about it before, and in fact, with her auburn hair, she did not think she looked good in yellow.

He laughed. "You're priceless," he said.

"So are you," she said, sitting cross-legged on a sofa in his apartment, watching him throw darts at a yellow and black board he had put up on the door to the hall. Sometimes, he would play by himself for an hour, touching each steel tip of a dart to his tongue, quietly counting down numbers as the darts hit the board. "You've got to not only learn how to count

down," he said, "you've got to think backwards."
She did not understand why he wanted to think
backwards or how he could watch darts programs
on the sports television network, sometimes for two
hours, hardly talking to her. He would glance at her,
as if he were going to speak, but all too often he had
the back of his hand against his mouth. He liked to
sit with his hand like that, and once she had said,
"Are you chewing your knuckle?"

"No, of course not," he'd said and he'd put his
hand defensively down on his knee, but she had seen
that his knuckle was red, almost raw.

"Do I frighten you?" she'd asked impetuously.

"Don't be silly," he'd said. "A slip of a girl like
you?"

"Do you want to arm wrestle?" she'd said.

"I'd break your wrist," he'd said, rubbing his
inflamed knuckle. "Yes I would."

"No you wouldn't," she'd said.

One evening, he asked to meet her a little earlier
than usual so that they could take a walk before
going out to supper. She wore a simple black raw
silk dress. His hair was cut. He was very erect as
they passed several expensive stores. He gave her an
approving smile and folded her arm under his. Then
he stopped by a jewelery store window and asked
which ring she liked, and when she said she wasn't
looking for a ring, he grew sullen and distant.

"I don't like diamonds," she said. "I like pearls."

"Diamonds are a girl's best friend," he said.

"Not this girl. And I don't like red roses either,"
she said, trying to take a light impish air. "Yellow,
white, anything but red." He said nothing. For some

inexplicable reason as they walked along the street in silence she felt guilty, as if she had failed him.

She asked him where they were going.

"Why, we're going to The Senator."

The Senator was an expensive supper club, a sophisticated jazz lounge. He led her up the stairs and through the door, and she let him hold her hand as if he were guiding her, certain that there was a grace in her stride because she had studied how all the models in the fashion films on television walked. She could see that he was pleased with her, because he walked beside her with his shoulders squared, an almost stern and disdainful look in his eyes that might have frightened her if she hadn't been so sure he was like this only because he wanted to have her.

The head waiter pointed to a side table, but Conrad took the waiter's arm firmly and nodded to the front. "We'll sit down by Mr. Jackson . . . thanks . . . he'll be glad to see us . . . "

"But sir . . . "

"No buts about it."

"Sir . . . "

"Thank you . . . "

Conrad, with a quick wave of his arm, almost as if he were directing traffic — which made her laugh gaily — led her through the close tables and then when they were seated he leaned across to her, before they ordered drinks, and said, "Today is my birthday."

"Your birthday . . . Why didn't you tell me . . . I should be taking you out . . . I don't have anything for you."

"You're all I want," he said, looking directly at her.

She put her head in her hands for a moment and let out a low quiet wailing sound. He looked perplexed, "What was that?" he asked.

"That's how I whistle in the dark," she said, trying to laugh.

He looked very grave and she thought he was watching her as if he were trying to trace her thoughts. She sat back in her chair. The week before, he had told her that she had to make up her mind about their future, and he had given her until his birthday to decide, but she was sure he hadn't told her when his birthday was, and she hadn't given it any thought at all. Only now, with the steadiness in his eyes, did she realize that he had been serious.

She pouted. It was ridiculous to suddenly thrust such a decision on her. How could she decide? Though they had been close, though they had had wonderful moments in which she'd felt both safe and free, and though they'd made love several times, he had never really talked about love. He had never said that he loved her though he had said one night that he valued her more than anything he had in the world. She had wanted to cry when he'd said that, but now she thought, he's never said that he actually loves me and she resented his restraint and his self-assurance. "Well," she thought, "when he mentions it we can talk it out."

J. J. Jackson, the pianist, came to their table. He greeted Conrad warmly, calling him Connie, and then said, "You got yourself a fine-looking lady. *Fine.*" Conrad asked him to sit down, and before she could say tartly that she thought she had a *fine*-looking man, Jackson told her that he had met Conrad in

Night Traffic Court. He said he'd been charged with "something really stupid, entering into a left turn lane when the light was already yellow, stopping and then turning against the red." Conrad, he said, had suddenly offered to appear as a witness for him. "He was some kinda brilliant," Jackson said. "He had that judge all turned around inside his head, with the time of this and the time of that, and how this and that were impossible, and finally, this here judge, he says, 'How do you know all this?' and he says, 'Because I designed the whole system, your honor,' and I thought I'd laugh till I died at the look on that judge's face." Jackson smacked him hard on the back. "My main man," he said. "My ace boon coon." Conrad accepted this display of warmth with ease. He looked so satisfied that she wondered if he hadn't seen Jackson's wry, belittling smirk and wondered why he would let anyone smack him so hard on the back. When Jackson left, Conrad settled into his reserved aloof air, the back of his hand against his mouth. She reached out and touched his free hand that was flat on the table and he smiled again, looking directly at her, a silent resolve in his eyes.

She shrugged and said, "What's it like being a boon coon?" and then, indignantly, she enjoyed the music, clapping enthusiastically after one of Jackson's solos, and the crowd around her was clapping loudly, too, so she put two fingers in her mouth, and she whistled. She was frightened that she might be acting like a young girl but it was the only way she felt she could maintain her sense of herself, her sense of her own dignity. So she whistled again and wanted to cry. She couldn't understand why she wanted to cry and why he refused to say anything to her about their relationship.

They left the lounge and walked home, taking the side streets that were quiet in the night. It had turned cool and she was shivering, yet she didn't cuddle against him as they walked. She didn't feel she could, because he was walking with his hands in his suitjacket pockets. He talked about baseball and a woman who was trying to swim across Lake Ontario for charity, for crippled children, and he seemed not only concerned about the children but quite content with her, but she knew he was not content and she thought he was not being honest, not being fair. She was angry and refused to walk all the way home in resigned silence.

"Would you like this to be our last night, Connie?"

"That's up to you . . . "

"No it's not," she said fiercely and wheeled away, furious, but somehow she knew that if she said any more he would just smile at her. She knew she would never forgive him if he smiled at her in her rage. She remembered how he had smiled at her in The Senator, as if he were being patient with her. She was tempted to put two fingers in her mouth and whistle at him. Instead, she punched him on the arm. "You're something else," she said.

"And so are you," he said.

They stood at the bottom of the stairs to her veranda. He was suddenly talking to her again, as if they had not been silent almost all the way home, and he was talking about how he hoped to move out of traffic control into policy planning for the whole city. "But never into politics," he said. "You just get your brains beaten in in politics and beaten in by any clunkhead who comes along." He told her it took courage to plan the future, to go to the top. "That's the way it is at city hall," he said, "the politicians, the dorks who don't know what they're doing, they are on the ground floor, the planners are on the top floor." He kissed her lightly on the cheek. Then, after a moment in which he held her hand, looking down as if he were meditative and shy, he said, "Goodnight, Marie-Claire . . . "

He began to turn away.

"Connie . . . just a minute, Connie ... . "

There were tears in her eyes.

"Connie, don't go away yet . . . "

He turned to her eagerly, expectantly, and she felt very young, very unknowing, beside him. He seemed to have counted on her calling out.

"Connie . . . "

He touched her cheek, as if his touch could help her out of her confusion, but she didn't feel confused. She felt bullied by his silence. She wanted to slap his face and tell him he was pig-headed and arrogant. "I guess I'm just yellow," she said.

"What?"

"Yellow."

"There's no need to be scared," he said.

"Who said I'm scared? You don't know what I'm talking about, do you? You don't know where the hell I'm coming from."

She turned and walked calmly up the stairs and into the house, leaving him standing on the walk.

For a moment, as she peeked through the lace curtains covering the small oval glass window in the door, she thought he was going to come up the stairs and her heart leapt, but then he turned and walked across the street and stood against the cemetery wall. At first, she thought she could feel him willing her out of the house, to come to him and she was afraid, but then, as she watched him stand for so long in the shadows with his back to the wall and his hand to his mouth, she thought he looked lonely and lost and she was sure he was waiting for her, as he had waited all night, because he couldn't bring himself to cross the street, couldn't say that he wanted her, couldn't say that he loved her. She felt a sudden urge to comfort him, to go to him and hold him and say, "You want to arm wrestle, never mind, you win," but then she thought with contempt, *He'd be scared stiff if I ever took him off into the graveyard at night.* She turned away from the door, closed the hall light and went into the kitchen where her mother and father were having their bedtime cup of tea.

As she saw them sitting so quietly at the table, as they had sat for years, she felt young and even more confident about her life, and yet she also felt ashamed that she had not been more of a friend to her mother and father in their home. She kissed her startled mother on the forehead and then, full of a strange new mellowness, she draped her arms around her father's neck and said, "You're right, it doesn't work."

"What?" he asked, astonished.

"The stop and go, it doesn't work."

She went upstairs to bed. She couldn't wait to go to sleep and then wake in the morning to the call of the train whistle coming to her across the graveyard.

Everybody Wants
To Go To Heaven

A man can die of fright in his dreams. That's what Cecil said he did, describing how he had died and how being one of the living dead was just like doing the dead man's float, face down into the water, drifting with his eyes open. He'd sit in his chair for hours staring straight ahead, slumped where his wife sat him every morning before she fed him cornflakes, a poached egg, and toast. Once a day she mourned for him. She stood in the kitchen with her eyes closed and she rocked back and forth on the balls of her feet, holding a slice of bread before she put it in the toaster, moaning low, a deep moaning for a woman so small. Sometimes she crooned to him. He seemed to like that, which wasn't surprising, since he'd always been a crooner around the house himself. She still dressed him in his green golfing slacks and canary yellow sweaters and his shoes with the little leather tassels. He'd been an actuary for an insurance company. Cecil Klose, the actuary, calculating the odds on death. "I'm always the first man in with the odd man out," he'd said. "Cecil," she said, "you were a heroic man. Until the day you died you lived a totally boring life." She chucked him under the chin.

He didn't look at her. He didn't blink. Then he said, "Transfer, please. Transfer. I want to change cars."

"I work hard looking after you," she said, glaring at him. "I'm steadfast to you, and I always was, working hard like I was about to go out of my mind, and now you talk to me like you've gone out of yours." She stroked his damp brow with a terrycloth hand-towel. "You may have died to all intents and purposes," she said, "but I know you're still in there, thinking." She stirred a glass of orange juice that had been standing so long that the pulp had sunk to the bottom. "Real fresh squeezed," she said, as she stirred the juice with a swizzle-stick. "Good for the vocal chords."

He had always sung around the house, especially after he'd closed an insurance contract. "You want to know who stands between the beginning and the end?" he'd always said. "It's me, Mister Inbetween," and then he'd stood crooning like one of the Mills Brothers, *Don't Mess with Mister Inbetween*. He had a dozen Mills Brothers albums. "It's not the voice, it's the timing, the phrasing," he'd said, "it's like me doing a deal, the nuance is everything."

She made him drink the orange juice and then wiped his lower lip with her finger.

She took a deep breath.

She puckered her wet lips and ran her hands along the inside of her thighs as if she were aroused. She was not aroused. Both of them now slept in the winterized back porch that was just off the kitchen — he, on a sofa-bed that hadn't been closed back into itself for a year, and she, on an old camp cot. She sat down beside the small back porch windows. There were streaks of sunlight on her face. The square windows were screened by climbing sweet peas and hollyhocks and there were colored wicker baskets full of thimbles and balls of wool on a pine table. She put brass thimbles on the fingers of her right hand. She started thrumming on the table, a steady rolling as if she were trying to find a tune, something he would remember and like, *The Boulevard of Broken Dreams,* and she began to whine as she thrummed, and this whine became a low keening wail. Then, without warning, she pulled the thimbles from her fingers and lifted his arms so that they stretched, open-handed, straight out from his body. "Time to do something useful. Time to do the wool," and she dropped a loose coil of red wool over his left hand, and then across the gap, over his right hand. In a dry whisper, he said, "I'll tell you how I died . . . " She drew the skein of wool taut. "No," she said, "not now, there's work to be done, three balls to get done this morning, red, yellow and green." She glanced at the huge hamper in the corner. It was full of balls of wool. "I'll tell you how I died," he whispered. She tried not to look at him. There were tears in her eyes. "You can die later," she said. "This is not a game."

"I was washing," he said, "taking a shower, the steam piling up, clouds . . . "

"That's no fun, talking about that, not now, Cecil. No games."

He'd been good at games. He'd liked dressing up in his green slacks to go out and play golf. He'd liked to play games with children.

His favorite game with the children on the street had been to stand on the sidewalk and let them see a cellophane-wrapped peppermint candy in his hand. In his open hand. He'd held his hands over his head like a boxer being introduced, he'd shown them his closed fists, and then his open hands, empty, and he'd laughed heartily, always pleased when the children had reached for his empty hands, pleased that once again he'd fooled them. "They know I'm a fun guy," he'd said. "I fooled them."

"Fun," she'd cried once, "what the hell is fun, what is fun?"

"Fun," he'd said, looking at her as if she were crazy, "is when you feel good and you feel good when what's good for you gets done. The trouble is," he'd said, looking directly at her, "some people like to feel bad and feeling bad spreads around like the common cold. The next thing you know, you're in bed for a week, or for life."

"In these arid hours," she'd said.

"What?"

"These arid hours."

"Arid, arid, what kind of word is arid?"

She had never answered that question. She'd taken a deep breath and had never answered the question. She took a deep breath now and kept unwinding wool from the skein around his hands, making a ball. She looked through the porch glass into the tendrils of sweet peas and morning glories. She saw petals of light. Radiant light. And delicate stamens held in the silence of the light in the glass. She knew how to hold on to silence. She would keep silent for days. "You're a windsucker for silence," her father had told her when she was a girl, "but so is God in these arid hours."

She took a deep breath.

"His Word. What'll it be like?" she'd asked her father.

"It'll be like one of those water bugs you see on a dead calm day on a pond, coming at you like a snub-nosed bullet . . . "

"I stepped out of the steam," Cecil said, "I stepped out and took a towel and wiped a big circle clean in the mirror and suddenly I was enclosed, enclosed by the circle so that I didn't know where I was except I was gone . . . Just like that, I was gone, into a dream. I knew it was a dream because I've never felt so right about anything in my whole life, like everything was where it was doomed to be, so I was terrified."

"Terror," she said. "What do you know about terror?"

He said nothing. She said nothing. He stared straight ahead, his hands wrapped in another coil of wool, yellow. Often when they sat like this, so still that she thought she could hear dust falling in the sunlight through the windows, she would begin to laugh quietly, a dry crackling laugh, and then her laughter would become deep and throaty. When he'd first known her he'd thought that every time she laughed she was going to tell him a secret, but she had never told him anything, not anything he thought was a secret, not anything deep, nothing dark or shameful. He had yearned to hear something shameful. But there'd never been anything dark about her. She had beautiful pale skin and pale blue eyes and was sparrow-breasted.

"Little birds for breasts," she'd said ruefully after they'd made love on their wedding night in a motel, "and I don't think they'll ever sing." He'd sat alone in the toilet until dawn getting drunk on a mickey of Alberta Premium rye whiskey and then he'd told her that a bird in the house means a death in the family and as far as he could see she had twin death for tits. He'd fallen asleep, snoring. She'd put a quarter in the vibrating machine and had watched him shake on the bed for twenty minutes. She was angry because she couldn't find any more quarters in her purse. She remembered her mother had told her, "You want to set a man straight, you give him a good shaking." She had cried for three days as they'd driven through the countryside from inn to inn, honeymooning, and for three days he'd said over and over again, "I don't know why I wanted to sound like I hate you. I don't." She'd stopped crying and said, "You do. You hate me." And then she'd said, "Why did you marry me?" and he'd said, trying to laugh, "You were the only woman I ever saw who wore open-toed shoes — your big toes sticking out, painted red." He'd laughed. He had a measured laugh. Like a metronome. *Heh huh, heh huh.* She'd said, like she was suddenly talking about something else, "Remember Jayne Mansfield?" And he'd said, "Why?" And she'd said, "Decapitated. She had the biggest birds in America and she got decapitated in a car accident."

"*Heh huh,*" he said.

"At times like this it's just best to take a deep breath," she'd said. "Breathe in, breathe out, like a breath of wind in the garden."

She sat, breathing, deeply in, deeply out.

"The garden's full of nests," she said, peering through the porch glass and the climbing flowers.

"And I could hear a bird that morning," he said, staring straight ahead. "I could hear one lone bird once the circle had closed and it wasn't singing, it was whispering. Everything was all steamy white and there was a bird whispering and the bird was so big that all the whiteness was inside the beak of the bird. I could see the sun in the bird's throat. But it didn't give off any light, only a glow with no reflection, and then it went out, so there was only a dim, gold, band-like rim, but though there was no sun I could still see walls of sheer ice a way off in the distance. I knew they were the walls of the universe. I knew I was in the mind of God. I was so scared I wanted to cry but everything was so brittle in the cold that I was afraid to cry because my bones would break if I even breathed, but then I saw how lucky I was, because I knew I had died and nothing could be worse than being afraid of God, being dead and not knowing that you had died."

"I'm not afraid of dying," she said. "And I'm not afraid of God."

He said nothing. There was a little spittle at the corner of his mouth. She tossed two balls of wool into the hamper and wiped the spittle away from his mouth. She wiped his brow with a damp cloth. He had always been meticulous and now she was metic-

ulous with him. There was an arborite tray attached
to his chair. She put both his hands on the tray,
palms down, fingers spread, and then unzipped a
small black leather pouch, taking out scissors, tweez-
ers, and a short pearl-handled nail file. She began to
clean his nails, to probe under the nails and to push
the cuticles back, so fiercely that thread-lines of
blood appeared along two of the cuticles. She
dabbed the blood away with cotton batten. "No,
God means nothing to me," she said as she stood up,
went to the sink, and took down a mug, soap and a
straight razor. She had learned how to strop a blade.
He had always used an electric shaver, but she liked
the sound of stropping. There was something sensual about it. It aroused her. And she liked to strop the
blade in front of him, though he never altered his
gaze, never looked at the leather or the blade. But
once she'd got a lather in the mug and had brushed
it on to his jaw, what she really loved was shaving
him, the clean track through the white lather, the feel
of the sharp blade against the stubble, the rasping
sound. It was the sound, and the feel of the sound in
her fingers, that she loved best, as she shaved his
throat clean, particularly around a mole that was
over his Adam's apple, a mole she'd never noticed
until she'd had to shave him.

"I don't know how I never saw that mole," she
said.

There was so much about his body that she had
never noticed, had never seen before. "Transfer,
please," he said. "Transfer, I want to change cars."
She took off his slippers and put on his brown shoes
with the leather tassels. She changed his clothes

every morning after breakfast and every evening just before the eleven o'clock TV news. She always washed him before bed, washed him and examined every part of his body, surprised each time by the hard boniness of his feet, the yellow of his toenails, the patch of black hair in the small of his back. She had spread his legs and stared for a long time at his scrotum and penis, soft and shrunken back into his body. He was not circumcised so she'd drawn the skin back, washed him with a hand cloth and found herself smiling at his limpness, and one testicle hanging lower than the other. It was the left. Her mother had told her that a woman's left breast was always lower than her right because of the sorrow and disappointment in a woman's heart. She wondered if the hanging testicle was the mark of a man's sorrow and disappointment, too. She suddenly bent down and gave his penis a pecking kiss. She'd never kissed his penis. He'd never asked her to. Now, she kissed and stroked him but nothing happened. She couldn't arouse him. She was enraged. "Look at you. Mr. Inbetween, Mr. Fucking Inbetween," she said, astonished at hearing herself say *fucking*. She had never said the word aloud in her life, she had only mouthed it in the dark, and she stood up and folded her arms and began to moan and sway and rock back and forth on the balls of her feet as if in deep pain, a pain in her marrow, and then she slowly drew the blanket up over his still body stretched out in the sofa bed, tucking the blanket to his chin as she said bitterly, "Death was always in you."

"Transfer, please."

"No, you don't get off that way."

"Transfer, I want to change cars."

"No, you've got to live with the truth just like I've got to live with it. The truth is the truth. You can't change the truth, we can't change anything else, why should we want to change the truth? That baby died in my womb. That baby had death in him, the death that's been in your seed from day one, the death that you've got in you."

"Transfer, please."

"That life in me, that breathing life was dead before it had half a chance. You're a carrier. I miscarried because you're a carrier."

"Transfer, please, *heh huh*. Transfer." He blinked, blinked again, and began to sweat.

"Oh Cecil, Cecil," she said, suddenly laughing and patting his hand. "It's all in the phrasing, isn't it." She let out a piercing scream. And then another. And another.

The phone rang.

She answered the phone. It was an automated voice, the telephone company offering new long distance rates. *Stay on the line for further information* . . . "No thank you," she said and hung up.

She stood drumming her fingers on the phone's cradle.

"And I stood waiting, waiting," he said, wrenching her away from the phone. "The bird was whispering but it wasn't words, and then I saw what I knew was one of God's thoughts, a thought for me. It was right there, standing in front of me, in front of the hollow sun. It looked like a wolverine, one of the animals of His mind, who'd come to have a word with me, slavering, an amber light in his black eyes.

For such is my beloved. That was the word, the words
I heard as the wolverine drew his claw like a razor
from my throat to my gut and opened me up, hauling my innards out, and then the animal entered into
me, closing the wound behind him, until I could feel
it, this living cannibal thought, possessing me from
within, devouring me, until at last I knew I was seeing nothing with my own eyes, I was no longer me, I
was terrified and dead and born again as this
wolverine, and I knew that the landscape I now saw
was blood red, as red as it had been white, and I
heard the word, *live in the blood,* knowing I had died,
that my body was like that gold rim of the sun, a
closed circle, empty at the core . . . "

He lifted his hand and drew a circle in the air.
She put her hand up and touched the line of the circle. He'd always loved circles. That's why he'd
always given children on the street soap-bubble
blowers. "There," he'd said as children surrounded
themselves with the diaphanous globes, "is perfec-
tion in the air." He'd also been able to draw perfect
circles and he'd always carried newly sharpened HB
pencils in his breast pocket, and whether he'd been
at work or whether he was watching re-runs of *The
Honeymooners* on television on Sunday mornings,
he'd always drawn circles on a legal-size pad, saying, "Leonardo da Vinci could draw perfect circles.
He was a southpaw, too. Said it was the sign of the
greatest artist in the world, freehand circles." And
he'd carried three stainless steel half-shells in his
suitcoat pocket. His insurance clients had loved to
play the shell game, trying, as he'd moved the pea
around under the shells, to guess where the pea was.

He'd been very quick. "The pea is like your heart," he'd said. "If you could find the pea real easy, there'd be no mystery." That's why, when he'd held candy in his hands over his head, he had told the children, "Go ahead, find my heart." He'd happily shown them an empty hand after they had guessed wrong. Then, to make them feel foolish and grateful, he'd always given them the candy anyway, with his little laugh, *heh huh, heh huh.*

"That's really what I can never forgive you for, Cecil," she said as she lifted his arms and began to wind more wool.

"I'll tell you how I died," he said.

"Never mind," she said.

"Doing the dead man's float."

"Grateful, Cecil, you wanted me to be grateful."

"I'll tell you how I died . . . "

She wound the wool taut. "When I wash you, clean you, I don't want you to feel grateful."

"Transfer, please."

She took the wool from Cecil's hands and put his hands down in his lap. She listened for the postman's step. It was very quiet. She listened hard. The postman didn't pass by. The disability cheques were late. She was angry. She looked at his fingernails. They were clean. She thought she might cut them back even closer. She began to hum, and then sing:

Love and marriage,
love and marriage,
go together like a horse
and carriage . . .

He stared straight ahead, a little spit at the corner of his mouth. The spittle reminded her of one of her spinster school teachers. The spittle disgusted her, the more she looked at it. She was seething with anger. She suddenly screamed, "Wipe your mouth." He didn't move.

She took off her gold wedding band. She was surprised at how easily it came off. His ring was more difficult. She yanked it over the knuckle. She weighed the two rings in the palm of her hand and then held them up to his eyes between her thumbs and forefingers, like spectacles. "Look," she cried. "Look. Just like the sun, just like the sun you saw in God's mind. Empty. What do you think about that?"

"Please," he said.

"What?"

"Please. I want to get off."

"Oh, yes, I bet you would like that wouldn't you."

"Transfer, please."

"You'd like me to really look after you, wouldn't you?"

"Please."

"But I can't kill you, you're already dead."

"Heh huh, heh huh . . . "

"What else can I give you?"

"Such is my beloved," he said, and she laughed and crooned, *"I can't give you anything but love."* Then she sang:

> *Dream awhile,*
> *scheme awhile,*

you're sure to find,
happiness, and I guess . . .

He began to growl. He had never growled before. He sounded like an animal, an angry animal. He was wide-eyed with no expression on his face, growling.

"Stop it," she yelled.

He growled again.

"You stop it," she said, as if she were warning an animal. "You better stop it."

His growl turned to a guttural snarl.

She got up. She thought she should make some toast. And tea. And take a deep breath. Instead, she went to the kitchen drawer beside the dishwasher. Years ago, he'd put a handgun in the drawer. He'd been worried about someone breaking into their house in the dark. But no one had ever threatened them, almost no one had ever knocked on the front door at night. The gun had never been fired. She wasn't sure if there was a bullet in the chamber.

She stood facing him with the gun in her hand. "I'm telling you to stop it," she said, "to go away with your growling." She looked hard into his eyes. They were bloodshot. The snarling grew louder, there was drool at the corner of his mouth.

She lifted his left hand, because he was left-handed, and put the gun in it, closing his fingers around the butt, and then she turned the gun back toward his mouth. "I'm warning you," she said, "for the last time." He curled his lip, snarling. She pushed the snub-nose barrel into his mouth, her hand on his, her finger on his, up against the trigger. "Stop it," she cried. His head was tilted, his eyes wide open, and she was sure that she saw him, saw him hiding down a deep hole inside the dark pupils of his eyes. "Cecil," she said, "I knew it. I can see you. You're in there. There you are."

The bullet blew out the back of his skull. There was blood all over the chair but none on her. She stepped back, leaving the gun in his hand. "Cecil," she said, "Cecil, dear Cecil."

The police found her standing on the front porch wearing only her kimono, holding a feather duster. She was dusting the air. The open kimono had slipped off her shoulders, so that she was naked to the policemen as they came up the walk, startled by her being naked, by her big bush of black hair for so small a woman, and how boyish her body was, and one of the cops said, "Jesus, she's got no tits at all." She was crooning quietly:

> *I can't give you anything but love, baby,*
> *That's the only thing I've plenty of, baby,*
> *Dream awhile . . .*

NOBODY WANTS TO DIE

Willard Cowley lived with his wife Kate in a sandstone house. There was a sun parlor at the back of the house and the windows of the parlor opened on to a twisted old apple tree.

"Everything alters," he often told her, "under the apple tree. One by one we drop away." He was a well-known scholar, big boned and tall, with closely cropped grey hair. "It's the job of wizened old teachers like myself," he said, smiling indulgently at his students, "to tell the young all about tomorrow's sorrow." He was told to stop teaching, to retire. He was sixty-five. Kate came down to his office. "You needn't have come," he said, but he was comforted to see her. She said the sorrowful look in his eye made him even more handsome than he was. "A lady killer, Willard, that's what you are."

"I've never felt younger," he said, as they walked home together.

As the weeks went by, they went for a long walk every day, and he talked about everything that was on his mind. "A mind at play," he said to her one afternoon, "and I don't know whether I've told you this before, but it's not a question of right or wrong, really — a mind at play is a mind at work." She had soft grey eyes and a wistful smile. "Yes, you've told me that before, Willard, but I adore everything you tell me, even when you tell me twice." They often stopped for a hot chocolate fudge sundae at a lunch counter that had been in the basement of the Household Trust building since their childhood. She loved digging the long silver spoon down into the dark syrup at the bottom of the glass.

"You and your sweet tooth," he said. "It'll be the death of you."

"Someday you'll take death seriously," she said.

"I do. I do," he said.

"How?"

"I think I'd like to die somewhere else."

"Wherever in the world would you like to die?"

"It's strange," he said, "we've always lived in this city but now I think I'd be happier somewhere else, out in the desert."

"There's no ice cream in the desert," she laughed, softly humoring him.

"Well, it's only a daydream," he said. "It's not how I dream at night."

"What do you dream at night?"

"About you," he said.

"But I'm always right here beside you."

"Yes, yes," he said, "but think of where we could go in our dreams, think of what it would be like watching wild she-camels vanish into the dunes."

She threw her arms around his neck and said, "Yes," kissing him until they were out of breath.

"What a couple of crazy old loons we are," she said.

"Thank God," he said.

Her eyesight was failing, so at night he began to read the newspapers to her. They got into bed and he read to her as she lay curled against his shoulder. "Oh, I like this," he said, "a politician is like a football coach, he has to be smart enough to understand the game and stupid enough to take it seriously."

"I like that too," she said, laughing. "I don't like football but I like that."

"That's why you'll never be a politician," he said, "thank God," and he linked his hands behind his head, letting his mind wander, suddenly perplexed because he couldn't remember the name of the pharaoh at the time of Moses. He heard her heavy breathing. Before turning out the light, leaning on his elbow, he looked down into her face, astonished that she had fallen so easily into such a sound sleep because in her younger years she had often wakened in a clammy sweat, panic-stricken, mumbling about loss, about eyes that had not opened, saying she could hear her own screaming though she was not making a sound. He wondered what dreadful fear had welled up within her during those nights, what darkness she had sunk into, and he wondered how she had managed over the years to stifle that fear, tamp it down. Perhaps in her fear she had gotten a dream-glimpse of their stillborn child. He wondered why they had never tried to have another child. He wondered why he had never wanted another woman, but he had not, and this gave him sudden joy and a sense of completion in her. He was close to tears as he looked into her sleeping face, afraid that she would go down into a darkness where she would not waken and he whispered:

> *Child, do not go*
> *into the dark places*
> *of the soul,*
> *there the grey wolves whine,*
> *the lean grey wolves . . .*

In the morning, after he had two cups of strong black coffee, he read the newspapers aloud. Any story about old ruins and the past lost in the dunes of time caught his eye. A few months before he'd retired, he had written in *Scholastics: A Journal of New Modes* that the psalms of David were actually based on a much older Egyptian sacred text, now almost entirely lost, and this meant that David was just a reporter of what he had heard somewhere on the desert trails, and so Willard was pleased one morning to read in the paper that nearly all the archaeologists at a conference in Boston had agreed that the Bible was not history, that no one should pay any historical attention to anything written before the Book of Kings. "The whole thing," he said to Kate, "may just be theological dreaming. The whole of our lives, our ethical and spiritual lives, may be a dream. A wonder-filled dream in which we defeat death by turning lies into the truth." When she asked him how a lie could be the truth, and how everything that was true could be a dream, he said, "I think that maybe all through history we have become our own gods in our dreams. We create them and then they turn around and taunt us. Maybe Christ on the cross is really a taunting dream of death and redemption, a dream in which Christ has to stay nailed to the cross because we don't dare let him come back to us again, we don't dare let him come back and live among us like a normal man because then there'd only be a dreamless silence out there without him in it, a great dark silence." As he said this, he felt a lurch in the pit of his stomach, a slow opening up of an old hollow deep in himself, but this hollow didn't frighten him. It was an absence that he had long ago accepted, just as he had accepted the absence of children in their life. He had learned to live with this absence but he could not bear to see Kate in pain. One morning when he was wakened by her moaning in her sleep he felt a frightened pity as he looked down into her sleeping face, pity that she had had to suffer her own attacks of darkness, attacks of absence, in her sleep. He touched her cheek and whispered, "Kate, you're my whole life. Thank God."

One afternoon, when the apple tree was in bud and the hired gardener, who had tattoos on his arms, was cleaning out the peony beds, Willard laughed and pointed at the gardener and told Kate that he'd been studying a book of maps of the Middle East that a friend had given him years ago, and he'd discovered that there was a small city near the Turkish border that was called after Cain's nephew, Enos, and since the men there had always marked themselves with tattoos, he said, "The mark of Cain was probably just a tattoo."

"You mean Cain's pruning our rose bushes?"

"Yes."

"Willard," she said, "you are a notion," and she smiled with such genuine amused pleasure and admiration that tears filled his eyes. He held her hand, breathing in the heavy musk of the early spring garden.

"With you Kate," he said, "I always feel like it's going to be possible to get a grip on something really big about life before I die. I'm very grateful."

"Oh, no," she said. "No one in love should be grateful."

"I can't help it," he said and he felt such an ache for her that he had to take several deep breaths, so that he sounded as if he were sighing with sudden exasperation.

"Don't be impatient," she said.

"I'm not, I was just suddenly out of breath."

"And soon you'll be telling me you're out of your mind."

"That goes without saying," he said, laughing.

"That's what everybody says happened to Adam and Eve," she said. "That she drove Adam out of his mind because she wanted the apple and she ate it . . . "

"And look at us now," he said.

"A couple of old lunatics," she said, lifting his hand to her lips, "and that's not gratitude, that's love, Willard. You've always been the apple of my eye."

He stood beside her with tears in his eyes.

"Some day," she said, brushing his tears away with her hand, "I'll tell you what I really think."

"I bet you will," he said.

"Yes."

He riffled through a sheaf of papers on a side table. "You know what, you'll never guess," he said, fumbling the papers. He was excited. He wanted to please her. "I've come across the most wonderful creation story . . . "

"Creation?"

"Yes, yes," he said, flattening a piece of tawny onionskin paper on the table. "Professor Shotspar translated this for me years ago, from a flood story, it was written down somewhere around 1800 BC, in Akkadian, which in case you don't know is one of the oldest languages in the world, and it's exactly the same flood you'll find in the Gilgamesh, but this is about the gods and how they got around to creating man — Lullu, they called him — how do you like that, and it's about how they created all of us so we'd knuckle under and do their dirty work, their mucking up . . . "

> When the gods, before there were men,
> Worked and shed their sweat,
> The sweat of the gods was great,
> The work was dire, distress abiding.
> Carping, backbiting,
> Grumbling in the quarries,
> They broke their tools,
> Broke their spades
> And hoes . . . .
> Nusku woke his lord,
> Got him out of bed,
> "My lord, Enil your temple wall is breached,
> Battle broaches your gate."
> Enil spoke to Anu, the warrior.
> "Summon a single god and make sure he's
> put to death."

Anu gaped
And then spoke to the other gods, his brothers.
"Why pick on us?
Our work is dire, our distress abiding.
Since Belet-ili, the birth goddess, is nearby,
Why not get her to create Lullu, the man.
Let Lullu wear the yoke wrought by
Enil.
Let man shed his sweat for the gods.

"Maybe that's where *he's a lulu* comes from," she said, laughing.

"That's good," he said. "Damned good. I guess we're a couple of lulus."

A week later they were sitting in the sun parlor having a glass of dry vermouth. There'd been a heavy pounding rain during the night and it was still raining. The garden walk was covered with white petals pasted to the flagstone. He should have noticed that Kate was growing thin, eating only green salads, Emmenthal cheese, and dry toast. At first, sipping her vermouth, she'd grown giddy, and then, as if sapped of all energy, she said, "I'd love to be sitting somewhere south in the hot sun." He turned to her and said, "But you've never liked the sun." She was sitting in a white wicker chair with her eyes closed. He touched her hand. She didn't open her eyes. He went back to reading Conrad, a novel, *An Outcast of the Islands.* Suddenly he stood up, staring into the stooping branches of the apple tree, bent by the weight of the pouring rain, and then, just as abruptly, he sat down.

"Listen to this," he said: *"There is always one thing the ignorant man knows, and that thing is the only thing worth knowing; it fills the ignorant man's universe. He knows all about himself . . . "*

Willard dropped the book.

"What's the matter?" she asked, opening her eyes.

"Can't you see?"

"See what?"

"If I seem to know so much about everything, maybe that's only a kind of ignorance, maybe I don't know anything about myself."

"Don't be silly," she said sternly.

"Silly?" he said. "I'm deadly serious."

He sat staring out the window, into the downpour as tulip petals in the garden broke and fell. He stared at the headless stems. She rose and went upstairs and took a hot bath. She lay in the water a long time, slipping in and out of sleep, until she realized the water was cold and she was shivering. When she came back downstairs he was still sitting by the window, facing the drenched garden.

"Willard, for God's sake, what's the matter? You've hardly moved for hours and hours."

"I don't know," he said, "it's a kind of dread, or something like that. A dread . . . "

"It's silence, that's what it is."

"I suppose it is. The vast silence. Maybe we live in silence forever. Maybe when we die that's all we hear. Silence. The word is dead. Maybe that's what hell is."

The next morning she didn't get out of bed. He brought her toast and tea, but she only drank her tea. "Perhaps it's a touch of flu," she said, but she had no temperature and no headache. Her hands were cold.

He sat holding and rubbing her hands. She smiled wanly. "Oh, I missed our good talks yesterday," she said.

"It was only a pause," he said, trying to be cheerful. "A pause in the clock."

"That's right," she said, and she closed her eyes.

"It was a hard day on the garden, too," he said.

"Yes."

"All this dampness, it's not good, not healthy."

"No."

"It gets into the bones."

"Yes."

"Dem bones, dem bones . . . " he sang, trying to be gay.

"Dem dry bones . . . " she whispered.

"Did you know Kate," he said, leaning close, seeing that she was drifting off into sleep, "that they've started digging near to where most people think the garden of Eden was, and there's an actual town that was there around 6000 BC. And that's a fact," he said, wagging his finger at her as she lay with her eyes closed, "because there are so many ways of actually dating things now, what with carbon 14 and tree rings, dendrochronology they call it, when they cut across a tree and read the rings, and then of course they match it with an older tree, and that tree with an older tree, all the way back to the bristlecone pine, to 5,000 years ago, in fact even longer. And then . . . "

She was sound asleep, smiling in her sleep. Her smile bewildered him. He had never seen her smile in her sleep before. He wondered what secret happiness, found in sleep, had made her smile.

One week later, she was taken to hospital. She had a private room and a young doctor who spoke in a hushed monotone with his hands crossed inside the sleeves of his smock. "It's a problem of circulation," he said. "The blood's just not getting around."

"Oh dear," Willard said, and sat in the bedside leather easy chair all day and into the early evening until Kate woke up and said, "You shouldn't stay here all this time."

"Where else should I be?" he said.

The day she died, her feet and lower legs were blue from gangrene. She'd been in great pain and had quickly grown thin, the skin taut on her nose, her eyes silvered by a dull film. She panted for air, rolling her eyes. "Willard, Willard," she whispered and reached for him.

"Yes, yes."

"Talk to me."

"Yes, Kate."

"There. Talk to me there."

"Where is there?" he asked desperately.

After her cremation, to which only a few old scholars came and none of his former students, Willard wandered from room to room in the house talking out loud. He kept calling her name, as if she might suddenly step in from the garden, smiling, her hands dirty from planting. In the late afternoons he sat by the open sun parlor window, talking and reading and gesturing, but then early one evening he got confused and said, "What did I say?" and because he couldn't remember what he had said, and when Kate did not answer, the dread that he'd felt the month before, the fear that the hollow he'd so easily accept-

Barry Callaghan

ed was really a profound unawareness of himself,
seized him in the chest and throat so that he was left
breathless and he thought he was going to choke. He
was so afraid, so stricken by his utter aloneness, that
he began to shake uncontrollably. He sat staring at
her empty chair, ashamed of his trembling hands.
He was sure he heard wolves calling and wondered
if he was going crazy. He decided to get out for some
air, to go down to the footbridge that crossed over
the ravine and then come back. Later that week, he
went for a long walk in the downtown streets, along
streets that they had walked, but he couldn't bring
himself to go into the lunch counter. All the faces
reflected in the store windows as he passed made his
mind swirl, but when he stepped through the subway turnstiles, to the *thunk* of the aluminum bars
turning over, he told Kate as clearly as he could that
he was now absolutely sure, as he had promised her,
that he was on to something big, a simple truth, so
simple that no one he knew had seen it, and the truth
was that all the great myths were based on lies. He'd
actually been thinking, he'd said to her at the cremation, that to live a great truth, it is probably necessary
to live a great lie. "After all," he said excitedly, as he
stepped through the last turnstile, "the Jews were
never in Egypt. There was no Exodus. The
Egyptians were fanatical record keepers and the
Jews are never mentioned, and the cities that the
Jews said they built, they did not exist. They were
not there, there was no parting of the sea, no forty
years of wandering in the desert . . . I mean, my
God," he said, shaking his long finger as he forgot
where he was going and went back down an escala-

tor, "what does anyone think Moses was doing out there for forty years? Forty years. You can walk across the Sinai in two days. And Jericho, there was no battle. No battle took place because there were no great walls to tumble down. There was no city there back then, not at that time," and he threw up his arms, full of angry defiance, standing on the tiled and dimly-lit platform of the St. George subway station. Several people were staring at him.

"Sorry," he said, "I'm very sorry." He hurried back to the escalator, travelling up the moving stairs, craning his neck, eager to get out into the sunlight. "I just don't know what I'm going to do, Kate," he said in a whisper. "Talking to you like this, I forget. It's so fine, I just plain forget, people looking at me as if I were some kind of loony."

It was painful for him to stay at home all day. He kept listening for her voice in the rooms, embarrassed by the sound of his own voice. He sank into grim, bewildered silence, sometimes standing in the hall in a trance, a stupor, certain that he was losing his mind. Sometimes he slept during the day and dreamed that he was walking on his shadow, as if his shadow was always in front of him, and his shadow was made of soot. It whimpered with pain. He stomped on his shadow till he was out of breath. He was afraid it was the soot of a scorched body. He heard her voice, and he saw her sitting with her elbow on the window sill, picking old paint off a glass pane. She was feverish and kept calling for ice. "Ice is the only answer." He woke up terrified. He locked their bedroom door and made his bed on the sofa in the upstairs library. For a week, he slept on the sofa, drinking several glasses of port, trying to get to sleep. He could see from the sofa a hem of light under the bedroom door. He'd left the light on, a bedside reading lamp that she'd given him for his birthday, a porcelain angel with folded wings. On two evenings he was sure that he heard her voice in the bedroom, a voice so muffled that he couldn't make out the words. Then, one night while he was keeping watch on the hem of light, half-tipsy, half asleep, it went out. He was panic stricken. He took it as a sign that she was in trouble, that she was really going to die, and he fumbled with the old key, trying to get it into the lock, whispering. "Hold on Kate, hold on, I'm coming," cursing his own stupidity and cowardness for trying to close off the bedroom. He felt ashamed, as if he had betrayed her. When he got into the room, breathing heavily, he discovered that the bulb in the lamp, left on for so long, had burned out. He had seldom cried before, and only once in front of her. Now, standing before her dressing-table mirror, he discovered that he was disheveled and haggard and he was crying. He began to sing as cheerfully as he could:

If I had the wings of an angel,
over these prison walls I would fly,
I'd fly to the arms of my poor darling,
and there . . .

He moved close to himself in the mirror and curled his lip with contempt. "You're a coward," he said, and then he lay down and fell asleep on their bed. In the morning, he dressed with care, putting on an expensive Egyptian cotton shirt and camelhair jacket and he went out into the bright noon hour and found he was relieved to be walking again with a sudden jaunt in his stride, downtown among the crowds. He began to sing: *I'll take you home again Kathleen* . . . But then he grew suddenly wary and stopped singing, trying to make sure he heard himself before he spoke out loud. He kept looking for himself in mirrors and store windows to see if he was singing or talking at the top of his voice.

In the Hudson's Bay underground shopping mall, he came to a halt so abruptly that an old woman bumped into him, spilling her bag of toiletries. He didn't notice. He stared at a portly black man standing by the checkout counter. The black man was talking into a walkie-talkie, and farther along the mall, another man had a walkie-talkie or a cellular phone close to his cheek. Willard realized that for weeks he'd seen people all over the city talking and nodding into phones and no one paid any attention to them. "Nobody knows who they're talking to," he cried, "maybe they're not talking to anyone," and the old woman, picking up her rolls of Downy Soft toilet paper scattered around his feet, looked up and said, "You're not only rude, you're crazy," but he hurried off.

He tried to persuade a young salesman at Uruk Sound Systems that he needed only one cheap child's walkie-talkie, a black one, not a pair, but when the salesman said sternly, "Look, there's no point, you can't talk to yourself, you can't talk to no one. Someone's got to be on the other end," he quickly agreed, bought a pair, and strode out of the store.

He walked home, flicking the *Send* button as soon as he got to the footbridge, talking and laughing, telling Kate an old joke he'd told her years ago: "How these two old ladies had promised each other that the first one to die would come back and tell the other what Heaven was like, so after Sadie died Sophie waited and waited, and just when she gave up, Sadie appeared in a halo of light and Sophie said, 'You came back, so what's it like?' And Sadie said, 'You get up in the morning and eat and then you have sex, and then it's sex before breakfast and afterwards sex, and before lunch and then lunch and more sex and sex before a snack before goodnight and then sex,' and Sophie said, 'Sadie . . . Sadie, this is Heaven!' But Sadie said: 'Heaven, who's in heaven. I'm a rabbit in Wisconsin.'" He laughed and laughed but with the walkie-talkie tucked against his cheek, so that no one paid any attention to him. "Oh, I'm in fine fettle," he said. "This walking clears the lungs."

He stood on the footbridge over the ravine. He had never stopped and looked down into the ravine before. He'd always been in a hurry to get home, his head tucked into his shoulder against the wind. He was surprised at how deep the ravine actually was, and how dense and lush the trees and bush were. The city itself was flat, all the streets laid out in a severe military grid, but here was the ravine, and of course there were ravines like this one that ran all through the city, deep, dark, mysterious places, running like lush green scars through the concrete, the cement surfaces, and he felt sheepish. "All these years, and I've never been down in the ravines. Who knows what goes on down there. Can you imagine that, Kate?" He began to walk slowly home. He looked up and down the street. "All this is beginning to trouble me. Everything's beginning to trouble me," he said. "Everything seems to be only the surface of things. Everything is not where it's supposed to be. I mean, Abraham was always Abraham, some kind of old desert chieftain from around the River Jordan, but that's probably not true. All the actual references that I can find say he lived in Heran, in Anatolia, and that's a place in southern Turkey, close to where Genesis says Noah's ark ended up, settled on Mount Ararat, and that's not in Jordan, that's in eastern Turkey. The whole thing seems more and more like a Turkish story, a Turkish delight," and he laughed and quickened his pace, "because Abraham's descendent, a man called Dodanim, became the Dodecanese islands, and a guy named Kittim is really Kriti, which is Crete, and Javan is really the Aegean, and Ashkenaz . . . everyone knows the Ashkenazi are from north of the Danube. The whole thing, the whole story, took place somewhere else farther north. It's not a desert story at all, that's why the Jews weren't seen in Egypt . . . they weren't there, they were out on the edge of the world."

He was so out of breath from talking and walking at the same time that he had to stop walking. He had a cramp in his wrist from clutching the walkie-talkie to his cheek. He was relieved. There was no one on his street of tree-shaded homes. He put the walkie-talkie in his jacket pocket. Then, he suddenly shuddered and choked back tears. All his talk, he

felt, was wasted. He was alone. He was alone in a
well of silence. "Jesus," he said, "even Sadie came
back and said something." He felt abandoned, he
wanted to hear what Kate thought of all his talk, all
his daring insights. A man coming around the corner with his dog on a leash hesitated because Willard
looked so frantic, but Willard shouted, "And a good
day to you." The man hurried on.

Around noon on Easter Sunday, Willard put on a
lightweight tweed suit that he hadn't worn for years.
He went across the footbridge and strode along
Bloor Street, revelling in the strong sunlight. He
hadn't been out of the house for days because he'd
been working in his study on several cuneiform
texts. He'd hardly eaten. He'd done very little talking to Kate, but now he felt fresh and bold and self-
confident as he walked among well-dressed women.

"It's a wonderful day" he said to Kate, holding
the walkie-talkie close. "And I've got wonderful
news. I've finally figured this thing out, yes ma'am
. . . the answer's right there in what looks like a con-
tradiction that's built in at the beginning, right there
at the start of Genesis, where God says he's made
man in his own image, and then, in the second chap-
ter, there's no one around. Everything's empty. So
whoever he'd made has flown the coop." As the red
light changed to green at Church Street, he stepped
off the curb, saying, "The whole place is empty, man
is gone and what that means is that for nearly a mil-
lion years, man trekked around chasing animals,
naming them, hunting them, but suddenly he got
smart. Ten thousand years ago he got smart. He
wanted a garden. And a closed garden is something

you've got to cultivate. And man shows up in Genesis again, and he was Cain the cultivator, who'd taken off from the old happy grazing grounds of Eden to work the earth in a new place, the new civilization where there was nothing. That's what the new Eden was, not a paradise of two witless souls lying around under an apple tree, but Cain, the tattooed man who had the courage to build a closed garden, a city out there on the edge of the world, Cain the civilized man, the marked man . . . " and Willard raised his arms, facing into the sun. The women in their Easter outfits shied away from him. "That's when man became magnificent, Kate, that's when he went into the dark to create his own world, to create himself. That's the first time he had the guts to take his own word for everything."

"Oh, yes, yes," a tall, lean woman with big owl glasses said. "Oh yes." She was smiling eagerly. He quickly brought the walkie-talkie up to his chin. He wanted to be left alone. He wanted Kate. He waved the woman with the owl glasses away and as he did so, his thumb slipped from the *Send* button to *Receive*. He had never pressed the *Receive* button before, but now he suddenly heard Kate. She was calling him. "Willard, Willard, what's been the matter with you?"

"It's you."

"Of course it's me."

"I knew you were there. I knew it," he said triumphantly.

"You knew. You knew where I was!"

"No. Where are you?" he whispered, stepping through the crowd of women on the sidewalk.

"I'm here. Right where I said I'd be. I've been screaming at you for weeks, and you didn't hear a word."

"I never dreamed that all I had to do was flick the button. I never tried the button, I never heard you."

"But I heard you," Kate said. "Can you imagine what it's been like listening and listening and I couldn't say a word . . . "

"But I never thought . . . " he said.

"That's all you've been doing, Willard," she said, calming down. "Thinking."

"I've been talking to you."

"A blue streak, I'd say."

"Don't be upset," he said.

"I have a right to be upset," she said. "Sitting here like a dumb bunny for weeks."

"Never mind now," he said.

"I mind. And locking our bedroom door, that didn't help. I was yelling so loud at you I thought I would die. I was hoarse for two days, I lost my voice."

His thumb was sore from flicking back and forth. "We're just wasting time talking like this," he said.

"Time is not my problem," she said.

"I've been dying to know for weeks what you think."

"What I really think."

"Yes."

"Truly?"

"Yes."

"I think you are, Willard," and she paused, and then said with quiet gravity, "simply magnificent. I can't imagine living without you. I hang on every word."

"You do?" he said.
"I would never lie to you," she said.
"Thank God you're still alive," he said.
"Nobody wants to die," she said.

THE STATE OF THE UNION

*I*don't know how to tell a story so I'll tell what I
know. This is what I knew when I was sixteen:

> *The spider's kiss,*
> *a wrench in the womb,*
> *a petal falls,*
> *my face in the water by the white reeds.*

I was sitting down in the rocks by the pond. The
house was up the hill. We lived on Humberview
Crescent. It was dark. At my feet there was a
branch, and a spider waiting in the white throat of
the branch.

There were always frogs in the big pond. I
always listened to the frogs at dusk. There were
hundreds of them on all sides of the pond — shrill
lost souls drowning in the darkness — frogs who'd
suddenly found themselves upright with hands and
feet, sinking, clutching at the water, trying to walk
on the water, flailing, beating the water with their
tiny hands as they sank, and at my feet, a spider in
the white throat of a branch, waiting.

It was the white throat, the white reeds, the whiteness that fascinated me. And the frogs trying to walk on the water.

We could see the pond from our living room window, an elbow of black water, black because it was so deep. More than a hundred years ago, when the pond was on the edge of the town limits, a company of grenadiers on a forced march, trying to get into town before night fell, cut across the pond in a mid-winter mist, marching in single file through the deep snow over the ice. The ice broke and they all died, drowned. They went down like a long chain into the cold water. In the summer time, when swans on the pond ducked their heads into the water, I always thought they were looking for the dead soldiers. They weren't. Still, there are some people who say they can hear the soldiers crying out at night. I can't. But I could hear my mother. She often cried at night in her bedroom in the dark. I think my father beat her though I never saw bruises on her body. He did not look like a man who would beat a woman, so clear-eyed, a good nose, and his white hair. He was too young to have white hair but it had turned white during the war, Korea, and he had medals from the war. A row of medals. He wore them on police parade or at police funerals; otherwise, they were kept on the living room mantelpiece. She polished them. If anyone spoke admiringly of them, however, she smiled and her wry smile seemed to enrage him. "Never laugh at a policeman," she told me. "It's like laughing at God, he'll never forgive you." I never laughed at my father but there still seemed to be something he refused to forgive me for. "He is a man, that father of yours, who's got a lot of secrets," she said, and she had a lot of secrets, too.

One day, she had just let the screen door slam behind her when she told me, as if I weren't her son who might be shocked, that she was in love. She was feeling sorry for herself, or not so much sorry as vulnerable — soft, she called it — "I'm a soft woman," she said to me, "so soft you see . . . and I want only the best for us all" — as the door slammed and no sooner had she said how soft she was than a red beetle crossed the concrete stoop, a hard-shelled beetle, and I said, "Should we kill it?" and she said, "Yes," and she didn't blink an eye and stomped it dead with her shoe.

"That'll do it," I said.

"You bet," she said. She scraped the sole of her shoe against the stair. "I'm going out," she said.

"Will you be back soon?"

"Maybe."

"Should I lock the door?"

"No."

"Why don't you ever lock the door?"

"I never have, not in all the years, it's just not been my way, no matter how strange it seems, no, I've never locked a door in this house, never, and it's not because I'm looking for loads of family or strangers to come in, I'm certainly not looking for that, no sir, but as for locking people out, you can't lock a thief out. You can lock a fool out, but not a thief if he really wants to get in, and besides, I keep all the locks off the doors, not because I want to keep evil from getting in, but to make sure evil can get out . . ."

She touched my cheek, looking wistful.

"Now do your mother a favor and give her a big kiss."

•

*T*here was a snow storm, the snow thick and wet. At about three in the morning it stopped. It turned cold and a crust hardened on the snow. My mother and father were asleep. I pulled on my high black boots and went out walking down the center of the street. There were no lights on in the house windows. There was only the deep white snow, and the crust was a brittle shell shining in the light of the street lamps. The crust bellied and broke under my boots, black boots that sank into the clinging softness of the snow and the only sound up in the black branches of the trees was the cracking of the crust, breakage, the sound of small murders, and I could hear the half-tone of hands whispering in the dark . . .

•

*M*y father bullied his way out of my heart. At least he tried to. He was a big man, a sergeant of detectives. He broke men's legs, two or three times, he said. He was never charged. He told my mother, not as a confession, but just as a matter of fact across the breakfast table, that he'd broken men's legs with a crowbar. He was a burly man who would moan and pout if his eggs were not properly poached. He would also glower at himself in the mirror. And then touch his face in the mirror gently, as if he expected his face to shatter. "There's a tiny little criminal, a real creep, a puppet, dancing in all of us all the time," he said. He saw darkness in everyone. Sometimes he said he saw faces in the mirror, black faces with popping eyes. Black faces enraged him, not because they were black, but because the faces were always there in the mirror. Sneering at him. He said this to me one afternoon. He told me that he couldn't tell anyone else how he saw them sneering because they'd call him a racist. The men whose legs he broke were black. They were cocaine dealers. Black snowbirds, is what he said. "I broke their wings. I told them I'd rip their beaks off, too." But the worst, he said, were the Vietnamese. Saigon shivs, he called them, his voice shrill. Sometimes when his voice was shrill like that he sounded afraid. Womanly. It was hard to imagine him ever being womanly and afraid, not with his pale pale eyes, crystal colorless eyes. But often when he was afraid his hands trembled. "Shakey Jake," he said, trying to laugh. "Shakey Jake McDice." That's when he got most cruel, when he was afraid and his hands were shaking and he was trying to make fun of himself.

"Most of the time a man gets what he deserves," he said, as he sat gripping the arms of his wingback chair.

"Sometimes he does," my mother said. She slipped off her shoes, studied the turn of her ankle, and said, "I wonder what our boy John'll be like when we're dead."

"More like us than we'd like to know," he said.

"In that case, I don't want to know," she said.

"You don't?"

"No."

"You don't want to know."

"No."

"You don't want anybody to know anything."

"Nope."

"You don't want anybody to know how crazy all this is?"

"Nope."

"I'll tell you how crazy this is. This is as crazy as it gets. It's like you never letting us lock all our doors, that's crazy," he yelled. He got up and strode from the room and locked all the doors. "Safe and sound," he said. "I'm a cop. I know what's going on." She got up and threw his golf clubs through the windows, breaking the windows one by one. "I'll break your legs," he yelled. He closed his eyes and began to tug and pull at his hair. "Not likely," she said, "not bloody likely," and she went out and got in her car and drove off. She loved her car. She loved her racing gloves. She wore her racing gloves in the house. She loved to talk about camshafts and carburetors. "I love empty roads," she said, but she didn't want to go anywhere, she just wanted to drive, full throttle, by herself. She'd drive along the lakeshore expressway in the middle of the night and get speeding tickets. They were yellow ribbons that she laid out beside his poached eggs in the morning. He put them in his pocket and said, "What you better remember, what you want to remember about freedom, is that you get nothing for free." He narrowed his Forever eye. The leper's squint, my mother called it when he narrowed his eyes.

"Nothing," he said, "Nothing, nothing, nothing. Forever."

•

Waking in the morning, I was always excited, always sure that something crooked in the air was about to correct itself. I was an optimist. I believed that there was something like an open seam in space, a seam that opened on to a scream of outrage, a silent scream that I could almost hear. I could feel this scream. I could feel the outrage. It sometimes made me cringe with pain. But whenever I was in pain I took a cold shower, shivering afterwards as I put on a heavy white terry-cloth robe, certain that I could outlast, outlive this pain. Every morning I was certain, certain that the crooked would be straight. That's when my father went to work. Unless it was raining, he walked to work. On those good mornings I opened my bedroom window, always surprised by the slant of morning shadows on the lawn, shadows that were a dun color, earth tones full of promise. "Dun is the color of my true love's hair," I used to sing, trying to make a little joke. "Dun is the color of shit," my father said, the one time he heard me. I could see our flagstone walk from the window. I cranked up the silver lever to the sound system in my room as my father came out on to the walk and I sang along with Engelbert Humperdink, singing as loud as I could in front of the open window, the street booming with our blended voices, a splendor of sound that my father took as it was intended, as a taunt. He said I had no voice, no talent. "A good-looking kid, bright and all, but no talent. Not for singing anyway." Feeling the reverberation trembling my bones, I lifted my arms and my robe fell open and I saw myself naked in the long mirror on the closet door. I went off key and then silent, startled by how dark my crotch hair was, black against my pale skin, and in the reflected light I saw that I was having an erection.

•

*T*he moon trailing flowers is the clock's nursery rhyme. From the other side of the moon the world is in a blind (a half-rhyme . . .). I made a list of my father's favorite songs. I called it the Humperdink list: *Release Me; Our Love Is Here To Stay; Someone To Watch Over Me; There Goes My Everything; But Not For Me; They Can't Take That Away From Me; The Last Waltz; I'll Never Be Free; Time Out For Tears; Please Send Me Someone To Love; Am I That Easy To Forget?; So Lonely I Could Cry; Mixed Emotions; I Apologize; A Man Without Love; Don't Say You're Sorry Again; In My Solitude; Don't Explain; Winter World Of Love; Can't Take My Eyes Off Of You.* These are the songs of Engelbert Humperdink. My father knew them all. He loved Humperdink. He loved my mother. He loved golfing. He swung at my mother with a golf club. Such is love, such are the songs of love. The frogs are good dancers.

•

*M*rs. McGuane lived down the street. She had married late, in her early thirties, and then her husband, who she said was a mining engineer, had died in a north country plane crash in the winter. "Icing on the wings," she said with a look full of bemused sadness. "Icing on the cake, now it's around my heart." She told me this with a sensual laugh, as if she really liked the sound of the words, and of her laugh. My mother told me some months later that none of this was true. She refused to tell me what *was* true, except to say that Mrs. McGuane's husband had some kind of connection with the church but was in fact dead, and her own family had left her well-off. Mrs. McGuane hired me to dig up her garden, and on hot days I stripped down to my waist and I sweated and I sweated until I was sopping wet. She used to watch me. One day she invited me in for a glass of water. She didn't bother with the water. She drew her finger down the sweat on my chest and opened my trousers and began stroking me, slow at first, and then hard as I stood there staring at a kind of glee in her face until three or four jism shots went looping through the air to the tile floor. "Surprise, surprise," she said, and went to get me a glass of water. My thighs were shaking. I thought I was going to fall over. She held the glass of water out to me, smiling benevolently. I knew she was not benevolent. I could feel that. She would be good to me, but not benevolent. I worked every second day in her garden. On those days she took off her blouse or her sweater and sat cross-legged on the floor of the breakfast room. She didn't take off her shoes. She had light freckles between her breasts and her left nipple was larger than the other, and darker. She said her husband had never noticed that. One day, she draped a silk shawl around my bare shoulders, and the next day she made me wear a single strand of pearls at my throat. Then she asked if she could make up my face — eyeliner and lipstick. The lipstick was bright red. She gave me a silver hand mirror from her dressing table so that I could see my face and she told me to watch my face while she knelt and took me until I came in her mouth. I watched my face, or the face that was in front of my face, the parted red lips, the socketed eyes. The next time, I watched her, a woman who might have been my mother, on her knees before me, moaning at prayer. I told her that I wanted to make love to her, that I didn't understand why she wouldn't make love with me even if maybe I really didn't know how to make love, but she said, "Why would you want to do that?"

"Don't you like sex?" I asked.

"Not afterwards," she said.

"Maybe I love you," I said.

She sat very still, staring at the floor, and then narrowing her eyes, she said, "If you keep that up it'll change everything for the worse. No talk about love allowed."

She asked me what I thought about when I was coming. I said I didn't think, I heard things.

"What?"

"Frogs," I said. "I could hear them drowning in the darkness."

•

*M*y father always looked at you like nothing could be simpler than what he was thinking. He had a mind that was machine tooled. He had a turnstile in his head, whipping around back and forth, *gu-thunk, gu-thunk,* a head full of contradictions, at least they were contradictions to me, which is why I could not read the map of his mind. Maybe my mother could. Not me. He said he hated TV, how TV got inside your head, yet on Sunday mornings he always sat watching the *Crystal Cathedral of Tomorrow,* "The Hour Of Power," glass on glass walls, piles and piles of glass sheeting and mirrors, the smarm of salvation, a salvation that was all coiffure and self-esteem. And he always brushed his hair before he sat down to watch, as if someone in the Crystal Cathedral might look up from a pew and see him on the other side of the tube. But he didn't watch because he was religious. He watched because he had a yellow-dog eye, a jaundice in his eyeball, and a contempt for preachers and he relished his own contempt. He could get high on his contempt. Almost nobody deserved his admiration. Nobody. Except maybe General Westmoreland and Ronnie Reagan. And Gordie Howe. He liked Gordie Howe. But he thought all preachers were a crock. That was his word. Billy Graham was a crock, and politicians like Nixon and Trudeau were a crock, but the Pope was even worse. He was "a buckraker for every pooch in the world in a black suit," and as for the local politicians, he would lie back in his La-Z-Boy chair and say, "The mayor's a bumper sticker, got all of what he knows off the back of a puffed wheat box, you can buy him by the yard — give him

a set of used dining room furniture and he's yours."
He felt he was going good when he said things like
that, and when he was feeling real good he would
insist on taking me golfing or bowling, but I didn't
like going bowling because even as a child I thought
that anyone who wanted to run quick short sprints
in rented shoes while carrying a twenty pound ball
was slightly demented. Still, he was smart, he was
meticulous, his nails pared and his pants pressed,
spanking clean and talced. He was attractive, and
mysterious, because you never knew what was
going on behind those pale pale eyes. He was the
worst kind of secretive man, he seemed so open, so
abrasively friendly. He liked to say, smacking me on
the shoulder, that he had the common touch, but if
anyone said that he was common, then he was on
them as quick as white lightning in a water glass.
That's what my mother told him, sitting in her bath
soaping herself and she blurted out as if she'd been
brooding on it for years, "You're common, Jake, common." Then she yelled to me in the next room, "Your
father's totally common." I walked into the room
and stared at my father. He looked like he'd been
slapped behind the ears with a two-by-four, he was
so furious he was smirking stupidly. He had a right
to be furious. After all, he loved her, at least he said
he did, and he insisted she loved him — though
she'd told me she also loved somebody else. "I've
taken somebody else to my heart," she'd said. My
mother's breasts were splotchy with soap. She slid
down into the water up to her chin to hide them from
me, her head floating on the water, and he said, "I
will kill you, I'll lop your fucking head off." He

laughed. A tinny, high-pitched laugh. She had sloe-eyes. She looked up and said, "You don't scare me, talking to me like that. God scares me, I'll admit that. I don't know how to talk to God and He doesn't know how to talk to me, but you don't scare me," she said. No matter what she said, she was always smiling, smiling though she was more often than not hurt and bitter. Smiling was something that she had learned in school, along with two and two are four and little ladies don't sit with their legs apart. Smile! She nursed a powerful sense of being wronged. "Your mother," my father said, looking at her like he was looking at a criminal, "and all her friends like her, are only busy being busy, busy while they're unloading all their hyped-up complaints and self-pity and grief on any unsuspecting stiff who'll listen to them, bleating on and on about how something pure inside themselves has been defiled. Defiled, the goddamn cock-wallopers."

The next day he sent her roses in the morning, roses in the afternoon. "Your father is crazy," she said. She was slicing bread with a long bread knife, wearing her leather driving gloves. "You know what's the matter with him," she said. "He feels he's been overlooked. That's what really gripes men like him, they're all fascists, they feel they've been overlooked. That's all Hitler was, a man who felt overlooked." I looked out the window. There he was in the garden. I wondered if he felt overlooked. What did he really know? Did he know that she was soft, soft in love? It was Sunday afternoon. Every Sunday afternoon she played somebody with a Russian name playing Chopin's *polonaises*. He was standing in the backyard by the peonies, wearing golfing trousers tucked up at the knees, leaning on his putter. He looked ridiculous, especially for a cop, a hard-nosed cop. I went out to talk to him, to ask him how his game was going. "My game, my game," he said. He whispered to me about the menace of rootless, homeless men and women in the cities, and how the government was like the homeless, always looking for a place to roost in our lives. He hunched toward me as if he were afraid of the flowers, as if they were insidious listening devices. It was the first time that I ever felt sorry for him. "The walking dead are loose in the land," he said. "Fucking bureaucrats." My mother was in the window, smiling. I wanted to break the window, break her glass face. She was smiling as if she'd just looked in the Lost And Found and found that we were gone and she was glad. I was surprised at such anger in myself, particularly as I loved my mother more than my father. I hated him for the bullying yet seemingly sad man that he was. It was the sadness in him that made the bullying so false, so brutal, so much a cover-up. As he broke a man's legs, I knew that his heart couldn't have really been in it: he always wanted to cry when he hurt people, he was always feeling too sorry for himself.

•

Mrs. McGuane had a collection of ceramic frogs. They sat on her kitchen window sill, on their haunches. They had bloated round bellies, small heads, mouthpiece lips, and holes in their haunches. Ocharinas. I learned to play them. I played *Somewhere Over The Rainbow, Blue Moon,* and *Harbor Lights*, Mrs. McGuane's favorites. She said she'd bought the frogs in New Orleans, that she'd gone there after her husband's death and that she'd fallen in love with a black woman. "Actually, I wouldn't call it love," she said. "I just wanted to look at her, look at her naked. I didn't want to touch her, didn't want her to touch me. It was more like adoration."

She said she'd decided that she wanted me to look at her; and I agreed not to touch her. She led me upstairs to her bedroom. It was a long narrow room, pearl gray, the walls, the carpeting, the covers on the bed. Pearl grey. She told me to sit with my back to a big bay window that overlooked the garden. "That way I can hardly see you in the light." She slipped off her dress and was naked except for high heels. She had shaved off all her pubic hair. She stood about three feet in front of me with her hands on her hips, her legs apart, staring over my head into the light. She didn't move. She had a bruise on the inside of her left thigh. She said, "You can do yourself if you want. Don't young men like to do themselves?" I said no. She said, "Good, you can just look at me."

The next time, she was waiting for me in the back porch room with her make-up kit and she made up my face again, lipstick and eyeliner and led me upstairs. After slipping off a silk robe with a shawl collar, she told me to put the robe on over my own clothes. I sat wrapped in red silk, licking my red lips. Then she handed me one of the ocharinas. As she

stood in front of me, naked, I played *Somewhere Over
the Rainbow* on the frog.

"You look very much like your mother."

"Excuse me?"

"Though not as beautiful."

•

*I*sn't our soul the spider which weaves its own body in
the throat of the branch?

•

*I*t was my mother who insisted I was a singer. She
wasn't stupid. She knew better. And I knew I
was not a singer, though as a child I had been a boy
soprano, a beautiful voice in the choir at St. Peter's
Church who sang the solo at Christmas and at Easter.
It was *The Seven Last Words* that we sang on Holy
Thursday that I loved best, and it was a time when
all the images in the church, all the crosses, were
wrapped in purple shrouds. Seven last words inside
the shroud. *Eloi, Eloi lama sabachthani. It is finished.
Father, forgive them, they know not what they do.* "They
know not . . . " No one listened, not back then, and
not in the church, and that is really what betrayal is,
the refusal to listen. Knowing what to do is something else altogether. Guys like Hitler are the guys
who know what to do. Stalin. Churchill. Guys like
Popeye, Pete Rose . . . the guys "who know how to
put the puck in the net . . . " After *The Seven Last
Words*, on Good Friday they took the mourning
shrouds down, and there was the cross. The cross

fascinated me, the rigid dove-tailed intersection of the lines, the precise intersection of pain, in suspension. And I saw that the hanging body made a different shape than the cross itself. The crossbar went straight out, east to west, but through the sag of his body his arms were uplifted, his body hung like a Y . . . feminine, in his dying he was like a singer, maybe Judy Garland, singing his last defiant silent note . . .

Then my voice changed. The hair on my body turned black, abdomen, knuckles, toes. I waited for my voice to deepen, and it did, but when I tried to sing it slipped in and out of alto, falsetto, baritone. I'd lost my voice. It could not be found. That's when I began to sing along with other singers, especially my father's favorite, Engelbert Humperdink (his other favorite was Zamphir, the man who played echoing wooden shepherd flutes) and my mother joined me. We were a duet. She had a throaty, husky voice for a small woman. Standing by the window in my bedroom we'd sing *Time After Time* and *A Sunday Kind Of Love* and *What A Difference A Day Makes*:

> *twenty-four little hours,*
> *only sun and the flowers*
> *where there used to be rain . . .*

My father resented it. I had no talent. He'd said so. I had the aptitude for talent. That's what he said. "The world's full of men who'd like to be Lucky Luciano but they can't cut it. They hold up one gas station and spend the rest of their lives in jail. All they got is an aptitude." He'd come home and stand on the lawn and stare up at the window. I sang. One day, he went to the garage and got out the old lawn-mower. As I stood there singing along I opened my arms to him and he scowled as if he'd been sullied, as if someone had dumped dirt on his head, and he put his head down and began pushing the old mower across the lawn, the blades clattering, pushing it faster, louder, till I stopped singing but he didn't seem to hear that I'd stopped and he kept pushing the mower till mother stepped out on to the stoop and cried, "Jake, your heart, you'll hurt your heart."

•

*I*t was right around then that I acquired a limp. It was like a hitch in my thoughts. It was quite funny. Every time I had a serious thought I had to laugh, I was limping so hard. That was also the time I saw an old black blues singer, Brownie McGhee. And he had a huge limp, one leg shorter than the other, from polio it looked like. And when he left the stage he was singing *Walk On*, riding his hobble leg up and down and everybody wanted to cry at his pain but I wanted to laugh because he knew how to play his own pain into a performance, into pleasure, and I went out of the club limping a huge limp, and laughing, and someone told me I should be ashamed, imitating a man with a mockery like that, and I was ashamed, not because I was limping, but because I couldn't sing. So I went home and sat in total silence in the empty house and I remember saying to myself, "All I want is to be happy." I was in my mother's room, staring at one of those glass globes of hers, those glass balls, and inside the globe there was a house under a perpetual falling snow. I realized I was never going to be happy, not in that house. Still, it was my home, my family, even if in the summer time the snow still fell. But the swans would never duck their heads and look for me. That was clear. There were three tall urns sitting on the floor at the far end of the room, filled with dried flowers and bulrushes. I picked up the globe, rocked on the balls of my feet, took a stride, and bowled the glass house down along the carpet, crashing the ceramic urns, *KaPow*, a dead hit.

•

"You never know what the hell's going on," he said.

"You're the cop," she said.

"Cut the shit. This is no time for fucking around."

"I don't fuck around."

"I'm not talking about you. I'm talking about an internal investigation."

"Surprise, surprise."

"It means maybe they found out, but it don't mean they got me."

"Too bad."

"Too bad what?"

"Too bad."

"That's all you got to say, too bad?"

"Too bad I married you, how about that? I never should've married you. Never."

"Yeah, well, never's just a bus stop, lady, a bus stop in Never Never Land. This is us, this is real, this is the state of the union."

•

*T*hat summer, I read the following statement in a book. "Dying each other's life, living each other's death." — Heraclitus. I didn't then know who Heraclitus was, and frankly didn't care. A few pages on in the same book I found a diagram. I liked it, though I'm not altogether sure why. I took it to a copy shop and had a copy enlarged 300 percent and pinned the copy up on my bedroom wall.

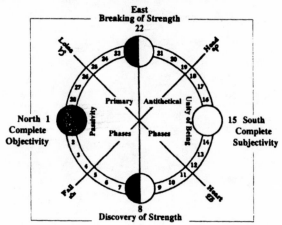

*M*rs. McGuane phoned and said the sky was a strange teal blue. I still haven't bothered to find out what teal blue is. She asked me to bring one of my mother's silk robes and a pair of her sunglasses to the house. "You mean a dressing gown?" I asked. "Yes," she said, "and her pink bedroom slippers that you just step into, with the little pump heels." I didn't know how she knew about those pump heels but I brought them in a Shopper's Drug Mart plastic bag. As soon as I stepped inside the back porch door she told me to take off my clothes. I did, and then she slathered my cock with a clear liquid grease from a tube, *H&R Sterile Lubricating Jelly*. It was exciting, the slipperiness. Then she led me up to the bedroom, the drapes were drawn, it was a summer afternoon but it could also have been winter in that air conditioned shadowlight, except that I could hear cicadas in the heat. She was naked under her own robe, wearing only a garter belt which she took off and put on me. I was surprised that it fit me so well around my waist, and looking down at myself, so erect between the loose black straps, I felt an intense rush of pleasure in my loins, a satisfaction with myself. She draped my mother's blue raw silk robe over my shoulders, closed a little clasp at my throat so that it was like a cape, and then she told me to put on the sunglasses as she carried the slipper-pumps to the full-length mirror on her closet door and set them down on the carpet facing the mirror. I stepped into them and wobbled for a moment because they were too small. She stepped between me and the mirror, with her back to me so that she could see us in the glass, so that she could hold my eye as she bent forward toward the glass while reaching back between her legs, drawing my cock toward her buttocks, one of her hands up on the glass, and then with my cock up against her, she put her other hand to the glass and said with a fierceness that almost frightened me, "Fuck me." I took hold of her hips and entered her and reached for her breasts and began to fuck her. I had to kick out of the slippers. She didn't notice. She was smiling, and then, as I really began to hump her from behind, she cried, "Fuck me . . . " and then began to sing almost blissfully, at least it sounded blissful to me, "Georgia, Georgia, the whole day through . . . "

Georgia, my mother's name.

•

*P*ale, pale footprints of the barefooted trying to find their pale way in the snow. I dreamed that. A step, a step, toward something someone might call a truth, a word or a glance. A bullying curse. The bite of truth. Sometimes that's the way my mind worked, and works. Still. Bop. Bop. Bop. Word. Word. Word. That afternoon I went down the hill to the pond. The swans were swimming. There were several old men sitting on benches and children playing along the walkway and a Mister Softie ice cream vendor was parked under a weeping willow. The old men were smoking White Owl cigars. One was wearing a paper White Owl wrapper as a ring. In the two o'clock heat the still pond had an oil-like sheen. Hues and tones of pond-slime green and yellow. And old men smoking, swans swimming. It was very peaceful. Standing beside the Mister Softie machine, there was a life-sized Coca-Cola bottle.

It was made out of some kind of vinyl, except for the cap, which was wood. It came walking toward me. I could see the shoes underneath the bottle bottom. It walked right up to me, and just above the hyphen, there were two eye-holes. I was sure I could see two eyes inside the eye-holes. Eyes. I heard a deep, not harsh, but gravelly voice. "You tell your father, we're gonna get him. He won't see us coming any more than you saw me coming, and he'll get his." Then, the Coca-Cola bottle turned and walked away. I didn't know what to do. I couldn't call the police, or attack a bottle. Maybe he had a gun. I went back up the hill and into the house and sat in silence in my room for a long time, and then I put on Engelbert Humperdink and I opened the windows and just before six o'clock as I was singing my father came striding along, looked up, went into the garage and got the mower and started mowing the lawn. He seemed to be furious with me, thinking whatever he was thinking, *gu-thunk, gu-thunk*, whereas I had felt only afraid for him, hardly thinking at all, and so I went downstairs and out on to the lawn, the Humperdink song still blaring out into the street, and I told him about the warning from the Coca-Cola bottle. He looked at me a long time, a hard, almost disdainful, disbelieving look, and then he punched me hard on the shoulder, a short crossing punch that sent pain shooting down into my finger tips and he said, "I told you when you were a pipsqueak kid, never talk to strangers and above all, never talk to Coca-Cola bottles, and if you do, then make sure they take the Pepsi Challenge first." He laughed hard at his joke.

•

Mrs. McGuane blamed everything on sunglasses. She said that Aristotle didn't wear
sunglasses. Luther didn't wear sunglasses. But her
husband did. He was John Cletuse McGuane, a
Presbyterian preacher, and he wore sunglasses.
That's what she finally told me. He wasn't a mining
engineer whose bones were now encased in the
somewhere ice. She said he'd risen quite rapidly in
his church, both as a preacher and because of the
pamphlets he wrote, especially about Judas. In one
of his pamphlets that she gave to me to read while I
was sitting in the sunroom, he wrote: "In the early
church, in Egypt — and mind you, the early Church
was much closer to the present spirit of
Pentecostalism than anything in Catholicism since
the authoritarian Council of Trent — Judas was
regarded as a saint. The argument was simple and
straightforward. Jesus, the Christ, the Son of God
on the Right Hand, was all knowing, and therefore
knew what He became Man to do; His end truly was
His beginning, His intention was to die, and so early
believers said that He came to kill himself for our
sins. In His own mind He was a suicide. The apos-
tle who understood this was Judas, who took upon
himself the mantel of scapegoat, and out of love for
Jesus, and in perfect imitation, hanged himself. As a
matter fact, the great theme at the heart of sacrifice
— running through Judas to Jesus to Peter — is the
efficacy of betrayal." I could hear frogs running for
their lives across the pond water. She said that after

he delivered a sermon like this on Judas on Easter Sunday, a shouting match took place in the church. Though the sermon was startling to the parishioners it was nothing compared to the shock of his suicide a year later. His body was discovered at dawn in Gzowski Park on the lakeshore, facing the water, hanging from a tree. His hanging had its own peculiarity. He had climbed into an old maple tree, had tied his ankles to a branch so that when he fell into the air he was hanging upside down. He'd then slit his wrists with a razor, his blood draining out of his outspread arms. She showed me some newspaper clippings. Someone had suggested that his suicide was an imitation of the death of Peter, who had asked to be crucified upside down because he was not worthy to die as his Lord had died. Someone else said his suicide was a deliberate mockery of the Cross and the Church by a man who'd lost his faith or his mind or both. Several neighbors were interviewed and among them, my father, who said, "All you can say is he did it his way."

My father had discovered Frank Sinatra. He'd started singing *New York, New York*, and *Bring In The Clowns* around the house.

•

When I was a kid, I used to go down to the pond and catch frogs. Every ten minutes I could catch a frog. I'd rub my finger down its back, soothing it, and then I'd put a straw up its hole and watch it swell and swell until it was swole up, and then quick as a whip, I'd stuff a little cherrybomb firecracker in where the straw had been and I'd light it and lob it out over the still pond, toward one of the swans, like a hand grenade, and if I'd got the timing right it would explode in mid-air. I didn't know why I did it. I didn't know why I enjoyed it. I just listened to the shrill cries of the frogs at dusk and knew I'd never run out of frogs. One day, an old man stopped by the water's edge and told me I was evil. I knew I was not evil. Whenever I came home from the pond I felt heart-broken. All I could see before they exploded was the little arms of the frogs, wide-open, embracing the air, full of hope.

•

*I*t wasn't until my mother started wearing tailor-made buckskin suits with beading on the sleeves and came home with a hickey on her neck that my father turned really sullen and silent. He had nothing to say. It looked like whatever he'd had to say had been taken from him. He'd sit there and stare at her and she'd stare at him but he didn't do anything. She'd brush her teeth and then hunker down over a plate of dry toast, looking blacker and blacker. She'd brush her teeth again. Late one afternoon I saw in her eyes for the first time the laughter like a skull laughs. Knowing laughter, the laughter of someone who's come unlatched. Finally, he said to her, "What's that on your neck?" and she said, "Love bites, love bites back." Every day, she ordered boxes of cut fresh flowers. She kept putting flowers all over the

house. "Why don't you order in some coffins, too?"
he said. He looked like he was going to cry. I felt
sorry for him, and hated him. I didn't want to feel
sorry for my father. She put on and then took off her
driving gloves, going nowhere. He started prowling
the house, opening dresser drawers, sifting through
her underclothes, opening closets, not looking for
anything, just sifting, like he was rehearsing his
training at cop school, sometimes talking out loud.
She said, "I loved you, maybe I still love you, but I
don't care." He took his putter out of his golfing bag
and went into the living room. "You don't care. You
don't fucking care." There was a lime green portable
plastic putting hole on the rug in front of the fire-
place. He dropped a ball on the rug and lined up a
putt. "If it's any consolation," she said, "it's a
woman." He stroked the ball straight into the hole.

"A woman," he said.

"Yes."

"Anyone I know?"

"Yes."

"Who?"

"Eleanor McGuane."

"Eleanor Fuckin' McGuane?"

"Yes."

He broke her head with his putting iron, blood
all over his white shirt and the white rug. He called
the police, warning me not to interfere. "Don't fucking interfere. Don't get in the way." When the police
came, and the ambulance men, too, he was sitting up
close to the television set though it wasn't turned on,
staring into the blank gray tube, and he was listening
to shepherd flutes, softly humming along with

Zamphir. I wanted to haul the old lawnmower up into the room and mow everything there was on the floor around the room to make him stop his humming. I could feel a silent scream in space, my space, a scream of outrage. I knew nothing was going to correct itself, no seam was going to be healed, nothing crooked was going to end up straight. He just sat stiff-lipped, hardly said a word to the police and they treated him with something that looked like baffled awe. I was suffocating, swallowing words although I didn't have anything to say, almost hysterical, as they wheeled my mother out on a stretcher. She was still breathing. I could see I was going to be all alone. Whether she lived or not. Alone. Like one of those grenades gone down to the swans. As my father stood up to go to the patrol car, I cried, "Don't worry about me, Dad," and he said, "I am not worried about you, I'm worried about me," and a cop standing beside me said without looking at me, "The goddamn selfish fuckhead," and I said, "No, no he doesn't mean it like that, not like that, that's just Shakey Jake talking."

•

I think: my father tried to kill my mother and then I am swamped by shame, which makes me laugh, and then I fall silent. I limp home.

"Despair is silent. But even silence has a meaning if the eyes speak. And if despair speaks, then we are not alone." My mother's eyes are on me, my father's eyes are on her, I watch as they watch me.

We are not alone. We are a family.

THIRD PEW TO THE LEFT

A man of about seventy came into a downtown
 bar every late afternoon, a small man who
wore slacks and a sports shirt in the summer and a
cardigan sweater over his shirt in the winter. His
hair was white. There was a feeling of wry benefi-
cence in his smile. He seemed to wish people well
and to wish himself well. This had something to do
with his being an old priest who drank, and sometimes he drank a lot if people at the bar bought him
drinks.

The woman who was the bartender always
called out cheerfully when he came in, "Hello,
Father Joe." He smiled, pleased to be welcomed,
but perhaps not wanting everyone to know that he
was a priest. He took a chair by a small table in a
corner, a table almost no one ever sat at unless the
bar was crowded and usually it was crowded late at
night, long after he had gone home to St. Basil's, a
residence close to the bar and close to the university, a home for young seminarians and old retired
priests.

I had gone to the university, and I had been married in St. Basil's Church so I called out, too, "Hello, Father Joe." He smiled but it was the smile of a man who expected to be left alone. Sitting by myself at the bar I always sent him a drink, a scotch and soda over ice.

"Cheers," he said quietly.

One day I was feeling so alone at the bar that I couldn't help myself. I sat down beside him. He was surprised, but at ease. "You're a fine-looking amiable old priest," I said. I had been drinking since noon.

"You're a fine-looking ruin of a man yourself," he said.

"Perfidy's upon us," I said.

"Not likely," he said. "Relax."

I did. I told him that I'd been a student. He said that he'd been a teacher. I'd studied languages and literature, I said. He said he'd taught philosophy. I asked him how, after all these years, he liked being a priest. He said he liked it fine. I asked how he liked the new right-wing bishop, Father Ambrosionic.

"I dunno," he said.

"The mad Pole's given us a stern Serb," I said. "Now, now," he said. "Let's be looking on the bright side, at least you know now exactly where you stand. You can thank the Pope for that."

"Thank you, Pope," I said.

"Have you been drinking?"

"A little," I said.

"I drink a lot," he said. Then he touched my hand. "Don't worry," he said. "It has nothing to do with any spiritual crisis. I don't go in for that class of thing."

"Where you from?" I asked.

"Pittsburgh," he said. "Many long years ago, when it was a tough town. My father was a tough man, a steel worker. How about you?"

"Here," I said.

"You're from here?"

"Here."

"I haven't met anybody from here for years," he said.

"Well, you have now," I said.

"Good. It's good to be in touch with roots," he said.

"I'll tell you the truth, Father, as far as I'm concerned, that's a shoe store."

"Well, at least you've got your feet on the ground," he said, trying to stifle a laugh. I wagged my finger at him and he winked at me and I waved at the bartender, telling her to bring us two more drinks.

"I've a weakness for cheap jokes," he said.

"I've a weakness for cheap whiskey," I said.

"You might say that makes it even between us," he said. "Myself, I lean to the good whiskey, when I can get it."

"Well, they don't serve you slouch whiskey in here," I said.

"No, they do not," he said.

We smiled at each other.

"Well, now that we've got that settled," he said, sipping his fresh scotch and soda, "what's your claim to fame?"

"Advertising. Consulting," I said.

"Which is it?"

"Both," I said. "When I'm not consulting I advertise that I do."

"You do?"

"Yes."

"And this is where literature gets you?"

"Like a patient etherised upon a table," I said.

He laughed.

"I used to know some poems by heart," he said.

"What happened?"

"My heart gave out," and he laughed again, saying, "Forgive me, I can't help it."

"Neither can I," I said.

"Do you know what forgiveness is?" he asked.

"No," I said.

"When you know you have nothing left to lose and you pass it on."

"Boy, I should've studied with you," I said.

"Maybe not," he said.

"What'd you teach?"

"Philosophy, for openers. Plato, Aristotle, Thomas Aquinas . . . it was wonderful, talking about how God's mind worked, and then I used to leap right up to the twentieth century, to our own time, to Maritain . . . "

"What happened to what's in between?" I asked.

"Nothing," he said.

"Yeah but where'd it go? Where'd Descartes go?"

"Nowhere. I left him right where he was."

"You can't do that," I said.

"I did," he said.

"Didn't anybody say anything?"

"They did not. Anyway, I used to tell them, 'We all know the trouble with Descartes, he put de cart before de horse!' "

"Oh, God, you didn't!"

"I did," he said. "And why not? It's a corny joke, but it's got me out of some tricky situations. Anyway, when you think about it, this business about 'I think therefore I am' is rather profoundly dumb. After all, God thought and therefore we are and since we are, we think. What else could we do but think — go bowling? And if we think too much we probably end up like your man Woody Allen, talking ourselves to death. It's what the wise boys call ennui . . . "

"The wisdom of hell," I said, laughing with him.

"I don't know a lot about hell," he said. "That's why I drink. Any time I get anywhere close to hell I take a drink. "

"But you're in here every day," I said.

"Yes," he said.

"Jesus."

"Yes," he said, lifting his glass, "and isn't He a help, a wonderful fellow. Forgave us, and died for our sins."

"You're kidding," I said.

"I don't kid about Jesus," he said.

"I don't mean that, I mean the way you said it."

"How'd I say it?"

"Like He was the guy next door."

"You drink too much," he said.

"Says who?" I said, drawing a circle with my finger in the dampness on the table.

"Never mind, I don't want to ruin our nice talk. I don't want to know why you think you drink."

"No?" I asked, disappointed.

"I might be interested to know why you think you love," he said. "But that would take a couple more drinks and they're not going to give me any more. Orders from on high, eye in the sky."

"You really think I drink too much?" I asked.

"How do I know? I hardly know you."

"Maybe it's true," I said.

"Maybe."

"Maybe a lot of things are true."

"Could be, you never know. Not until you know."

"Not until the fat lady sings," I said.

"The only fat lady I ever knew," he said, "was my mother, and she lived to a ripe old age. Ninety-two. She had a fine philosophical bent," he said.

"I used to like talking philosophy," I said.

He smiled, his mouth taking a little turn, wishing me well.

"You did, did you?" he said.

"Yep," I said.

"If a tree falls in a forest when there's no one there, does the tree make a sound? . . . That kind of thing?" he said.

"Yeah, that kind of stuff," I said. "And poetry, the half-deserted streets, the muttering retreats of cheap one nights in sawdust hotels . . . Something like that."

"I never went in much for poetry. Limericks were my speed," he said.

"There was a priest who taught me, Dore or Dorey, something like that," and Father Joe nodded as if he knew who I was talking about, "and he had that whole poem off by heart. He'd stand up in front of us and roar that thing out, I never liked to admit it back then but I envied him, he had this light in his eyes like he was lifted right out of himself. And then, he said something I've never forgotten. I mean he said about the end, where you feel like you're a pair of ragged claws scuttling across the ocean floor — and I don't know about you, Father, but that's exactly how I feel when I've drunk too much — he said, Hell probably isn't fire or anything like that, it's probably being those claws inside your own head and hearing them . . . "

"Don't be so hard on yourself," he said.

"Hard?" I asked.

"Yeah," he said.

"My father always said I was too easy on myself."

"Well, it's a matter of perspective. The truth is tricky."

"Do I dare to eat a peach?" I blurted out.

"There's a time for everything," he said.

"I guess there is."

"Time for me to go," he said, standing up, "I think."

" . . . am not Hamlet, nor was meant to be," I cried. "Am an attendant player — "

"Thanks for the drinks," he said, straightening his shirt collar.

"Right. Any time," I said.

"And the chat," he said.

"Any time."

I was wounded. I was sure that he had grown tired of me. Then he said gravely, "It's a long time since you've been to confession. I can tell, a long time."

"I suppose it is," I said, startled.

"After a long long time it's harder," he said, leaning close to me.

"I don't know."

"Listen, the time'll come when you'll want to go to confession . . . "

"I doubt it," I said.

"Sure. It'll come, but don't worry about it. When the time comes, I'm your man."

"You think so?"

"I know so."

I stared at the circle I'd drawn on the table. Then I said, "Yeah well, do you want me to go to confession or do you want me to tell you the truth?"

"Confession," he said, laughing. "I told you, the truth is tricky."

Over the next three or four months, we saw each other almost every day. We got used to knowing that at the end of the afternoon, for about forty-five minutes, we were together in the same room. We said a word or two but we never had a long talk again. I never went to confession. I bought him drinks. He drank them. I consulted. I drank and told myself one or two small truths and turned down a free ticket to see the new Woody Allen film. "It's got to do with Descartes," I told my friends. "He and Woody . . . put de cart before de horse." Nobody laughed. "Get off the bottle," one of them said.

Then, Father Joe was not there. I asked the bartender if she knew where he was. She said, "Father Joe's been sick, he died, the funeral's tomorrow." I went to the funeral at St. Basil's Church. The bishop, Father Ambrosionic, didn't go. I didn't mind. I knew where I stood. Third pew to the left.

NEVER'S JUST
THE ECHO OF FOREVER

And I went unto the angel, and said unto him, Give me
the little book. And he said unto me, Take it, and
eat it up; and it shall make thy belly bitter, but it
shall be in thy mouth sweet as honey.
And I took the little book out of the angel's hand, and ate
it up; and it was in my mouth sweet as honey:
and as soon as I had eaten it, my belly was bitter.

Apocalypse 10: 9-10

1

*A*s Albie Starbach stood at the foot of the stairs
to the stone house, he heard a lone sweet fiddle high in the bare trees. He had dark red hair,
hazel eyes, and strong bony hands, and as he stared
at the melting snow and the slush in the flagstone
gutters, he pulled on his heavy saddle-stitched
sheepskin gloves. He liked to keep his hands warm.
He picked up a round paddle that had STOP paint-

ed on it in fluorescent red, and he wore a red vest that was fluorescent, too, saying softly to himself *sashay, sashay*, liking the sound of the word but he wasn't sure whether a man should ever want to sashay, so he strode down the walk, pretending to ignore a grizzled old desperado who was standing in the snow under the apple tree, an old desperado who craned his neck and whispered, "Albie, Albie, there are people dying who've never died before." Albie shrugged, not breaking his stride though he knew the slush would soak a salt ring into his black cowboy boots, and the salt would then rot the leather, but there was nothing he could do because he knew salt was tougher than leather. "Cowboys don't go in for wearing rubbers," he had told his mother, but she'd scowled and said, "You ain't no cowboy, you're a caretaker. You got cowboys beating on your poor addled brain." He tucked a chaw of Old Chum tobacco in his cheek and said, "Salt is even tougher than love." A red snow shovel stood against the trunk of the apple tree. The blade was rusted. There were twisted black apples on the tree. The old desperado began to sing, "*A-may . . . zing grace, how sweet the sound . . .* " as Albie looked at the shovel and then back to the big house, the old cut limestone walls stained by the weeping iron in the stone and the tiny crab-like tracks of the ivy he'd ripped from the walls, enraged at starlings who'd built hidden nests in the leaves. He laughed. "Some caretaker. If I was the owner, I'd goddamn well fire myself."

2

*H*e had nervous hands and quick eyes. He narrowed his eyes whenever he walked alone into a bar in the early hours of the morning, trying to slit his eyes like a snake. He was sure that all the old gunslingers had looked down at the dead lying in the dust like that. Snake eyes. And cops, too. Snakes were smart and so were cops. Nobody played cops or snakes for fools. As a boy, he'd had a snake tattooed on his left forearm and he had thought about being a cop, a cop packing a snub-nose .38 in a shoulder-holster close to his heart because he wanted to see and feel things with the hard-nosed grit of a cop, and he had watched all the gunslinger and gumshoe shows on television, all the re-runs of *The FBI in Peace and War* and *Dragnet*, and *Kojack*, looking to see who had the most grit, but then one afternoon he'd been arrested for shoplifting. It was the day before his twentieth birthday. He had got up in the morning and with his finger he'd drawn 19 in the film of dust on his bedroom window, intending to wash the window clean the next day, and intending to start a whole new life as his own man in his twenties, and then he'd gone out to buy himself a birthday present. He had picked up a white stetson hat in a western clothing store, but he'd also seen a pair of turquoise cuff links set in silver in a glass showcase, and not wanting to soil the hat on the top of the showcase, he'd stuck the hat on his head and studied the veins in the turquoise and then he'd bought the cuff links and walked out of the store. He'd started to sing:

The redheaded stranger had eyes like thunder,
and his lips they were sad and tight,
his little lost love lay on the hillside
and his heart was heavy as night:
Don't cross him, don't boss him,
he's wild in his sorrow . . .

They'd stopped him on the sidewalk, the fat waddly
owner of the store and a cop. He'd narrowed his
eyes. If he'd been a snake he would have bitten
them in the throat. He couldn't understand the
shopkeeper's anger. He couldn't understand the
cop's sneering contempt. He tried to tell the cop as
calmly as he could, "I forgot. The hat was on top of
my head." An old desperado sidled out of the
boarded-up Le Coq d'Or saloon and laughed. He
laughed loudly and he had brown broken teeth.
Albie could see that he was a desperado who had
come down through the dog years of dust and tumbleweed in the old ghost towns, a desperado who'd
earned the right to sit with his arms folded in the sun
and wait for the noon train, but even so, Albie told
him to shut up. The burly cop slapped Albie and
Albie said with bewildered astonishment, "I wasn't
talking to you." The cop snarled, "What are you,
some kinda slopehead? There ain't no one else but
us here, you fucking smart ass." Albie saw the
saloon's padlocked door and the sign, CLOSED.
The cop shouldered him into a corner, and so he said
again, "I forgot, that's all. Hell there's things even
on top of your head you got to be able to forget."
The cop snickered and said, "If your momma don't
screw your head on to your neck, you'll forget it,

too." The cop had a line of sweat pimples on his cheek. Albie believed pimples were the sign of a wanker's brain. He believed men got pimples from too much wanking and then stuffing their semen-shot socks and handkerchiefs down behind steaming radiators in the winter. He knew the reek of semen on his hands. He also knew the smell of women. He'd tasted the smell of women. It was like the damp earth where mushrooms cluster at the foot of hemlock trees and at the same time it somehow tasted of sweetened saltwater, like the raw fish he'd once eaten in a restaurant where he'd said, "This tastes just like you Elizabeth," smiling warmly at a waitress he often talked to, and he was sure — looking at the pimples on his cheek — that the wanker cop didn't know about things like that, didn't know how to think in any way delicate about them, and he was so hurt by the cop's contempt that he kept his head down, staring at the desperado's boots, secretly satisfied because he knew that the cop would never be able to see the old unshaven gunslinger either, not the way that he could see him, the lines in his leathery sun-creased face, lines that came from sleeping lonely and travelling light for years with a weight of grief in his heart. Albie hunkered down into a weary, sullenly pained and sorrowful resignation, as if he'd known all along that the cops would disappoint him, and he thought it was a sign of his own growing up and grit and backbone that he'd so quickly come to accept such disappointment with a wry smile. "Disappointment's like your Buckley's cough medicine," he'd told his crippled mother, "you swallow it to kill the tickle."

After the arrest he'd come home and washed the dirt and the 19 from the window in his room and he'd turned twenty quietly, but he'd also decided that nineteen would be his unlucky number for the rest of his life. A month later when he was working as a bicycle courier, he got fired because he refused to make a delivery, refused to get off an elevator at the nineteenth floor. And then, that same week he was convicted in night court by a bald-headed judge who didn't even bother to glance up at him. He was convicted of shoplifting. "If I'd wanted to be a criminal, I'd have been a criminal under my own hat," he'd said to the judge as the judge gathered his robes and read out in a low sonorous voice, "Since they tell me this man Starbach has no history, suspended sentence," and after that, Albie had always spoken resentfully of the cops and courts. "They don't know dick, they don't know nothing, which is why they're so dead-certain about what they don't know." He now refused to watch cop shows on television and he was glad when he heard that J. Edgar Hoover liked to wear a dress and to hold Clyde Tolson's hand. "The fucking dick-licking fraud. They carry on like they're smarter than every other dickhead wanker," he said. If cops drove through his traffic crossing lane when there was a lot of traffic he acted like he didn't see them and tucked his STOP sign under his arm and stared grimly ahead. If the street was empty, then he waved them through, furiously wig-wagging his STOP sign like he was directing them to the scene of a crime. The puzzled looks on their faces, as though they thought he was harmlessly crazy, made him laugh. He knew he was not harmless and he believed he had every right to be crazy and laugh, just like he had the right to hear sweet fiddle music in the high branches if he wanted to. After all, it was his crossing lane, and he knew he was a good crossing guard, always on time, three times a day.

He had applied for the job after seeing it posted on the telephone pole in front of the stone house, but then he had been afraid that they would find out about the shoplifting conviction, that it would show up on a computer. Computers were how they knew about everything and everybody. He didn't care about the conviction itself and he could hardly remember the mustard-yellow courtroom or the bald judge. He remembered the hat. He was haunted by the hat, a white stetson with an orange and black oriole's feather in the black braided suede band. He saw the hat in his dreams. Sometimes he dreamt of trees full of hats, hats fluttering like birds, mourning doves. Though his favorite country singers all wore hats, and though he wore tailored western clothes with pearl-gray piping on the pockets when he went out at night to the local clubs or to the Zanzibar saloon on Saturday afternoons, he'd never worn a hat again, not even in the winter sleet or freezing rain. In fact, he liked the cold clarity of rain water running out of his dark red hair and down his face. He could vision himself standing tall on a shelf of stone in the high country, standing against the long low clouded sky over the tundra. Staring into the wind. Narrowing his eyes against the grit on the wind, swollen with anger, an anger that sometimes pounded at the back of his head and gave him a

headache. A jack-hammer headache. He could bear
headaches and the cold wind on his bare head and
he didn't mind his wet feet soaking in his cowboy
boots. But cold hands frightened him. When his big
bony hands were cold, he lost all feeling in his fingers, and this, he thought, this numbness was as
close to death as he could come without dying, not
being able to feel the trembling of his own body in
his fingertips.

One night, after he'd been with a woman in a
dark hallway, a woman almost as old as his mother
in her middle forties, a woman he'd picked up in a
bar and had fondled up against the wall, probing
and pushing deep into her with two fingers until
she'd said, "I'm happy. I'm happy. I don't want to
fuck. Men weigh too much," he'd gone home and
studied his fingertips under his bedside lamp light,
prodding the pads of soft pale flesh that looked withered and drawn and bloodless after so long in the
wet heat of the woman, and he'd been frustrated at
not being able to see the inward swirl of lines he
knew were there in his skin, so the next day he'd
bought an ink pad at Woolworth's and had taken his
own thumb prints on a sheet of blank white letter
paper. "It's like seeing who you are," he'd told his
mother, "your prints are pasted on the empty air."
He'd thumb-tacked the paper to the wall at the foot of
his bed, and sometimes he went to sleep staring at the
two smudges in the dimmed light, his hazel eyes
flecked with yellow. His mother had told him when
he was a child that the yellow flecks were blind
spots. There were things, she'd said, that he would
never be able to see or understand. He had refused

to believe her. One night when he'd found her alone and drunk and crying in her bed, he'd said, "I can see everything real clear, and look at you, you're a mess. You're drunk." She'd wiped her nose with the back of her hand and said, "You got a cruel eye, you're a cruel boy." He'd resented that, so he said, "No, I'm not. I love you because you're my mom. I only said I can see what I see, and you're sick drunk," and he'd broken into tears and gone back to his own bed where an hour later he suddenly sat up and that was the first time that he saw through the tumbleweed blowing across the end of the bed an old desperado gunslinger, his arms folded, his eyes full of wilted flowers.

3

*A*lbie didn't sleep well. He never slept well, dreaming of swollen waters full of broken tree branches and drowning fish, and he shifted from shoulder to shoulder when he slept, twisting his sheets, twisting through bloated bodies in his dreams. Women with fish tails, thrashing. He had to untangle his legs from the winding sheets in the dark and straighten the bedclothes. Sometimes when he got out of bed he wasn't sure that he'd got out of his dream. The walls were somewhere within reach, they were black mirrors at the edge of his mind. He reached out for the walls but never turned on the bedside lamp. It was a game he played with himself. Almost gleeful. Except he never smiled because the dark was a test, it was dread country. The dark was his night-time woods.

With no moon. Unless his clock was the moon. He was serious about his big old round-faced clock, ticking *tock tock tock* and serious about the things he could do well in the dark woods. He could find his cowboy boots. He could piss in his toilet and never wet the floor. He could dial his telephone. "The darkness and whoever's out there line dancing in the dark don't frighten this old shitkicker," he said aloud to himself, and he wondered why he never saw any old desperados sashay up out of the dark, their lips sad and tight, because he knew that down in the dark, on the other side of the clock there was a deep hollow place where they came from, their hearts as heavy as night because he knew that all the old desperados had been born to live lonely and to die lonely while waiting in the sunlight of high noon and if they didn't end up nose first and dead in the dirt, then more than likely they'd end up their lives sitting wild in their sorrow in the sun looking for a noon train that was always late, sitting close by the long wooden legs of the lone water tower that cast a slim shadow toward the faraway blue hills, singing *Sa-loon, Sa-loon* into the badland winds. Tumbleweed winds that blew hot and dry and the thought of the winds that blew against the faces of all the old desparados left him soured and then enraged whenever he walked into the wind in the narrow downtown canyons staring at the tall glass bank towers at King and Queen Streets. The wind whistled between the towers. It was a whistle that had no words in it, no song, none that he could hear. A train whistle had words. A train had moaning words on the wind. He believed that he would never die till he heard a lone-

some train whistle blow in the night and so he sometimes sat alone in the dark for hours without closing
his eyes, angrily pitting himself against the dread,
against the dark hollow behind the clock, waiting for
the whistle, taunting death, listening, moaning and
singing *Don't cross him, don't boss him, he's wild in his
sorrow*, bunkered down in his three small dry-walled
rooms in the basement of the stone house.

Before the house had been divided and rewired,
it had been heated by a forced-air oil furnace, but
now everything in the house was electrical. The
cumbersome old furnace and the asbestos-wrapped
pipes were gone, but all the air ducts were still in the
walls, tunnels of tin sheeting that angled down
between the floor joists to the furnace well. The wide
air vents with their wrought iron gratings were still
in the floors of the rooms. He sat in the dark in the
square furnace well under the ducts and listened to
voices from the upper ranges, to whispers and cajol-
ing and laughter, and sometimes to screaming rage
or whimpering. He'd heard a hundred voices in the
dark and thought he'd heard almost everything
there was to hear about love. "Yessir, I heard it all.
Love's like a skeleton trying to dance itself out of its
skin," he said to himself one night. He liked that.
He'd seen a movie once where a boy who'd been left
all alone in a prairie sod house had scared off out-
laws in the night by painting a skeleton on one of his
mother's dresses, his mother having been shot dead
by a toothpick-chewing gunslinger, and he'd run out
into the night wearing the dress straight at the out-
laws, who rode away, terrified, and Albie could hear
the boy's laughter as he waved his white bony arms

after them in the dark exactly like Albie waved at
cops as they drove through his crossing lane, waved
at them with a curl to his lip. "Tell it to Tolson, boys,
tell it to Tolson."

Cops, he was sure, never heard music in the high
branches. He believed it was possible some priests
could hear sweet fiddling in the trees. He knew
there was a priest who came into the Zanzibar every
day late in the afternoon, dressed in slacks and a
sweat shirt, furtive and hoping no one would recog-
nize him, and there was fiddle music in the priest's
eyes. Priests fascinated him. Priests in black.
Crows. Sad lonely crows in white-face. Or doves
who'd dyed themselves in mourning dress, lone-
some doves who knew how to stand tall and calm
and benign at the end of the steel and glass world as
it collapsed in on itself, crying, whispering and crying, like all the voices in the stone house that collapsed in on him as he sat in his chair, voices that
tunneled in on Albie in the furnace room, down
through the air ducts and into the long spells of
silence in the cellar when all he heard was the ticking
of the big alarm clock he kept on a table in front of
his chair. The clock had a luminous round face, and
as he sat hunkered forward in the dark to listen with
his eyes open, he sometimes saw a smile on the
clock's face. There were blasting wires attached to
the clock. And the first floor, back and front, had
been wired, too, through the ducts and the old floor
vents. "There's standard time and daylight savings
time. This is bomb time," he said and laughed to
himself, alert suddenly to an anxious voice in the
duct from the second floor. It was a woman who

seemed to have a different man in her bed every night and her moaning cries came down the shaft and swirled around his head in the empty furnace well where he sat in a maroon leather easy chair. Her moaning aroused him, but he never masturbated in the dark. He'd always done that in the light, with the television blaring, alive to himself in his fingertips, but now that his mother had come to live with him he didn't do it at all.

4

*B*ack on his ninth birthday, as he'd blown out the candles on a round Kresge cake, his mother, Emma Rose, had told him that he had no father, not a father anyone knew by name. "There was a man who you are the seed of but I have no idea who he is, and neither does he." She wasn't even sure what town Albie had been conceived in. "It's not that I was fast into the bed, I'm just an inch short in the memory, that's all. And besides, there's no point worrying," she said. "The world's full of worry-warts, and warts'll pester your skin, pester your mind." She had bright blue eyes and a pouting bruised mouth. She had a strong grip. She could break a walnut in the squeeze of her right hand. She'd given Albie her hands. Big-boned, and a big middle knuckle. As a teenage girl, she'd wanted to go on the stage and had joined a dancing troupe, but she had never been light on her feet. Her feet were too big. She thought her feet were beautifully shaped, like the feet she saw on stone statues in the museum. Long sculpted toes. Still, they were too

big. She'd been fired, but because she had several
sequined costumes in her Samsonite suitcase, she'd
persisted, hung in, and managed to travel the small
mining-town Bingo and Big Top show circuit keeping the company of a knife thrower named Mike
Doov, and she'd been billed as Mike's Emma Rose.
To steady his nerves he'd snorted cocaine and said
the rosary while she drove them from town to town.

At a miners' fundraising pageant, he'd pinned
her hand to the wall in the basement of St. Barabbas'
Church in the copper mining town of South
Porcupine. She said she'd felt no pain in the palm of
her hand; instead, she felt it was like a trap door that
had sprung open, as if the earth had broken apart,
leaving her hanging over the gap, by her hand.
Through the years her scar sometimes opened and
her palm bled. She was sure there was a reason for
that, sure that her hand had a memory all its own of
the knife, but the doctors at Mount Sinai Hospital
said there was no reason. None. They were firm.
"Hands don't think," they said. "Neither do some
people," she said, "no matter how many scars they
got." She'd quit Doov the knife thrower and had
worked for two years as a hostess out on the airport
hotel strip, at Dade's, a dude trucker saloon that had
a huge blackjack boot bolted to the peak of the roof
and chrome hub caps wired to the backs of chairs
around the bar, but she'd finally been fired after finding two barrel-chested men, the chef and the bouncer, whacking each other off behind a WonderWorld
pinball machine. She'd laughed and yelled *TILT
TILT* and then had put a quarter in the machine and
begun to bang away at the flippers. "Don't nobody

forgive you for laughing at them, so they fired me, but it didn't matter," she said, "because some guy had already pulled down the night shade beside my bed and he'd whispered sweet nothings in my ear. Nothing. Nothing. Nothing. I had a weakness for wise guys."

She'd got pregnant, had never once thought about an abortion, and had passed her confinement quietly, working the phone for a bookmaker in a hairdressing salon until Albie was born in Grace Hospital, the Salvation Army wing. She said the horse that had won the third race while she was lying there in labor was called Fox On The Prowl and the first word she'd heard anyone say in the delivery room was, "Jesus." She had taken that as a sign. She was not exactly sure of what, but just a kind of blessing over his head. Albie insisted that he could remember the first word he'd heard from her: it was *Sa-loon. Sa-loon.* She laughed and said his memories were lunatic. "It must have been salon," she said because that's where she'd worked, in the hair dressing salon, and because after all she'd taken no drink and known no men all through her pregnancy.

Then, once she'd weaned Albie, she'd travelled for several months with a man who sold aluminum-siding and storm windows, leaving Albie in a foster home until she'd been hired on as the supervisor of a lakefront assembly line, spray-gunning lead finish on to the plug-end of television tubes. She liked being a supervisor. After six years, all the workers were warned that their lungs and innards were probably clogging up with lead poison. She'd lived at the time with Albie in a small studio flat but was sleeping on weekends with the divorced owner of another factory and so she went to work for him in his peanut plant, keeping the traffic and tonnage books on all the burlap sacks that were stuffed with unshelled peanuts. It was a dry musty building of tall ceilings and old windows with panes of marbled glass. She'd liked the quiet in the old building, and the bent light. She'd worked there for years, long after she'd stopped sleeping with the owner, and as long as Albie could remember, she'd had the smell of dust from peanut shells in her hair. He smelled it when she hugged him and she'd never stopped hugging him, not even when he'd turned twenty and come home sick-drunk, crouched over in the morning with the dry heaves, and not even when he'd come out of night court that evening wearing his turquoise cufflinks that he'd bought, blinded by the ceiling glare of the fluorescent strip lighting in the mustard-yellow hall, GUILTY, but then, not long after that he'd gotten the job as caretaker to the stone house, the caretaker also being the rent collector for the dozen rooms and small flats, and she had fallen down the loading elevator shaft at the factory. "I didn't have no time to say *oops*," she said, "so I just yelled SHIT and fell."

After nearly a year in hospital, strapped to wheels and pulleys, "just splayed out like a fool spider caught in my own web," she'd said she would gladly come to live with Albie in the three rooms in the basement, giving him her small disability pension. He decided her money would pay for their monthly whiskey bill. He liked whiskey. Old Crow or any bourbon. He lifted a glass of bourbon to her health and heard himself say, "From here on in, home base is the basement." He was often surprised hearing himself say things that he hadn't planned to say. Afterwards, she sat all day in the basement in a wheelchair, sitting hunched forward, two spit curls stuck down on her forehead, bobbing her head like a seasoned old boxer as she watched television, talking back to the talk shows. "You see those suckers on *Cross Fire*, they don't think a thing through to what they're supposed to be thinking, they just yell over each other," she yelled at Albie, and then she tilted her head coyly to the side and said, "This is fine, I never before felt so fine with you, Albie."

Every night and every morning for nearly three years, he'd wrapped a tartan mohair blanket around her limp legs and he'd carried her in and out of what had been his waterbed in his bedroom, settling her into the wheelchair, where she sat surrounded by broad-leafed rubber plants, popping caramels into her mouth, or exercising with the Ladies Trim Torso barbells she'd ordered by direct mail, pushing them straight up in the air, and sometimes he thought she looked like a fugitive from the law practising to surrender at gunpoint. One night, as she was about to lift the barbells, he pretended to fast draw, slapping his hand off his thigh. "Bam," he yelled, pointing his finger at her. "Bam, my ass," she muttered, and then he heard low whiskey laughter and he saw the desperado step out of the room's long narrow shadows, whispering to Albie, "You're a horse's ass. That's your mom you just shot." He said nothing. She slumped and dozed and then fell soundly asleep.

Albie picked her up and carried her to the bedroom,
but she began to whimper and whinge as he tucked
her into the waterbed and so he sang to her from the
foot of the bed:

> *Love is like a dying ember,*
> *till only memories remain,*
> *and through the ages I'll remember*
> *blue eyes crying in the rain . . .*

He slept on a fold-out sofa bed under the broad dark
leaves of the rubber plants, and every morning he
made her breakfast of toast and low cholesterol
EggBeaters that were good for the heart. "Because
we don't want no fat around the heart. Lean and
mean is what we want," he said, and then he laced
up his yellow work boots and took care of the big old
house, vacuuming the dimly lit hallways, making
sure the Tough-Tuft wall-to-wall broadloom was
carefully tacked down so that no one could trip on a
loose corner and sue the landlord, and he changed
dead light bulbs, replacing them with special long-
lasting bulbs he bought from the Crippled Civilians'
Society, and he fixed cracked walls with Polyfilla and
semi-gloss paint that he'd mix to the right color himself. He liked painting walls. Very few things gave
him as much satisfaction as the smooth unblemished
sheen of a wet wall newly painted, seen by the light
of a bare 100-watt bulb. Sometimes, he'd decide to
change the color of a flat when a roomer moved out
just so he could paint the walls. If it was necessary,
he'd use a roller but he preferred a brush, and he
kept several expensive camel's hair brushes in a

turn-of-the-century glass-doored cabinet in the furnace room. He never let anyone handle his brushes.
Not even Emma Rose. Emma Rose had never been
in the furnace room.

5

On sunlit and warm Sundays, Albie took Emma
Rose by taxi down to the harbor docks and
then by ferry across the city harbor to Ward's Island
and Hanlan's Point and back. Otherwise, she sat in
the basement flat and watched television all day.
"You mark my word, TV is time travel," she said.
"It's me and Captain Spock, the eyes and pointy little ears of the world belong to us." She watched All-
Star wrestling in the morning, giggling as a bellow-
ing hulk with pink hair wearing a rhinestone bow-tie
slammed a fat bulbous bonzo in black studded boots
to the mat, both wrestlers snarling into the camera
and yelling *kill, kill*, or she'd watch *The Dating Game.*
"Albie, Albie, can you believe this moron-looking
woman," she cried with a grim look of satisfaction,
"can you believe it?" — pumping her barbells up
and down, excited and breathing hard . . . *phum,
phlum . . . phum, phlum* . . . till Albie said, "You're
gonna get arm muscles like a piano mover." She
grinned and switched channels, pointing the remote
at the red eye in the television Wonder-Box as if it
were Spock's ZAP gun. "Albie, these days everybody's watching everybody, all them bird watchers
are out there and the night watchmen and the watch
makers, but you and me . . . " *Blippety-blip-blip. Pip-
pip. Blip-blip.* Applause for *Wheel of Fortune. Blip-*

blip. "You and me, we're the watch to end the night," she said, and then she blip-blipped back to *Wheel of Fortune*: *"Can I have an N . . . ?"*

"No," Emma Rose cried. *Tk, tk, tk, tk, tk, tk, tk, tk, tk,* of the wheel: — *"Five hundred."* — *"Can I have a D . . . ?"*

"No." — *"Yes, there is a D."* — *"Can I buy a vowel, an E."* — *"There are three E's."*

"Morons," hissed Emma Rose — *"I'd like to solve the puzzle."* — *"Go ahead."* — *"TOMORROW IS ANOTHER DAY."* *"Right, right, and that's worth six thousand, two hundred dollars."* "Albie," she said, as he peeled open a silver foil of Old Chum chewing tobacco and tucked a chaw into his cheek and picked up his STOP paddle, "Albie, don't you dare forget it, what that fellah says there, tomorrow is another day." He was getting ready to go out for the noon-hour crossing.

"Don't bet on it," he said.

"Bet on what?"

"On tomorrow showing up like you'd like it to."

"It'll be what you make it, Albie."

"In a pig's ass."

"Never mind no pigs now. I got no notion about pigs, but I been thinking a lot about you Albie, I was thinking about you this morning."

"You was were you?"

"Yes I was."

"There's nothing to think about me."

"I was thinking about the child you were, a real off-the-wall child."

"I wasn't so off-the-wall."

"Yes you were, carrying on like a little old man who'd never had no childhood, and now that you're older there's something kinda like a child coming out in you."

"No child I ever knew," he said and laughed.

"Well, not exactly like a child."

"What then?"

"I don't know. Maybe your father."

"My father ain't nowhere."

"But I been dreaming him, he's been coming to me in my dreams every night now for six nights, he knocks on the door and there he is."

She shunted back and forth on the big gray rubber wheels of her wheelchair.

"So what's he look like?"

"I'm not sure. He ain't at all like my own father but he's got my father's face, except I'm sure he's your father, but I still can't exactly tell who he is."

"What's he want?"

"To come in out of the rain. He's standing in the rain, and it's sloshing down outside and you're standing behind him with water running down your face. I'm the only one who's not getting soaked in the rain, and his face is like soap that's been soaking in water, kind of separating and coming apart in creases, what you'd maybe call a weathered face, a weathered face on a thin stick of a man who's all angles with a boy's smile, a big smile that's very obliging-like so you shouldn't ever know how hard-bitten he could be, but then his eyes lost me, they just let go of their hold on me before I could read their expression and when I spoke out loud to him it was like when you wake up after falling asleep in front of the TV and there's only that great big silver gray nothing glowing at you and humming in your ears."

"And what was I doing?"

"What?"

"Where was I? Still standing in the rain?"

"I don't know. I didn't look."

"You didn't look."

"No."

"I'm no goddamn dummy," he said angrily. "I don't stand out in the rain for nobody. Not for your dreams or anybody else's." He closed the brass fasteners to his fluorescent red jacket and adjusted the white vest cords around his waist, making himself comfortable, tying the cords in a bow. *Sashay sashay.* He was in his stocking feet. "You and your dreams and those people you watch on TV are the dickheads of the world who don't mean shit."

"Don't talk dirty to your mother."

"I'm not talking dirty. I'm talking facts."

"Yes you are, with your dick this and shit that."

"Jesus Christ, Momma. I'm twenty-nine years old."

"Then act your age and speak nice."

"I do speak nice."

"Let me give you a piece of advice, Albie. Free. You make sure, no matter what you think's going on, you make sure that you always say good words, and then eat some honey, and that way you'll never get a sore throat."

"I don't get no sore throats."

"You will and you'll be sorry."

"I'm not sorry for nothing, Momma. That's what you don't understand. I ain't killed no one. I haven't done a damned thing to anybody yet to be sorry for."

"We've all done something to be sorry for," and she pounded her fists on the arms of the wheelchair. "I am good and darned sorry for a whole lot of things, things I can't do nothing about."

"Neither can I."

"Neither can you what?"

"Do anything about what's done, except look after you, which I do."

"Yes, you do Albie."

"And I look after this house, and I look after all the kids who cross the street with me every day. That's a whole lot of looking after."

"You just make darn sure you look after yourself," she said, as she picked up the remote. "Don't you be a sap and a fool for nobody."

He closed his eyes. He saw drowning white-bellied fish. He was no fool, not for anyone. "Not even Jesus H. Christ had better fuck with me," he said to himself, welling up with anger, an anger that was always there inside him, an anger lying like a low fog hugging the ground. "You want to know how come I'm angry sometimes, I'll tell you how come I'm pissed off," he'd told Emma Rose. "It's like I haven't been doing nothing all day, not since I got up and washed myself off real clean, but suddenly right there, when I look, I got all this dirt under my fingernails, black dirt that didn't come from nothing or nowhere but it's just there, black, and that's what it's like when I find myself mad as hell."

It was a rage that he had no release for and no root that he could put his finger on. It just seemed to rest in him until it was roused, like an angry twin hanging on inside him to his ribs. One night after drinking whiskey he'd decided that this twin was called George. "Just plain George," he told his mother. "And you know how hard it is having a brother who don't say nothing, not a word. Speechless and dumb. You ain't deaf, George, but you're dumb and that's tough, man. That's hard. That's no fucking fun at all." Then he heard beyond any question the word *grief*. A sound like an echo inside his bones. *Grief.* He felt a terrible loss. It was always like this. Whenever he was full of rage he felt the veins in his neck swell and an ache all through his shoulders, and then he was quickly drained, as if he'd been sucked dry and left shrivelled, in a cold sweat. He heard the word *grief* again but he didn't know what he'd lost and didn't know what grief is, though he'd often stood facing into a mirror wondering why he alone seemed to hear sweet fiddles in the high bare branches of winter and why he had this dumb clinging child in his chest and also the memory that haunted him of a man with a raspy voice singing, "Love, O love, O careless love . . . " *Pip-pip. Blippety-blip-blip.* Flares of light, *SOSs*, channels flipping. He pulled on his boots, listening for a train whistle in the distance, in the foothills. Instead, he heard *Every shitheel's got to stand tall for something.*

"Who said that?"

The grizzled desparado winked at him.

"What?" Emma Rose said as she stopped channel-surfing and locked in on the evangelical station and sat bolt upright for the preachers. "Nobody said a word." She wiped her hand across her face. She liked to talk about God. She liked to talk about God and stick out her tongue. "You want to find God," she said, "you check out the list of missing persons. We should put up posters of Him in the post office . . . WANTED, DEAD OR ALIVE: — GOD. Haw, the poor son-of-a-bitch probably don't even know He's wanted, stumbling around out there in space with his thumb in the air, hitching a ride from here to Moose Jaw and back. Amnesia, He's probably got amnesia, stunned like some animal from staring into too many headlights in the dark, because those headlights'll do it to you, you get lights in your head just like these pop-eyed TV motormouth preacher fools, they seen the light, too much light for me, right in their own goddamn heads." She chuckled, and then laughed and hooted and went *Haw, Haw*, punching at the air as the TV preachers pounded their Bibles.

Albie loved her laughter, but seeing her in the nest of shawls in the chair, punching the empty air, upset him, the way her barbell weightlifting upset him, the way the black apples on the apple tree upset him, finding a fallen withered apple in the snow right where he was looking for a desperado's footprint, right where he'd seen two men standing the day before, standing there eating what looked like a dried fig taken from a side coat pocket stuffed with dry figs, but then he too suddenly laughed as a baby-faced blonde woman, her eyes bright with the beamish light of salvation under a beehive hairdo, appeared seated on a mangy old camel outside the walls of Jerusalem, the camel led by short reins into a heavy swell of orchestral violins by two smirking men in striped ankle-length skirts, the camel carrying her down the stony hillside *bumpety-bump, bump*, as she tried to lip-sync a hymn, lipping the air with

Twelve Gates To The City, Hallelujah, and as her husband's pious squirrel face suddenly appeared superimposed over her bobbing hairdo, crying *Lord forgive us, we know what we do,* Emma Rose began to howl with laughter, so that Albie, who'd leaned forward, squinting, realized that not one but two old suntanned desperados were out there on the desert hillside, smirking, dressed up in long skirts, and Albie, snaking his eyes to slits so he could see their faces and their silver-tipped shitkicker cowboy boots sticking out from under the hems of their skirts, said to himself, *Ain't they a motherfucking pip* as she yelled, "Heal, heal," whamming the flat of her hand against the air as if she were hitting the top of some poor sinner's forehead, *Bam* — "You jess step up here and slope your head for Jesus, *Bam,* heal."

6

On his twelfth birthday, just as he'd blown out the candles on his cake, she asked him if the men in her life, the friendly strangers, upset him, and he said, "No, I don't think about it, I think about me."

"That's good," she said, "you go on thinking about you, because in the long run, you is all you got."

At thirteen, when she asked again, he said, "No, I'm not upset."

At fourteen, he said, "No, nope."

At fifteen, he said, "No," as one of her lovers moved in and lived with them for two months, a sallow-faced man, Yuri, who had dark shadows that looked like old bruises under his deeply socketed eyes, eyes, as he slumped beneath the hanging kitchen lamp, that were dark as the ebony stone in his mother's big ring where Albie believed he saw slivers of light go swimming and then drown, and whenever Albie looked into Yuri's eyes he thought of a ring of ebony water and silver fish and drowning, though he had never been swimming in his life, and so he told Yuri while they were talking at the kitchen table that he knew he would never die by drowning because he would never make the mistake of going swimming, but Yuri smiled and said, "Never mind, we drown, you'll see, we drown in our own puddle."

"No I won't."

"Why won't you?"

"Because I dream about water and fish but I never die in my dreams."

"What else do you dream about?"

"Dynamite."

"You ever seen dynamite explode?"

"Nope. Except in the movies," Albie said.

"But you see fish?"

"The dynamite'll blow up all the fish."

Yuri said that he'd spent a long time in a place where everything seemed to have blown up and come to an end, where everything was always night, where even at high noon you saw ash that was just like pollen in the air and you saw the night in a man's eyes, and there in that place he'd learned that the very end of things could happen every day and over and over in a man's head until it became only a dull hum, and men forgot all about the end and never needed to know what the beginning was, because men could forget what they'd been through almost as fast as they could spit, and that's what he'd learned when he was a boy himself, just a little older than Albie, working in the camp, what was called a concentration camp, where he'd learned to concentrate, to think, and it had been a camp attached to a stone quarry, so he knew all about dynamite but he never dreamed about it.

"Why not?" Albie asked.

"Don't know."

"What do you dream about?"

"God. I try to concentrate on God."

"You ever see Him?"

"No. And I'm not sure I want to," Yuri said, laughing. "I might try to kill him." Yuri repeated the word *concentrate* over and over when he talked about his life, and Albie discovered that he himself saw yellow, or rather, felt he was being invaded by yellow, when he heard the word, the yellow of pus as it broke out of a soft and almost healed wound, and he remembered Yuri as a hulking man who sat in a cold sweat of sadness at the kitchen table, a man thinking so hard his mouth hung open.

He also remembered Yuri wore cowboy boots and said he was Ukrainian, "What not very nice stupid English call *hunky*," and that he'd been put in the concentration camp to learn how to think because he'd gambled with a Jew, gambled the gold in the Jew's teeth against a loaf of bread. The Nazis had arrested him and the Jew because they said he'd tried to steal state treasures, since all Jewish teeth belonged to the state. "This was so crazy it made sense," Yuri said. "All laws are laws only because they make sense with such logic." The people had been brought into the camp on trains in boxcars and he'd been put to work, because he was so strong, with a Jewish labor gang, a Commando, who helped unload incoming Jews, leading them to the gas chambers. "Jews leading Jews, the blind leading the blind," he said, "and I was only Uke." This gang, because some had pouches stuffed with watches and diamonds that they collected from the incoming Jews, was called Canada. It was the Canada Commando, the dream Commando, so he'd always thought of himself as Canadian, and he'd dreamed of Canada, of western cowboys, and horses and cowboy boots. After the war, he'd come to Canada, but he'd never gone out west. "I liked the picture shows better, the movies. In movies, there are no checkpoints. I am proud citizen of this new country, Movieland Canada." He wore brown tooled-leather cowboy boots and he polished them every day, and on Saturday afternoons he took Albie to cowboy movies. "You know what it is for me that I like to see about American movies?" he said, "when you take all gunfire away, there is only silence, and it is this silence that could kill you, kill you badly." He loved seedless mandarin oranges. He would eat one after another, piling up the torn peels on the kitchen table. It frightened Albie when Yuri sat, sometimes for hours, eating oranges and saying nothing, lost in silence. "But there is silence and then there is silence," Yuri said, "and the only silence you got to watch out for is the silence before the calm of the kill."

"Did you ever kill anybody?" Albie asked him.

"This is not what you need to know, for such a small boy, beginning."

"So what do I need to know?"

"That during the daytime when you look up, because there is so much sunlight, you don't see the stars. But at night, when the dark is darkest, this is when you see the stars."

Sometimes on the weekend Yuri would get up in the morning and say to Albie, "She's asleep. Your mother's still asleep."

Albie would go into the bedroom and look at her.

"She isn't sleeping. She's pretending."

"No she's not," Yuri said.

"Her eye is open."

"How do you know?"

"It's white. She's dead," Albie said.

"No she's not. She's sleeping."

It was always around nine o'clock in the morning when they talked like this, and Yuri made thick black coffee and ate a mandarin orange and paced back and forth in the narrow front room, bumping into furniture, talking to himself, pointing to the window. Sometimes he'd go back to bed and kiss and bite Emma Rose. She'd shriek and bury her face in his neck. Yuri yelled that he was tired. "I am very strong but I am tired." She'd get up and brush her hair, the brush thick with hair, and soiled. If Albie came into the room she'd close one eye.

"I'm only half-awake," she said.

"You look like you're awake to me," Albie said.

"I'm only pretending."

"Is Yuri asleep?"

"No. He's dead."

"No he's not," Albie said.

"How do you know?"

"Because he's in his bare feet."

"Of course, he's in bed."

"He told me that when he died he'd die in bed with his boots on."

Then, one weekend Yuri packed his small leather suitcase with its wrap-around belts and told Albie that he would always send him postcards from wherever he went in the world but he would never see him again, because he and his mother Emma Rose had nothing to say anymore, and Emma Rose stood leaning against the doorjamb looking tired, because they'd been up all night talking and talking until they had nothing left to say, so he took Albie downtown for the last time and bought him a pair of boots. Albie, who was almost seventeen, stared at himself in the mirror, and the cowboy boots with their high heels gave his angular body a lean line, and he liked being so much taller, and liked the look of himself in the mirror and the look of Yuri smiling in the mirror behind him. He'd never forgotten Yuri's eyes, the old bruises. One day, he realized that they were the same eyes as the eyes of the desperado who'd appeared at the end of his bed, eyes full of night wind and wilting flowers. Sometimes, when he took off his boots and was sitting in the furnace room, he felt the hollow behind the clock turn into a well of dark flowers and sometimes, when he attached the blasting cap wires to the timing device on the alarm clock and sat listening to the ticking, he saw Yuri's eyes in the face of the clock, his mouth hanging open, concentrating, and he heard Yuri's soundless laughter.

7

"Television," he said to Emma Rose, "don't mean dick. You and me, we watched that Desert Storm war day after day and all night long, and we ended up watching a war we never saw, except dickheads are discussing it like they saw something in the pictures that weren't there. Shit, if they want real pictures, I got pictures. I got pictures they've never seen, moving in my mind all the time." He laughed and slapped his thigh. "But I ain't like one of those loonies you see on the street, talking out loud to themselves, their brains bungholed and all screwed up. No sir. And I ain't no preacher." He knew what he was talking about because he heard words from deep in the back of his mind, luminous words, as if they spoke from inside mirrors, like razor cuts of light that tattooed the inside walls of his skin so that he winced and slitted his eyes and stared straight ahead, his body taut, as if he were trying to focus, to concentrate, absorbing an intense aching awareness behind his eyes, and when he was sitting with Emma Rose watching the evangelicals and one of them said that *God saw all there was to see with the freshness of vision in which nothing was hid, a vision in which the waters parted,* he wondered if God wasn't in him, God's words, because out of nowhere, the dark waters at the back of his mind would part and he'd see with utter clarity a telephone pole, or a dragon fly, or a lampshade on the other side of the room, or a twilit gunslinger, and there'd be nothing else there but the pole, or the fly etched in the air, alone in itself, or when he was walking down the street he'd fasten on a crease in the face of a weathered old man, or an unlaced shoe, and wings, white wings, and flying fish, he saw flying fish, and sometimes he wondered why he never saw angel wings as he sang *bird in the sky flying high flying high* but then in his heart he was sure that angels, though there was no question that they had lived and flown and fought with each other once in the sky, they were gone now. The sky was like an emptied cutout book, full of holes, with the angels that had once been there all scissored out. What people used to believe in was full of holes. He was sure of that. He was sure because he believed he could see everything that was actually there to be seen, though he had no clear idea what all the things he saw meant or why they were so intently and suddenly lodged in his eye or whether other people saw things in the same way. And he always heard that word *grief*.

It came like a whisper outside the window. Like a dry leaf or dead branch blown against the glass. It was a strange sound against a cellar window. He never tried to say the sound of the word. He had never tried to tell anyone, not even his mother, about the gift he had for hearing sounds and words or for seeing things, and as for any blind spots, as for the possibility that something might be there that he couldn't see, he didn't ever doubt his own eyes. Only the feeling of loss left him wondering, the pangs so acute that he could feel an invasion of yellow in his bones and he knew, without knowing why, that sorrow was yellow. "Yes, yellow," he said, brought to a halt by a wild and prickly burning under his skin. The pins and needles of sorrow, his body gone to sleep. The burning made him furious. He chewed on his fingernails. He began to hum *It takes a worried man to sing a worried song* but he had no words, the letters lost on the wind like torn paper. Or flying fish. Once, he'd gone to church because TV preachers said the lost words were there, *holy, holy, holy,* but he'd felt an awful lethargy and a sourness in the church because what he'd seen was not God but people hiding. Faces shut tight. Dark mirrors. Like the walls of his room at night. He decided church was a place where people felt good because they were supposed to be able to talk to God. But he didn't see God in their faces. God wasn't talking back to them. He saw pews full of people talking to themselves, all of them stern, just like the police were stern. He was sure the church was a comforting place for the police, because it was punishment that kept cops and priests in lock-step, but Albie didn't want to punish anyone. Cops punished people. They didn't care who they hurt. Or beat. He'd seen cops beat up kids, kids who talked back. Cops didn't care if they were wrong, or the judges were wrong. The baldheaded judge hadn't even looked up. Albie was sorry that he had ever wanted to be a cop. He was sure his nameless father — who might have been anything — had not been a cop, just like Albie was sure that he himself was no thief, because he had never intended to take the white stetson hat on his birthday, and any damned fool could have seen that, but the judge hadn't bothered to look up, the judge had never seen him because the judge had never bothered to look. But Albie had seen the judge. He'd seen that the blue veins at his pale temples were too blue, and the skin of his neck, under his flushed face, was the white of a garden slug. When he'd left the courtroom that night, a policeman at the door had said, "Sorry," and Albie had said, "So am I, that man is dying."

8

*A*s he hurried down the street, passing a row of lean red brick houses, his black jeans tucked into his black cowboy boots, he began to hum, a humming so sensual in his throat that if he held on to a deep note it eased the spasms of anger which wrenched him so much that he hacked for air. He hummed, trying not to step on the sidewalk cracks. He remembered a little rhyme-song his mother had sung: *Step on a crack and break your mother's back*, and he walked carefully, skip-stepping between cracks so that he seemed to be a light-hearted man out for a stroll, swinging his STOP sign, and as he walked he sang out loud to the two old desperados that he'd last seen dressed in long skirts leading a camel downhill outside Jerusalem, but now they were in black jeans and black shirts, dressed just like Albie. They kept stepping out arm-in-arm from behind trees in the morning shadows, tipping their hats. Nothing desperados did surprised him anymore, not since the morning he had seen the gunslinger with the wilting flowers in his eyes, beaming at him benevolently as he swung in the breeze, hanging by his neck from the branch of an old elm tree, another desperado beside him, and Albie had cried out, holding his sign in front of his face, but then when he had inched the STOP sign down and looked again, the hanged desperados were gone. The air was empty. "Maybe that's how angels used to appear and disappear," he decided, pretty sure that the desperados had swung into sight just to taunt him, to fill him with a melancholy that he'd only recently learned to turn to a bittersweetness by singing, indifferent to anyone who sneered or looked quizzically at him as he passed:

> *Nobody slides my friend,*
> *It's a truth on which*
> *You can depend.*
> *If you're living a life*
> *It will eat you alive,*
> *And nobody slides my friend.*

He only got upset and nasty if someone barged up out of nowhere and stared at him, stared at the chaw of tobacco bulging in his cheek or stared at his cowboy boots and his fluorescent vest, someone who soured his song, making him break stride so that he squinted into the sun, his eyes full of the snake spit that comes from knowing what it's like to sit with morning whiskey on your breath, rolling a cigarette on a hot, hot day, licking the flimsy pale paper, waiting for the noon train, singing:

> *Been looking through the dictionary*
> *For a word that's running through my mind.*
> *Though I like the sound of brother,*
> *I've been looking for another*
> *That nowhere in its pages do I find.*

Can it be that all its glories are forgotten
And are buried in the language of the Greek?
If it is, 'tis always buried in my memory
As the first word that I heard my Mommy speak:
Sa-loon! Sa-loon! Sa-loon!
It runs through my mind like a tune.
Now I can't stand cafe, and I hate cabaret,
But just mention saloon and my cares fade away
For it brings back a fond recollection
Of a little old low-ceilinged room
Of a bar, and a rail
And a dollar, and a pail . . .
Sa-loon! Sa-loon! Sa-loon!

As he got to the southeast corner of his crossing-lane, he faced an Army-Navy War Surplus store. The window was cluttered with ammunition pouches, fold-up aluminum fry pans, flare guns, flack-jackets and nylon pup-tents. A big inflated yellow rubber life-raft hung from a second floor fire escape. As he stood on the corner, singing *Sa-loon* to himself, he saw a middle-aged man in front of the store. Though the sun was shining, the man was wearing a clear plastic raincoat and a red scarf, and he had a brown paper bag full of crushed soda crackers. He threw a fistful on to the sidewalk. There were five seagulls on the corner. "Goddamn seagulls," Albie said. "We're goddamn five miles from water and we've got seagulls shitting all over the place and you're feeding them."

"No problem," the man said.

"It's a problem, I'm telling you, shit's a problem."

"So say it nice," the man said. "It won't hurt you to say it nice."

"In your face," Albie said, angrily slitting his eyes.

The man spun away and stared back into the surplus store window, saw himself, and touched his cheek. "There's nothing in my face," he said. *This guy's a real lunatic*, Albie thought, looking at his watch. *Real.* He was always acutely aware of the time. It was ten to twelve. The school children would be along in ten minutes. Trying to ease down his anger, Albie walked to another doorway, a LOVECRAFT lingerie shop, the windows filled with black and red garter belts, sheer brassieres, lace panties and feathered pasties. A hand-lettered sign over a box said *Orange-Flavored Condoms*. He looked hard at the box, and saw a woman taking into her mouth a cock sheathed by a condom. *Orange-flavored rubber.* He stood transfixed. *That*, he thought, wagging his sign at the window *is fucking insane*, unaware that the owner of the store, a woman standing inside the door, was scowling at him. She wore a lapel button that said *Safe Promiscuous Sex.* She waved Albie out of her doorway. He shrugged and went back to the corner, to the man with the paper bag, but the bag was now empty and he had crushed it into a ball and was tossing it from hand to hand. The seagulls had flown to the other side of the street. Children were coming along the sidewalk. The man looked in the window glass again, then turned on Albie. "You're telling me I'm in your face."

"I told you," Albie said, "you're in my face."

"You're telling me."

"Right."

"You're telling *me*, you're telling *me*, on a public corner to get out of your face." He backed away to the curb. *"Me,"* he said, buttoning his plastic rain-coat and stepping backward into the crossing lane.

"Don't go backwards," Albie yelled, afraid the man would get himself killed.

"Backwards? What're you talking about? The whole blessed world is backwards."

"Don't walk backwards," Albie said sternly.

"I can go anywhere and I can walk any way I want," the man cried, "and you better believe it."

The man waited for an Acme Distilled Water truck to make a right turn and then hurried across the street. He threw his balled paper bag at the seag-ulls.

"I don't better believe nothing," Albie said and turned and held out his arms to the cluster of laugh-ing children who were hurrying toward him, and some were shouting, "Albie, Albie."

He lined the children up in a row, telling them to hold hands, and then he stepped out into traffic, holding his STOP sign high. He knew how to look hard-faced and dangerous at drivers who encroached on the crossing lane. He waved the chil-dren forward, shielding their bodies as he walked beside them to the other curb. A few weeks earlier, a boy had given him a St. Christopher medal, a gift from his mother, and another boy had sneered, "That Christopher ain't a saint no more, they kicked that jive-ass out of heaven." Albie didn't care. The boy, tugging at his sleeve, making him lean down, had whispered in his ear, "That's you. My mother says you're my St. Christopher." Albie was so moved he'd wanted to cry, and he'd attached the medal to a silver chain. He'd bought the chain from a skin-head girl who was selling stolen jewellery in the stripper saloon, the Zanzibar, and he'd double-looped the chain around the alarm clock so that the medal hung suspended in the middle of the clock face. One night, he suddenly knelt on one knee and said, "It's you and me," and he kissed the medal before going to sleep and he'd slept well and now he kissed the saint every night and blessed the children.

"You going to sing today, Albie?" one of the little girls asked.

"No, no. We're too late today."

"Aw come on Albie," the girl pleaded.

As he led the three girls across the road holding the STOP sign over his head, he let out a high-pitched nasal wail:

> *I'll always be with you*
> *For as long as you please*
> *For I am the forest*
> *And you are the trees.*

9

*A*lbie sat in the furnace well in the maroon chair. The leather was dry and cracking. It had been his mother's chair in the Cabbagetown apartment they'd lived in for years, four rooms in an old frame house that had been torn down to make way for First Permanent Place, two glass insurance towers that the newspapers said gleamed like gold in the late afternoon sunset because the sheets of reflecting wall had been fired with gold dust when they were in the state of molten glass, great gleaming towers of hundreds of thousands of dollars of dust. Albie dreamed of gold dust, of panning for gold with sourdoughs along crystal clear river beds, crouched over cold water at the foot of a dark ravine, watching for bears and wolverines in a ditch as dark as the foot of the stairs in the cellar where his mother had made him stand as a child, reciting his arithmetic tables, and whenever he'd made a mistake, she'd bolted the cellar door and left him alone in the dark where he'd dreamed of water in the walls and of dark forests planted in the fields of his skin. He never died in his dreams. He was steadfast, like the dark rich soil behind the stonehouse at the bottom of the garden, soil that was alive with worms, and his chest heaved under the constriction of the roots of pine trees, and the birds in the trees sang from the branches and the more they sang the deeper the trees sent their roots into him, drilling down between his bones and throttling him, and desperately he tried to reach up and catch the birds, tried to wring their necks, to stop the throttling, but the birds flew away to nests hidden in his mother's hair, and when she cut her hair she clipped their wings so that they had to stay in the low branches of the trees, still singing, but only one incessant note. *Dark. Dark. Dark.* Emma Rose insisted now that she couldn't remember putting him down in the cellar. "I wouldn't abandon a child to the dark." He told her not to worry, he didn't mind remembering the cellar now because he'd learned that, except for the tunnels in his dreams, the quietest and safest place in the house was the cellar, in the dark, and he confessed that sometimes as a boy he'd deliberately tricked her by leaving out multiples — particularly sixes, he didn't like the look of sixes — so that he would seem stupid and be left alone to himself. He'd quickly learned to walk through the cluttered cellar without banging into boxes and rusted old garden tools. He'd become sure of himself in the dark. And now, sitting in his mother's chair, he cupped his bony hands before his face, spat quickly into the palms like he had done when he was a kid playing sandlot baseball, and he rubbed the saliva into his skin and settled back. His hands had a sure sticky feeling. He liked that feeling. "Six times six is thirty-six," he said, and laughed. "I always knew that."

10

*F*our air ducts opened on to the empty furnace well. He had made hinged lids for the square ducts out of plywood covered with white acoustic tiles so that he could close off any sound he didn't want to hear from the rooms above, particularly the stronger, shriller voices from the first and second floors. Very little sound ever came down from the third floor where there was a small three-room flat with sloping ceilings. It had apparently been lived in for several years by three dwarfs who worked in the local carneys. The carneys had closed down. Now, a big, heavy-set man who was an ambulance driver lived there. *The man upstairs,* Albie called him. He had no idea what went on up there, or what the man was like, except that he shaved his head clean and performed what Albie thought were Tai Chi exercises in the backyard early on Sunday mornings (Emma Rose said he looked like a man wig-wagging SOS signals in slow motion), but the rooms in the rest of the house often sent down so many overlapping voices and so much TV talk and music, that he slumped down in his chair and felt he was travelling a night time road listening to an old car radio out in the country, the stations drifting in and out of his head.

He was excited and alert when someone new moved into the house and he'd take off his boots and settle in the leather chair and try to hone in on the new voice. He knew where each duct went in the walls. He'd made a map of all the ductwork and vents in the house when he was laying down the wiring and the caps, drawing the wiring through the ducts to the clock. Still, it sometimes took him a week to hear the new voice, to separate intonations. He didn't try to see the face, it was the voice he wanted to know. On his rent collecting rounds, he was flustered and shuffled his feet when he looked into a face in a doorway and heard the voice, so flustered that the air in the doorway warped. It was like peering through flawed glass, the face and voice veering apart, and he was sure that the voice he heard in his head was much more real than the face in the doorway. He didn't trust the face just like he didn't trust the faces that appeared to his mother on television. "Tonight," she would say, "Johnnie Carson appeared to me. He was very sweet tonight."

"He didn't appear to you."

"Sure he did."

"Only angels appear to people."

"Are you outta your mind? That's what stars do, that's why they're stars, they make appearances."

"They make movies, Momma."

"Right, they appear in movies."

"And they talk to you?"

"Who else are they talking to?"

"Each other. They don't know you from Adam."

"You know the trouble with you, Albie?"

"No."

"You got an unkind streak, you got an eye that likes to hurt."

"Yeah?"

"Yeah. You like to hurt, you like your own hurt."

"I like my own hurt?"

"Right, you're a loner who likes too much to be alone, like being alone is better than being with someone."

"I'm with you, I got you."

"I'm your mother Albie. I'm your mother, you don't got me."

"Whatever I got, I got, and I like it. I like it like that, I like it alone."

"You know the trouble with you Albie?"

"No, 'cause I got no trouble."

"I don't want to say what the trouble is because I don't want to hurt you."

"Say what you want to say."

"You think your ass is a star."

"I think my ass is a star . . . listen to you, listen to you talk, and I'm supposed to be the one who talks loose, and listen to you. My ass is a star, but I'll tell you something, since you think the stars talk to you, I'm talking to you, this here star is talking to you. These are dangerous times, very dangerous, and you got to be on your guard the whole time, otherwise the bogeyman'll get you. You remember the bogeyman, Momma. You told me about the bogeyman. The whole world's full of bogeymen. Bigshot bogeymen who'd just as soon break my balls as look at me. Except I see them coming. Except I got myself bunkered and I'll blow them beyond kingdom come before they can whisper through the walls how sorry they are, and sad, you ever noticed that Momma, how sad people are? Even the bogeyman, I'll bet even the bogeyman is sad."

11

*I*t was only voices emerging from the dark that could unnerve him, the intimacy of all the words he heard, not the love words or the moans of lovemaking, but he thought that hearing voices the way he did, so close, so intimate, without his own body being there in the room beside the voice, was probably like being inside a woman without her knowing it, as if somehow a man like him could do that, could have that wet inner intimacy without even touching, a warmth like early morning rain that broke open to him as painlessly as a flower breaks open, or shells, oyster shells or peanut shells, all breaking-open, with the words that he heard popping out just like peanuts, and he laughed because that meant his mother had spent all her years counting up burlap bags of unshelled peanuts, unshelled words. Bags and bags of words that had never been opened, never heard. But he heard the wrangling arguments in the house, the weeping into the phone of a placating woman lying on the floor, her phone beside the grille, whispering *Oh I want I want and I'll do anything you want because I just want you to want me* that was like being with people inside the words they mouthed, and if it was true, like the TV preachers said, that God overheard every word in everyone's heart, then maybe God, when He dreamed, dreamed He was Albie, and the Holy Ghost was actually a cop, an undercover cop who whispered the word that got someone killed. But unlike the cops, he didn't go in for mug shots, he didn't try to fix words to a face, didn't want to hold what he'd heard against anyone. He just cradled up in the hollow of the well, humming to himself, wanting to wish the lonely old desparados in his world well before he said goodnight.

Sometimes, before he stumbled to bed, in the shank hours of the morning when he couldn't sleep, when the house was completely still, and when his rooms were silent except for the light snoring of Emma Rose, he sat on the edge of the sofa bed with his boots off — the toes of the empty boots always turned inward — and the silence seemed to contain, like a seed, the word that he thought would unlock a question he didn't know how to ask. No matter how wonderstruck he was at all he had heard coming down the air ducts, that unasked question always hung out there in the shadows and sometimes the question seemed to haul him forward, so that he sat on the edge of the mattress, wary and alert and even afraid. Sometimes he thought the answer to the unknown question must be the word he always heard, *grief*. He peeled open a foil of Old Chum and tucked a chaw in his cheek, trying to soothe himself. He listened for the train whistle, or more frightening, listened for someone who was going to speak directly to him through the ducts, a voice that was going to name his name, throttle him, and at first he thought that this desire to hear a voice he did not know, a desire filled with dread, was a punishment for putting his ear to the secrets in the walls in the house, but then, because he had hurt no one, because he had not even told his mother what he had heard in the darkness, because he had kept the dark words as holy as a priest could keep them, he decided that what he was really afraid of was hearing his father's voice. Perhaps his father was on a train, whistling, coming back for him, to kill him. Or be killed. Ever since his mother had told him about her dream, he wondered when he would come in out of the rain and cold and hear from his father, too.

12

On Saturday afternoons, Albie went downtown to the Zanzibar, a strip saloon on Yonge Street that had silver stars stencilled on the black walls, a stage studded with flashing lights, and a glass shower stall on stage. At the back of the long narrow room, a blind old black man played the organ, rhythm and blues. Two huge wooden canary cages hung from the ceiling and naked girls danced in the cages. The bar-room was crowded with working men and women hunched over round black arborite tables, staring deadpan at girls dancing on the stage, and other girls sidled from table to table carrying shoebox-stands, charging five dollars to shuffle on the box beside a table and strip, or ten dollars if they got up on the table and danced.

Albie always tried to sit at the same table. He liked the slouching indifference of the girls, their hard baby-doll faces. He drank draft beer with a jigger of tequila in the beer. This drink was called Colorado Cool Aid, from a song by Waylon Jennings, a song about a bully who liked to spit beer laced with tequila in people's ears and then one day the bully got his own ear razored off by a Mexican who handed him back his sliced ear with the attached sideburn and told him the next time he wanted to spit, to spit in his own ear. Albie laughed out loud whenever he thought of that song and he felt so good he paid one of the girls to dance on her shoebox, cupping her breasts, stroking herself, parting her legs and bending over, touching her toes, so that he could see her vagina.

One afternoon, a girl who had skinny thighs, bent over and held her ankles and said, looking at him upside down, "Ya wanna kiss this? Fifty bucks." He looked sternly at her, unblinking, offended. He wanted to be left alone to his own thoughts. She straightened up and spun around, her pubic hair shaved and trimmed to the shape of a black diamond. He looked up into her pale eyes, eyes drained of light, and turned away to the stage where another girl had stepped into the chrome-encased stall wearing only lucite high heel shoes. She stood inside the glass walls soaping herself in a shower of water. The organist played *Night Train*. Albie was aroused by her glistening pale body as she drew handfuls of white soap suds up her thighs and between her legs. He felt the swell of an erection and leaning close to the table so that no one could see, he took hold of himself, feeling a rush, a connection with himself. The shoebox dancer bent over again, looked under the table, leered and said, "Gotcha." He was furious. She spread her legs, pulling her buttocks apart so that he could see the rosebud of her ass. He knew the girls called this the Moon Shot. He ignored her, staring at the girl in the shower stall, her breasts sloping with fullness. Then the water shut down in the shower stall and the blind organist stopped playing. The shoebox dancer said, "So what'll it be?" He ignored her. She picked up her box and went to another table. "Gotcha my ass," he said. "Don't nobody get me that easy."

A dancer wrapped in a sequined shawl and sitting with the owner, Horace the Hop (he had a gimpy leg), a woman whose heavy-lidded eyes made her seem sensually sure of herself, stepped on to the stage. Albie hunched forward, unbelieving. He'd rented a second floor room in the old stone house to her, and for a week he'd been listening, trying to find her voice in the air ducts. He'd only heard a distant crying and someone somewhere sitting close to a floor vent, muffled words, and there was no way to know if it was her. As she shimmied on stage, her body seemed swathed in sweat, sweat pearling on her breasts. She slipped off her black halter with a coy laugh that mocked shyness. She was high-breasted, almost boyish. Sweat ran down her throat, between her breasts. She seemed to be suffering some intense inner heat, but under the sheen of sweat her skin was pale and there was no strain in her face, only an amused wry smile. A bead of sweat on her left nipple caught the light, caught his eye, and then it fell as she spun slowly on the balls of her bare feet, her palms joined together over her head, her head thrown back as if in ecstasy, but then Albie saw that she was watching herself in the ceiling mirror, and her wry smile was for herself. The men in the front row had become silent and Horace the Hop looked around, wondering what was wrong. Even the girl was aware, despite the bass peddle swell of the organ, of a deadfall of silence over the front tables. She looked back, as if someone might be behind her.

A man with a bulging neck, his fleshy mouth puckered, pointed and bawled out, "For Christ's sake, she's bleeding." Horace the Hop cursed. A hairline of blood had stained the girl's white sequined briefs, and it was widening. "Goddamn, that's disgusting," a woman sneered. Horace hobbled up the stairs, grabbed the bewildered girl by the wrist and hauled her down from the stage. The organist stopped playing and Horace snarled, "Tell that blind fucker to get back on the pedals." Albie, arms folded, holding his elbows, yelled into a sudden pocket of silence, "Hey, Hop, that's the only human goddamn thing that's ever happened in here." Albie was taken aback, shocked at the loudness of his own voice. The owner was, too. He knew Albie was a regular who kept to himself, and for a moment he paused, but then he pulled the dancer toward the dressing room door and a mulatto hurried up to the stage. Albie ordered another Colorado Cool Aid, but he felt sour and glum. He spat his last mouthful of beer back into the glass and went home. He was home two hours early. He unhooked the blasting wires.

Through the week, as he worked around the house, tacking new rubber treads to the stairs, digging up flower beds that were spongy as the last of the frost eased out of the earth, he wondered whether she'd heard him yell in the saloon and whether she had been hurt and ashamed. In the furnace well, listening for her voice, he dreamed of drying her body with heavy towels, drawing a white towel down the runnel of her back bone. As the days passed, he listened for her step on the stairs as he checked the electric radiator thermostats in the halls, turning them down, and he glued down a corner of battleship linoleum in the vestibule. Once, at twilight when he was carrying a ladder from the back yard, he caught a glimpse of her hurrying into the house with an armload of groceries. The landlord did not allow cooking in the small single rooms, and that evening, in his stocking feet Albie stole to the top of the second-floor stairs, to the corridor where her room was, and he smelled frying sausages that could only mean she had a hot-plate in her room, a danger to the old wiring because only the three-room flats had been rewired for appliances. But he said nothing and turned and went quietly downstairs. His mother, squinting at him, slumped in her wheel-

chair. At last she said, "Albie, what's eating you?
You got some kinda bother on your mind."

"Windows," he said. "We only got goddamn cellar windows that aren't like real windows, where
you can look out and see what's going on, or at least
see out on the lawn."

"It's raining out."

"I'd like to sit and watch the rain."

"We got the whole world to watch," she said and
switched on the channel selector. An electric sizzle
fanned out across the gray screen.

"You got to be kidding," he said as the *Evening
News At Seven* came on and he hunkered down into
the easy chair beside his mother, who said, "I don't
kid about the news, Albie. No sir, news is what
makes the world go BANG." She hoisted her Trim-
Torso barbells . . . *phum . . . phlum . . . phum . . . phlum*
. . . "That's because our whole friggin' world is on a
short fuse," he said, as the newsreader reported that
several thousand desert tribesmen, after random
testing, showed tumors on their lungs from breathing in the smoke and ash from oil well fires that con-
tinued to burn out of control in the desert.
"Surprisingly," the newsreader said, "doctors say
their lungs look as if they'd been working as coal
miners for twenty years, and there is, of course, no
coal in the desert." Albie smiled. An old gunslinger's soot covered face was superimposed on the
screen, singing *with whiskey and blood all around, not
even the wind heard a sound, since nobody prayed my
friend* . . .

"You know the first thing I wanted to know
about you when you were born, Albie?"

"I don't know nothing about first things," he said and began to sing along *since nobody prayed my friend* . . .

"Whether you were left-handed."

"What'd you care about that for?"

"Because of what I always wondered."

"Which was?"

"Why God's got no left hand."

"You mean," *with whiskey and blood all around* "you mean God's a gimp?"

"He's got no left hand to sit on."

"Only dumbheads sit on their hands."

"It's in the Book," she said *with blood all around* . . .

"So where's His left hand?

"The angels always sit on the right hand, right?"

"Right."

"It's the devil."

"What're you talking about?"

"His left hand" *since nobody prayed my friend* "is the devil. You know how hard for me it was to find out that you were left-handed?"

"This is stupid, Momma."

"Stupid to you, but not to me," *since nobody prayed* "it wasn't stupid to God," *my friend* "look what's happened."

"Where?"

"Look how godawful the news is."

"Yeah well, what they say is going on is not necessarily what's going on."

"You think they're saying it wrong?"

"Who says they're saying it right?"

"I say." *and not even the wind heard a sound.*

"Who're you?"

"Your mother okay?"

"It's not okay." *and nobody prayed* "Maybe you're wrong, too, okay? Why not?"

"Because the right people," she said, *with blood all around* "know the right things."

"The right people know shit."

"There you go."

"There I go what?"

"I'm talking fifty-six channels of how the world is whacking the world and bonehead saints are setting fire to themselves with gasoline and it turns out the stars in the sky are clusterbombs blowing the hell out of everywhere in the air and you're talking shit."

"You're talking TV talk," he said scornfully, and he stood up and yelled, full of defiance, at the soot-faced gunslinger, "And you, you're just some friggin' dead ghost, you're not my dad," and he buttoned his fluorescent crossing guard vest, and then said with grim control to his bewildered mother, "You know what the last thing a man wants to do is?"

"No."

"The thing he does."

13

*A*t the beginning of each month Mr. Timko came for the rent money, came and put it in his green leather pouch. Mr. Timko had shining pellet eyes and he always smiled, his heavy lower lip wet, and there was a tiny split in his lip. Albie thought it looked like an overcooked sausage. He liked spicy sausage and he liked Mr. Timko. When Mr. Timko had hired Albie, he'd warned him, "I only vork for landlord. Anybody late vith rent, then no vay, no vay for dem, and if too many too often, then no vay for you. Vee understanding each other because I have understanding vit landlord and he vit me same as vit you."

Albie kept careful accounts in a neat hand in a Kresges' *Date and Data* book. There were epigrams and quotes on each page for each date. He liked to see his trim rent figures lined up beside some true saying out of history. He had never been short on the rent, and he liked to think his book had its own precise historical order as he entered a final Saturday notation and read: "Some of them believe in the immortality of the soul, while others have only a presentiment of it, which, however, is not so very different; for they say that after their decease they will go to a place where they will sing, like crows, a song, it must be confessed, quite different from that of angels." *Samuel de Champlain, Voyages, 1618.* As he touched the lead pencil to the tip of his tongue and wrote PAID beside Room Six, he wondered who de Champlain was, and then he wondered why he'd written PAID. He'd only paid for the rent on a room out of his own pocket twice before, and that was after roomers had skipped out in the middle of the night, leaving him responsible, something that he'd never explained to Mr. Timko. He never wanted to be held responsible, to explain. He didn't want to be held, period. That's why he liked strippers and hookers. It was an intimacy without really holding. Room Six was the dancer's room and he hadn't seen or talked to her face-to-face since the morning she'd moved in. Troubled, and feeling melancholy because it was a sombre rainy afternoon, Albie greeted Mr. Timko glumly, but the cheerful collector said, "Albie Starbach, dis is good day." He was smiling broadly. He had little teeth. "Dis is good day for you, for me, a day ven landlord says vell done, dat Starbach man does not steal from me, so give him raise, ten dollars a week, and raise to you too Timko for finding such a man who don't steal." With great formality, Mr. Timko shook Albie's hand. Albie was taken aback: "The land-lord?" he said.

"Landlord, yes."

"That's great, that's great."

"Yes, is great."

"Mr. Timko . . . "

"Yes?"

"You don't mind my asking?"

"You ask. Ask avay."

"Who is he?

"Who's to know?" Mr. Timko shrugged and tugged at his lower lip.

"You don't know?"

"I never see," Mr. Timko said. "Is all phone. I have tiny office and is all phone for landlord who is to me a number."

" A telephone number?"

"No, no," and Timko laughed loudly, as if Albie had just told a big joke, and then he pulled at his lower lip again, saying, "Corporation number. Ontario 672160. You look your check vat it says."

"That's the boss?"

"Dis is boss."

"Son-of-a-bitch."

Mr. Timko smiled. It was pouring rain, steady sheets of rain in a rising wind. He wasn't wearing a raincoat or carrying an umbrella. He said goodbye. He didn't run or hunch up his shoulders against the heavy rain. He went down the walk and strode along the pavement with a measured pace.

14

*A*lbie was sure all the school children had crossed the road but in the late afternoon he waited as long as he could for stragglers. He had given himself twenty-six minutes to get home. Then he saw a child, a boy about nine years old with thick blond curling hair. The boy had a long-legged loping gait, and then Albie thought, *what an angel baby-face this kid is,* until he looked into eyes so unflinching that Albie blinked.

"You're new," he said.

"Yes sir."

"Well, I'm Albie."

"I need to cross the road," the boy said. "Will you take me across the road?"

"You bet your sweet life," Albie said, holding up his STOP sign as he led the boy out into traffic. It was early rush hour and drivers honked their horns.

"What do they call you?" Albie asked.

"Sebastien."

"I never knew no kid named Sebastien."

"No? Neither did I."

They paused on the curb.

"Where do you go from here?" Albie asked.

"That way," the boy said, pointing toward a small tree-sheltered park and a street that was a cul de sac.

"See you tomorrow," Albie said.

"Yes sir," the boy said, and went down the street. He turned and waved, and Albie waved his paddle, the red fluorescent STOP catching the falling afternoon light.

Because he was late, he hurried along the sidewalk, folding his fluorescent vest under his arm, pausing only for a moment on the front porch steps to the stone house because he still hadn't seen the girl, but then he went into the house and down the narrow stairs to the tubular bar of light above the door to the furnace room. As he took hold of the doorknob, he heard his mother hacking heavily for air in his flat. *Jesus, maybe she's dying*, he thought as he yanked the furnace room door open, rushed to the alarm clock and pulled the wires out of the timer, and then ran into his flat, stopped, and stood dumbfounded. Emma Rose was walking around the room on her hands, her bare limp legs waggling out of her underwear, and she was grinning at him upside down. He yelled at her, "Goddamn, you scared me half to death. I thought you were dead. If you're going to do that, then do it out on the street so I can sell tickets." She stood still on her hands, her face flushed from the blood rushing to her head.

"You don't want me to go for a walk, Albie, not even around the room?"

"For Chrissake, this is awful. This is a goddamn scream."

"This is the way it is, Albie."

"You're talking to me topsy-turvy, Momma," he said. "It don't have to be this way."

"It doesn't, eh?" She rolled her eyes. They disappeared up into her head. Then she took three hand-strides toward the wheelchair, paused, and somersaulted in mid-air, landing in the wheelchair.

He gaped.

"Where the hell did you learn to do that?"

"You think I just pooch around watching television all day?" She touched her two spit curls and then slapped her hands on the arms of the wheelchair. "No sir, Emma Rose does not rest. But you take it too slow and easy, Albie. You worry me. I end up thinking about you all the time. Like you should have a woman. A woman. Why don't you have a woman, sitting alone in there in your dark room for all hours, doing what I wouldn't ask."

"You got a dirty mind, Momma," he said, and stepped into the alcove kitchen to turn on the microwave oven.

"I got a natural mind," she said.

"Natural nothing." She always ate supper early, so he slipped a day-glo TV dinner box out of the freezer tray, a picture of green beans and fleshy-white pasta gleaming on the box.

"You're a nut and you know it," he said.

"I don't know no such thing."

"If you weren't a natural nut, Momma, I wouldn't love you."

She drew her mohair tartan shawl around her shoulders, stared straight at him, but said nothing, tucking the tail of her shawl under her knees.

"Do you want the TV?" he asked.

"Whatever you want."

"It's not what I want," he said, turning on the TV.

"Sure it is," she said.

"No it isn't."

"Yes it is."

"I don't want dick," he said at the ping of the microwave oven. He brought her a segmented white plastic plate of baked lasagna and greyish green beans.

"I don't like to eat alone, it's no good," she said.

"Good food's good food."

"No it's not."

"It's too early to eat," he said. "I'm not hungry yet."

"It's not too early to talk."

"About what?"

"I can see you got a lot of stuff on your mind," she said, "I can tell."

"You can't tell nothing."

"Yes I can."

He turned up the sound, sheltering himself in the rising pitch of TV talk, Channel 37, CNN. He wanted to be alone to think, cocooned, because faces and sounds had been verging in on him for several days, unnameable things, and he could feel their wing speed, like insects, like dragonfly angels flying in the dark, and he sat trying to shuffle his thoughts into some order, wondering if what she said was true, that the upper daylight air, the daylight blue, really was filled with clusterbomb stars about to explode in the coming night. He was acutely aware of Emma Rose lifting a forkful of lasagna to her mouth, touching the lasagna to her lips, testing the heat while still watching him out of the corner of her eye, never letting him slump back and be alone, never giving him a moment alone though she seemed to be completely absorbed in badgering the man who was talking on television: "Bunk," she snarled, *at what simply has to be done, and what has to be done, as Solzhenitzyn says somewhere, is . . . there's an inevitable increment of victims . . .* "Bunk, it's all bunk, whatever he thinks he's saying," she cried, *whose homelessness is in the heart.* "Bunk. Bunk. Do you hear that Albie?" and she banged his arm with her fist. "Do you hear that?"

"No."

"You don't?"

"Sure I hear it. Goddamn fucking noise."

"What do you think about what they're saying?"

"I'm not thinking about it at all."

"What's increment mean?"

"How would I know?"

"Albie, I'm worried about you."

"Don't worry."

"Why not?"

"Momma, I thought you were dying, when I came home I thought you were goddamn well dying for sure."

"I ain't about to die. I never was no quitter, I never led no lickspittle life," — *but now what we are forced to face about those victims who survive* "because I got along with or without knife throwers all my life," *is that they not only know nothing about other victims but they don't care* —

He opened a pine cupboard on the wall beside the basement window-well, a narrow window that shed a damp gray light, and took a bottle of bourbon

from the shelf, poured two drinks, turned the TV
sound down so that there was only the pale silent
flickering of faces, shrugged at his mother's quizzical
look and dropped a Willie Nelson cassette into the
tape deck.   "He can't be no down home country
singer," Emma Rose had said.   "I seen him on the TV
and he wears his hair in pigtails, a little girl's pigtails."   Albie stood behind her wheelchair, sipping
whiskey in the muted light of the TV shadows shifting
on the broad leaves of her rubber plant and he began
to sing, lifting the tape deck's silver sound lever up
until he was wailing in the dark, staring down at her
lifeless legs dangling out of her shawls and sweaters,
his high-pitched cry hitched to Willie Nelson's:

> *Take the ribbon from your hair*
> *Shake it loose and let it fall,*
> *Play it soft against your skin*
> *Like the shadow on the wall.*
>
> *Come and lay down by my side,*
> *Till the early morning light,*
> *All I'm taking is your time,*
> *Help me make it through the night.*
>
> *Well I don't care who's right or wrong,*
> *And I don't try to understand,*
> *Let the devil take tomorrow*
> *For tonight I need a friend.*

She sat with her eyes closed, letting on that she
was asleep, and Albie knew she was pretending
because one eye was open slightly, a white slit, just

like when she had pretended to sleep with Yuri, so he sat down beside her and leaned his head on her shoulder, acting like he was asleep, too. After a while, he tucked her shawl close to her throat and then, as if he'd been caught doing something too intimate and shameful — like the afternoon when he was a boy and his mother had caught him in his room wanking — he smiled sheepishly at an old grizzled desperado, a desparado who had a rope burn on his neck, a man whose face — the color of gristle — had suddenly come up on the screen like a face coming up from under water, and he was watching Albie with a knowing look, and Albie turned up the sound to hear what the old man was saying, but it wasn't a man he heard, it was a falsetto, singing:

> *Rise Charlie rise,*
> *Wipe your dirty eyes,*
> *Turn to the east,*
> *Turn to the west,*
> *Turn to the one*
> *You love the best,*
> *Go in and out the window . . .*

"Who the fuck is Charlie?" He didn't understand why the old desperado, singing to him in some strange child-like voice, was calling him Charlie. "Albie," he yelled, "Albie," and his mother, bolting upright in her chair, astonished at the anger in his voice, said very quietly, very carefully, "Why are you calling yourself, son? Why are you calling to yourself?"

15

On Sunday afternoons the island ferry was always crowded with women and children who wore rubber thong sandals and carried hampers, soccer balls, and six-packs of beer and wine coolers. The two-hour cruise in the harbor stopped at Ward's Island and Hanlan's Point. Albie and Emma Rose stayed on board. They enjoyed the light on the waves. Sometimes, if there was a strong wind, he'd get a head cold. He didn't get head colds on shore but he did in the harbor, so he had started wearing a cap. He didn't really think of it as a hat. He still refused to wear a hat. It was a cap that he had bought at the war surplus store on the corner of the crossing lane, a paratroopers' camouflage cap. "Maybe," he thought, "when I'm wearing this cap no one'll be able to see my head, not even Emma Rose," who wasn't worried about the wind, or where his head was hiding. She loved the sailboats and clapped her hands in the late afternoon when the water was crowded with boats sailing out along the concrete and stone breakwater past the tall pines of Hanlan's Point. "Handkerchiefs," she yelled. "If you were God you could blow your nose all day." She laughed out loud at her own joke, hunched forward in her wheelchair, her head over the rail, the hand-brake clamped against a gray rubber wheel and a safety bolt jammed between the spokes. The rolling of the ferry soothed her, and it soothed Albie, too. He sprawled to the side on a bench behind her, one leg crossed over the other, an eye half-cocked on her while squinting sleepily into the sun. Sunlight made him drowsy. That's how he had got his head cold. He had fallen asleep under a strong wind, misled by the heat of the sun, so he did not trust the sun and he kept a watch for rising wind. And he watched while she bawled out whatever was on her mind, eagerly taking the wind-spray in her face, rubbing and stroking the spray into her skin, and when she hollered to Albie as if no one else were standing close by, he yelled back, indifferent to anyone on either side of him, but still, in his bones, he knew it was wrong not to narrow his eyes and pay attention. He always paid attention on shore, but he liked to think that out on the water he could be free, free to be alone, because being out on the water was like being out in the wilderness, and in his mind's eye he could see the desert badlands being water, and himself standing on a shelf of stone over the badlands. But that was in his mind's eye. With his actual eye, he knew that they were never alone and eventually they talked less and less. It was easy to stay silent because of the soothing rocking of the ferry as it crossed the protected harbor, and one day when they had not spoken for nearly an hour, she suddenly lifted her right hand and curled and wiggled her fingers, joining the tips, as if she were throwing animal shadows on the wall of the sky, and, amused by herself, she turned to see if Albie had noticed, and he had and he made finger curl signs back to her, as if they were talking sign language. They laughed and signed and scowled and pondered, and then she signed at him rapidly, as if she were making a stern maternal point. He nodded contritely, looked like he

was pouting, and closed his eyes, seeing animals on
the walls of his eyes, panthers, a cheetah, and what
he thought was a wolverine though he wasn't sure
what a wolverine looked like, but he saw teeth, he
was sure of the teeth. He was sure of the dread. He
clenched his fists, full of resolve, braced himself for
the worst, and then he opened his eyes, but saw only
that his mother had drawn her shawl close to her
throat and she was staring out over the water, looking very happy, peaceful, like she had seen a bird in
the sky flying high, flying high. He sat for a long
time with the heat of the sun on his face, snuffling
and snoring though he thought he was alert and
awake, his mind drifting, teasing him — now that
the animals were gone — with glimpses of the girl in
the Zanzibar, as if she were standing on her toes, on
the water, naked, not dancing but standing still, dis-
creet, the beads of sweat on her bare body exploding
in the sun the way he'd seen water droplets landing
on a hot plate explode. Detonations. He made little
muffled explosion noises, *phugh, phugh,* expelling air
out of his cheeks. A baby sitting upright in a carriage that had been parked beside him while he
dozed, watching him, went *phugh, phugh.* He
opened his eyes. The child went *phugh, phugh.*
"Mind your own business," Albie said. The child's
mother said, "Oh, I thought you were deaf and
dumb."

"I'm not deaf and dumb," he said, shaking his
head, disgusted with himself, because he had decided to ensure a silence in which he could hide and rest
by pretending for the rest of the ferry ride that he
was handicapped and could only sign. "I'm not deaf

and dumb, I'm just goddamn fucking dumb." He got up and went over to stand behind his mother, to lean on the back of her wheelchair, saying, "Let's get off for once, see what's what."

"Okay, I don't mind."

"I feel like I wanta kill somebody if I don't get off."

"Jesus, Albie."

"Jesus nothing. I just want to get off. Damn baby's drivin' me nuts."

"What'd the baby do?"

"Nothing."

"You just want to kill it?"

"Making fun of me."

"A baby can't make fun of you, Albie."

"The baby was making the same sound I was making, that's all, like it was in my mind, reading my mind."

"Nobody wants to read your mind, Albie."

"You know lots but you don't know that," he said, "you don't know what they'd love to know, what we're all thinking."

"I think you make a lot of trouble in your own mind for yourself."

"You think I'm dumb."

"I think you think too much."

"I think like I got to think."

"Sometimes you don't got to think, that's what you got to learn, Albie. You don't got to think, you got to relax your mind."

The woman pushing the baby in the carriage edged up beside them as the docking ferry let down its bumpers and reversed engines, easing into the wharf at Ward's Island. *"Phugh, phugh,"* the baby said, staring up into Albie's eyes. *"Phugh, phugh."* Albie glanced at the child, cocked his thumb and forefinger and pointed it at the child and said BANG and then laughed. He laughed very loudly. "See," he cried to Emma Rose, "he understands me, he knows exactly what to say, *phugh, phugh,"* and he leaned down and kissed the child's forehead and the mother was about to pull the carriage away but then thought better of it, smiling warily, saying to Emma Rose, "He be your son?"

16

*A*s he sat alone in the evening hours in the furnace room he began to drink heavily, full of rancor and resentment at the whispers he heard in the ducts, yet he was even angrier if there was only silence, so angry he thought he would retch, except there was nothing there, and he thought that if he were a woman, if he could ever be a woman, he would find he was barren . . . and sometimes there were tinsel lines of glittering light in his eyes, and floaters — dark spots, like dust, like stardust, he thought, laughing out loud to himself, taking another drink straight from the bottle — watching the shadows in the dark of the window-well shape themselves into hollyhock flowers and then into a bird hung by the throat from a horn in the moon, the moon rolling back and forth like an illuminated crystal ball in the dark glass box. He stood up and felt limp and took a deep breath before going to the window, peering into the glass, shading his eyes, as if he were looking far into a distance. He shook his head, discouraged, and folded his arms and shifted his weight to one foot, and with one foot in the air he suddenly felt relaxed, he had taken a weight off his body. He smiled and was about to hop back and sink down into his armchair but stopped, afraid that his chair would not be there, that he had no place to rest, that he would never have a place to rest, and rather than take a chance at sitting down he reached out for the wall, still standing on one leg, balancing, as if he were on a dark peak, water behind him, water before, and he was happily fondling the stamens of a strange island flower. He realized that he had hold of himself. He looked around though he knew no one was there, not wanting to be seen fondling himself, and fell back into his chair. He took a long hard drink and felt that his chest was full of tiny enflamed roots and he sat back down and folded his knees up against his chest, embracing his legs, the roots, staring straight ahead, hearing a woman's voice, sweetly singing.

He knew it was not a voice coming down the ducts. It was not a voice in a room. It was a voice in his head. His head was a room. He tried hard to keep calm. He knew he had to keep calm. He couldn't hear words. It was just a voice. A sweetness. An excruciating sweetness. A woman's voice as sweet as the little boy Sebastien's face. He leapt up again and went to the window, stood on tip-toe as if he might be able to see the crossing lane, though he was several blocks away, and then he shuffled back to the chair, sat down, embraced his knees, looked up and saw in the dark a black tulip open like a parachute in the ceiling. As it drifted down to the floor he said, "Holy shit, I must be losing my fucking mind. That flower's booby-trapped, it's gonna kill itself." He closed his eyes. When he opened them, the parachute was gone. He smiled. "Safe," he said, as if he were an umpire at home plate, and took another drink, determined to finish the bottle and get out of the basement room, get away from the empty furnace well, the blank face of the big round clock, the arrowhead hands holding the St. Christopher medal. It was two in the morning. He staggered as quietly as he could out the door, hoping that he wouldn't wake his mother, going up the stairs to the second floor, feeling more and more exhilarated with each stair, as if he were travelling in the tunnel of his childhood dreams, escaping sur-veillance. He tried to draw air into his lungs as he knocked on her door and when she opened the door and saw him standing in the half-light, grinning, holding a fresh bottle of bourbon, he said, "Remember me, I thought you might like a drink, we gotta talk about the rent and all."

She was wearing a beige slip, no stockings, high heels, and no make-up. He was surprised at how pale her face was and surprised at her thin lips, lips like an incision, a tiny cut that he could feel, a paper cut, and he winced, but then quickly smiled, and she smiled. She had fine white teeth, and she waved him into the small yellow room, saying, "Sure, sure, you're the caretaker guy down in the cellar."

He stepped in, swaggering a little.

"You shoulda been down to see me last weekend, and a couple of weekends before that," he said. "The rent, right, you're supposed to leave off the rent, like if you intend to go on living here."

"Well, I had some hard weeks, you know," she said, smoothing her slip. "So what's your name anyway?"

"Albie."

"Albie who?"

"Albie Starbach."

"A'll be a son-of-a-bitch," she said, and laughed. She had a deep, throaty laugh, the laugh of an older woman. *That's a laugh that's been used,* he thought, and said, "That ain't so funny," peering into the black glass of the back window, as if he were looking to see if there was anyone on the garage roofs. But he wasn't looking for anyone, he was looking at himself in the dark glass. "I know the whole score," he said.

"What score?"

"What's goin' on."

"Yeah?"

"Yeah, like the world, the Zanzibar. Take your pick."

"Oh yeah."

"Yeah," and for a moment as he looked into her blue eyes he wondered if it could be possible that she hadn't seen him while she was dancing, when he had called out to her, though she had been staring straight at him. She put two glasses on a small table and he poured drinks.

"Ellen's my name."

"Yeah, I know, I got it in my book, I got it from you."

"Yeah, right, right, I got my name in a few books." She lifted her chin, saying, "So you like dancing girls, eh?"

Barry Callaghan

"I like watching you," he said, sitting on a straight-back old kitchen chair. She sat with one leg crossed over the other on the edge of the small table, so that he could see the underside of her thigh. The covers on the single sleeping cot close to the window were rumpled. He wanted to fix her covers. He looked around. There were a lot of things he could fix in the room. Cracks in the wall plaster. Polyfilla. He heard a hard whiskey laugh. It was one of the old desperados, the one with the brown broken teeth, eyeballing him from the other side of the glass. He said as sternly as he could inside his head so that only the desperado would hear him: "Fuck off outta there." Then he told her how hard it was keeping track of people in a rooming house. "People come and go, come and go. Like goddamn ghosts. Nobody sticks close to nothing anymore." He took another drink and wished that he could lie down. He wished that he could lie down on her cot and be cradled by her. He wanted to be comforted. He was bone tired of being angry. The blood was tired of banging in his head. He was tired of his headaches. He took another drink from the bottle, his glass empty on the table beside her. He knew she was watching him. He couldn't remember how long she'd been watching him. He wanted to remember that. To be exact. To play Xs and Os with each moment. He closed his eyes for a second and before he could open them he saw himself spinning on a giant nipple, God's nipple, with his paper wings suddenly on fire, since nobody prayed my friend, and he began to laugh. "Jesus," he thought, "I'm really losing it." He opened his eyes as fast as he

322

could, saying, "Your mother ever seen you dance, I mean, a girl like you, where you from anyway?"

"Petawawa," she said. "Camp Petawawa and she's dead anyway, though she just didn't up and die. She died a long time. Took a long time. She stuck with dying longer than anything else in her whole life."

"Shit, I'm sorry," he said and poured her another drink.

"Nothing to be sorry about."

"No?"

"She done okay for herself while she was still alive." She lit a cigarette and stood up. She had long legs and good ankles. "What do you do anyway, I mean aside from sitting down in the cellar?"

"Traffic guard."

"What?"

"Crosswalks, you know. I stop traffic."

"You mean if I made myself a little girl again you'd walk me across a crosswalk?"

"Right. Right," he said eagerly.

"Except, right now I'm as old as my mother was when she had me so no chance of my being a little girl again."

"Yeah," he said, charmed by her openness. "I'd look after you. I sometimes look at them little kids, and I feel sorry, sorry 'cause I figure someone must be treating their lives all shitty. That's what most people do, treat others shitty."

"Well," she said, as if her good sense of herself and her mother had been offended, "nothing's shitty about my life, no shit on my heel, I got along good with my mother."

"Me too," he said, reaching for her hand. "Me, too." She let him hold her hand for a moment. He could see the shadow line of the inside of her thighs under her slip. He was sure she was not wearing panties.

"Hell of a way to spend a Sunday, eh?" she said.

"Sunday's always the worst," he said. "Nothing to do."

"Not much."

"Fucking boredom's a bugger."

"We could pray," she said.

"Sure we could," he said. "I ain't said a prayer since I was a kid." He was wonderfully drunk, and at ease, and so loose that he felt unhinged from himself, free-floating, like the spots he'd seen in his eyes, stardust, or like the guys he'd seen in TV commercials for beer, hang gliding through the air on the wind. She was twisting the satin string of her slip, one hand on her hips, staring with an amused brazenness at him, as if she had realized how hungrily he was eyeing her.

"What you say your name was?" she said.

"Albie, it's Albie Starbach."

"Albie," she said, and dropped one shoulder, keeping a hand on her hip. "How do you like it, Albie?"

"Any old way, any old . . . " he whispered, "god-damn, you're so goddamn beautiful."

"Oh yeah," she laughed and spun slowly on the balls of her feet, "and I bet you wanta see my tits, eh?"

"Yeah," he said, "yeah."

"Do I got tits as good as your momma?"

"Naw, naw, you don't look nothing like my mother."

"She's got no tits?"

"No, she's got no legs."

"Gimmee a break, man."

"No kidding."

"Gimmee a fuckin' break," and turning away from him, looking over her shoulder, she said, "Takin' my clothes off don't bother me, you know."

"It don't bother me either."

"Why should I be bothered?"

"No reason."

"The only thing I don't like about stripping in the club is the dancing shoes I wear, they smell so bad at the end of each night, I got to buy new shoes all the time."

"You want dancing shoes. I'll buy you shoes," he said as she turned around, her breasts bare. She had small pink nipples. *Little girl nipples*, he thought, *with an old woman's voice.* He stared at her. She smiled and cupped her breasts.

"Taking my clothes off, see, it don't mean nothin' to me."

"No, no, why should it?" he said, edging forward on his chair.

"I like to be looked at," she said. "Men, women, don't make no difference to me."

"No. Me neither."

"Sometimes some of the women who come to watch us in the club, I know they figure us for some kind of whores or secret dykes, they got these squinty little eyes, but when I dance I don't think like I'm naked, right, 'cause naked's my costume, you know what I mean, like right now, you think I'm next to naked, but I feel just like when I was a little girl and put on high heels for the first time and a man looked at me and I knew he didn't see no little girl legs, and that gave me pleasure, bein' a woman, cause there's nothing better than bein' a woman."

He slid off the chair on to his knees, an imploring look in his eyes, and as he reached toward her, he said, "I'd like to kiss you. I'd like to give you something really good, like really kiss you. You know."

She shied away, out of reach, his yearning gentleness making her wary, as if she sensed that his only chance for any intimacy with her was a selfless offering of himself for her pleasure, letting her have her pleasure alone.

"Yeah, I'd really like to kiss you," he said, nudging forward on his knees. She put her hands on her hips and spaced her legs, her calf muscles taut as she stood waiting in her high heels, her fingers gathering her slip, slowly running it up her thighs until he could see her black hair trimmed to a diamond, as all the dancers did, and for a moment he rested his head on her belly, smelling her skin in the folds of her slip, wanting to taste the smell of the woman, the damp earth of mushrooms and sweetened saltwater, and then as he sank lower, her hands were on his shoulders, pushing hard, and his head snapped down and then she disappeared out of his sight and he felt only a crushing hot, damp weight on his neck and blood rushing into his ears, realizing his shoulders were against her thighs and that she'd pushed his head through her legs and she'd spun around and was sitting on his neck, yelling, "Ride 'em cowboy," squeezing his neck so hard that he was gasping for breath, and she smacked his back, kicking her heels. "Ride that fuckin' cowboy . . . "

He struggled, gripping her ankles, moaning, "No, no." Then he screamed as if he were in pain, "Stop. Goddamn, stop, please stop." She swung off him and stationed herself against the wall away from the door. He stood up, tears in his eyes, blinded by humiliation, his lips quivering. "I wanted to kiss you," he said, stupified. "I just wanted to do a little something for you." He stumbled toward the door, and as he went out, she cried savagely, "You think I'd let a guy like you do me for the fuckin' rent?" She slammed the door. He stood very still, stunned, listening to see if the slamming door had wakened anyone. He took off his shoes so that he'd be quiet in his stocking feet, and he hunkered down as he went along the hall, enraged, grinding his teeth, but thankful that the desperado had not stayed outside the window to see him. The house was still, except that he could hear a gentle *tock tock tock* like a metronome in the back of his head, a voice singing, that same voice, a sweetness so sweet he wanted to cry.

17

*I*t was pouring rain. Albie was wearing a heavy oilskin rainslicker. The rain was so heavy there seemed to be a mist inside it. It was hard to see. All the cars had turned on their headlights. Albie's feet were soaking wet. He was worried that the toes of his cowboy boots might curl when the leather dried.

There were large, deepening puddles of water at both curbs but he stepped through them, being very careful as he took the children through the traffic. There was such a water slick on the road that the cars cast an arcing spray. His trousers were soaked. Anyone walking in the distance seemed to be a shadow. He had always liked the cold chill of rainwater against his face, but everything, the trees, the telephone poles, the doors to stores, people, the children were underwater shadows. He said as he stood in the pelting rain, "I can't swim." He knew it didn't make any sense and he laughed. But he was serious: he couldn't see: his mind felt full of swollen waters and his dreams of drowning fish: the rain was a flood of water in his eyes. He blinked. He blinked again. He was sure that he saw two shadows down the street, a man, a child, and for a minute he thought it might be his father in his mother's dream, hunched but not hurrying, a hand on the back of the child's neck, holding and then hauling the child up on to his toes, a small boy, a big man in a tent-like plastic raincoat, but it was the man with the bag of stale crackers who had stepped backwards into traffic, and the child, the boy with the angelic face, Sebastien, who — as they stopped in front of him — looked up into the rain, into Albie's face, and said, "My father," and for a moment Albie was rattled and confused because he thought the boy had meant that he was his father, but then he understood that the man in the raincoat was his father and Albie was appalled. He heard the word *grief.* A sound like an echo in his bones. He turned away but the man said loudly, "Watch yourself," and Albie turned back, unsure if it was a warning cry to him or an alert to the child or just a cry in the dark rain, so he took the child's hand and held up his STOP sign and said, "Come on Sebastien," and stepped into the cross-walk. The child kept close to him. He was wearing yellow rubber boots, a yellow raincoat and rain hat. He did not look back nor did Albie. "That was my father," the child said. "Still is, I guess," Albie said. Cars had stopped, the headlights, blurred by the unrelenting rain, made their faces shine. When they got to the curb Albie looked back. The man was gone. "What's he do, your father?"

"I dunno."

"What d'you mean you don't know?"

"He's looking for my mother. That's what he says he does."

"Where's she?"

"Don't know. She just wasn't there six months ago."

"So he's looking?"

"Says he's a private detective. I don't like him."

"Don't talk like that, not about your father."

"I don't want to be like him."

"Maybe not, but don't talk like that."

"Why not?"

"Because, that's all."

"No it's not."

"What?"

"That's not all. I want to be like you."

"Me?" Albie said in consternation, stepping backwards.

"Yeah, the way you look after kids, all the kids, me, that's neat."

"Jesus," Albie looked up, for fiddlers in the trees. He didn't know why he was looking for fiddlers. There was no music. He was flustered. "I got only nine or ten minutes, I gave myself only nineteen minutes . . . "

"What for?"

But Albie, turning, strode away, yelling back through the rain, "I'll see you tomorrow. Tomorrow there'll be time," hurrying home.

18

The next day, in the afternoon after school, Albie and the boy stood on the sidewalk. There were broken branches on the lawns, brought down by the weight of the rain, but the lawns were fresh and green, and so were the leaves on the trees. They were standing in strong sunlight, the boy smiling, holding Albie's hand.

"I left us some time to talk today," Albie said.

"Can I walk along?" Sebastien said.

"Sure. But don't hold my hand," Albie said firmly. "You don't hold my hand anywhere but when we're in the crosswalk."

The boy looked at him, narrowing his eyes, but then he shrugged, and they walked on down the street, Albie holding his STOP sign in his folded arms, the boy holding his hands behind his back, like a little old man.

"So you want to be just like me?" Albie said.

"Sure, why not?"

"Why not? Because no one's ever told me anything like that before."

"I wish I had cowboy boots like you, too."

"Oh yeah."

"Yeah, except my father says they're stupid. He doesn't think my yellow raincoat is stupid but he says cowboys are stupid."

"He does does he?"

"Yep."

"I know a couple of old guys who'd tie a tin can to his tail for talking like that."

"You know some real cowboys?"

"I've seen an old gunslinger or two," Albie said, smiling.

"No kidding. Where?"

"Around."

"Where?"

"I been around. They been around."

"You talk to them?"

"When I want to."

"What do they say, what do they say back?"

"Back?"

"When you talk to them?"

"They talk mostly about themselves, tell me about themselves, about what it's been like waiting for the noon train . . . "

"Yeah . . . "

They were standing by the porch stairs to the rooming house, beside the apple tree. He could hear fiddle music in the high branches. He took it as a sign, a good sign. He snaked his eyes and turned to face the house and the boy did, too.

"This is where I live," Albie said.

"Neat," the boy said, as Albie was asking, "You ever see some people?" He put his nervous hands in his pockets, "You ever see people that may not be there?"

"Sure."

"You sure?"

"Sure I'm sure. One day in the winter when it was all deep snow I saw four red noses on the lawn in the snow, and I thought there were four clowns lying down under the snow but when I told them to get up they didn't get up and when I went and picked up the noses they were just round red sponge noses you put on your nose if you're playing clowns so I decided the clowns must have gone away under the snow . . . "

"Oh yeah?" and Albie led him up the walk and into the house, down to the furnace room, to the square well under the ducts. He unfastened the wires to the luminous clock. "You sit there," he said, "and I sit here. This is my room. My special room. Everything that I think special I think in here."

Sebastien, on an old pine work bench, looked around the dry-walled room in wonder, peering into the shadows beyond the well.

"You're not scared," Albie said.

"Naw."

"Some kids'd be scared, coming down into an old furnace room."

"I got nothing to be scared of. Safe as a church." He smiled so sweetly at Albie that Albie wanted to kiss his forehead but stiffened instead and drew back into his big easy chair. "That's right," Albie said, "and don't ever forget it. With me, you got nothing to be scared of."

Suddenly, they heard a loud voice singing down through the air ducts . . . "*You been gone twenty-four hours and that's twenty-three hours too long . . . "* and Albie, tracking the sound in the map of his mind, leaped up and left the boy and hurried to the second floor, knocked on a door, didn't wait for an answer, and strode into the bedroom of a fat little black woman who was lying on her bed in her slip, her legs bent and spread, and Albie went directly to the CD player sitting on the grate and turned it off, saying, loudly, firmly, "Don't play this thing sitting it on the grate and don't play it so loud," going back out the door before the astonished, embarrassed woman could say anything. When he got to the furnace room the boy said, "I heard you, heard you talking. Where were you?"

"Upstairs."

"What's upstairs?"

"Rooms. The rooms I look after."

"You look after the whole house?"

"Yep," saying "Yep" again as he closed off the ducts, latching the little doors and singing:

> *and if anyone finds us*
> *let them all be forewarned*
> *that you are the thunder*
> *and I am the storm.*

19

The boy came to the house almost every day and stayed for exactly an hour. Albie gave him one can of Coca-Cola every day, and only one, and he never let Sebastien stay for more than the hour, watching the clock carefully, and watching the dark

behind the clock because he didn't want any desperados sneaking up on them behind the boy's back,
surprising and frightening him. "No mistakes," he
said to himself happily as he sat back in the chair and
talked to the boy, about school, and about the different people who lived in the house, but mostly about
the desperados, his desperados, and how old Sam
McCabe, the one he'd first seen come through the
tumbleweed at the end of his bed, the one who had
come out from behind the tree, the one with the eyes
full of wilted flowers, had told him how he used to
ride into a town when he was young in the early
evening, and you could look to the left and look to
the right and pretty much trust what you saw as
much as you trusted your own horse in those days,
which was a lot, because without your horse, without the trust, you were lost, and it made life easier if
there was some trust, though it was hard living in
terms of the getting of food and all, but if you were a
red-headed stranger it was easier to know where you
were coming from back then and where you were
going, back in the days when a man was his word,
pretty much. And men looked each other in the eye,
pretty much. Of course, some desperados did some
bad things that left him with a troubling mind, like
Billy Bob Monroe who had the scar over his eye and
sometimes showed up with Sam and one time for a
joke was out there hanging with Sam from a tree, and
the boy asked, "Was he dead?" and Albie said, "No,
no, it was a joke, just a joke on me to see if they could
surprise me, but then he told Sebastien that he figured this was how angels appeared and disappeared
in the Bible and people were always talking to

angels, some of whom he knew were hard and couldn't be trusted, and so it was, he said, with Billy Bob, Billy Bob was a hard man to trust, and in fact, he wasn't too sure at all about Billy Bob because he was a man who just said bold as brass that he'd shot and killed, in his lifetime, two men, two men who, he said, deserved to die, and were — he said — found to be so deserving, deserving to die, by a sheriff, but Albie said that he didn't know whether to believe Billy Bob or not because old Sam always made a sour face when Billy Bob told that story, and one day Sam had come right out and whispered to him that Billy Bob had shot the sheriff, too, but it was impossible to tell if this was true because they were two old competitive proud men who poked fun at each other a lot and Sam often sang:

> *If you're living a life*
> *It will eat you alive*
> *And nobody slides my friend*

saying that all he and Billy Bob really wanted was to be left alone and left free to say what they wanted to say and go when they wanted to go, from town to town if they wanted to, and they didn't want anyone trying to take their guns from them for no good reason and there was never a good enough reason to take a man's gun, so they were living out what was left of their lives in towns where no one could find them because the towns were forgotten, lost forever except inside their own heads as they sat in the noontime sun by the old water tower waiting for a train to take them on home . . .

The boy, sitting with his arms folded and one leg crossed over the other, staring at him from the shadows of the well, unblinking, left Albie disconcerted for a moment — worried that he was talking not to a child but to someone who, behind the wondering eyes, was wise and could take all his secrets and use them against him. But then the boy said, "I knew I was right when I wanted to be like you."

"Every now and then I get a postcard from this one," Albie said, and he showed the boy a small packet of cards held together by a broad rubber band. He snapped the band off and flipped over the top card that was a photograph of a fish and he read aloud, *"Follow the Madonna, She Doesn't Eat Meat."*

"What's that mean?" the boy asked.

"I don't know. Sometimes desperados talk strange, like they're talking to themselves. That's all he ever says on the cards, things like that. He wanted to go west, all the real desperados do, but he never got there, not that I know of, not yet. He only got there in the movies. Bought me my first pair of cowboy boots, took me right downtown and bought them and then lit out of town. Couldn't stand being closed in, because he'd once been closed in in a big stockade, a camp, like there are always camps in wars. And what he loved was seedless oranges. Always ate an orange, cause he told me that what you love is what you can't have. And the worst silence is the silence before the calm of the kill. He told me that, too. And soap. He loved soap so much he said prayers over it . . . And what's awful is people like him were given numbers, so they were just never more than numbers, numbers given to them by people like my boss, whoever he is, the boss who owns this house, who is also just a number . . . but men like old Sam McCabe, as far as I can make out, they didn't put up with any of that stuff, they just shot the numbers out of everything every chance they got."

"Maybe my mother went out west, too," the boy said.

"Maybe," Albie said. "It's possible."

"I like to lie awake thinking of her out west."

"Well, if that's what you want maybe it's the way it is."

"If I say my prayers?"

"Prayers might be good. I used to say prayers, prayers for my father. I think my father, though I've never seen my father, I think he might be in the west, but he's coming this way though."

"He might meet my mother."

"He might."

"That'd be neat."

"Yeah, but if he's coming he ain't stopping, and if your mother's going I'll bet she'll be going on ahead."

"My father thinks she's right here."

"He does does he?"

"Yep. That's why he's at it all the time, trying to find her."

"What's he gonna do if he finds her?"

"He doesn't say. I think he wants to hurt her. You want your father to come home?"

"Well, he's never been here so he can't come home, but I sometimes think or maybe I sometimes dream he's coming."

"To take you away?"

"I'm too big to get taken away. And my mother wouldn't take kindly to my leaving her."

"Where's your own mother?"

"Next door."

"Your mother?"

"Yep. She lives with me. She's sick. She's got no legs. Not so you'd notice."

"Can I see her?"

"Maybe."

"You love her even if she's got no legs?"

"Yep. You should always love your mother a lot."

"I do. Sometimes I sit at her dressing table and look at myself in the mirror like I'm seeing her, and sometimes I put on her lipstick and I am her the way I see her. And I talk to me like I'm her in her mirror."

"How d'you know what she's saying?

"I know."

"What's she say?"

"She loves me."

20

*T*hree days later Albie took Sebastien downtown and bought him a pair of tooled leather cowboy boots, made especially to his size. The next day, two policemen met Albie at the crosswalk. They were polite but stern and sour and cold.

"You Albie Starbach?"

"Yes."

"Instead of young Sebastien Bawden we're the ones who're gonna walk with you back to your house today. If you don't mind . . . "

"Sure I mind. So what?"

"That's right. It don't make no difference. Just trying to be polite."

They walked along the street. Albie was sure they were being shadowed by at least one of the desperados but he didn't look back.

"So what's this all about?" Albie asked.

"It's not necessarily about anything," one of the cops said.

"On the other hand, it may be about everything," the other said.

"We were asked by the boy's father to have a talk with the boy."

"Yeah?" and Albie began to sweat. He could feel black mirrors at the edge of his mind. The trees were filling up with hats. "So you talked."

"You know what he said to us?"

"No."

"He said he loves you. He said he loves you because you're crazy, you really believe dead old cowboys talk to you. Now why would a kid like that love you?"

"He said that?"

"Sure."

"That I was crazy?"

"Aren't you, talking to dead cowboys? You really do that?"

"Talk's cheap."

"We don't care about the talk, we care about the boy, you and a child in your cellar, and all this love talk. What's that all about?"

"Nothing."

"He says it's everything. He tells his old man that he loves you, that his old man should be like you," one cop said.

"You like little boys?" the other cop asked, trying to sound casual but sounding sinister.

"Don't be disgusting," Albie said.

"It's not us who's disgusting."

"Look," and Albie stopped in front of the house, his arms folded, the STOP sign flat against his chest, feeling so wronged that he wanted to cry, as he said again, "Look, I look after kids. I take kids across the road . . . "

"To your little room in the cellar."

"Fuck you," Albie said.

"Don't talk like that to us," the cop, who smelled of Brut said. Albie saw snake eyes, two little crap-out dots, in the cop's eyes. "Don't ever talk to us like that, bonehead, or we'll stick your dick face so deep in the shit you won't be able to tell the roses from your asshole."

Albie felt so distraught, so disappointed at what he'd been told and so invaded by the cops, the actu-al physical smell and sound of them, that his legs were shaking, thinking he was going to collapse. Yet he was angry, rage welling up in his chest, in his lungs, and he drew in a sudden deep breath, gasping with his eyes wide open and his shoulders back so that the policemen, startled, stepped apart defen-sively. Albie knew he had only about eight minutes, maybe less, so he asked very abruptly but politely, "What's the day today?"

"The nineteenth," one cop said.

"Why?"

"So I figured," Albie said, and then he said, hop-ing that they would leave him alone so that he could hurry into the house, "Anything else, gentlemen?"

"No, no, not for the moment, but you'll hear from us."

21

*H*e sat staring for a long time at the luminous white face of the alarm clock, listening to the heavy *tock tock tock*. He watched the hands with their arrow heads move. He counted the numbers on the face, backwards and forwards. He had made supper for his mother, but he had not been hungry himself. He had not been able to talk to her. She had wanted to talk about monarch butterflies, the beautiful butterflies she'd seen on television, how they had flown thousands of miles south to roost in one or two trees, millions of butterflies in a few trees, and someone had cut down the trees and the monarchs had fallen out of the air, their bodies settling around the tree stumps, piling up and covering the stumps, piling up and heaps of dying, suffocating butterflies, all because some idiot had cut down a tree. Albie had stared at her. "What the fuck is she going on about?" he'd thought. She had wagged her finger at the TV. He'd wagged his fingers at her. She'd wagged back. "Holy shit, we're nuts," he had said to himself, making a small mound of white Reddi-Whip cream in her bowl of cherry Jello. He'd licked some Reddi-Whip from his fingers and then poured himself a Jack Daniels, and at last, after she'd asked, "Aren't you hungry, aren't you going to eat?" he'd said, "Follow the Madonna, she don't eat meat."

"What?"

"Never mind. I don't know what I'm talking about, I'm going across the hall."

He sat in the furnace room. He could feel time

ticking in him, speeding up, *tick tick tick,* and because
there was no sound in the air ducts, he thought, "I
wonder where that ambulance man is, maybe out
doing his Tai Chi," and he got up, re-wired and
timed the clock and headed for the back door though
he knew his mother, sitting trapped in her chair and
left alone without explanation, would be thrashing
her arms back and forth, upset and worried about
him, but he couldn't explain anything to her. He
couldn't explain anything to himself. He couldn't
explain how he felt, except that he felt betrayed,
deeply betrayed, and humiliated . . . he felt like he
was a puke, a puke, a puke — he kept saying over
and over — a puke at the hands of a jerk in a raincoat, and he was angry. He knew his anger. He
could talk to his anger, it was somebody in him, it
was George, his twin, a wild dwarf of a man who
had settled into the right side of his rib cage, teeth
like a slavering dog, leering, full of rage, Albie's rage,
feeding and feeding off Albie's rage, getting fat,
bloated, and suddenly Albie cried, "Jesus Christ, the
little fucker's having a shit, he's taking a shit inside
me, I can feel it," and Albie leapt out the back door of
the house hoping he was a skeleton leaping out of his
skin. He landed on his two feet. He knew he was
still in his skin. He began to moan, a long low sorrowful moan, a moan that rode like a chill on the
wind. It was a yellow wind but the chill soothed
him, made his skin clammy though it was still warm
out; it made him shiver, and he stopped moaning
and said, "Never mind, I can think straight if I have
to, fucking right I can," and he thrust his shoulders
back like a soldier and he walked in a straight line to

the back of the garden, looked at the dark house, dark except for one or two windows, and he decided he would wire the back of the house, too, that he had enough wiring and more than enough explosive, and he strode briskly in a straight line to the house, to the side alley, to the street. "What I'd really like to do is wire the fucking cop shop," he said out loud as he turned to go downtown, to Yonge Street, to the Zanzibar.

22

*T*he club was not crowded. There were two paratroopers at the bar. He could tell they were paratroopers. He knew most of the military insignia. He had studied them in the war surplus store. They were dead drunk, trying to pop beer nuts into each other's open, gaping mouths. Nuts were bouncing off their cheeks and foreheads. Then, one threw a fistful of nuts at the girl dancing in the shower stall. The nuts rattled off the glass walls and the paratroopers roared with laughter. Albie thought, "Fucking jerks." The bouncer, a bull-necked man who wore a black T-shirt with the arms cut out and black gloves with silver studs in the knuckles, went up to the troopers, put his hand on their backs as if he were being friendly and said, "You guys may think you're tough soldiers but I'll bite your ears off before you get off your stools." Albie laughed. He knew the bouncer had just been convicted in court, and had paid a fine for biting the earlobe off the ear of a Devil's Angel biker. He'd read about it in the papers. The bouncer had swallowed the ear lobe.

He had said in court, "If he wants his earlobe he can look for it in my shit." One of the troopers turned, going to throw a punch. The bouncer whipped their two heads together with a slam of skull to skull. It sounded like a pistol shot in the night. The two troopers toppled off their stools to the floor. Albie felt a strange exhilaration. He despised stupid soldiers. He despised stupid cops. He'd seen soldiers before, yelling and drinking and vomiting as if they couldn't care less that there really was an enemy out there. "Pukes," Albie called them, staring at their half-conscious and jerking bodies, blood in their crew cuts, and he laughed, thinking he'd like to jerk off over them, he'd like to see every boy he'd gone to school with lined up and jerking off over them. "Weird, man," he said as he went to the back of the room, back beside the stall where the blind black organist played, back where there was a row of little round-topped tables in front of fake plush chairs.

He sat down. It was a dimly lit section set aside for lap dancing. There was an old man in the chair nearest to him and a girl was straddled across his legs, naked, rubbing her thighs against his. He was giggling, giggling and bobbing his head. "What's so funny?" she snarled, "what's so fucking funny?" He kept giggling and trying to touch himself. She kept slapping his hand away. Girls who were caught whacking a customer off were fired. The girls could rub against a man but the man could not touch a girl, or himself. It was the law, the liquor licensing law. Albie stared through the brown light and smoke. She was coming down from the stand. He signalled the cruising hostess. "Her, I want her," he said.

"Thirty bucks," the hostess said, took the money and went and stopped the girl, who shrugged, and turned toward Albie. For a moment, he felt upset in his stomach . . . not so much sick, as empty, as if he had been pumped empty. He watched her walking toward him in her high heels, her panties, bare breasted. She hadn't come to see him about the rent. There was nothing he could do about that. There was nothing he could do about her, not now, not with what was going on, not with the cops wanting to jump on his head and shit in his hair. If he threw her out, she might go to the landlord and say that he had tried to get her to fuck for the rent. What could he say? He had been in the room, on his knees. He had seen films of pilgrims people on their knees, walking on their knees toward holy waters. No one was going to listen to him now, not even if he walked on his knees. No one, not with a couple of cops prowling around asking about little boys. He was stuck with her, and stuck with the rent. He hadn't done anything, not a thing, but he felt the walls closing in on him, the girl, the cops closing in. *You think your ass is a star. I'll pay, okay . . . for now,* he thought, smiling grimly as she hesitated, startled to see that it was him, and then, with a wink she stepped out of her panties and straddled his thighs. She moved her buttocks slowly against him to the rumbling beat of the organ. "Hello again," he said very quietly. She didn't answer, staring at a spot on the wall above his head. "You don't need to talk," he said, leaning close to her breasts, whispering, "I didn't pay for you to talk. I don't want you to talk." He had an erection and he tilted his hips, pushing up against her through his trousers. "Congratulations," she said without looking at him. He took a deep breath, inhaling her sweat and a musky perfume she was wearing. "I can pay for you anytime," he said. He loved the sheen of the sweat on her body, wanting to feel it on his cheek, the wet softness of her skin, and he clenched his fists and said again, "Any time," feeling her push and grind down on him, as if she could break him, hurt him, not moving to the beat of the music, but grinding, and she flattened her hands against the wall for leverage, leaning so that her breasts were so close that they brushed his face. He closed his eyes. He saw animals. Teeth. Smelling her. He could taste the smell of her. Apples and asparagus, he didn't know why he thought of that. He hated asparagus. It was a taste that filled him with a sadness, a yearning, but he didn't know what he wanted. *"What the fuck do I want,"* as he pushed his hard-on up against her again, feeling bitter and so disappointed because he had only wanted to give her pleasure in her room. He heard the words *give* and *grief.* He opened his eyes. She was moving faster and harder on his body. He flicked out his tongue and tasted her sweat, tasting smoke and salt, knowing that she was trying to make him come in his trousers, trying to humiliate him as he felt the urging rush in his loins. He didn't care. He touched her nipple with his tongue, tip to tip. She stiffened, surprised. He suddenly took her nipple in his mouth, held it hard, sucking in. "Ow," she said and hit him on the neck with the heel of her left hand. He held on, sucking, taking more of her nipple into his mouth. "Ow, Jesus," she cried and chopped at his head. He let go, her body springing back but before she could get her balance, before she could get up off his hips, cupping her sore breast, he grabbed her by the shoulders, grim with a hard triumphant anger, and he pulled her toward him and bit her shoulder, not breaking the skin, but taking the skin between his teeth, clamping down and then letting go, leaving his mark. Howling with shock and pain she whirled away and ran toward the front of the room but the owner Horace the Hop and the bouncer were already running toward Albie, who sat very still, his head down, trying to go blank as fast as he could so that whatever was going to happen to him would happen before he knew it. He heard the bouncer, who he remembered had a snake tattooed on his upper arm, yell, "I'm gonna break you fucking in half," but when it didn't happen right away, he came out of his blankness and looked up and saw that the owner had a hand on the bouncer's arm, right by the snake. "How come you?" he asked as Albie shook his head, shrugging, saying, "I don't know. I don't know . . . Look, just lemme leave, don't hurt me, I'll never come back . . . " The bouncer reached for him and lifted him out of his chair but Horace the Hop said, "Never mind, Ronnie . . . let him go, he'll go quiet."

"You saw what he did to Ellen?" the bouncer said, aggrieved, and whining at the owner.

"What about it?" Horace the Hop said.

Albie stepped quickly between the tables of staring men and the standing naked girls, trying not bang into anything, trying to shift his hips as smoothly as he could between tables, relieved — and almost unable to believe that he wasn't going to get beaten up, thinking *Snake Eyes* — as someone swung open the front door, holding it open for him, and "At least she didn't make me come. No sir," as he stepped through the door, heading north toward home, suddenly in quick stride with one of the desperados. "No sir, she did not do that. Did she?"

23

*H*e was standing close to the crosswalk curb, in the sunlight, his hands linked, holding the STOP sign, sure that all the children had come through the lane after lunch and now they were safe in their school chairs, all except Sebastien — he hadn't seen him for more than a week — and Albie knew that that did not bode well, but the sun felt surprisingly good on his face. He didn't feel drowsy at all. He took a deep breath as he heard a voice say, "Mr. Starbach?"

"Yes."

There was a portly, heavy-jowled man standing beside him.

"Mr. Starbach, I'm Mr. Cather, the school trustee. I hope we can do this smoothly, Mr. Starbach, but in light of the police and all, questioning the children about you, you see, I mean, we can't have that kind of suspicion and consternation, can we, you can understand that, so while all of what's going on is going on, we've decided, the school trustees that is, that it's better that you don't do the job you're doing here at the crosswalk, for the sake of the children, you can understand that, what with how confused the children and all must be about you . . . "

Mr. Cather had reached out, attempting to take Albie's STOP sign, but Albie had stepped sideways, almost backing into the LOVECRAFT doorway, holding it behind him, edging away, saying grimly, "Okay, okay, I understand, I get it, okay . . . ," catching out of the corner of his eye: FRENCH TICKLERS AT HALF PRICE.

He hurried home. He was sure that he had seen Sebastien far off in the distance but he couldn't be sure if his eyes were playing tricks on him, and he went straight into the furnace room to his chair in the well. He closed his eyes, trying to find a place of calm in his mind. *Tougher than leather.* Salt was tougher than leather, tougher than love. The boy, standing in the distance, was salt. Suddenly he leapt up, yanking the wires attached to the clock. "Jesus," he said, sitting down, "I'm losing it. Kill my god-damn self if I'm not careful." He took a deep breath, leaned back and stared at the ceiling, realizing that the sound lids for the air ducts were still in place. He opened them and listened. Not a sound. The house seemed to be completely empty. *That stripper bitch is probably still asleep,* but then he forgot about her almost immediately. *I know the score, six times six is thirty-six,* but how was he going to hide all this from his mother, how would he ever tell her that he'd brought a little boy to his furnace room? Day after day? He broke into a sweat. And what if the police went to Timko, or even to his boss, whoever 672160 was, because the police could find out things like who a number was, and what if Timko had to fire him and had to tell him to get out? What would he do then? What would he do with his mother? "How the fuck're we supposed to live if they do that?" he cried. He opened up his Kresges' *Date and Data* book. Everyone was paid up except the girl. He wrote PAID beside her name and read the entry note for the date, May 21: "On May 21, we set out with a west wind and sailed north as far as the Isle of Birds, which was completely surrounded by drifting ice . . . The great auks are as large as geese, black and white in color, with a beak like a crow . . . our longboats were loaded with them in less than half an hour . . . " *Jacques Cartier, Voyages, 1534.* He touched the lead pencil to the tip of his tongue. He had never heard of an auk. He knew the awk. Awk was how he felt, it was what people said in comic books when everything was turning to rat shit in their lives. "Awk, awk," he said, and then, feeling better, he began to sing, *bird in the sky flying high, flying high.* He got suddenly calm. He didn't know how that had happened, how he had found the place in his head, but he had. He had found a piece of the sky in his head. He took a deep breath. Then he thought of the bay, of the water, he and his mother, their laughter, making finger signs. He wondered if it was as silent under water as people said it was, as silent as the sky. He didn't know. He couldn't fly, he couldn't swim. He'd never really been under water anywhere, not long enough to listen. He found it hard to believe that there was no noise, that the fish didn't hear things, all those scaly minds talking, and what did the sun look like from under water? Like it was drowning? And what did people look like to a bird? He knew a song from school:

If I had the wings of an angel
And the arse of a big black crow,
I'd fly over these prison walls
And shit on the people below . . .

No one he knew had ever talked to him about these things although his mother had once told him about how we had all millions of years ago come up out of the sea. Tiny little things looking like snake heads with nubbly legs, but it was hard for him to imagine the old unshaven desperados being nothing more than a tiny head on nubbly legs. The closest the desperados had ever got to water, he figured, was the water tower by the railroad line. They had never had anything to say about water. They had little or nothing at all to say these days. The desperados seemed to be hiding out. He hadn't seen one since he'd fled from the bar and even then that desperado had broken stride and had crossed the street and walked parallel to him all the way home, as if he were walking shotgun for him, watching out for him, and then he had ducked down a laneway that ran off the empty street near the house and since then he hadn't seen anyone and Albie began to sing:

I'm going to leave here running
because walking's most too slow . . .

He felt a lot better, much calmer. He had hardly said a word in days to Emma Rose. He went into the apartment. She was wrapped in her shawls, watching television, the *Geraldo* talk show. She called him The Lamprey Eel; the Eel was talking to two big black women dressed in silver lamé, one explaining that she was a crack dealer and the other woman was her "muscle" — her hit-woman who beat up on men, homeless junkies who didn't pay up, and The Eel then brought on a man the women had beaten up and the muscle ran across the stage and tried to beat on him again until The Eel revealed that like many young gangsters and gangs in Miami, the two women videotaped all their street action and he showed the first beating of the junkie as the woman clubbed him down to the ground beside a lamp post and then the audience applauded as The Eel broke for a commercial.

"America in the afternoon," Albie said.

"He just showed before that," Emma Rose said, "before the two women, he just showed some gang kids shooting a guy in the middle of the street after they stole his car . . . "

"You know how goddamned sane we are?" he asked.

"No," she said.

"No! You're watching that crap and you don't know. Neither one of us could ever get as crazy as that guy Rivera."

"It's the way life is," she said.

"On the other hand, maybe it's all fake," Albie said.

"Naw, naw, it's real. It's right there."

"But he could pay them to pretend all those things."

"Naw, this is no pretend Albie. You and me, we pretend about things, Albie, but this is no pretend."

"I don't pretend," he said.

"You been pretending nothing's bothering your mind," she said.

"Nothing is."

"Nothing?"

"Nope," he said. "Anyway, it's all nothing."

"Don't seem like it to me," she said.

"It don't, eh?"

"Nope," she said. "What we're into here is forever."

"Two nopes make a dope," he said.

"Haw. Haw."

Geraldo had appeared on the screen again so Albie said, "Well, got to go," and he picked up his fluorescent vest and STOP sign and went out. He stood on the front walk beside the apple tree and buttoned on his vest and then wondered what to do, where to go, walking up the street toward the crosswalk. There was somebody already there, somebody standing by the curb holding a sign. "Holy shit," he said. "Holy fucking shit." He turned and walked the other way. He walked about eight blocks. One of the desperados, Billy Bob — whom he hadn't seen for a month — stepped out from behind a maple tree, wagging his arm, like a railroad wig-wag, pointing Albie out into the traffic and Albie held up his sign, STOP, and the traffic stopped though there were no crosswalk lines painted on the roadway. *Sashay sashay.* Albie waved at Billy Bob, yelling, "Come on, come on, then," but the desperado stepped back behind the tree. A car honked just as an old woman stepped into the stoppage and crossed over and as she passed Albie she said, "Thanks, sonny," and he said, "Think nothing of it." After half an hour of stopping traffic he went home.

He went back to the same place for the rest of the week, three times every day. Whenever anyone wanted to cross he stopped the cars and took them across. A couple of people recognized him from the school crosswalk, but no one asked why he wasn't there, or why he was stopping traffic where there was no giant white X painted on the pavement. They smiled at him, glad to see him, glad to cross safely. The cars stopped. No one objected. No one honked. He was efficient at helping elderly people. Every day the same little old woman he had helped on the first afternoon came by, pulling a little wire shopping cart on two wheels. She always said, "Thanks, sonny," and he always said, smiling happily, "Think nothing of it."

Then, at noon hour of the second Tuesday, he held up the sign realizing that he was staring through a windshield at the ambulance driver, the man upstairs from the third floor in the house. The driver was staring back at him, and checking to see if there were any crosswalk signs, and after Albie let the traffic move, the ambulance pulled over to the curb and the driver got out and waved him over. Albie stopped two cars and went across the road.

"What you doing, man?" the driver asked.

"Nothing."

"No way," he said laughing and rubbing his clean shaven head. "There is no crosswalk here."

"I know," Albie said wondering whether he was rubbing his head for luck.

"But you're stopping traffic."

"Yeah."

"Fantastic," the driver said.

"Right."

Then the driver looked at him and said, "You okay, I mean, you're okay?"

"Sure."

"Well, it's not everybody who decides to spend the day stopping traffic any old place."

"It's not any old place."

"No?"

"It's my place."

"Right. Right, I shoulda figured. Well, listen, it's great. Love it," and he laughed again and got into the ambulance and then said through the open window, "You're okay, you're not in trouble?"

"No."

"Well, like, if you feel in trouble gimmee a holler."

"Naw, there's no trouble."

"Right. There never is," and the ambulance man drove off, but as Albie watched him go he felt himself welling up with panic, with dread, afraid for himself, for everyone, "Big trouble, fucking big trouble," and when the ambulance was about a hundred yards away he yelled, "Deep shit, man," and he stood in the center of the road and started waving the STOP sign back and forth and up and down but the ambulance kept on going and Albie was afraid that he was about to cry, he felt so sorry for himself, and bewildered, sure that the ambulance man must have seen him in his rear view mirror, and he said, "He probably thought I was doing my own Tai Chi stuff." He laughed wryly and looked to both sides of the road. There was no one there. Not Sam and not Billy Bob. "The sons-of-bitches," he thought, "they pick their own time and place."

24

On Thursday, he got a phone call from Mr. Timko, asking if they could meet on the next Saturday, at the house in the morning. Albie, trying to sound jovial and relaxed on the phone, said, "I guess the boss wants to give me a bigger job, eh?" Mr. Timko just laughed and hung up. Albie was rattled. He walked back and forth in the furnace room. "This is it," he said, pounding a fist into the palm of his open hand. "This is fucking it." He waited for the dark waters in the back of his mind to part. They didn't part. He went out into the backyard. There was no one there. There were no lights in the windows on the third floor. There was no music in the trees. "This is it." He took an angry swing into the empty air. He hauled a triple-section ladder from the garden shed, a roll of wiring, his tool case, and a sack of Amex. He ran the wires up the corner drainpipes and secured the explosives under the eaves. "Top and bottom, back and front," he said, and put the ladder away. Inside the apartment, his mother said, "Let's ride the ferry this Saturday, if it's nice, in the afternoon, okay Albie?" He put his arms around her and said, "Sure, sure, babe." She held on to his arms for a moment. "It's gets more and more lonely down here, Albie, you know that? Lonely as hell, when you get right down to it."

"Well, you got me, Momma."

"Sure, but I can't have you forever. I don't want you forever. I want you to have a life, Albie, a real life, without me."

"So, what're you going to do?"

"What I've always done. Look after me. I can look after me."

"Sure. Sure."

"Don't sure sure me."

"Right," and he wiggled his fingers at her and she wiggled hers back and they both burst into laughter and she cried, TILT and he said, "Saturday for sure," as he picked up his STOP sign and went out singing *don't cross him don't boss him he's wild in his sorrow . . .*

25

*A*t around one-thirty in the afternoon, as he was about to go home, he saw a man on the other side of the street, a man who was watching him. The man had been there for about ten minutes. He had a camera. Then, without waiting for Albie to stop traffic, he crossed the road, side-stepping the moving cars. He had bushy hair, a moustache, and a big easy smile. He walked right up to Albie. "Hi," he said, "Tom Sloper's the name. I wanna talk to you if it's okay."

"Okay for what?"

"For the paper. I'm a reporter, a photographer, for the *SUN*."

"I'm no Sunshine Girl."

"Naw, we heard about you. It's a great little story. Stopping traffic, helping people all day just for the sake of helping them, it's a terrific human interest story. It'll cheer our readers up."

"You want to take my picture?"

"And know all about you. I want to know all about you. Everybody'll want to know about you, it'll do you good, too."

"Jesus Christ," Albie cried, and turned on his heel and hurried down the street. When he was far enough away he turned and yelled, "You take a fucking picture of me and I'll kill you."

"I already did," the photographer yelled, waving his camera over his head, smiling happily.

Albie got home and told his mother that he was sick, that it must be something like a flu, his head was pounding and he wanted to bring up but he couldn't, he had the dry heaves, so he wasn't going anywhere, not for a day at least, he was taking Friday off, and what he needed to do was sit in the dark, in the quiet, he needed to calm the nerves in his stomach. "Keep calm no matter what," he said as he watched her hoist her Trim-Torso barbells . . . *phum* . . . *phlum* . . . *phum* . . . *phlum* . . .

"You should try lifting weights, Albie," she said.

26

O n Saturday morning, shortly before Mr. Timko was to arrive and just after Albie had made his morning attachment of the wires to the clock, there was a knock on the furnace room door. He had made up his mind to slip out and go down to the corner 7-Eleven to buy the *SUN* to see if his picture was in the paper, so that if it was he could be ready for what Mr. Timko might have to say. He didn't bother to press the lever on top of the clock or move the alarm hand. He opened the door. It was the two cops. "Hello, Albie, mind if we come in?" one said, as he came in.

"Your mother told us you were over here," the other said, holding a handkerchief. "She can really move in that chair, your mother."

"Yeah, nice woman, and this looks like a real nice room you got here, Albie."

"Yeah, well come on in," Albie said as tight-lipped as he could, falling back into his chair.

"Your mother says you're sick."

"Naw, I'm not sick."

"She trying to put us off?"

"She thinks I'm sick."

"Maybe you are," the cop, wiping his nose with his handkerchief, said.

"Very funny," Albie said.

"We're not here to be funny, Albie."

"Yeah, so what're you here for? You got a warrant?"

"Save that warrant shit for the movies, Albie. We're just here to talk, maybe more."

"So."

"So, we got a problem," and he blew his nose.

"Like what?"

"Like my allergies, like I got allergies to everything."

"Too bad," Albie said.

"Yeah meanwhile, we also got a very respectable father who wants to kill you, and we can't have that, can we?"

"So lock him up," Albie said.

"We make an arrest," the other cop said, snickering, "and it's gonna be his nose that we'll be arresting."

"What?"

"Him," the cop said, pointing at his partner. "It's his nose that's on the run," and he laughed loudly. He was wearing Old Spice. Albie wanted to ask him why he had switched from Brut to Old Spice but, thought better of it. *Bird in the sky flying high.* he sang to himself, *bird in the sky . . .*

"Yeah, yeah," the snuffling cop said, "except we still got this kid who says over and over he loves you but he never did nothing with you down here."

"That's exactly right."

"Maybe it is. Maybe it's not," the cop said, his voice muffled behind his handkerchief. "I got a little experience with these things, you know. Maybe the kid's too scared to say what really happened . . . "

"Not likely . . . "

"Maybe you got so deep inside the kid's head he liked what went on here and he don't want to tell us that, maybe he really does love you . . . "

"Maybe."

"That's the way we look at it," and the cop blew his nose again, his eyes watering.

"Look at it any way you want, though if I was you I'd watch out for yourself. You look terrible."

"I do, Albie, I do."

"I'll bet."

"Don't bet, Albie, don't bet on nothing. Didn't your father ever tell you that, don't bet?"

"I got no father."

"You got a father complex?"

"What the hell is that?"

"You like little boys."

"Get off it."

"Get off what?"

"Get off me. You fucking ruined my goddamn job, they took my job, you know that, so now what're you gonna do?"

"Get to the bottom, Albie."

"There's no bottom. You got it all wrong."

"I tell you what, Albie," but the cop sneezed. They waited for him to blink and get his breath back.

"See, this is the mystery for me," the other cop said, "this is the thing that don't fit. Why should a kid, a beautiful intelligent kid like that, why should he think he's in love with a skuzzball like you, a nothing little creep, eh? Answer me that."

"You got all the answers, you answer it."

"No, no. That's the point. I don't have all the answers, and that's what really bugs me. Why you? The kid's got a wonderful father, why you?"

"The father's a nutcase," Albie said, "he feeds seagulls so they can shit all over the place and walks backwards into traffic."

"Yeah, yeah, you're a big time authority on traffic. But I tell you what I figure. I figure the kid is never gonna break, he's never gonna tell us the truth. He's gonna protect you and protect you, you insidious little shit. You think I haven't dealt with guys like you before, goddamn misfits trying to fuck kids?"

"You're fucking crazy."

"Yeah, and Mona Lisa was a man."

"So what we think we're going to do, Albie," the watery-eyed cop said, muffling his mouth with his handkerchief again, "is we're gonna take you downtown, give you a taste."

"A what?"

"A taste. You get away with this one, okay. But you guys chasing sweet meat, you never quit. There'll be another, and we'll get you, and this is what it's going to taste like, a little time in the can, time behind bars."

"You can't do that."

"We can't, eh? You fucking well watch us."

"I got things I got to look out for today and tomorrow. Who's gonna look after my mother?"

"See, Albie, see what happens when you want to dick around, you want to molest kids."

"I didn't molest nobody, you're molesting me."

"Jesus Christ, listen to him . . ."

"Get what you're taking, Albie, and come quiet, don't cause no more trouble than there's gonna be."

Albie got out of his chair. He looked into the dark behind the clock. It was full of black tulips, but there was no one there, nobody. He said, "You want to play your game, go ahead, I don't got to take nothing. I go clean."

"Good, Albie, good."

"Sure."

He stepped between them, and then, when the cop blew his nose again, he reached out and touched the St. Christopher medal that was hanging over the clock's face, and moved the alarm hand to three in the afternoon. "A stitch in time saves nine," he said, shrugging, and the cops looked at the old clock and shrugged, too, and then Albie said, "I'll just tell my mother I'm stepping out."

He leaned forward on one leg into the apartment, using the door to shield the cops from her sight, and said, "I'm just going out, Momma, don't worry about nothing, no problem. The two Dick Traceys were just looking for a place to put parking tickets. It's ferry time for sure."

He walked between the cops to the patrol car that was parked at the curb at the end of the walk. As one of the cops opened the back door, Albie said, almost in a whisper, his hand on the roof of the car, "You'll be sorry, Jesus H. Christ don't fuck with me," and he looked back at the house, a house he had done so much work on, a house that he thought of as his home — even if he had had to live at the bottom in the cellar — and then the whole house was awash in his eye in a yellow light and a surge of sadness and remorse and loss hit him and he turned and got into the car. The cop put his hand on top of Albie's head to protect him, "Watch your head." Albie saw that Mr. Timko was standing down the sidewalk, looking distressed, and Albie waved, crying, "Don't worry, don't worry Mr. Timko, just go home," as he ducked his head, laughing as he heard the word *grief* and said over and over again, huddled in the back seat of the car, staring at the bulletproof glass shield and steel grill-work between him and the two cops in the front seat, "Oh Jesus, Jesus, Jesus . . . "

27

"There's no charge for the room," the cop who smelled of Old Spice said as he closed the police station cell door. Albie stood holding his trousers up with his hands. They had taken his belt and shoelaces. "And there's no charges, either. We're not charging you with nothing, Albie. So you stay here a few hours, and then we're sending you downtown, to Don Jail for the night, to hustler's row, you'll love it. After they hose you down for lice and go up your ass looking for little plastic bags, you'll spend a night with the boys. You'll love it. Educational. We're all for education Albie. Just think of us like we're taking you safely to school." Albie didn't say a word. The other cop, who had taken a clean dry handkerchief from his desk on the way to the holding cells, was singing *Mary had a little lamb his fleece was white as snow* but Albie was trying to get his mind to go blank, to shut down the anger that was paining him in his chest. He was sure he had gone beyond anger, that it didn't matter anymore. He was sure that he was tougher than leather as he looked across the hall, over the snuffling cop's head and there, in an opposite cell, the two desperados were hanging by their necks, grinning. "You bastards," he screamed. The cop opened the door and punched him in the face. "Who the fuck you calling a bastard?" He lay on the floor for a long time. It felt good. The floor was cement. It was cold. He lay with his eyes closed. There was blood in his left eye. He didn't want to think about blood, he didn't want to think. He refused to think. He counted, 1-2-3-4-5-6-7-8-9-10-11-12-13-14 . . . He stopped counting. Six times six is thirty-six. It was stupid. He hummed. He crossed his ankles, he uncrossed his ankles. Though he was humming, he could see numbers. Numbers on the clock, the arrowhead hands, and St. Christopher's face between the hands, a silence. He closed that off. Like a shutter across his mind. He didn't want to think about the clock, the *tock, tock, tock.* He thought about Yuri's face in the clock, laughing. He wanted to laugh at the cops who thought they were so smart. The stupid cops. "Shit for brains." He'd set the timer right in front of them. He didn't want to see the time. He wanted to see a blank face. A clock that was blank. He heard a voice. He refused to look up. The bald-headed judge had refused to look up. "Since this man Starbach has no history . . . " This man. "No history . . . " In that dreadful light, tubular neon, it was the same neon in the cell, he could tell through his closed eyelids. "That man is dying." He heard a voice. "Rock-a-bye-baby, in the tree top, when the wind blows the cradle will rock . . . " opening his eyes, there was a priest standing close to the other side of the bars. "Hello there," he heard the priest say. He closed his eyes. Crows. *Caw. Caw. Grief. Grief.* "He can't be real."

"Hello."

Albie refused to look. He saw a sad lonely crow in white face.

"Hello, hello."

It's the fucking Bell Telephone hour, he thought.

"Just doing our Father's work . . . "

Holy shit, he thought. *I'm losing my mind.*

"He is your Father. And He loves you . . . "

Albie rolled on to his side. He opened an eye. The priest was there. "You're still there," Albie said.

"Where else would I be?" the priest asked.

"Alaska," Albie said, sitting up.

"I'd like to speak to you about our Father, your Father, how He loves you."

"No, no preaching."

"No, I'm not going to preach. I'd just like you to know, in these very difficult times, that there is a love, a love as pure as a child's love."

"What else you want?"

"Nothing."

"Nobody wants nothing."

"No, no, I just want to give you these."

"So you want me to take them."

Albie sat up close to the bars, the priest was holding a basket, a Sunday collections basket, except it was filled with tiny brightly colored books. *Gimmee an E . . . TOMORROW IS ANOTHER DAY.*

"Take some," the priest said, and thrust the basket between the bars. Albie reached and took a handful. "What are these?" he asked.

"Parables."

"What?"

"Each little book contains one parable. They are for you to read. The parables are wonderful stories."

"You're kidding."

"No. Otherwise I wouldn't give them to you, would I?"

"How would I know?"

"These are the stories of His son who died for our sins."

"You guys never do what you say you're going to do. I said no preaching."

"I'll just leave the stories with you, and wish you well, and let you know that I'll be praying for you."

"Don't pray for me. Pray for my mother."

"Okay."

"Emma Rose. Say a prayer for Emma Rose."

"Right," and the priest, making a sign of the cross in the air, left Albie alone, clutching the little books. He opened his fist. Chicklet books. He laughed, they looked like the two-chicklet Chicklet boxes from the time when he was a kid, and he thumbed the pages. Tiny books and a big print. *The Little Parable Of The Barren Fig Tree, The Little Parable Of The Mustard Seed, The Little Parable Of The Narrow Gate.* He closed his fist around the books and got up into a squat on his haunches. He knew a lot of time had passed. He wasn't sure how much. He had no idea how long he'd been lying on his back wild in his sorrow. He narrowed his eyes, trying to see real clear again to part the dark waters at the back of his mind, trying to focus on a little nub of nothing until that nub amount of nothing would go away, disappear, and he would be left with only a clarity, an absolutely clear sense of the absence of everything. Concentrate. He tried so hard to concentrate that he was actually thinking of nothing, or almost nothing. But every now and then he saw his mother, Emma Rose, doomed — he was sure — to a life with The Eel and doing flips into the air in her chair. He blinked back tears. He could tell that he was weeping. There were tears down his cheeks. He was not sobbing. He was just weeping, overwhelmed by sorrow, thinking of the cops, how pathetic they were, the way they saw nothing and would never hear fiddle music in the trees, misunderstanding everything, and then, an enormous sense of relief took hold of him as he felt his twin, the little dwarf in his chest, cocooned in his rib cage, shrivel . . . shrivel and shrink into a little stone, like a peach stone, wizened the way his awful little face had always been wizened, shrunk to a stone pit, but suddenly he heard the two cops laughing and calling out, "Hey Albie, Albie, your picture's in the paper, in the *SUN* . . . " and they held the tabloid page open on the other side of the bars and there he was standing in the center of the road, holding his STOP sign high with one hand and pointing with the other as the little old lady walked between cars . . . *"Thanks, sonny . . . "* and the heading over the big picture on the page opposite TODAY'S SUNSHINE GIRL was THE CROSSING GUARD NOBODY KNOWS. *Think nothing of it.* The cops laughed again. "Wouldn't they like to know who the real Albie is, eh?" One of the cops smacked the newspaper against the bars. "This makes me as angry as fuck," he yelled, "you'll be sorry you little pervert shit," and Albie said very quietly, "You know what the last thing a man wants to do is?" and the cop, sniffling, his eyes swollen, said, "No," and Albie said, "The thing he does." The cops left him as he tucked his head down to his knees and began to rock on his haunches, rocking and rocking, humming the same sound over and over, waiting, thinking in the silence before the calm, *She'll know nothing, she'll know nothing, blippety — blip — blip* . . . rocking, rocking in the night behind his closed eyes and he could see stars, *The stars in the sky are clusterbombs*, a dark sky full of starlight, and then it was a little tremor that he felt first in the floor, a tremor throwing him back on his heels, followed by a rumbling that shook the building and then hearing it, even though it was fifteen or twenty blocks away, a huge erupting explosion, a sound bigger than he had ever imagined, a sound that sucked the air around him and blotted out everything, the floor, the walls, the station, and it blew open the black walls of mirrors at the edge of his mind so that he saw long lines of air ducts, bent and folded to move around corners, shooting up into the air, sound tunnels, and tumbling between them, smiling and sending hand signals, his mother, Emma Rose, beaming, flying high, rising up into the air . . . *go in and out the window*, FOLLOW THE MADONNA . . . and then everything was still, though he heard yelling and phones and sirens, but everything was still, the floor was still, so he stayed on his haunches.

All his bones were shaking in his body. His body felt like a bag. An empty bag full of shaking bones. Bones dancing out of his body. He had to do something but he didn't know what to do. If he didn't do something he thought he would explode, the bag would explode and his bones would go all over the place. The two cops would play chopsticks with his bones. He began to laugh, his jaw moving up and down. He opened his fist. He popped one of the little books into his mouth, biting down hard on it, chewing and chewing and this began to soothe him, the hard work of chewing soothed him, and he began to hum, *Double your pleasure double your fun, chew Wrigley's Doublemint chewing gum*, as he swallowed and then popped another little book into his mouth and started chewing. He ate three of the little books. He felt totally calm. He touched his legs, his chest, his mouth. He couldn't feel them. He couldn't feel his fingers. They were cold, ice cold. He tried to say *fingers*. He couldn't. And he couldn't think of an angry word, there was not an angry bone in his body, and he tried to spit in his hands. He wanted that sure sticky feeling. He felt a swelling in his throat, the paper, the wet words. He began to choke. He had no spit, no air, and the pressure of no air made him feel like his eyes were pushing out of his sockets and there was pain in his lungs that spread to the joints, his bones separating, and as the whole of everything began to go black in his head, he heard singing in his chest, steady and mournful, sung from far away in the hills and he heard a train whistle out by the water tower and he thought, *It's the noon train, it's come, there's no one here but me.*

ACKNOWLEDGEMENTS

Several of these stories appeared previously in United States and Canadian magazines and anthologies, often under different titles. These stories appear here in revised form. The author is grateful to the editors of the following:

Exile for "A Kiss Is Still A Kiss," published as "Second Timothy, One: Seven," and "Up Up And Away With Elmer Sadine," and "Never's Just The Echo Of Forever."

Toronto Life for "Nobody Wants To Die," published as "Willard & Kate," and "Because Y Is A Crooked Letter," published as "A Motiveless Malignancy," and "Intrusions," published as "The Way The Heart Is."

The Ontario Review (Princeton, N. J.) for "Intrusions," published as "The Way The Heart Is," and "Because Y Is A Crooked Letter," published as "A Motiveless Malignancy."

The Pushcart Prize, XV, 1990:1991 for "Because Y Is A Crooked Letter," published as "A Motiveless Malignancy."

"Because Y Is A Crooked Letter," published as "A Motiveless Malignancy," received a National Magazine Award: The President's Prize For Excellence.